Mist Falcon

Book One of The Warrior Poet
Archives
Ryan J. Doughan

Mist Falcon
Book One of The Warrior Poet Archives

Second Edition. October 2021.
ISBN: 978-0-9962062-3-5

---

1. http://www.ryanjdoughan.com

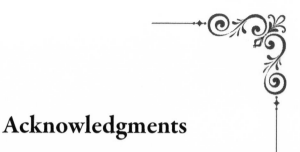

Acknowledgments

In shaping the story and, ultimately, the book of MIST FALCON, I have been helped along by a great many people. First, a huge thank you to my dad, Larry, for reading to me every night of my childhood and offering me the keys to Narnia, Middle Earth, and more. You taught me the magic of storytelling and the written word, so thanks, Dad. Also, thank you to my mom who always encouraged me to reach for the stars.

A big thank you to all of my early readers: Katie, Colin, Aaron, Bob, Larry, Connie, Matt, and Amanda. Your comments and critiques helped me in all my blind spots. And a special thank you to Becky for your incredible help in editing. This book would not have been the same without all of your help.

Thanks are due Les at germancreative for her incredible cover artwork for MIST FALCON. The presentation of this book would not have turned out nearly as well without her hard work. A thank you is also owed to authors Derek Benz, Brent Weeks, Melissa McPhail, and Holly Lisle, whose advice and experience has been most beneficial.

Finally, though it sometimes seems mere ritual or cliché to thank one's spouse for their efforts and support, I need to give an enormous thank you to my wife, Katie. Your encouragement through such a long process is truly incredible. I would be lost without you. So from the bottom of my heart and with love, thank you.

1

For my beautiful bride, the mother of my children, and the love of my life.

Chapter 1

I write this now, chiseled in Stone and wrapped in Wind...

He was just squatting. The house wasn't his. But then, as far as Aiden knew, the house wasn't really anyone's anymore.

No one had lived in most of the country homes surrounding Oustenbasch since the revolt and the most recent Princes' War had ravaged the entire territory. The once-grand estates were now little more than burnt-out husks, long since pillaged, offering their shelter to small animals and the occasional squatter. Squatting, as it turned out, just happened to be Aiden's specialty.

"Go out to the estates," Old Kempt had told Aiden two years past now, "best thing in the world for a young man starting out."

Aiden had nodded in agreement holding the fear from leaking onto his face. Some of his feelings must have bled through his determination, though, because Kempt had winked at him and leaned in closer. "Don't you mind the stories, lad. Superstition, young Aiden, that's all it be. You mind old Kempt, now. Go out to them estates and have a look around. You find something out there that someone in the city might want; you bring it back to my shop. I'll fix you up with a fair sum for it. Could be a fine living for a hard-working young man, you mark my words, a fine living."

"Yeah, alright," Aiden remembered saying, and that had been that.

4

Aiden had settled down in this particular home, what was once the Lanchestor Estate according to the still-standing stonework of the front entry, nearly a month ago. He found himself loathe to leave. The roof of Lanchestor Hall still stood, defiantly repelling rain, and Aiden had grown used to the dry sleeping conditions. He hadn't known such dependable dryness since the Touch had killed his father, burned down his home, and taken Jansen, Aiden's older brother, all as payment for what Aiden's father had owed.

Aiden forced thoughts of the past away, focusing on the here and now. He looked again at the great stone entry as he passed beneath its grandeur. The vast doors had long since been torn down and hauled away, but the entry still stood, gaping wide—inviting any who dared enter. He liked it here at this quiet estate. Still, other than shelter, he had gotten about as much as he was going to from the Lanchestors.

The state of previously being pillaged didn't mean there was nothing left of value in the estates surrounding the city, and Aiden was one of the few who would brave the stories of ghosts and grummels to seek out any treasures left behind.

"Superstition," he said aloud to no one in particular as his eyes swept over the still-dusty floorboards and empty shelves of the main hall. Ghosts and grummels may have been superstitious children's tales, but bandits, mercenaries, and bounty hunters were only too real to this outer rim of Oustenbasch. One couldn't be too careful when the rule of law extended only to the strength of a man's own arms or the keenness of his blade.

Aiden made his way back through a hallway into what must have once been a study or office of some kind. Here he had set up his own quaint living area filled with his few possessions, including those treasures gathered from the estate. The Lanchestors and those who had previously looted the house had been kind enough to leave behind several items that Aiden was sure would fetch a tidy profit for him.

Upon arriving, Aiden had found a handful of coins tucked beneath a loose floorboard in this very room. He smiled to himself, remembering: that was when he had decided to stay on as the Lanchestors' guest for a while. In the last month, Aiden had collected a slightly chipped, wide-mouthed ceramic bottle with a worn cork to close off the top, two silver steins, and several sheaves of paper that had somehow avoided all of the small fires the estate had endured, along with an assortment of other small prizes. All in all, it would be a decent take, and Aiden should be able to trade old Kempt in Oustenbasch for enough supplies to get to the next estate on his list.

"It should be enough," he said aloud, willing the truth into the words as his eyes moved from his tiny treasure trove to stare at the Lanchestor grounds out the cracked window glass. The mist was turning to rain out there, clouds obscuring the two moons of the Twin Angels, and Aiden truly didn't want to go out in the rain and mud.

Once finished with the main house, Aiden had moved on to a few of the buildings and dwellings that sat scattered on the property. Most of the buildings had proven useless, empty of anything of value—a couple of horseshoes in the stables a small tarnished plate in a servant's room—nothing that would sell for much.

Now Aiden had come to the end of his circuit around the grounds. He was nearly back to the main house with only one final servant's dwelling to be gone through. Aiden sighed, poured a drink from his jug, drained it, and headed back into the hall. Wrapping his cloak tight about himself to ward off the chill and the rain, he splashed his way through quickly forming mud puddles to the last of the Lanchestors' buildings.

The small, one-room house looked much like the rest of the buildings—pillaged, very pillaged. Aiden made his way through the room methodically all the same. This was, after all, what he did—looked for things others had missed.

He searched the single room for the better part of an hour, finding little enough of value. With a sigh, Aiden pushed his hair back out of his face, accomplishing only to streak his forehead with soot. That was it then—time to move on. As he turned to leave, Aiden's eye fell on the cold ashes of the fireplace. Fine, one more try, he thought, moving across the room.

When he reached the hearth and bent to poke through the ashes, Aiden placed his hand against the brick to steady himself. This particular brick, however, didn't hold Aiden's weight, but gave to his push, receding into the wall. A series of metallic clicks sounded. Then, with a groaning, dusty, pop a door swung free from the wall paneling adjacent to the fireplace. A small compartment, sheathed in metal, lay revealed behind the door. Cradled in that compartment nestled a delicately carved box, adorned with a single precious blue stone on its clasp.

Aiden took the box gingerly, but firmly as if scared it might both break and vanish from his hands. Kneeling, he placed it on the dust-covered floor before pressing the blue stone. He was rewarded with a faint click. The lid opened, revealing more wealth than Aiden had ever had a right to hope for: rings, bracelets, a gold necklace, two pea-sized clear stones that Aiden believed were diamonds, and a ruby the size of a small grape. There was also a smattering of golden eagles, each coin worth ten silver pennies. It was a fortune. Beneath the bed of coins, Aiden uncovered a small knife in a leather sheath whose pommel was shaped into the head of a falcon. On the sheath, just below the crossbar, a clenched talon had been embossed into the leather. Drawing the blade, Aiden found it still well oiled, and if scavenging and trading had taught him anything, it was how to recognize a metal. This blade was silver as surely as the coins were gold eagles. Still, it was light—half of what it should have weighed, maybe less.

As the tip slid free of the sheath, Aiden thought the blade vibrated ever so slightly. It was only for a moment, but in that moment, he was sure he could feel the stones in the ground beneath him. The moment passed, and Aiden snapped the blade back into its sheath.

Even through his awe at the discovery, Aiden couldn't help wondering what all this was doing here. Someone had gone to a lot of effort to construct a secret door and mechanism just to hide this box. Had Master Lanchestor put it here, or had one of his servants been stealing from him? Maybe the master of the house had a secret lover who liked gifts. In the end, it didn't matter overly much how it got here. It was Aiden's now.

After looking over his treasure for another few moments, Aiden removed his right boot, reached in, and pulled the small cord toward the bottom. This old hut didn't hold the only secret compartment. The cord allowed a little flap to open in the lining of the boot. Aiden usually used it to store a few extra coins or small valuables he might find. One could never be too careful when working the outer estates. He slipped the sheathed knife into the pocket of his boot. Normally the pocket closed so seamlessly you would be hard-pressed to find it if you didn't know to look for it. This time it proved a bit of a challenge to get the lace to pull tight, but Aiden managed in the end. That done, he closed the lid on the box of his new treasure, and after consideration, shut the hidden door again for safe measure. With his windfall cradled tightly under his arm, he headed back to the main Lanchestor house and his room.

Once back in his private sanctuary, he pulled the small box out once more just to ward off disbelief. Now the question: what to do?

He was done with all of his scavenging at the Lanchestor estate; he knew that. Still, it was hard to leave behind this safe seclusion and head back into crowded Oustenbasch. The city wasn't a place for a man to flaunt wealth without swordarms to keep him safe. Aiden had no time to hire swordarms, and it would draw too much attention at any rate for a poor scavenger to looking for hired muscle. He'd draw every gang to him like gawkers to a Delrethi Cobra fight. No, he'd just have to be careful.

With a sigh, Aiden retrieved his leather bag from the corner and began packing up his belongings. When he came to the small treasure box, he paused. Aiden had had things taken from him by the gangs in the past, especially in those early days when he didn't know any better. It was never good to appear overly laden with goods if you weren't also overly protected by swordarms. Aiden opened the lid of the box and was again stunned by the wealth inside. No, he couldn't keep all of this together, just in case.

Aiden grabbed a few of the golden eagles and dropped them into his coin purse, enjoying the extra weight in the small bag that usually felt so light. He slipped a few more into one of the pockets sewn into the inside of his cloak. He dropped the ruby and diamonds into another cloak pocket, and wrapped the necklace, bracelets, and rings into his extra shirt before packing them. After considering, he dropped the remaining coins into the bottom of the ceramic bottle and then stuffed in the rag he used for washing to keep the coins from rattling and clinking around.

After packing some of the less valuable things on the top of the bag, Aiden flipped the flap over the opening, tied it down to the clasp on the bottom, and shouldered his life's fortune.

He was just passing from the Lanchestor grounds onto the road with his pack over one shoulder and his small hunting bow and few arrows over the other when the question hit him: what was old Kempt going to say about all the riches showing up in his shop? Would he even be able to move the pricier jewels and rings? Kempt had always treated Aiden fairly, never cheating him out of his goods, or at least not cheating him like he cheated other, unwary customers. There were other, more dangerous options, but Aiden wasn't sure he was ready to go to the Barons, not yet. His father had been their man, but where were they when the Touch had come to call? Absent. Easily absent.

Aiden sighed and started toward town. He would begin with Kempt as he always had, and decide on the rest if the old man couldn't help him.

He only traveled a mile toward town before veering off onto a diagonal cart path that would lead him around the north wall and through a maple grove to the western gate of Oustenbasch. This entrance was otherwise known as the Serpent's Tail; Aiden supposed it was for the meandering route one was forced to take to get through the first quarter-mile of the city before other avenues branched off.

The quarter-mile of Serpent's Tail lay riddled with shops and vendors—*free* shops and vendors. Neither Baron had a hold on the space. It was too hard to hold or maneuver easily without the regular back-alley traffic. And because the Barons were mostly absent, genuine smiles bloomed on the vendors' faces along the path. It felt unnatural to Aiden, so used to seeing the ice in the eyes behind a smile. Still, the Serpent's Tail gave Aiden the perfect route in and out of the city—no Baron swordarms to harass him, and old Kempt's shop sat to the side of the square that the short stretch spilled onto.

Aiden crossed the square, careful to keep his speed to a brisk walk. He had business to attend to, not desperation to run from—nothing to hide. Willing this persona into being, Aiden passed the large fountain in the square center which depicted some fiery angel, probably Sansol or his vengeful brother Antice come down from their lunar throne to do battle, sword drawn over a two-headed water demon. The image was supposed to be uplifting, Aiden knew, good vanquishing evil, but he always found it a little disturbing.

Another dozen quick steps and Aiden approached Kempt's shop. Kaine, one of the shopkeeper's swordarms, leaned lazily against the building. "Well, if it ain't the little sparrow," Kaine sneered, spitting. "Come to push more chipped cups and blunted knives on Master Kempt, have ya?"

"Good to see you too, Kaine. Just doing business. I'm not looking for trouble."

Kaine spit again but offered no rebuttal as Aiden entered.

Aiden gained another glance from Pax, Kempt's other swordarm, upon entering, but nothing more. Aiden had never been worth more than a cursory glance. With his pockets filled with more fortune than he had ever dreamed of finding on the estates, he was grateful for his overlooked nature.

Old Kempt finished his dealings with a haggard woman in a faded, green dress selling off a few trinkets. Her shoulders fell as she let her head drop in a slow, defeated nod. From the counter, she pulled the few drab pennies Kempt had offered, turned, and passed Aiden on her way to the door. Not good; Kempt must be in one of his moods. There was nothing for it, though. Aiden wasn't leaving without at least attempting the sale.

He smiled as he stepped up to the counter. Looking up from a giant ledger book, old Kempt hesitated for only a moment before recognition lit in his eyes, and he smiled as well.

"Little Master Aiden, you've grown. I barely recognized you standing there."

Aiden ground his teeth, bristling at the *little* comment, though he hoped it didn't show. Aiden had always been small. He didn't think of himself that way, but at seventeen, he understood there were a lot of people bigger than him. He also doubted he had grown much since old Kempt had seen him last and thought his change in appearance had more to do with his not bathing for the last couple of weeks. Still, Aiden smiled all the broader in response.

"And how are you, Kempt? Stolen any sweet treats from small children since last we met?"

Kempt gave a wounded frown, furrowing his bushy, gray eyebrows. "Come now little Aiden, that was ages ago and a simple misunderstanding." He smiled at the end to show the wound was superficial at best.

Aiden offered a short laugh. "And as for you? How's business?"

"Oh, business is business, as they say. It's much as it always has been." Here Kempt tilted his head slightly as if trying to get a better view past his beakish nose. "Speaking of business, what can I be doing for the little Master today?"

With a slight twist of his shoulder, Aiden spun his bag from his shoulder and to the floor at his feet. He undid the tie and pulled out the steins and sheaves of paper. Better to start small, he thought. Setting them on the counter, he eyed Kempt as if this was his whole take.

Old Kempt looked over the steins and flipped through the paper before making his offer. "A silver penny apiece for the four sheaves of paper and twelve drab pennies for the two steins together," he said.

Aiden shook his head. The paper price was fair, but the price on the steins was a bit low, even for old Kempt. The shopkeeper could turn around and sell them in two days' time for three times what he was offering Aiden. This wasn't the big piece of Aiden's sale today, but he couldn't just let the offer go uncontested.

"Eighteen drab pennies for the steins," he said.

"Fourteen," Kempt countered so quickly he must have been expecting Aiden's refusal.

Aiden could get more, maybe even sixteen or seventeen drabs, but he didn't want to push, not yet. He hadn't gotten to what he had come for yet. Trying to seem resigned, Aiden nodded his head once, and Kempt smiled. It was apparent the old shopkeeper thought he had just won. He counted out a small pile of coins and pushed them to Aiden who slid them from the counter and into his money pouch without thought.

"Is that all then, little Master?" Kempt asked, already moving to his giant ledger.

"Actually, there is something more."

"Hmm," Kempt looked up distractedly. He had clearly been under the impression that the meeting was over.

Aiden reached slowly into the inside pocket of his cloak and pulled out the ruby and diamonds. He set them on the counter between himself and old Kempt. They glittered entrancingly in the shop's bright lantern light.

Old Kempt's eyes bulged for just a moment before he reined in his shock. "Well, young Master, it seems you have been busy since last you were here." Aiden noticed *young* had replaced *little* in Kempt's vernacular and had to fight not to smile.

"There's more," Aiden said, "jewelry and the like, but I wanted to know if you can move this kind of thing or if I should go elsewhere." Aiden tried to sound sure of himself, but he wasn't really sure where else he would go. He had always come to old Kempt's shop, and old Kempt had always bought whatever Aiden had brought to him.

His brow knitted tightly together, Kempt lifted one of the diamonds to the light and squinted at it. Then he looked at Aiden as if pondering. Aiden thought he might be deciding on whether he should bluff the boy or not. Aiden knew what the treasure was worth, though, or at least knew that it was real and worth a lot.

Eventually, Kempt returned his eyes to the diamond and nodded slowly. "I could make some inquiries," he said slowly, his gaze drifting back to Aiden. "It would be helpful to hold on to these, of course. Maybe some of the other...goods, too, just so I'll have something to show. Shouldn't take more than a couple of days and then we can—"

Aiden was shaking his head. He didn't want to leave his new wealth. Kempt had always been mostly fair with him, but money did strange things to people.

"I'll leave one of the diamonds with you for proof to your buyers. Two days enough time?" Aiden was already stowing the ruby and the remaining diamond inside his cloak.

Old Kempt looked like he wanted to argue, his wrinkled face reddening slightly, but he didn't want to lose the deal altogether either.

In the end, he nodded. "Afternoon, day after next. I'll make some inquiries, and see what turns up. No promises, mind you, but we'll see."

It was Aiden's turn to nod. "Alright," he said as he turned to leave. "Play this straight, though Kempt. Neither of us wants trouble." The old man swallowed but gave no other answer. So Aiden left.

He was breathing heavily by the time he reached the angel fountain. Aiden had two days to spend—to waste, really. Aiden hated waiting, but the dice were tossed and he would see how they landed. Working his way through the crowded streets, he stopped at a vendor's cart and bought two skewers of lamb chunks and a small cup of milk for five drabs. It was a bit extravagant for what he could usually afford, but the food took his mind off the waiting. More than that, it took his mind off of what, and whom, he knew he would fill the waiting with.

He spent the next few hours working his way from vendor to vendor and shop to shop, gathering the few items he would surely need on the next estate. He bought a small box of salt and some apples from one shop and a half-dozen straight arrows from another. He had never quite gotten the hang of making his own. They usually ended up slightly crooked, causing him to miss the wild game that made up his primary food source. He also bought some thread, two needles, and an extra shirt from a vendor who was just closing up shop. He even picked up a new blanket—his old one layering him with more holes than warmth at night. Such frivolity made Aiden's stomach twist, but he had the coin in his purse for once, and if things went well he would have even more.

With his shopping finished, there was nothing left to keep him from her any longer. He paused inside a momentarily abandoned alley and worked carefully in his pack until he pulled free one of the bracelets from his treasure. Tucking it carefully into another of his inside cloak pockets, Aiden moved back onto the main street and started off for the north side of Oustenbasch.

Less than an hour later, just as the sun was dimming enough for the Watch to light the street lanterns, he was standing outside of a two-story brick building bearing a sign that read *The Pearl—Food, Song, Lodging* hanging on an iron bracket above the door.

"Well, here we go," Aiden said quietly to himself as he moved forward and pulled open the large wooden door. He was met immediately by the warm mix of pipe smoke and cooked meat. Letting it wash over him a moment, Aiden breathed deeply. This was as close to a sense of home as he ever came.

There were several people at the bar and a few scattered around the tables in front of the large stage. It was still early. Aiden knew the tables would be filled in the next hour or two. His eyes drifted for a moment, taking in the scene. He passed over two merchants leaning over a game board, deep in a game of Crown Me, before his attention fell onto two men sitting in the far corner. One was thick chested with a bald head and dark beard. The other was slim with sandy hair. They were dressed in black and gray with silver falcon brooches standing out from leather jerkins. The falcons' wings were spread in flight. Aiden's breath caught. If the brooches weren't enough, the muskets slung over their backs would have screamed the truth. No one else carried muskets. No one else even had the weapons, and Aiden was sure there was a sword slung at each of their waists to match. These were Mist Falcons, heroes out of story and legend. Aiden had only seen one once before, and that had been years ago. Some called them mercenaries, but they were as far above the standard thug swordarms Aiden had seen as those mercenaries were above the beggars of the street. He wondered what would bring Mist Falcons to Oustenbasch and to The Pearl.

After a moment, the door swung open again, and Aiden was jostled the rest of the way inside by a new group of patrons. Snapped back to reality, Aiden staggered slightly and then made his way to the bar. Jace, the barman and owner of The Pearl, looked up and seeing Aiden, his eyes narrowed.

"You better be drinking tonight, boy. The shows aren't free, and there'll be no space for lollygaggers," Jace said.

Aiden matched the barman's stare while he reached into his coin pouch and slapped a silver penny on the counter.

"I'll have a tall beer, and whatever the special is for supper," he said.

Jace looked at the coin for a moment, then slipped it off the bar and started filling a large mug.

An hour later, with The Pearl's main hall full, Aiden was through with the beef stew and side of over-cooked beans and was well into his second mug of beer when the first performance of the night started, and *she* stepped onto the stage. Her name was Semlie, and she was as lovely as Aiden remembered. They had known each other since they were young. Semlie's mother did the sewing for Aiden's family after his own mother's death. Semlie had been singing at The Pearl since she was fourteen. Her voice entranced and uplifted. When Semlie sang, Aiden felt his heart fettered to her and set free from life's toiling at the same time.

Aiden blew out a slow breath, his beer forgotten as he listened to Semlie sing a Dala Ballad, her favorite, he knew, from a hundred years ago.

> "At night, the moon, a lover's kiss—
> bathed glory just for thee.
> This night, this moon—a forest pool—
> reflection for my lover's plea.
> So come dine with me, my sweet, my love.
> Come dine with me and know—
> that none will come here e're again
> as long as north winds blow."

The song sounded fresh coming from her lips—new as spring after a long winter. By Sansol, she was beautiful.

Semlie finished her ballad and sang two other songs, folk music that had everyone singing along. Then she was off for her break as a flutist stepped up, offering background noise as conversations rekindled.

Setting down his mug, Aiden stood and made his way to the door. He saw the two Mist Falcons disappearing down the street as he exited the front door of The Pearl. They, apparently, had had enough Pearl hospitality for one night. Aiden let them go without comment, his mind firmly fixed on the prize. He knew he only had a few minutes before she'd be gone. Striding to the side ally, he worked his way to the top of the low wall halfway down The Pearl's exterior via some of the looser bricks. From there he made the short leap to a window ledge before landing on the ground. All the buildings along this alley had these half walls, offering the illusion of privacy from the main road. He had done that little climb on every visit back to Oustenbasch for the last two years.

"I was starting to think you forgot about me," said a woman's voice that Aiden knew well. "How are the estates, Den?"

Aiden looked up from brushing the mortar dust off of his cloak and found Semlie leaning against the frame of The Pearl's alley side door, a shawl pulled tightly around her shoulders to ward off the chill. He smiled a big, toothy grin as if invisible hands were pulling upward hard on his cheeks. By Sansol and Antice both and by their winged lord, it was good to see her, to hear her say his name.

"The estates are as they have always been, quiet, peaceful. You should come with me sometime, Semlie. You'd like it." The extra beer had made him brash, and he added, "Let me show you the sunrise without the city smoke to obscure. It is almost as lovely as you."

Semlie laughed—a high, melodic tone. "And if I went with you, you'd lose both the quiet and the peace. I couldn't steal from you." Her smile took the bite from her refusal. It was no more than he expected anyway. She always turned him down, and he always asked the next time again.

Aiden smiled back, warmed by her very presence. "I have something for you," he said. This was also tradition. At his first estate, Aiden had found Semlie a small silver pin worth at least two golden eagles. Since then, none of his gifts had been quite so extravagant—a small decorated vase, a silk scarf, and the like. He brought her anything he thought she might like, but none of it compared to tonight's gift.

Kneeling to add some flair to his presentation, Aiden slipped his gift out of the inside pocket of his cloak and held it out to Semlie on an upraised, open hand. The rubies that ringed the gold bracelet danced with the lantern light. The bracelet was worth a hundred times everything else he had ever given her. Semlie awarded Aiden with a slight gasp as her large brown eyes widened further.

"Den," she managed to say after a moment, "it's beautiful. Is it real?"

Aiden nodded, a smile playing across his face.

"But how...I mean, where did you get this?" Her eyes moved to Aiden's face for a moment before leaping back to the bracelet, as if scared it would disappear if her gaze didn't hold it in place.

Wordlessly, he moved closer and fastened the bracelet around Semlie's wrist. There was so much Aiden wanted to say to her, so much he wanted her to understand, but words were failing him as they often did when he was around Semlie. Her beauty was like a befuddling spell, and he lost his way while enchanted.

After a moment he simply said, "Come with me. There is more to the world than The Pearl and four performances a night." Aiden hesitated and then repeated, "Come with me, Semlie."

Semlie, for her part, fell speechless for a full twenty count. Then she whispered, "I don't know, Den. The bracelet's lovely...." She trailed off and was silent again for a moment before she pulled her gaze from the glittering rubies and once more focused on his face.

Then it came bursting out of her like water that had strained against a dam for too long. "Aiden, you've asked me so many times, and I know it was kind of a game, but each time a piece of me would say *yes* so fast, but then the other part, the big reasonable part of me, would say *no*. I didn't think...I mean, with what you do for a living, and I'm not judging it or you. I know it's been hard since the Touch..." She seemed to catch herself here. Aiden and Semlie had had a huge, screaming fight over this two years ago. It had sat along the side of their meetings ever since, a silent observer, not mentioned but ready to spring if given enough opportunity.

Semlie bit down on her lip in the adorable fashion that announced she was worriedly considering. But her hesitation stretched only a moment. "The truth is, I never thought you would be able to afford a wife, and that's okay. Life isn't always fair. We had our meetings, our glimpses of time when you were back in the city. I had resigned myself to them being enough, and Jace is good to me here. I get to sing and have room and board. I've even saved a little of my pay.

"But now...Aiden, I need you to tell me: Have things changed? I mean, can you afford now...Oh, for Antice's sake, this makes me sound trite and self-seeking, and I don't really care about the money, but I've grown attached to eating. What I'm saying is, Den, we could buy a house with this bracelet, but I need to know if this is the end of it. Can we really go off on our own? Is there more where this came from? I need to know, Den, please."

There was real longing, real hope kindled in her eyes, begging him not to disappoint, and Aiden's heart swelled at what he knew his answer could be. He didn't have to disappoint. Of course, there was more. He had pulled a whole box of it out from the blessed Lanchestor estate.

But he didn't get the chance to fulfill the hope in those eyes; because at that moment, another voice shattered the hopeful excitement and joined their conversation.

"Don't you think you should answer the girl?" said a raspy voice from the far end of the alley, the one opposite of where Aiden had climbed in. "We're all dying to know the answer, Aiden." And now his voice turned cold, "Is there more?"

Aiden swallowed hard as he watched a half dozen men approach from the far end of the alley. Each man had a red cord tied around their upper arm. These were Raz's men then. Raz was always the quicker of the two Barons. He was the rasher of the two as well, but he nearly always got places first.

The man in the front of the group was bald with a long, beaded, scar running from brow to chin. He had a sword at his hip and a knife in his belt but hadn't drawn either. The same couldn't be said for the bald man's companions; two of them had swords in hand, two had clubs, and the last was a straight-shot with a crossbow balanced lightly in his hands, bolt aimed at Aiden.

This was bad, really bad. They knew about the Lanchestor treasure, or at least they knew he had treasure. Antice take old Kempt's shriveled black soul. He had sold Aiden out.

"Semlie, go inside," Aiden said quietly, taking a step forward and around her without allowing his eyes to slip away from the lead bald man.

Semlie hesitated a moment but then took a step toward the door. The bald man's icy, raspy voice pulled her up short, however. "Wait. I'm afraid there is still the matter of that bracelet, sweetheart."

"What business do you have with her belongings?" Aiden asked, forcing steel into his voice to match the man's ice.

"My business is with the stolen property you are carrying, boy. Don't give me any of your lip, or I'll take more than the gold."

Anger boiled inside Aiden's chest. This man calling him out for stealing in front of Semlie, planting the seed of doubt in her heart as well as taking away the future they had just been dreaming, was just too much.

"We both know the only thieves here are you lot and the master Baron thief who sent you," Aiden said. "You can take my pack, as thieves in the night do, but Antice take your lies."

The bald man smiled, and there was something feral and dangerous in it.

"Be very careful now, little boy. I will have what I came for, one way or another." His gaze turned to Semlie. "Girl, the bracelet."

"No," Aiden started, but Semlie cut him off.

"It's fine. Here," she said, as she undid the clasp around her wrist and started toward the bald man. That was when everything went wrong, shattering the last joy Aiden had clung to in life.

Semlie was clearly shaken by the turn of events, and as she stepped up to the man she stumbled forward on a loose cobblestone. The bald man showed no surprise. Nor did he hesitate. He jerked his knife free of his belt in a blink of time and buried it in Semlie's chest as she fell into him.

At first, Aiden couldn't breathe. He remembered his knees hitting the ground, but didn't recall giving them the order to drop. All he could do was watch as Semlie slid free of the bald man's blade and fell into Aiden's reaching arms. Blood blossomed across her dress, staining the cobblestones around them.

"No...no...Sansol, no," Aiden whispered, his voice cracked and trembling, breath coming in short gasps.

Semlie tried a brief smile, but it turned quickly into a grimace. "Den," she tried to say but then coughed, offering fresh blood to the massive amount pooling around the two of them.

"Shh," Aiden hushed, offering a weak smile of his own in attempted comfort. "It's okay. I'm here. It's going to be okay. I'll...I..." Semlie offered Aiden one more pained smile and coughed up yet another round of blood before gasping a final breath and falling still in Aiden's blood-soaked arms. Her vacant eyes stared blankly past Aiden, up at the night's sky, the playful joy gone from them altogether.

"No," Aiden sobbed, rocking Semlie's body back and forth. "No, no, no..."

Only when the bald man reached down and took the bracelet from Semlie's limp, partially opened hand, did Aiden even remember the others were there. In that moment, something snapped in Aiden's chest somewhere near his heart.

He screamed as he leapt for the man. There was a twang, and Aiden felt fire slice across his cheek, but its pain was as nothing in comparison to the storm raging in his chest. Then he was upon the bald man, who swung his knife up, trying to skewer Aiden as he had skewered Semlie, but Aiden was ready for that move. He may be small, but he was quick, and this wasn't his first alley scrap.

Aiden slid left at the last moment, and as the bald man's knife slipped past him into open air, Aiden brought his fist down hard on the ear of the man's over-extended head. The bald man stumbled, and Aiden pressed his advantage, throwing two more quick jabs, one to the head and one to the neck. He leapt onto the still staggering man, crumpling him to the ground with Aiden landing on top. Aiden pulled back his fist for another blow, but then there was a blinding flash of pain to the back of his skull, and all went dark.

Chapter 2

... with the hope that you may yet be saved from my folly.

"Play us another tune, boy," a wizened, small man said from one of the back tables of the inn named the Wagon Wheel. It was a quaint, dozen-room hall in the town of Bellcross—a town notable only because it rested at the crossroads of the Prince's Highway and the Riverway Road.

Willem smiled and nodded to the old man, his long blond hair bobbing around his sharp face. His fingers ached, from the last two hours of playing, and *Hello Danter* was supposed to be their final song of the evening, but when the crowd asked for more, you gave them more. Besides, his group was taking ten percent off the top of the inn's sales that night. Willem wasn't sure how Thant had gotten that deal over the customary five percent. Still, he wasn't complaining either, and more music meant more sales.

So, with another nod, Willem allowed his fingers to dance their way along the strings of his guitar and his voice to fill the air. He played the simple frolic, *Dancing Willow,* and then slowed things down with the tragic tale of lost love, *Thelayta,* before ending with a classic folk song suitably about mead in a tavern, *Mind Me Once & Mind Me Twice.* The whole inn joined in on the second chorus, bellowing, *"So set the tap and roll the dice. You'll mind me once and mind me twice."* And with his fingers truly throbbing now,

Willem was able to dance the whole band off stage as the song finished a cappella.

"Not a bad take on the night, my friends," Thant said with his usual broad smile. He laughed as he slapped Willem on the back. "That was quick thinking with the encore, Will. You should have seen the Drabs clatter on the bar—music to my ears." He smiled again at his own joke, and the others smiled as well, though more because of the cut that would be coming their way than because anyone found Thant terribly funny.

Besides himself on guitar and vocals, their small troupe was made up of Tess on percussion and backup vocals and Jafin on pipes. Thant had a fair voice and was decent on backup vocals, but only rarely joined in on stage.

"So what did the split come out to?" Jafin asked in his typical, no-nonsense, way.

"Oh, it's too early to tell, my boy," Thant answered, refusing to be put off his good mood. He almost always referred to Jafin as *my boy*, though in truth, Thant was scarcely a year Jafin's elder. "We'll know better in an hour or two, once the end of the rabble has cleared out, but my guess is a couple silvers apiece. Not bad for a night."

Over the next hour, the Wagon Wheel slowly emptied of those not renting rooms. Willem was halfway through his second mug of mead and just beginning to show Jana, the serving girl seated on his lap, how he placed his fingers for each cord when the small bag of coins dropped in front of him on the table.

"Better than I thought," Thant chuckled as he flopped into the seat across from Willem. "Now the question is, what's next?"

Willem slipped Jana easily back to her feet. "We'll have to finish our lesson later, my dear," he said with a wink and a smile. She smiled in return before making her way toward the back room.

Willem returned his focus to Thant and the money bag in front of him. With a nimble motion, Willem slipped the bag from the table and weighed it knowingly in his upraised palm. "Eight silvers, fourteen drabs, and a halfpenny," he said.

"Two half pennies," Thant corrected. "I thought I might throw you off with that. Probably a quarter of that was made in that last parade you put on."

"In that case," Willem said, "I'll have a fourth of your cut as well."

Thant smiled as Tess and Jafin made their way through the nearly empty common room of the inn to the table and sat as well. "It would appear we are at a crossroads," Thant said with another chuckle at his own comedic presence. "We can go south toward Oustenbasch, north to Perry, or west to Frantelin."

Willem had been thinking of staying in Bellcross for one more night and then going north toward Perry. He knew of a few inns along the way that brought in decent-sized crowds each night. But he never got to offer that idea because it was just at that moment that the screams started outside.

"SWAAR! RAIDERS! SWAAR!"

The innkeeper, a barrel-chested man named Craul, burst through the door leading to the backroom, a cleaver in one hand and a rusted short spear in the other. He glanced at the four of them for an instant and said, "If any of yous can fight the same as sing, you may want to find your weapons." And with that, he was out, closing the front door firmly behind him.

There was a moment of silence between the four of them, but then a hammer burst through the window accompanied by a crash and spraying glass. Chairs toppled as screams of *"Raiders!"* and *"Swaar!"* rang clearly through the open cavity that had been the window a moment before.

The road could be a rough and dangerous place, so each member of their troupe had to double as guard. Jafin was a fair hand with a spear, and Tess could put an arrow through the eye of a scampering squirrel at forty paces. Thant carried a long sword and wore a knife at his belt, while Willem wore a short sword on his hip and a long knife in his boot. The boot knife was safely in place, and Willem pulled it free now, but his sword rested half-forgotten under the bed in his room; he found it made the crowd uncomfortable for him to perform armed. It also made dancing more difficult, so he usually stowed the blade away as soon as his group arrived at their evening's destination. He cursed not having it with him now, as he bolted for the steps that led to the upper floor rooms.

Willem heard the door of the inn burst open behind him just as he mounted the first few steps, and only one thought reverberated in his now-frantic mind: *Swaar.* The Swaar were said to be savages who would eat a man's flesh as like as to shake his hand. The Swaar's raiding parties looted the hamlets and villages too far out from cities for city watch to intervene. Since few towns smaller than the Nine Cities were large enough to boast any policing force of their own, it was left to the people to defend their own. Willem had never heard of a Swaar raiding party hitting anything as central as Bellcross, but that did him little good since here they were.

Footsteps thumped up the stairs behind him just as he twisted the handle and slammed through the door of his room. Willem didn't know if the footsteps were friend or Swaar, but it didn't matter. He wrenched the door back closed and fumbled with the key until he had the door locked.

Without so much as a pause for breath, he dove beneath the bed and retrieved his sheathed sword. A moment later, he was on his feet, strapping his sword belt on with scarred, fumbling fingers. When the voice spoke from his bed, it was only the awkward state of his armaments—knife held in his teeth, sword belt half buckled around his waist—that kept him from lashing out at the person.

"What's happening?" a girl asked, her head poking from beneath the covers.

Willem had to search his mind for the briefest of moments to come up with the girl's name. "What do you mean, 'what's happening?'" he snapped. "What are you doing in here, Jana?" The adrenaline and fear made him more cross than he had meant, and the serving girl seemed to shrink from his harsh tone.

There were footsteps in the hall outside Willem's door, but still, he tried to calm himself enough to deal with Jana. Another night, he may have accepted her company with an easy smile; now she was little more than another inconvenience in an increasingly inconvenient night.

"Jana, listen. There are raiders in Bellcross, Swaar savages from the sound of things. We'll probably be okay up here, but..."

At that moment, a thump shook the door behind Willem.

"Up," he commanded Jana in a no-nonsense voice as he turned away from her, slamming his weight against the inside of the door. He grabbed the only thing that sat near enough for him to reach, a wooden chair—not overly heavy, but any barrier would help. He braced the chair against the door just in time for the thud to come again. Willem felt the vibration run through him. He looked around wildly. Jana was up and had pulled her dress back over her small clothes—at least the girl had some sense. The only other furniture in the room was the bed and a wardrobe in the corner.

"The wardrobe, Jana, the wardrobe," Willem said through clenched teeth as another thud reverberated through the door.

To her credit, Jana didn't hesitate. She lunged for the wardrobe, but as she grabbed and pulled, it became apparent she would never have the strength to move it so much as an inch by herself. Willem had to decide, and he had to decide now. With a deep breath, he waited for the next thud, his weight still bracing the door. Then he too lunged for the wardrobe, and together, they heaved the monstrosity across the rough wooden floorboards.

Another thud came, bringing with it the cracking sound of wood. And then the wardrobe was in place against the door with Willem and Jana both leaning against it. Willem sucked at lungfuls of air and tried desperately to calm his mind enough to think.

A window sat in the far wall. It would be big enough for them to slip through, but then there would be the drop. The alternative was waiting and hoping the villagers could drive the Swaar away before whoever was outside could get in.

Another thud sounded and with it an even louder *Crack* than before. Willem didn't like his chances in a fight much. He was a fair hand with his sword and knife, but these were Swaar, and he couldn't tell how many would come through that door when it gave. It was the window, then.

"Jana," Willem said in as calm a voice as he could manage, "I'm going to have a look at the window, but I need you to push against this wardrobe with all your might. Can you do that?"

The look in Jana's teary eyes said she was being abandoned, but she nodded her head just the same.

"Okay," Willem comforted, "It'll be okay. I'll be right back." He was only taking four steps across the room, but when raiders were at your door, a step could seem a league.

Willem waited for the next thud to come and pass, and then he leapt to the window, nearly tripping over himself in his haste. Flipping the latch, he jerked the window open, allowing the night air to stream in, bringing with it the smell of smoke and screams of battle and death raging below.

They were only one story up, but still, the ground was twelve feet or more down with the soil slanting away in a gentle hill that now seemed to guarantee broken ankles. *The sheets*, he thought wildly, remembering a tavern story about a man trapped in a bed chamber he shouldn't have been attending in the first place. Another thud shook the door and the barricade in front of it. It was something out of a story, but by Dentar's golden strings, it could work.

Willem made a grab at the bed, throwing quilt and blankets to the floor. A pair of off-white linens lay exposed, and Willem snatched them up. He found a corner of each and tied a double knot. He then threaded the far end of the linens through the spokes of the headboard, tied another knot, and threw the remainder out the open window.

Another thud sounded, and with it, another crack. The door frame must be all but shattered now. Jana shook with the effort of pushing against the wardrobe, and Willem put his weight against the wood to ease her struggle.

"Alright," he said. "We're going to try something a little brave." Jana glanced at the window and then back at Willem.

"Will it hold us?" she asked.

Willem shrugged. "Let's find out." He couldn't think of another option beyond waiting for the Swaar to finally break down the door.

They waited for the next thud and then sprinted to the window. Willem helped Jana out through the opening and made sure she had a firm hold on the sheets before he let go of her completely. He was about to follow her out when he remembered his guitar, rushing for it like a parent who has forgotten his child. Willem slung the guitar over his back by the case strap and stumbled back to the window.

There was another thud and a loud crack. Then the wardrobe began to slide forward into the room. Willem dove for the window and got a hold on the sheet with both feet outside when the first Swaar appeared around the corner of the wardrobe. He was a squat, thick man with a drawn sword. Willem spun as he pushed himself

off the sill and grabbed the sheet with both hands. He just caught
sight of two more men racing into the room behind the first as his
head slipped below the window.

Then a sword swing cut through the space where Willem's head
had been and into the sheet-rope that was holding him off the
ground. Willem fell, his hands still grasping the sheet as if it could
still hold him suspended as his feet flailed, trying to find purchase.
He landed hard on his back; the air knocked from his lungs. There
was a sickening crunch beneath him—his guitar, he knew at once.
The pain of the surely-broken instrument was worse than that of
his aching ribs. He had worked a solid year, scraping and saving to
be able to afford this guitar, and now that was gone along with the
twelve eagles it had cost.

He felt tears threaten and knew their source to be ridiculous as
people were dying around him. Then the thick man from the room
above leapt from the window, and the fear that re-blossomed inside
him had a tremendous sobering effect on his sorrow.

Willem flipped onto his stomach and scrambled on hands and
knees to avoid the falling Swaar, who landed and rolled in an unbroken, easy motion. Willem pulled himself to his feet by the garden fence he had bumped into and drew his short sword from its
sheath.

The Swaar man was already up and had his sword back in hand
as well. At least the odds were better than upstairs, Willem thought
as the man charged with a cry. The Swaar swung wildly, but with
such ferocity that Willem was hard-pressed to deflect his blows. He
also hadn't counted on the awkward nature of fighting with a broken guitar strapped to his back.

Willem dodged left and swung right, trying to distance himself
from the fence behind him, but his opponent only sped up his volley of attacks. Right front cut. Left backhand slice. Right, left, right,
left, right, left. Willem had hoped the man would tire himself out

but instead found himself pressed back against the fence, only just avoiding the death that any one of those blows would herald. Finally, he made his choice. Timing the cadence of the attack, he dropped in between right front cut and left backhand slice. As the Swaar blade whistled just above his ducking head for the second time that night, Willem brought his own sword around with as much strength as he could muster. The blade cut deep into the man's thigh, just above the knee. With a scream, the man went down. Willem wrenched his blade free and ran for it without another glance back. There were stories of how Swaar would fight their opponents (or prey) to the dying breath. Willem was not willing to stand anywhere close to where this maniac savage would suck in his dying breath.

He ran and ran, rounded a corner, ducked into an alley, and finally leaned against a wall to catch his breath. Only then did he remember Jana. He probably should have tried to protect her. That would have been the chivalrous route, but Willem couldn't remember catching so much as a glimpse of her by the time he had hit the ground. She had most likely bolted as soon as her feet touched the soil beneath the window. So much the better; it would be one less thing he had to worry about.

Screams and the sound of battle emanated from every side of Willem's little alley haven. He needed to get out of here, but how, and to where? He wanted to find Thant and the others, but he didn't have the slightest idea where to start looking. For all he knew, the others hadn't even made it out of the inn. Willem shook his head. If they got through this one, his group would have to figure out a plan of rendezvous in case they were to get separated like this again.

He ran his hand through his hair and tried to think. Their wagon and horses were being housed in the Wagon Wheel stables, but it would be a sure death sentence to try and get in there. Stables were almost always the first thing hit by raiders. They could claim the horses for themselves while cutting off any speedy escape all in one motion. There'd still be half a dozen Swaar standing guard there even if the wagon was still intact and the horses ready. No, that wouldn't work at all. For a moment, Willem considered simply staying to fight along with the people of Bellcross, but he dismissed the idea almost as quickly as it had formed. He was a musician, not a soldier. The fighting for just causes was for someone else. He preferred a battle of wits over one of strength. One rarely died from the lash of a sharp tongue.

He would have to make for the woods on the far end of the river, then. It was as good a place as any, and his troupe had discussed stopping amongst the trees for hunting and foraging before moving on. It was as likely a place to find his friends as any.

His decision made, Willem tightened his grip on his sword, drew out his knife, and peered into the street from around the corner of the building he sheltered behind. There were ongoing fights in the street, and several fires blazed in buildings, but for the moment he thought he was safe to make a break for it. Hairs prickled on his neck, though, and he didn't move.

Then a horn sounded from the far end of the street, low and ominous. Willem pulled back as quickly and quietly as he could. He set a crate on top of a waste barrel and leaned against the wall behind them, hoping he would be out of sight of anyone on the street. He held his breath and waited.

Willem didn't have long to wait. Only a moment passed before there was the clatter of hooves on the cobbles and a dozen riders pulled up outside the alley, met by another half dozen from the other direction. "Report," a man said in a deep, resonating voice from the larger group, and Willem peered from behind his crate ever so carefully. His heart dropped. The man who had spoken was unmistakable—the Rock Giant. He was huge, seven and a half or eight feet tall, towering over the men around him. He made the steed he rode look like little more than a colt. Still, he sat tall, covered from head to toe in dark gray scale armor that seemed to be made of some kind of stone.

Willem gripped his weapons fiercely to stop himself from shaking as he listened.

"We have most of the locals rounded up, my lord Dal," the leader of the second group was saying, his voice marred by a thick accent that Willem couldn't place. "They put up a decent fight at first, but it was just as you said—they had little in the way of experience. We're finding the last of them now."

The big man nodded. "And put out those fires," he rasped. "It'll do us little good to move in if we've desolated the whole town."

"Yes, my Dal," the man said with as much of a bow as he could perform while mounted. The group split again, the big man giving orders to smaller groups before eventually riding off with a handful of honor guards.

That was all Willem needed to hear. This was no raiding party, come to steal horses, women, and food. This was an invasion meant to take and keep Bellcross. And at the invaders' head was none other than the Swaar king, Dal Tek, the man called the Rock Giant.

Willem turned in the opposite direction and ran. He didn't much care where he ended up as long as it wasn't here. He ran and he ran, stopping and caring for nothing else at the moment.

Chapter 3

These may be my final words to you...

Waking could be painful on a normal day, but on this occasion, Aiden felt like he had to swim through a sea of pain to find consciousness. Slowly, ever so slowly, he opened his eyes and emerged from nothingness into a dimly lit room. His body hurt all over. Apparently, the beating hadn't stopped with a club to the head. He tried to take a deep breath, to think, but there was a sharp stab in his side when he did. He wondered absently how many times the infuriated bald man had kicked Aiden's limp body. The thought of the man with the scarred face brought new rage into Aiden's mind. He thought of Semlie, dying in an ever-growing pond of her own blood. They had probably just left her there for Jace or the watch to find. *My fault,* he thought for the first time, and the pain from that realization hurt worse than his body's screaming nerves could ever muster. A single sob escaped him as Aiden felt tears pool and threaten in his eyes.

With an effort of will, Aiden took shallow breaths and refocused on his surroundings. The room wasn't large, but it was well furnished. A lantern burned on low in the far corner, revealing a plush sitting room or den. Two overstuffed chairs sat in front of a large, well-lacquered desk of some expensive wood, walnut maybe. There were also bookshelves and a few benches along the tapestry-hung walls. He didn't know if the costly setting was a good or bad sign for him. He supposed he would find out soon.

On that account, he was right. Within a few minutes of waking, a door opened somewhere behind Aiden, flooding the room with warm light from the hall. Aiden tried to turn his head to look, and the door closed. A few moments later, it opened again, and several people entered. First came a woman, dressed all in dark riding leathers. She was lean and tall with two long knives in her belt. Next came two large, grizzled men that Aiden assumed were swordarms, followed by the bald man and finally a massive man in an expensive tunic and cape. This last looked like he had once been built like a brick wall, but his body had gone half to fat with a small gut now protruding out from a once firm chest.

Aiden's eyes had little time for this last man, however. He was zoned in completely on the bald man with the scar running down his face. His breathing grew heavy upon seeing Semlie's murderer. The ache that had been throbbing inside him flared, and Aiden struggled wildly against his bonds as a scream of rage broke from his lips.

"You...you killed her! Murderer! Antice take you! You killed her! You stupid, crow-licking, son of a hag! I'll kill you! Dregs and drought, I'll kill you!"

His tirade continued as he struggled against bonds that wouldn't give. Still, he fought, knowing if only he could get free, the bald man would pay.

"Now that's enough," the huge man who had seated himself behind the expensive desk said in a quiet, stern voice, rich with warning. Aiden didn't care, though, and when he didn't settle, a fist came down hard across his face, snapping his head ferociously to the side. The chair must have been bolted to the floor because the force of the blow should have knocked Aiden over and the chair with him.

"Branke, why don't you give us a few moments with our guest. I don't think he likes you much, and things may go easier without you," the large man said with the same, quiet tone as if nothing had happened.

The bald man, Branke, nodded once and giving Aiden one last look, left back through the door.

Aiden's eyes came slowly back into focus, and he stared more intently at the large man behind the desk. The pain threatening to swell his right eye closed had jarred him back to his usual, calm demeanor. He was still angry, boiling inside, but having his face smashed in by heavy-handed swordarms wasn't going to do him any good.

No less than you deserve, he heard a part of his mind whisper. *My fault,* he thought again.

"Now, little Aiden," the man behind the desk began, and his voice had taken on a deeper warmth as if pleasantries had resumed. "You were Terrance's boy, weren't you? Yes, I knew your father—good man, good man. As you may have guessed, I am Baron Walter Raztumble, but you may call me Lord Raz."

Raz was intermittently popping his knuckles and steepling his hands in an absent manner. This motion accentuated the scars patterning Raz's fists. This man was a brawler, and most brawlers Aiden knew *liked* to fight. Aiden would have to be very careful now if he wanted to survive the Baron. There would be no salvation from this chamber if Aiden said the wrong thing. Count Endresi may technically rule the city, but everyone knew, between the two of them, the Barons controlled the Count and held most of the city watch in their employ. No there would be no salvation from without—there was no cavalry.

"My associate tells me there was something of a misunderstanding earlier tonight," Raz said. "I believe you have come into some of my possessions, by pure accident I'm sure, but I would like them back." At this last, Raz's voice took on that same cold, menacing note he had used just before the swordarm had softened Aiden's face.

Aiden looked back, meeting the Baron's eyes, willing his own face not to give away his fear or his anger. He wasn't sure what was expected of him, though, so he remained silent.

After a moment, Raz sighed and ran his hand down the length of his face in a weary movement. "Aiden, it's very simple. We have gone through your pack and your cloak. All I need to know is, is there more?"

Aiden held in the laugh forming in his throat, but couldn't help a slight, joyless smile from reaching his lips. "Shouldn't you know? You bring me in under the pretense that I have robbed you, and you can't tell if you got it all back or not. What did old Kempt get for selling me out? I wonder, did you tell him that your men would kill a compliant girl in the streets for the crime of stumbling over a loose stone?" His voice had been rising involuntarily as he spoke. Now it broke, and Aiden had to clench his teeth to hold in the tears of fury and loss. He was slipping again, dangerously close to losing it. It would cost him his life, but Aiden was finding he cared less and less as he watched Raz behind his desk. Semlie was dead, and Aiden's rage welled and welled at that unforgivable fact.

"Yes," Raz said in something remarkably similar to a sympathetic tone. "Yes, Branke told me of the unfortunate incident—how he instinctively tried to catch the girl, but his knife was in his hand, and, well..."

"Liar!" Aiden bellowed, the rage breaking like white caps on a beach, refusing to be held at bay any longer. "I'll kill him! I'll kill him and you too. You stupid, fat pig, I don't have any more treasure for you to steal, you slimy cutpurse. You set yourself up here like some kind of Angel-appointed king like everyone else should just..." Aiden's shouting ended abruptly as another blow fell to the back of his head and all fell dark once more.

Aiden's eyelids felt heavy as stones when he finally blinked them open—or rather, when he blinked his left eye open. His right eye was swollen to the point that it no longer opened at his command. Since he didn't have the energy to fight it right now, Aiden decided he would just let it hang closed for the moment. He was growing tired of waking with such a reverberating throb dancing through his skull. He *was* waking, however, and that seemed an unlikely treat as Aiden remembered his outburst at Raz. He shouldn't have said all he did at the end, especially the bit about not having any more treasure. That had been his only bargaining chip, his only redemption to the Baron. Aiden was just so angry. He could have killed Raz with his own two hands.

Raz. Raz meant the bald man, Branke, and in turn Semlie's blood washing the cobblestones. His rage returned in a giant wave, rushing the beach of his heart, swallowing it in a tremendous, booming cacophony. Then, from the center of that rage, the pain of Semlie's death stepped forward like a soloist to the front of the stage. Tears welled and fell from his eyes, even from his swollen, unseeing right. She was gone, and the world was empty. A small sob escaped his lips as Aiden cradled his head with his arms.

"It's okay, lad. It'll be okay," came a rough voice from Aiden's side.

Aiden was so startled, his tears stopped immediately. For the first time, he took in his surroundings. He was bumping along in the back of a wagon. He could just see over the edge to watch the countryside trees slide slowly by. Now that he was aware of the movements, Aiden could feel the throb and crash of his pain harmonizing with each bump of the road. He was sitting on the floor, and a manacle held tight to Aiden's right ankle, binding him to the wagon. His cloak, drenched in Semlie's blood, had been taken from him, and only a few streaks of the stain still clung to Aiden's home-knit pants and shirt.

Aiden turned his head now and found that he wasn't alone in his new captivity. A scraggly, bearded old man sat on the floor a few feet away. The man looked at Aiden with genuine concern in his soft blue eyes.

"It'll be okay, lad," the man said again. There was a very slight hint of refinement in his voice, suggesting that he had been educated to some degree or another. "You're young and handsome. You'll catch a fair price to some lord's household and be one of those servants who get to wear the nice clothes while carrying wine and opening doors, my boy. You'll see. It'll be okay.

Aiden's brow creased as if in concentration. "Who are you? What's going on?" he asked, hating not already knowing, but his mind was sluggish at the moment.

"My name is Japh, young master, and we are on our way to one of the other Nine Cities, or so is my guess."

Pieces were beginning to fall into place, and the horrible truth descended on him slowly like a gently wafting leaf. Aiden had never been to any of the other Nine Cities, though he had always dreamed of seeing them. Still, chained to a cart was not the transport he would have picked for the trip, and Semlie had always been in those dreams. With a glance at Japh's manacled ankle, Aiden forced the painful thought away, asking, "And what was your crime, that you were sold to the slavers?"

"Ah," Japh said. "Well, you see young Master...?" This last he left hanging as a question."

"Oh, sorry," Aiden said. "Aiden. My name is Aiden, but I'm no master."

"Very good," Japh said and smiled. "A habit of mine, Master Aiden. You must forgive me. As to my state at the present, well you see, I am a man prone to risk. I see opportunity but not always the cost should my opportunity prove less than promised." Japh paused and smiled again—a sad smile. "Let us just say I took a loan from an individual I should not have done business with, for an amount I should not have borrowed. When I could not pay, well...well, here I am."

Aiden understood. Oustenbasch was not the biggest of the Nine Cities, but that didn't make it a safe place. Unpaid debts often ended poorly for the debtor, primarily since most loans flowed back to the Barons one way or another. Still, being sold to slavers was a bit extreme. Usually, a merchant's profits or merchandise were just seized for a time. Sill, Aiden had heard stories of people, even entire families, disappearing during the night. He supposed he had just disappeared during the night himself. Perhaps he had just become a story.

Japh proved good company, far better than Aiden, himself. By the time they stopped for the night, Aiden had nearly forgotten he was chained to a slaver's cart, bound for a foreign city where he knew no one. The three men who appeared at the back of the cart changed that perspective quickly.

"Up, you mangy dogs," the first man spat. He had a broad chest and the largest mustache Aiden had ever seen. It hung down, framing his mouth and chin before dropping in a braid to his chest. Japh scrambled to his feet, but Aiden remained seated and earned a kick to the ribs for his mutiny.

"Dregs! I said, 'up' boy," the man growled as he gripped Aiden's jaw and dragged him to his feet. "You will learn to mind me, or so help me, I will turn your soft skin to mush. Do you hear?"

The man released Aiden and turned away without an answer. Japh and Aiden's hands were chained together and then tied with a longer rope to the cart. Aiden saw a handful of men, slaves now, he supposed, tied in the same way in the cart in front of theirs. They were all allowed to walk around and stretch their legs for a time. Aiden didn't believe it was a kindness. If their muscles atrophied on the trip toward slavery, he didn't suppose they would bring as many eagles.

To the same end, the slavers fed Aiden and Japh well that night. Aiden learned why the next morning when their left hands were tied to ropes, and they were made to run the first hour behind the cart as the horses set a hard pace. At the end of the hour, they were allowed to catch the cart and jump into the back. Aiden was breathing heavily, and his legs felt thick while his recent injuries screamed for relief, but his time living in the wild had toughened him. Japh, on the other hand, was in far worse shape. He wheezed and coughed as he lay sprawled on the floor of the cart, his thin frame shaking from the effort expended.

"Well, Master Aiden," the old man rasped after the majority of his trembling had subsided. "It would appear we survived that, unpleasant as it was." Japh smiled weakly, and Aiden shook his head.

"Optimism won't get us out of these chains, old man," Aiden said. "Optimism won't fix the wrongs of the world."

"Ah, but pessimism will?" Japh smiled again. "Optimism may be all we have to go on, Aiden. It's best we hold onto it with both hands."

Aiden sighed but said nothing as he sat back against the far wall of the cart and rubbed his sore legs. When he got down as far as his boots, Aiden felt a strange lump that he realized now had been paining him as he ran. When grouped with all of his other injuries, he hadn't noticed the lump rubbing his skin raw as anything out of the usual. Now, it seemed strange indeed.

He groped down into his boot with his untied hand and felt something hard materialize in his grasp just beneath the boot's lining. Aiden felt the falcon head pommel and the leather grip. He had assumed all of his treasure lost, but by some miracle, they hadn't searched his boots, or at least not thoroughly. The silver knife still lay nestled against his calf. The knife also meant there should be a few coins tucked away. Possibilities re-birthed themselves in Aiden's mind. Leaving the knife where it was for the moment, Aiden leaned back against the cart wall and thought of Baron Raz and his lapdog, the bald man, Branke. Aiden thought of revenge. He thought of using the silver falcon knife on Semlie's killers, and Aiden smiled.

Chapter 4

...and to those who come after.

The sun was rising by the time Willem stopped his fevered run and dropped to his knees to drink from a small creek in the northern woods beyond Bellcross. He had swum through the Silverwine River that cupped Bellcross on the very northern tip but hadn't stopped to drink, for the fear had still been on him. Even now, the thought of being trapped in the town with those unfortunates who hadn't escaped made him feel sick.

The Rock Giant. Dal Tek was said to cut his captive men into eunuch slaves, turn women into servants of his men's needs, put children's heads on spikes, and even roast infants for feast. Why the prince and other city leaders didn't send their soldiers down on the Rock Giant and his Swaar baffled Willem's understanding. The majority of Prince Greenlea's lands bordered those of the cities of the East, the land from which the Swaar rode. Willem was sure the prince wouldn't want to risk open war, but was the raiding of his people all that different from war? And what now that the Swaar had invaded, presumably to stay? What was the point of claiming vast swathes of land surrounding his city of Frantelin if one wasn't willing to defend it? Taxes, he supposed.

He shook his head. Prince Greenlea and the rest seemed just as scared of Dal Tek as Willem was. He also imagined the princes,

44

barons, and lords may have their hands full with warring, bickering amongst themselves in their ever-important game of politics. Regardless, Willem was glad he was well away from the Swaar and their terrifying, giant king.

His breath caught. It was only now that Willem remembered the instrument strapped to his back. Cursing by the golden strings themselves, he hauled the guitar case around, undid the clasp, and peered inside. The damage could have been worse. Things could have been a lot better too, though. The neck was cracked, which was probably the noise he had heard upon landing beneath the window, and the headstock was dented in at the corner. Still, the body all seemed intact and the strings unbroken.

Knowing that he shouldn't but not being able to help himself, Willem strummed first one chord, then another. He picked his way up and down the strings listening for any off sound that might betray a problem he hadn't seen. Then he let his fingers dance for a moment on their own. They played his sorrow from all that had happened the night before. They played his relief at escape from the Swaar. They played his joy at finding his instrument something more than kindling. And it felt wonderful to be so unbridled.

After a short time, Willem looked up to find that the sun had moved perceptibly in the sky. He had gotten lost in his music and sat here for far too long. Bellcross lay behind him, but only just, and Willem wanted to be leagues away from here before any Swaar decided to roam as far as these woods.

He strapped his guitar carefully back into its case, making sure it didn't get any more damage from the slightly dented form the case now held. That done, he slung the case onto his back again and started walking north and further away from Bellcross.

As he walked, he took inventory of what he had in his possession. Apart from his guitar, he had his sword and his knife, both safely tucked in their sheaths. He had been wearing a dark wool

spun shirt and pants last night while he played for the crowd at the
inn. He also had his boots, thankfully, but no cloak of any kind.
The Swaar hadn't given him much time to pack. Luckily, he kept his
extra coin purse tucked into his guitar case. He also had the coins
Thant had given him last night, so if it came down to it, Willem
should be able to buy some supplies and a cloak once he reached
the next town.

As far as food was concerned, he had stumbled upon an over-
turned basket of apples as he fled Bellcross and had grabbed three
as he scrambled past. If only he'd had the presence of mind to refill
and take the whole basket. He had eaten one apple on the stream's
edge and the other two wouldn't last long as he walked.

He had never been much of a hunter. When there had been
an opportunity, Tess had done the majority of the hunting with
her bow. Willem could forage, though. After several years on the
road, he could tell a berry you could eat from one that would make
you sick. When his little troupe would stop, Thant somehow always ended up guarding the camp while Jess hunted, and Jafin and
Willem gathered berries or collected firewood. Thant was just like
that—not lazy exactly, but good at getting other people to do what
he wanted.

Willem stopped and placed one hand against a trunk while the
other ran through his hair and rubbed at his neck. Tears threatened
to revolt and his eyes stung. The others. He had left the others, his
friends, to their fates. What did that say of him as a man? There
wasn't a whole lot he could have done. One more drawn sword
wasn't going to stop the Rock Giant, but still.

"They might have gotten out," he told himself aloud and then
nodded his head in agreement as if that could make it so. Still,
if the others had gotten out, he didn't think they had come this
way—maybe not north at all. He had seen no trace of them at any

rate, and they hadn't found him even when he had sent his tune out into the woods before him.

There was nothing for it now, so he made his feet to move again and forced his thoughts back to provisions. He would just have to forage what he could as he walked, eat sparingly, and pray the next village wasn't too far.

After a full day's walking, that night brought him to another small creek. Willem had one apple left and a handful of berries he had found a mile or so back down his path. He drank greedily from the small creek, wishing, not for the first time, that he had some kind of water skin, cup, or anything to hold water as he walked. He supposed he could have filled his guitar body with water, but that would be incredibly clumsy to carry without spilling or to drink later. And regardless, he was nowhere near thirsty enough to fill his precious instrument with sound-devouring, wood-warping water.

With a sigh, he took off his guitar case, sat down, and leaned back against a tree. Eating the berries, he decided to save his last apple for breakfast. His stomach still complaining for nourishment, he took off first one boot and then the other and rubbed his sore feet. Willem had forgotten how nice it was to have a horse do the walking for him. After a moment, he slipped the boots back on. His feet were getting cold, and there was really no other way to warm them.

With a chill breeze, the night was setting in, cool and harsh. Willem shivered, all the colder now that he wasn't moving. A fire was out, however; he didn't have any flint and had never gotten the hang of rubbing sticks together.

He yawned even through the shivering and thought that if only he could get to sleep, he'd be the better for it. Having traveled to Bellcross, performed, run for his life, and then hiked all day through the forest with next to no food and all without a wink of sleep since two nights back, sleep didn't turn out to be a problem. Willem closed his eyes and drifted off immediately.

He woke, shivering violently, some hours later. The sky was full black, clouds covering the stars. It was impossible to know what time it was, but he didn't think he had been sleeping very long. There was no hint of sunrise on the horizon at any rate. He had to move, sunrise or no. It was too late in the season to sleep in the open with no fire and no cloak.

Willem's head ached from sleep deprivation, but he had no choice. So, he strapped his guitar case back on, filled his stomach with stream water even as his chattering teeth complained, and headed out again.

He had only walked a few minutes, and warmth had just begun to prickle his toes again when he saw a flickering, red light ahead. "Fire," he whispered through chattering teeth and started toward it.

Merchants, Willem thought, approaching the fire. There were several horses and a couple of carts a little ways off from the fire. These men must have been traveling on some kind of road or path because their carts would never have made the trip over terrain like Willem had crossed that day. A road was good for Willem. A road meant civilization and warmth and food.

Laughter from the fire pulled Willem's attention back to the flickering flames. A dozen men sat in a ring around the flames. A few of them sat bunched up at one side of the ring of fire-sitters as if trying to get close to the fire to soak up the warmth but being denied a closer spot or a wider ring. Several wild birds that may have been turkeys roasted slowly on a spit. Blessed warmth and the smell of the food—Willem was moving toward the fire without remembering to tell his feet to walk.

"Hello," he said when he was within about ten feet of the circle of merchants.

The men spun, swords leaping from sheaths as these strangers found their feet. There was a pause and Willem was sure his eyes had grown to the size of the moons themselves. Then the merchant in front, a broad-chested man, said in a rough voice, "What'a you want?"

Willem wasn't a small man by anyone's reckoning, lean but strong and he had his sword at his belt. Still, he was tired and cold and there were six of these men with drawn swords and another coming up from behind him—the man on watch, Willem supposed. This could end badly for him if he wasn't cautious. He took a breath and fell into performance. He smiled his best smile and tried to forget there were swords leveled at him.

"Well," he said, "it's a cold night. I was hoping to share your fire with you for a bit. I am a lonely traveler and have lost my flint." He smiled again and after a pause, added, "I'm a musician. I'd be happy to trade you some music for some warmth."

The first man's demeanor changed as smoothly as water flowing into a cup. He smiled something toothy underneath a large mustache, sheathed his sword, and said, "I do believe some music would be right nice, but come over here and warm yourself by the fire. By the Angels themselves, it's a cold night, true enough. You must be half-frozen."

The man filled the step between them and took Willem by the shoulders. Some kind of warning bell was ringing in the back of Willem's mind, but he was too cold and too tired to care about that right now. He let himself be led to the fire and soak up its delicious comfort.

"So, Master Musician, what instrument do you play?" the mustached man asked as he seated himself across from Willem by the fire. Another man cut a drumstick from the roasting birds and offered it to Willem, who accepted the kindness with a smile.

"The guitar," he said. "I play the guitar."

"Ahh," the first man said, "you'll have to play for us—once you're refreshed, of course." Another man forced a cup of wine into Willem's hand. Willem glanced up and thanked the man. All of these men wore a broad smile that they offered easily to Willem whenever he looked in their direction.

He took a bite of the drumstick, and his tongue danced for the joy of it. The meat was perfect: tender and hot. Willem couldn't have asked for better. His bird devoured, he sipped his wine as he glanced around the fire. He was again met with all those smiles—toothy smiles that now seemed ever so slightly off. He tried to puzzle it over, but his mind was only just thawing, and he was still exhausted.

Then his gaze fell onto the small group of men huddled together at the edge of the ring. They weren't smiling. They sat on the far end of the fire, saying nothing, and for some reason two other men stood behind them, not seeming to relax the way the smiling men in the ring did. One of the smaller men from the huddled group looked young, no older than Willem, and he appeared as if he had been fighting recently. His eyes were sullen when their gazes met, and the small man shook his head ever so slightly. Willem had been about to take another sip of wine but stopped. What was this man trying to tell him?

The mustached man's voice snapped him back out of his thoughts. "Master Musician, you must drink up so you can play for us. I understand music is a thirsty business."

"That it is," Willem said with a laugh. He downed the rest of his wine and reached for his guitar. The drink must have been stronger than it seemed, for he fumbled with the case. Then his eyes grew bleary. Trying to focus, he looked at the mustached man and began to make some kind of apology. He didn't think he could play right now. The man's smile was still on his face, but there was no gentleness in his eyes. Those eyes were cold and dark. They were also the last thing Willem saw before passing into darkness of his own.

Chapter 5

Avoid my errors...

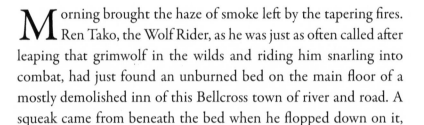

Morning brought the haze of smoke left by the tapering fires. Ren Tako, the Wolf Rider, as he was just as often called after leaping that grimwolf in the wilds and riding him snarling into combat, had just found an unburned bed on the main floor of a mostly demolished inn of this Bellcross town of river and road. A squeak came from beneath the bed when he flopped down on it, and Tako slammed his great axe into the floorboards, splintering them.

"Out," he rumbled in the common speech of these low dwellers.

The squeak came again and a girl of fewer than twenty winters scrambled from beneath the mattress and made for the door still on her hands and knees as if this would protect her from Tako's sight.

"Out," he said again, adding a growl to his voice. The girl sprang up and ran for the door. There were many among the Swaar who would have taken her for their own, but all Tako wanted right now was the comfort of this bed. He glanced back at the pillow and then at the door. With a sigh he stood and closed the door, turning the key in the small lock. The door wouldn't keep any genuine attacker out, but it would give Tako a moment or two's warning before anyone came barging in. Besides, none of these low dwellers would even dare a locked door in their own town. That was for more courageous souls.

He had just slumped down on the bed again, leaning his axe against the wall and making sure he had a knife close to hand when a beating came echoing at the door. Tako growled. How had they found him so soon? Could a man have no rest? When the pounding shook the door a second time, Tako rolled to his feet, knife in hand. He unlocked the door and yanked it open. The man on the other side stumbled back against the far wall of the hallway, forgetting even to lower his hand from knocking. Tako pinned him there, knife against his throat.

"By the All-Warrior and his crones," Tako whispered in his own tongue, biting off each word, "this had better be important, or I'll have your blood as payment."

The man hissed through the gap in his broken teeth, clearly fighting down the fear. Tako was sure the man had lost some bet or other to be forced to come find him so soon after a battle.

"Wolf Rider," he said, and slowly uncurled his clenched hand to reveal a smooth, round stone ringed in iron. The fist sigil of Dal Tek lay burned into the stone's flesh. So, the Rock Giant wanted him. Fine.

Tako let the man free, slipping his knife back into his belt and going to retrieve his axe. "Where is the Dal, boy?" he growled.

The man was not much younger than Tako, but he didn't blanch at being called 'boy'. *The coward should stab me for it. I bet no one would ever call him boy again.* But the man didn't stab Tako. He just stood there, gripping hard to Dal Tek's sigil and looking like he may dirty himself at any moment. Tako would never kill the man, not while he was carrying the Rock Giant's sigil. It was death to any man who killed one of the Dal's runners—even for the Wolf Rider.

Ren Tako turned back to him, shouldering his axe. He exhaled, trying to keep the growl out of it, and asked again, "Where is Dal Tek?"

Finally, the messenger found his voice. "He's in the great bell building with the two towers."

Tako smiled. The Rock Giant would have the gall to set his claim to the temple of the Twin Angels. And the All-Warrior wins again.

Leaving the trembling man, Tako made his way out of the inn and onto the cobbled streets. No man dawdled when the Rock Giant sent for him.

He twisted the silver ring upon his finger as he approached the temple, a bad habit that attached itself to him too many years ago to count. The ring had been passed from his mother before she died, the only family heirloom from her side, and it never left Tako's finger. The stone was pitch dark with spiraling white circles that almost seemed to glow in the dark. "As dark as night," his mother had said. "As dark as night and bright as liquid starlight; remember that, Tako." Still, it was a nervous tic and he was a Ren. Forcing his hand down, Tako focused on what lay ahead.

The temple itself was unimpressive compared to the larger cities Tako had visited in his youth. No marble pillars soared up to grasp a high entry. No triple-life-sized, chiseled stone statues with precious stones inlaid in the eyes stood watch as worshipers came to pray. Instead, the front of the building sat, unassuming and plain. If not for the two towers chasing each other an extra story into the sky, Tako would have taken the building for another two-story merchant shop and living hole.

Inside was a bit of a different story. Two marble pillars stretched from floor to ceiling at the front of a small walkway. The pillars served to frame two, marble statues of the Twin Angels, grasping each other's forearms while drawing blades with their free hands.

Tako knew the angels were supposed to symbolize the counteracting work of good and evil, but he found the concept ridiculous. *You fools, one would have killed the other a long time ago, instead of just scrabbling with each other like children.*

Dal Tek sat behind the altar in a big wooden chair adorned with delicate scrollwork and carvings. It had no doubt been some lord's prized chair yesterday. Today it was the Rock Giant's—perhaps tomorrow, kindling. The chair was large or would seem so with anyone else occupying it, but the Dal dwarfed it, making the chair appear fit for little more than a child.

The Rock Giant's chief men and war Grenats sat with the Dal. To Tek's right sat Olivat Storm Eater, and to his left, Gray Riller. Riller had been Tek's closest friend and fastest supporter all through the Rock Giant's rise to power. Olivat, on the other hand, was only a part of the Dal's inner circle for the last few years. He had come from even further to the east five years ago, and few ever came from the wastes that stretched to the horizon there. And the man could do things, sorcerous things: moving stones, calling up and vanquishing sand storms. After Tek himself, these two men were more feared than any others in all the Far East. As Tako thought about it, Ren Tako Wolf Rider may be reasonably far up that list as well.

On the altar, before the Dal and his guests was set a meal of roast lamb, new bread, cheese, an assortment of greenery that Tako had no doubt would go untouched by Tek, and, of course, wine. The Rock Giant always drank wine in plenty, thick and dark, prone to steal a man's senses and perhaps the legs out from under him.

Dal Tek never seemed to feel the wine's effects, however. Always calculating was that man, always thinking eight steps ahead. The only exception was the Dal's horrible temper—a rage created to rip down city walls and crush armies. When the calculation met the rage, a kind of cold fury was born that no man, no matter how brave or how strong, could withstand. Tako was wise enough to know that for all his own skill, he was not exempt from this truth. The trick, then, was always staying far enough in Dal Tek's good graces so as not to summon the cold fury.

"My Dal," Tako intoned, slamming his fists together and bowing his head for a moment as was appropriate.

"Ren Tako," Dal Tek rumbled like a distant thunderhead. "Come, sit. Eat and tell me of the day's events." The Rock Giant's voice was so close to monotone that it was hard to read his mood. It was usually best to take the Dal literally and wait for him to wave you off if his words had been in jest.

Tako stepped forward and pulled out the chair in front of an empty plate. A man hurried over from the wall—a local, dressed in the red and black robe of a priest of the Twin Angels. His robe was dirtied, and his face was swollen and bruising. With downcast eyes, the now-former priest cut a generous portion of lamb and some thick slices of bread to fill Tako's plate. When the man reached for some of the greens, Tako waved him off. Meat and bread would more than suffice. Tako doubted he would have much time to eat at any rate if Dal Tek was expecting him to talk. The priest skittered off quickly as if Tako had struck him.

Olivat laughed. "Oh ho, our little priest thinks you might bite him, Wolf Rider. Hmm, and from hearing the stories, perhaps he's wise to think so. I, too, am anxious to hear your telling of today's great victory." Grenat Olivat was a broad-chested man, big, not as big as Tek, but then, no one was. Olivat was mostly bald with a double-braided beard swinging from his chin. He almost always wore a smile as broad as his chest, especially in battle. Tako heard him say once that he just enjoyed his work, but Tako had seen the ice in Olivat's eyes, and he knew not all was laughter in the Storm Eater's heart. It was more likely that Olivat smiled and laughed because it seemed out of place, disconcerting his opponents and offering himself power through it. *But you can smile all you want at me, old man. You will see no fear from me.*

Tako cut a piece of meat, chewed, and swallowed. Dal Tek had said no more and had continued eating, but the huge man's gaze had never left Tako.

A quiet *tick, tick, tap* floated up from beneath the floor as if someone was knocking on a basement door. Taking a drink of wine to chase down what he assumed may be his only bite of this particular meal and trying to ignore the sound from below, Tako spoke. "My Dal Tek, today was a victory, but forgive me, Storm Eater, it was no great one. We butchered a hundred merchants, farmers, and fisherfolk. We cowed another thousand and have destroyed a third of what we came to take for ourselves."

He paused to allow Tek to agree or reprimand as he saw fit. It was best not to anger the Rock Giant, but Tako would not lie and weasel to win favor, either. All being equal, he would rather make his statements with his axe, but if he spoke, he would *say* something.

Gray Riller seemed ready to argue, but Tek raised his hand, forestalling him. "Say all you would, Ren Tako. You do not anger me with your words."

Tako took one more drink of his wine and continued. "I do not mean to criticize my Dal, and I will ride out whenever and wherever he commands. I cannot claim understanding in this move, though. The Swaar have courage and strength, but the people of the Nine Cities number greater by far. Bellcross is useful for traders and merchants, but it is not defensible, as the people found out here last night. We struck here. Fine. Why are we still here? Let's march on one of the Nine, Frantelin or Taalmor, and claim something we can keep, or let us return to Allisii with all we have claimed here."

A pause hung stiffly in the air of the one-time temple. Then Dal Tek smiled, actually and truly smiled. It was perhaps the most disconcerting of any expression he could have offered Tako at that moment. Something lit and danced behind the Rock Giant's pale gray eyes. Tako sent a silent prayer to the All-Warrior for strength if he had just called out Tek's cold fury.

When the huge Dal spoke, however, there seemed to be genuine amusement in his voice. As if knowing Tako's thoughts, he said, "Do not fear, my dear Ren. I commanded you speak, and you gave the best wisdom you had. This does not anger me. Tell me, Wolf Rider, have you heard of the Shield of Ammereth?"

Tako nodded. "What child has not heard the story? Konto, the warrior, was said to have worn it defending the siege of Tyrass. Senzmonde was also said to carry it during his conquest of the western isles. Myths. Power and protection for its holder. The claim of something special for others to rally behind."

"A good synopsis," Olivat laughed. "But stories come from somewhere, and history is little more than a myth until one experiences the things claimed true by the history. What are Frantelin and Taalmor but stories until one visits and finds them true and whole with walls, buildings, and people?"

Olivat paused to smile. It oozed out somewhere between knowing and ingratiating, and Tako could again hear the *tick, tick, tap, tick, tick, tap* from under his chair. Pieces began to reorder in Tako's mind. He had always been quick to discern situations. It was a part of why he was still alive.

"You think it's real," Tako said. It was not a question. "The Shield of Ammereth, you think it's real, and you think it's here." *Tick, tick, tap.* "You think it is in this very temple."

Olivat smiled, "Beneath this very temple, actually."

"We will see, Storm Eater," rumbled Dal Tek. "And then we will know, Ren Tako, if we should have come to this Bellcross or not."

Chapter 6

...and do not follow in my footsteps...

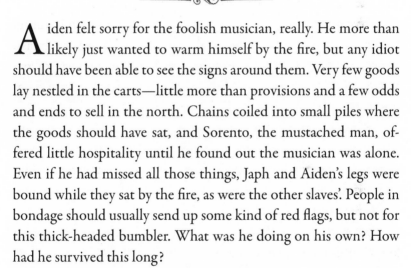

Aiden felt sorry for the foolish musician, really. He more than likely just wanted to warm himself by the fire, but any idiot should have been able to see the signs around them. Very few goods lay nestled in the carts—little more than provisions and a few odds and ends to sell in the north. Chains coiled into small piles where the goods should have sat, and Sorento, the mustached man, offered little hospitality until he found out the musician was alone. Even if he had missed all those things, Japh and Aiden's legs were bound while they sat by the fire, as were the other slaves'. People in bondage should usually send up some kind of red flags, but not for this thick-headed bumbler. What was he doing on his own? How had he survived this long?

Aiden shook his head. He and Japh had just finished their morning run which was a bit easier, though not easy, now on the fourth morning of it. No run that held your wrists tethered to the moving cart in front of you could truly be called easy. As they sat catching their breath in the bouncing cart again, they both stared at this blond music man who lay at their feet, still asleep from the effects of the drugged wine.

"The man must have the wits of a mule," Aiden said to break the silence. When he had seen the man come out of the trees with a sword at his side, Aiden had hoped he may be the escape plan Aiden had been waiting for. But no.

"He was just cold and unwary, Master Aiden," Japh said.

"Yes, cold and unwary and armed. At least he was until he passed out," Aiden said

Japh sighed. Aiden knew the old man was getting tired of listening to him complain, tired of the dark mood that rarely left him. To be honest, Aiden was tired of it as well, but he couldn't seem to help himself. Life just seemed unfair. And that truth was magnified at every new turn, like with this musician—armed and foolish, worthless now, chained to the cart like the rest of them.

They rode in silence for a time. Then the blond man began to stir from his drug-induced sleep. Aiden watched as the man's eyes opened blearily before slowly focusing. The man took in Aiden, Japh, and the cart with the slow efficiency of the genuinely confused.

"Wh...what?" he finally mumbled.

Japh stepped in with his usual comfort, as he had with Aiden not that long ago. "It's alright, young master. I'm Japh and this is Aiden. Just take it slow and get your bearings."

Aiden said nothing, just watched the man. He was sure the contempt showed easily on his face, but he didn't care. He was so angry. This man had strutted into a camp of slavers with a sword on his hip and a knife in his belt, but he hadn't seen. And, since he hadn't seen, he hadn't fought, and he hadn't fled. Aiden rubbed a hand over his face, trying for the compassion he knew he should be feeling.

"Willem," the man said a little more steadily as he pulled himself up to a sitting position against the side of the cart. He offered, or attempted to offer, a friendly smile. "My name's Willem. Where are we? What happened?"

Aiden sighed. "They drugged you. We're heading north to be sold on some slaver's auction. Fun, huh? Maybe you should have opened your eyes and put that sword of yours to use instead of that winning smile last night. Welcome to slavery, Will."

Now it was Japh's turn to sigh. "You'll have to forgive Aiden, Master Willem. It's been a trying time for all of us."

Aiden watched as realization bloomed from the chaos of confusion in Willem's eyes. The musician's face grew red as he began to struggle against the manacle that bound him to the cart.

"Hey," Willem called. "Hey, you can't do this. Do you know who I am? Hey!" He was struggling to see over the edge of the cart and yell more directly at their captors, but the chain was situated in such a way that he couldn't get both up and turned. Finally, he just slumped back to the floor of the cart muttering, "Oh, for Dentar's sake."

Then realization seemed to strike him because he sat bolt upright again. Willem groped at his own back. He patted his front. "Where's my guitar?" he asked of no one in particular. "Where's my guitar? Dregs and draught, by the golden strings themselves, if they've broken it..."

Willem tore at the manacles and chains, fighting an unwinnable battle. Finally, he flopped back against the side of the cart and slouched there as anger played its way across his features. The man's eyes looked sullen, and some piece of Aiden was pleased to see that no sign of the winning smile touched Willem's face.

That evening when Sorento, the mustached slaver, called a halt, it was left to Aiden and Japh to gather close by firewood and prepare the kindling from fallen branches of the surrounding trees. They weren't, of course, given flint or steel. One of the other slavers would take care of that when the wood was ready. Willem just sat on the cold ground, brooding. For a moment, Aiden imagined this is how Japh must view him, unhelpful and sullen. They had been left unchained for once. The night was already turning cold, and they were leagues from anything remotely civilized. There was no point in running. There was no place to run to. Aiden knew it, and the slavers knew it. He supposed life was easier with understandings that didn't have to be stated.

When Sorento came toward the group of slaves working on the fire, Willem was up in an instant. "My guitar," Willem said when the slaver was still a few paces away. "Where's my guitar?" It seemed odd that he was so fixated on his instrument. Aiden was sure the guitar held great value for Willem, but still. The man's freedom had just been stripped from him, his very life stolen, and all he could talk about was a box of wood and strings?

Sorento just smiled at Willem and something snapped inside of the musician. He swung an exaggerated arching hook at Sorento who seemed only too ready for this kind of attack. He tilted his head ever so slightly forward and to the side while his meaty arm came up to block the blow. Aiden was sure this wasn't the first time a captive had decided to fight their way to freedom and Sorento was prepared for it. What he wasn't prepared for was the quick jab that snapped out from Willem's opposite fist. The punch caught the mustached man right in the nose of his forward tilting face. The exaggerated hook must have been a feint, and for an instant, Aiden marveled at Willem's prowess.

Then the others were on them. Japh fell and cowered, but Aiden's body responded without prompting. He threw the small log he had been preparing to place on the kindling pile as he saw Willem lash out with another quick jab to Sorento's face. Aiden's log caught one of the charging slavers in the right shoulder, and the man stumbled and fell. Two others were on that one's heels, though, and Aiden didn't have much time. These two both had swords drawn, good Perrian steel from the look of it. Aiden hadn't seen the slavers in a fight before, but money for quality weapons

usually meant some amount of training. Even if they had no training, they still both had very sharp steel longing to slice into him.

Aiden grabbed a second log, just small enough for him to hold
and swing with one hand. The pine was only about two feet long
and was sticky from sap, but it would have to do. He forced a smile
onto his face and stared down the slavers, who had slowed as they
approached. Aiden and Willem had an advantage here. They were
mostly unarmed, but they were also the payday. If the slavers cut
them down here in the middle of nowhere, they would have that
much less to sell when they got to the slave market, and caravans
from Oustenbasch to the far north couldn't be cheap to fund in the
first place. Aiden knew it, and the slavers knew it. Again, understandings could be useful.

The two slavers moved to either side so that Aiden had to swiv-
el his head back and forth to keep them in focus. They would try
to grab him, subdue him, but if that failed, Aiden had no doubt
they would kill him before letting him escape, profit loss or no. He
would have to be very careful and very quick to survive the day.

Then, all at once, the calm of waiting evaporated. The man on
Aiden's right slashed out at him with his sword, and Aiden moved
away instinctively. He cursed himself as the slaver on his left made
a grab for him. With Aiden a full step closer after his dodge, it was
a very near thing. Only by pure speed and luck did Aiden avoid
the man's grasping arms. He spun at the last possible moment, the
wind seeming to aid his movement, and the log in his right hand
smashed into the man's ribs. The slaver grunted and doubled over.

Aiden dove and rolled further from the man who had slashed
at him and was rewarded with the feeling of the man's fingers just
sliding over the back of his shirt but finding no purchase. He was
back on his feet a moment later and staring down his pursuer.
Aiden bobbed his body this way and that, trying to be ready for the
impending sword swing. Then, the man smiled, and strong arms

closed around Aiden from behind, wrapping him in a fierce bear hug.

He tried to flail, to kick or bite, but it was of no use. He had been caught unprepared and had no leverage. Then the man in front of him was there as well, and a knife lay against Aiden's throat. He stopped fighting. Grinding his teeth, he knew it was over.

As they approached the cart to chain Aiden back to his manacle, he could see Willem was already bound. His lip was bleeding, as was his nose. He looked at Aiden and shrugged as the slavers moved back out of the cart. Apparently, two other slavers had tackled Willem as he had focused his energy on pummeling Sorento. The mustached slaver had offered Willem two heavy-booted kicks in repayment for his trouble once the musician was bound again. The man who had grabbed Aiden from behind was the first slaver who he had hit with the thrown log.

The slaves from the other cart hadn't done anything at all. Just sat like cattle going to slaughter. Japh, he supposed, had been no better, but fear worked that way sometimes—debilitating, petrifying.

"There were just too many of them," Willem said to Aiden. "We put on a decent show though, didn't we?"

Aiden was forced to smile. "It'll only be harder next time. They probably won't unchain us again until we're sold."

Willem shrugged again. "It was worth it to work over Sorento's face a bit. We'll switch next time so you can have the pleasure."

Aiden smiled more broadly this time. Next time's escape would be far harder, but as it turned out, he might like this pretty-faced musician after all.

Chapter 7

...save in greater preparation and wisdom than I have shown.

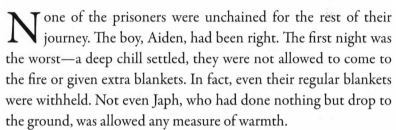

Nnone of the prisoners were unchained for the rest of their journey. The boy, Aiden, had been right. The first night was the worst—a deep chill settled, they were not allowed to come to the fire or given extra blankets. In fact, even their regular blankets were withheld. Not even Japh, who had done nothing but drop to the ground, was allowed any measure of warmth.

The three of them huddled in a tight group, trying to share body heat. Willem felt somewhat bad for the others, knowing he had started the fight. Still, he wasn't sure he would do anything differently if he were to do it over. He may have grabbed for Sorento's knife and ended the man instead of focusing on as many face shots as possible, but he hadn't been thinking clearly. Escape had only been a vague notion of sometime in the future. At that moment he had just been angry, and his anger focused unyieldingly on Sorento and his ridiculous, braided mustache.

The next day had been a bit better, even if the slavers were gruffer and warier than they strictly needed to be. The day after that was a near return to the disinterest that the slavers usually paid them, and Willem had no doubt the day after would have finally caught them up to being the best of friends, but instead, their caravan crested a hill, offering them their first sight of Perry's city walls.

According to Aiden and Japh, Sorento and his men had taken great lengths to avoid populated areas since they had left Oustenbasch. That seemed to indicate only one thing to Willem.

"Looks like we're home, boys," he said. "Welcome to Perry, home of the finest smiths, pubs, and entertainment this side of the Silverwine. Oh, and it's also got one of the largest slave markets anywhere in the Nine Cities." Willem and his troupe had been through Perry on a couple of different occasions. Big cities could be great for landing a big tip or having a rich patron pay for a private concert, but they were also dangerous for small groups without the funds for multiple swordarms. And that's not to mention the performers' guilds that had a hand in more or less every group or troupe in most of the big cities, from actors and jugglers to pipers and singers. Set your troupe to playing on the wrong corner at the wrong time, and you'd be lucky if your day's earnings were all the guild claimed. That's why his group had always made their way through cities but hadn't set up a permanent residence in any of them. It was easier to go unnoticed when you were only in a place for a short time. With Thant's ability to talk pretty much anyone into having their group play for profit, the system seemed to work well.

Now, however, Willem wished they had stayed put somewhere with people that knew them and could speak to little things like, *Willem's not a slave. He was born a free man, and I saw him playing at the inn two nights ago.* But that was all for wishing. Still, he could hope to find someone he knew or who knew him in Perry. He had a chance. It was small, but he had a chance.

The slavers stopped briefly outside of a small village where an old man brought out two young women, barely more than girls. The girls were chained in the cart in front of Willem's and the caravan started toward Perry again.

The city lay sprawled over a vast distance. Dauntingly high walls encircled the main city, or at least what had been the main city a hundred years ago. Perry had expanded as its reputation for opportunity and wealth had grown along with its standing as an educational hub. More than a decade ago Grand Duke Bentrial, who ruled in the stead of a true king, had commissioned a second city wall be erected to surround what were now more accurate city limits. He had possessed enough foresight to build the wall quite a distance from the existing, unofficial border so as to give Perry more room to grow. Still, the city had stretched nearly to the new Perry Wall.

Most of the buildings now inside the first wall in the space called "the inner circle," were large and lavishly constructed. Many of the homes and businesses there were as old as the original city, but many others had been built later as younger families had risen to power and influence and had wanted the respect the inner circle demanded. Smaller houses and establishments were torn down to make room for these new powers. Today most of the shops, markets, and dwellings of the city sat outside the first wall, in what was called "the outer circle." Willem supposed it would someday be called "the second circle," or something similar, once Perry grew beyond the second city wall.

Upon entering the city, Sorento led their small caravan along winding side streets and back roads, passing gray, unadorned buildings that stood one and two stories high. Willem guessed this was normal: slip the new slaves into the market as if they had been freshly baked in some oven that morning and were ready for sale. He had seen a slaver's caravan come through the main streets of Perry once. Some of the slaves had screamed for anyone and everyone to help them. "We are free men," one of the slaves had called out before a slaver had given him a boot to the side.

The crowd had simply watched the spectacle. They had done nothing. Willem had done nothing. And now it was his turn for the slaver's parade. They weren't even on the main streets, and the few eyes that looked at them had no warmth and little curiosity. He guessed the side streets cut down on the chance of running into a friend or relative, though, which could become a messy business.

Aiden and Japh held tight to their silence as the cart rumbled on slowly, offering only small grunts or nods to Willem's statements and questions. Willem was a nervous talker, and he knew it. Their silence was unnerving. He knew the slave market lay ahead, but bravado was far easier than sitting, brooding on what waited down that path. Of course, bravado was difficult to maintain in silence. That required true courage, something Willem was having a hard time marshaling at the moment.

So he talked on, filling their silence with his voice. It didn't matter much what he said, but rather how he said it. "Hmm, lovely neighborhood for a summer home," he jested when they rode through a particularly filthy back street. Sometimes, he would comment on things he actually did know about the city, "I think that run-down estate used to belong to House Rendling before they moved to the inner circle." He would pause from time to time, but then the fear would slink back toward him, and his voice would sound out to ward him against its evil presence.

Perry was large, and the trip to the slavers' market took most of the rest of the day. As late afternoon set in, Sorento called for an all stop in front of two large, metal gates with spikes on the top. The slaver jumped down from his seat to have a word with a man in a gatehouse that seemed to grow from the wall that held the gate. Laws stood in place that were supposed to protect free men from the slave trade. One was to have just reason for being sold into slavery, but with frequent travel between the Cities and little cooperation amongst the law-Keepers of the Nine, it was nearly impossible to prove you were not sold into slavery justly. A slave market was to have some proof of that justice before they admitted new slaves, but there was little to no enforcement of that law. Willem saw Sorento smile at the guard in the gatehouse, and a coin changed hands. Then, the guard called out, and the gates swung in slowly.

"And thus is shown the power of the law to protect the weak and innocent," Willem muttered.

Once their small caravan was inside, the gates closed again. The clang of their locking sent a chill through Willem. "Well, I guess that's that then, gentlemen. I think we really made it big this time. The slavers' market awaits."

They were unchained and unloaded at sword point, this latter to deter a last-minute attempt for freedom. They stood in a large, ringed courtyard with unadorned two-story buildings in front and to the sides, connecting to the wall and gate. To Willem's far-left he could make out stables and a courtyard watering well standing lonely and unattached.

After a moment, the slaves from the cart in front were led off to the left somewhere while Willem, Aiden, and Japh were taken right. They were led through a doorway where a thick wooden door stood ajar, down a passage with several turns, and finally into a cell where two other men already sat on the floor, leaning against the wall. A door, inlaid with iron bars for a window, slammed shut behind them, leaving them with only the dim glow of a lantern in the hallway to find their own seats against the wall.

Willem decided to keep things as light as possible. He knew they were bad, and that more than likely they would all be sold tomorrow or the day after, but lightness was the only shield he had—that and the sound of his own voice.

"So, what they get you fellas for?" he asked the two men who had been sitting in the cell when they arrived. The men looked up, showing features so near to the same it would be difficult to tell them apart even in the light of day. Twins then. The twins just stared at the three of them for a moment, and Willem braced himself for some kind of outburst. People usually ended up yelling at Willem for making light amid situations that scared or frustrated them. Then, as if the twins had been counting for synchronization, the two of them smiled at the exact same moment.

"We was helping ourselves to a bit of bread and the like at one of them swanky taverns over on the east side one night," the first twin said in a thick Perrian street accent.

Then the second twin took up the story. "It was late, see, and we didn't think no one was around down in the kitchens."

"We had a bag of provisions all filled up, and we was getting ready to leave again. Nice and quiet-like out the back alleyway," Twin One said.

"Nice and quiet," Twin Two agreed. "Then, this git tavern owner—big bloke—stumbles into the kitchen with a serving girl half his age, and her arms around his neck."

"She was probably more like a third his age, mate," Twin One said, turning to Twin Two.

"Well, whatever," Twin Two said. "The point is, this git, who has no business having any *business* with this maid or serving girl or whatever, doesn't even have the decency to overlook the light of our lantern."

"No," Twin One said, "he has to go and step forward out of his own ethical failing to call us out for the lesser moral crime of borrowing a few foodstuffs."

"Next thing we know," Twin Two added, "the big bloke with the girl has a knife and is calling for the red hats." The red hats, Willem knew, were the city patrol, the constables charged with keeping the peace in Perry. Willem was sure they would have been anything but pleasant to a couple of thieves stealing from an upper-end establishment in the middle of the night.

"Yeah," Twin One said, "and next thing we know we end up here to, 'pay our debts'. The crazy thing is we shouldn't have no debts, not with the big git with the serving girl at any rate. We didn't get to take none of that stuff we loaded up."

"By the Twin Angels themselves, didn't think they made you a slave for not stealing nothing," Twin Two added. "But then that's Perry for you, idn't it. I'm Rem by the way, and this here is my brother Lem, not that introductions matter much, being as we probably won't see each other after tomorrow, but who knows. We could end up in the same house, serving food or cleaning floors. We may even face each other in the tourney, but then we won't be talkin' over much, will we?" He said this last with a wink at Lem, who smiled all the wider.

"And how 'bout you lot," Lem said. "How'd you end up in the western bowels of our great city?"

"Swaar attacked Bellcross, drove me to flee," Willem said after a moment's hesitation. He hadn't spoken of it yet, not even to Aiden and Japh. The memory, the reality lay too heavily on his mind, the fear and sadness spread too thickly over his emotions. He didn't want to fall into those emotions and drown. Perhaps now these twins seemed too light, too willing to joke for that fear to be debilitating. Their jokes and laughter could anchor him like a lifeline, so he could talk. "I'm not sure what happened to my troupe, dead most likely...or worse. The Swaar aren't known for their kindness." He tried to smile but offered something closer to a grimace. "Next thing I know, I'm running into these fine gentlemen in the woods." Here Willem gestured at Aiden and Japh. "And it just so happened they were surrounded by half a dozen slavers. I suppose one thing led to the next, and here I am."

Japh spoke up next, explaining about his bad business deal, being swallowed in debt, and eventually ending up in the back of the slaver's cart.

When he finished, all eyes turned to Aiden, who had seemed to sink in on himself as the day had progressed. The slender man looked up with haunted eyes and slowly slipped his hand into his boot. A moment later, Aiden pulled his hand free, and with it came a knife in a black leather sheath. The knife's pommel was shaped into the likeness of a bird—a falcon perhaps.

"I found this knife and a small fortune in some ruins," Aiden said, his voice distant, removed. "I trusted the wrong person with the information, which led to me losing everything—my treasure, my freedom, and...Semlie, her life, our future. I lost everything but this knife," he said, drawing the falcon knife from its sheath. "And it was a costly treasure to buy—costly and worthless. I didn't even have the presence of mind to draw it when we fought the slavers a couple days ago. Worthless."

For a moment, Willem held a flash of fear that Aiden would take his own life with the blade, but the moment passed. Aiden sheathed the knife again and slipped it back into his boot. Before his head drooped back again to his chest in a resigned sullenness, Willem saw a tear slide down the man's face and thought, *perhaps there's no place for lightness in this after all.*

Chapter 8

I write this now, chiseled in Stone and wrapped in Wind with the hope that you may yet be saved from my folly.

A man danced out with a long, thin sword, trying to prick at Tako's chest. Tako swatted the steel away with a gloved hand and buried his axe in the attacker's neck. He let his off-hand slip to his belt, yank free a knife, and send the blade whirling into another onrushing opponent without looking. Two more to add to his count of the day. He laughed, feeling the glory of battle.

Then the world grew hazy, and the wind began. He knew this wind and dreaded it. Tako tried to take a step forward, but moving one foot off the ground pushed him back a step instead. The earth opened a gaping mouth behind him, falling away into abyss. He strove with his whole will, but to no avail. Another moment and he would be torn from his wide stance. Just as his feet found the very edge of the cliff, Tako cried out in frustration at his powerlessness against this foe. Then he slipped back, the last gravel crumbling beneath his boots, and he fell.

Tako woke. Sweat soaked his shirt, and the shadow of his cry still traced his mouth. The crones-cursed wind dream again. Dante sat up on his mat across the tent, looking at Tako with concern plain on the younger man's face.

"Water," Tako croaked out in as harsh a tone as he could muster in his shaken state. Dante tossed off his thin blanket, grabbed an empty canteen, and hurried out through the tent flap. Tako ran a hand over his face, trying to wipe away the lingering dream along with the sweat.

He had led a party of twelve riders north out of Bellcross six nights past on Dal Tek's direct orders. They hadn't found the shield of Ammereth that night in the Temple. Indeed, the excavation had taken two days and nights—a trap of stone had been sprung and collapsed all through the tunnel network beneath the Temple of the Twin Angels before the Swaar's arrival. Finally, the group of workers Tek had forced into service came upon a small, circular cell with a podium growing up out of the floor in its center.

Tako had escorted the Dal, Gray Riller, and Olivat Storm Eater, down into the small room. Olivat's excitement was palpable as they entered the cell and approached the stand. His joy turned to ash on his face as he stared down at what the podium held. It was not a shield, at least not in any form Tako had ever seen. A flat sheet of glittering stone lay on the rock plinth. A scrolling lettering flowed across the sheet in a metallic shimmer as if someone had chiseled out the stone and then inlaid melted silver. Though Tako could recognize several of the languages used in the Nine Cities, this was unlike any of them.

"What is this?" Dal Tek asked, and fear crept up Tako's spine, for the Rock Giant had not yelled or boomed. Rather, his voice slid out cold and hard as steel on a winter morning.

Olivat Storm Eater, stared down at the flowing script on the stone plate for a moment, his eyes narrowed in concentration and his lips moving in muttered silence. All the time, Tako felt Dal Tek's fury growing frostier until it was only by a force of will that Tako kept himself from shivering. One of the workers covered his mouth in an attempt to muffle a nervous cough. A knife leapt free of Tek's

hand and buried itself in the man's throat so quickly that Tako barely caught the motion at all before the man stumbled over, offering
a slow gurgle along with his life blood. The Rock Giant's eyes had
never left Olivat at the center stand, seeming oblivious to the now-
dead man lying across the room. Tako again reminded himself never to annoy, much less cross this big man.

Finally, the corners of Olivat's lips pulled up with the beginnings of his usual smile. He too seemed not to notice, or at least not
to care that a man had just been killed a pace away.

"Forgive me, my lord," Olivat said, turning, at last, to meet
Tek's cold anger with a warm smile. "This is not the Shield of Ammereth, as I am sure you can tell."

The Rock Giant's exhale came out more as a growl than a
breath, but to Olivat's credit, the man didn't lose composure for so
much as a blink. "This is not the Shield of Ammereth," Storm Eater
repeated, "but it is a clue to its location."

Glowering, Tek barked, "That is what you said of the crypt in
Allisii, wizard. What game are you playing?" At least Tek's anger
had stepped back from cold fury, but any anger from the Rock Giant was far from safe.

"As I said, my lord, you must forgive me," Olivat said, spreading
his arms and giving a small bow. "What we found in Allisii was a
hint to finding something to do with the shield. Here we have a
true clue, real directions. I had hoped it would be simpler than this,
had hoped we would find it here, but this is by no means a defeat.
We simply have more conquest to undertake to find the Shield of
Ammereth." His eyes flicked over to Tako. "That should please our
Wolf Rider, at any rate."

"Enough words," Gray Riller said, apparently out of patience.
"What does it say, Olivat?"

"Of course, of course," Olivat said, offering another ingratiating
smile that reinforced Tako's dislike for the man. He was too full

of words, this one—full of words and promises, lacking in action. "The script is in ancient Terrian. I will need more time for a full translation, but the essence of the tome is a description of two cities, one north, and one south. The southern city is called Kantavollie of the Eight Towers, which is modern-day Taalmor, of course, but the northern city is simply called, The Keep of the White Tower."

Storm Eater pulled gently at his beard. "This will need some thought and deliberation. Either way, the tome says that each of these cities holds a..." and here Olivat peered at the stone plate for a long moment. "It says they hold 'a word for the Shield of Ammereth and the defender.'"

And that was that. It had been clear that Dal Tek was not pleased by this turn of events, and Storm Eater had not escaped his displeasure entirely. Regardless, Tako had been sent north with twelve Swaar of his choosing to find this Keep of the White Tower, and whatever clues it had of the shield. It was apparent from the tome that the author—Brother Terriase, Olivat called him—assumed the reader would be familiar with both cities he described. Therefore, he gave only vague descriptions of Tako's path. 'Past the Twin Rivers and around the star of Mountain Bright,' Storm Eater had translated. It was little enough to go on. Fortunately, they traveled north and not further west. He was at least a bit familiar with these lands, but only a very little. This still stood as the land of the Nine Cites, and Tako had spent most of his life many leagues east of here.

By the time Dante returned with his fresh canteen of water, Tako had stood, dressed in fresh clothes and feeling much more himself again. The dreams always left him with an eerie sense of loss for the first moments after waking, but that was gone now. He was Ren Tako Wolf Rider, and he refused to be afraid of the wind.

"Thank you, Dante," he said, accepting the proffered water. He took three long drafts, letting the water cool his parched throat. Tako wished he had something a bit stronger to will away the spirits of the night, but they were traveling light and the wine they had brought had slid down throats quickly. "Let's get going as soon as everyone is packed and loaded with a bit of something in their stomachs."

Dante nodded and turned to leave, saying simply and quietly, "Rider." Dante Whisper, he was named. He could move more quietly than the lightest of breezes and spoke but little. He could sneak up on you, or your enemies for that matter, without moving a single blade of grass out of place. Dante also held the title of being Tako's closest, and more than probably, only, true friend. On the night that Tako had claimed his name of Wolf Rider, he had saved Dante's life, riding down and killing a man on horseback who was pursuing Whisper at the battle of the Three Hills. Dante had sworn himself doubly to Tako that very night through both fire and blood.

Since then, Dante had hardly left Tako's side, and been true even against odds when others had deserted. Whisper had paid back the life Tako had saved more times than once, but never did he relinquish his pledge. *He's a good man,* Tako reflected, *with more claims to that title than I have.*

Tako ran a hand through his long, unkempt hair. He had never quite taken to the fashion of the west as other Swaar had in recent years, with brushing their hair out flat and even oiling it down. *"The All-Warrior is who you ought to concern yourself with,"* Tako's father had told him once, when the boy had asked about gods of the west and why the Nine Cities didn't give offerings of blood to the All-Warrior. *"The gods of lesser men are beneath you, Tako. You are a man of the Swaar."* Tako bore his father's words with him to this day, long after his father's death. Frankly, he doubted very much if the All-

Warrior cared one way or the other about Tako's hair—not as long as his axe was sharp.

The men stood or sat in small groups. His Gray Pack, or so they had taken to calling themselves since they followed the Wolf Rider, had already assembled by the time Tako had dressed and left his tent. The plan was simple enough—they were to travel north until they found Brother Terriase's Keep of the White Tower, died in the attempt, or were summoned home by the Dal. For all their sakes, Tako hoped for the last of these least of all.

Tako's plan was indeed simple enough, but Dal Tek's plan for the large force of the Swaar remained something of a mystery to him. Tako's was not the only small force being sent out: north, south, and west. He didn't know if they all sought this same shield or if there was more going on, but it took no scholar to realize a shield was of little use but in battle. Something floated their way on the winds of time, and Tako didn't think it smelled much like peace.

His eyes drifted over the fast-flowing current of the river they had made camp beside. Before they had killed the farmer in the burned house two miles back down their path, the man had called this river 'The Twins'. Tako could just see places in the center of the flow where the ground still rose up into tiny, thin islands. It required no great leap of imagination to see how what was once two rivers, flowing alongside one another, slowly became one. And apparently, the name stuck. 'Past the Twin Rivers and around the star of Mountain Bright,'—at least they were going the right direction—now to find a way across.

"Mount up," he growled low, absent-mindedly spinning the ring on his finger and moving toward his own horse, knowing that Dante would see to the tent. It wasn't loud, but when the Wolf Rider speaks, his Gray Pack listens. Before the sun had moved another finger into the sky, they were off.

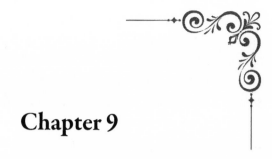

Chapter 9

Offer my apologies to the rest of the council...

———◦◦◦———

"Thirty-one, thirty-one. Do I hear thirty-two? Alright, going once...going twice...thirty-two—we have thirty-two," the auctioneer's voice sprung on rapidly in a mix of Perrian street and universal middle-class merchant with just a pinch of aristocratic snobbery mixed in, no doubt to make these wretches buying other humans feel more comfortable.

Aiden had been forced to stand and listen all morning. It was amazing how many people were for sale in this slaves' market of Perry. He had lost track after he counted the first hundred slaves sold. That had been several hours ago, and the number must be better than triple that now.

They had been woken early that morning and given a breakfast of eggs, bread, and water—all in all not bad food for a slave in a cell. Aiden knew they were just fattening the cattle up for sale, though. They were all dunked in a giant tub of water and then forced to stand and air dry. It actually felt good to have a bit of the grime washed off of him, even if he would have preferred a tub of hot water in an inn somewhere in Oustenbasch. Then they were loaded into carts and brought here to the slave market itself. Apparently, their stop of the day before had only been one of several holding houses for slaves meant for that week's market.

Each slave was announced with a number, which they also wore on a small sign around their neck, and a description of their crimes or previous experience as a slave. One older man, number four-nine-one, was being sold by his last master after serving that family as dish boy, server, and later, third house steward. He was being sold for "personal reasons, none of which tarnishing the steward's work for the house he served." In short, Aiden thought, the man's owner needed a few eagles, and the steward's life and service were expendable to him. What a wonder of humanity.

"Sold at forty-one eagles to the man in the black hat," the auctioneer chimed. The man, number four-nine-one, was led off stage to whatever new life awaited him. The twins, Rem and Lem, had been sold to a group of men near the back of the crowd two hours ago at fifty-two eagles apiece. Willem had gone to the same group a half-hour later for fifty-eight. Japh had been sold only a few minutes ago to a stout woman who had been carried in on a litter and who now sat in a chair near the front of the stage, like a queen being waited on by her subjects.

Now, Aiden stood alone, the last sale of the day. "Number five-one-six," the slave auctioneer called out, and Aiden stepped slowly up onto the stage, doing his best to savor his last few moments without an official master. "Slave five-one-six, convicted of theft of property and assaulting a lord's retainer in Oustenbasch." This lie stung, though an assault on his character really shouldn't matter to him when faced with a life of slavery ahead. "Shall we start the bidding at forty eagles? Do we have forty?" the auctioneer began.

The woman who had bought Japh was first to bid, followed by the men in the back who had purchased the twins and Willem. Then a younger woman, perhaps in her early twenties, bid forty-five, and the war was on. Japh's stout master dropped out somewhere around fifty, and it became a two-way battle. Aiden's eyes leapt from men in the back to young woman in the front as the bid rose slowly. The woman looked into Aiden's eyes each time she bid and offered a small smirking smile. Aiden had no idea how to take that look. Was it a promise of hope or a cold and uncaring threat?

Aiden caught himself trying to decide where he would rather go before he cursed himself for a fool and resigned himself to his helpless state.

The bid rose ever higher: fifty-six, fifty-seven, fifty-eight. The men in the back went to sixty and the woman countered with sixty-one without so much as a pause. The men in back did pause at that, though. They stood in hushed conversation as the auctioneer counted off, "Going once...going twice."

"Sixty-two," the men in the back said. Aiden found his eyes drifting back to the young woman in the front. The smirk still played across her lips as their eyes locked, but this time she offered him a tiny shrug, nearly invisible. It was as much as he was going to get for an apology.

That was it. The auctioneer counted off his sale and it was finished—Aiden belonged to the men at the back of the crowd. That was a surreal knowledge. Someone else owned him. The law would be on their side if he was caught trying to escape. It didn't matter how his enslavement had begun. To the peace keepers and constables, Aiden was now the property of those men in the back.

A guard led Aiden off the stage and around a side way to a covered cart. Inside the back of the cart, shackles held Willem, the twins, and two other men who had been purchased today. Aiden slid into place next to one of the twins, Rem, he thought, and across from Willem. Once Aiden had been shackled as well, it was only a short, silent wait until the cart lurched and they were moving, off to a new future. Aiden couldn't see where they were going. A hinged door had been thrown shut before they had left, and the new slaves were left with nothing but a tiny stream of sunshine silhouetting the frame.

An hour passed, or maybe two. The air grew stale and hot before the cart finally stopped, and the door was flung open again. Aiden squinted against the glaring sunlight as he was ushered out of the cart and into another dirt courtyard. A high, gated wall stood on one side of the yard, and on the other rose a massive structure that seemed to be built of a combination of stone, steel, and wood. Two giant pillars marked an archway at the bottom of grandly-cut stone steps. A guard flanked the set of pillars to either side, and Aiden saw several other guards scattered throughout the yard. A sinking feeling began to gnaw at his stomach. He had an idea of where he might be, and if he was right, this new life might not last terribly long.

Aiden, Willem, and the other new slaves were set in a line facing the daunting steps. After a moment, a man materialized over the edge of the topmost step and began his descent. He was tall and thin, gaunt almost, with high cheekbones, thick lips, and thinning hair. Around narrow shoulders was wrapped a dark red, velvet-lined cloak, and a medallion depicting a mailed fist clutching a broken sword swung easily around his veined neck. Aiden absorbed all those things in a moment, though, for it was the man's eyes that transfixed him. He supposed they were blue, but the coloring was so light they were nearly white and flecks of red stood out like burning embers. There was nothing warm about these eyes, however. Embers or not, these were the coldest eyes Aiden had ever stared into. Here stood a man who would torture you to death slowly and then follow you into the beyond just to make sure you found no rest there.

As the man's gaze swept over Aiden's small group of slaves, he paused to stare into each man's eyes. At his turn, Aiden shivered involuntarily.

Finally, the man spoke in a deep voice that was no less haunting for the slight lisp that accompanied it. "Welcome, you future

Champions. I am Master Gregor, Twelve Rings," he held up his thin arms displaying six fingers on each hand with gold and silver rings glistening from each. "Congratulations are in order, for today, you six are added to the list of honored Champions who will tread the sand of the Tournament Square. You will all offer blood to those Sands," Gregor paused and pointed up the steps behind him before continuing, "some your own, some that of your neighbor. And some of you may offer all, bleeding your very life into those Sands. Know this—there is no greater honor for you than to redeem your lives by offering them to the Tournament." Here Master Gregor, Twelve Rings, paused for what Aiden assumed to be effect. Then he added, "Welcome to the Tournament, Champions."

With that, the thin man turned his cloak flapping, and marched back up the steps. It was not the greeting Aiden had expected. He saw that Willem drew the same surprise. When he turned toward Aiden, Willem mouthed, "Scary," and nodded his head toward the stairs and the man receding up them.

Aiden offered a small, involuntary smile and nodded.

So, they had been bought by the Tournament of Champions, or as most of the public referred to them, the Death Games. And that thin, cold man was the Master of the Tournament, the rule maker and game former. Aiden's father had told him the tale once, not that it was any great secret. Every child knew the story of the Champions.

A century or more ago, the Tournament had indeed been one for Champions. Lords from all surrounding areas of Perry would send their knights and warriors to fight and win honor for their houses. The Tournament's popularity grew, as did the wealth and renown gained by the Champion. It grew to the point that the games drew fighters from all Nine of the Cities, and the City leaders would bestow lands and wealth on Champions from their city.

Then the most recent Princes' War came. The Land of the Nine Cities was in turmoil as lords flocked to one banner or another, backing the *prince* they thought had the best chance of reuniting the Nine into one nation or the one that offered them the best riches. Three princes emerged, all claiming lineage from the dead Renillion kings of old. All the warriors were needed for the war, Champions most of all. The war ended in a shaky peace, leaving the nation few enough strong arms for rebuilding and fewer yet champions for the cities to rally behind.

The Tournament Square had closed for several seasons following the war. Then Gregor, Twelve Rings, a one-time Champion of Perry, came forward and was awarded the medallion of Champion Master. At first, Gregor tried to recruit Champions from the heroes of the war and past contestants in the games. There lingered such hostility and mistrust between the Cities that Gregor's call went unanswered, however, and there were too few warriors in Perry to risk their lives on the sand.

The Tournament remained void of life, the Square Sands unwarmed by human feet. Then Master Gregor, Twelve Rings, struck upon an idea while out walking the Perrian streets. If the stories were to be believed, Gregor saw two slaves arguing over a dropped and broken package. The argument grew lively, and one slave struck the other, turning the argument into a fight. Neither slave had been trained in battle, but still, they raged against each other until the constables arrived to haul them away.

Gregor had gone immediately to Grand Duke Bentrial and explained his vision. After some convincing, Bentrial had given Master Gregor all the prisoners from his dungeons that were already slated for execution.

He took them and trained them, at least trained them enough to put on a good show. The public seemed hesitant at first. It was, after all, a fairly large mental switch to move from watching the greatest Champions of Nine Cities battle for prestige and glory to watching condemned criminals fight for their lives. People came around quickly when the bloodletting started, though.

Now, decades later, the Tournament of Champions was a tournament of slaves and criminals. The Death Games had become a far better description as well. The fatality rate of participants had gone from occasional and unfortunate before the war to a near certainty. Master Gregor seemed to take pleasure in pushing even the best of the *Champions* until the match was so set against them that their death was guaranteed.

This was the life Aiden now found himself in. This was the death that awaited him beyond those daunting steps.

Aiden was snapped from his thoughts as a whip flew in from the side, uncoiling like a Delrethi Cobra and cracking out in front of the six slaves. Heads turned just as fast, and Aiden found a new man awaiting his attention. This man seemed to counterbalance Master Gregor so perfectly there was nearly something comical about it—nearly, but not quite. As tall and thin as Gregor was, this man grew short and thick. He was even shorter than Aiden, which really took something. Of course, he was also three times as thick as Aiden, and Aiden noted the man's bare forearms rippled with dense muscle as he recoiled his whip. The man didn't remind Aiden of anything so much as a boulder.

"I am Sevion, and I hold the whip," the man said. "You are mine now, and you will obey as a dog does his master, or I will beat you as a man does his dog. Do we have an understanding?" Six heads nodded in unison, but no one said anything. "Good." The man smiled, but there was nothing friendly about that smile—joy in the eyes but no warmth. "Now, to the Sands."

Sevion led them, not up the stone stairway, but around to the side. Two guards fell in to either side of their small parade as they walked. At the far side of the Tournament compound, two large wooden doors stood ajar, and their group passed through without comment. Beyond the door lay a perfectly square section, perhaps eighty strides from end to end in either direction, of fine, soft sand. Around the square towered a stadium of seats rising like a funnel from the earth. Aiden felt that the heavens couldn't help but stare down at these focal-pointed Sands. Thousands of people could sit and watch the battles that raged in this square, and each person would be able to see, not missing a moment of the bloody spectacle.

They walked the Sands slowly, childishly playing follow the leader with the stout man at their head. Silence ruled as they zigzagged this way and that across the square before stopping in front of a rough wooden stand of weapons.

"Know the Sands, my Champions, and you may survive a while in the Tournament," Sevion said in his slightly lilting accent.

"Yeah, well, that's great, idn't it," one of the twins said. "That way Gregor can bleed us slow and painful like instead of all at once."

"A right pretty idea, that is, mate," the other twin chimed in. "Not that I'll complain too loudly. I'd rather live than die when given the choice, but who knows once the pain starts..."

Lem and Rem were cut short as Sevion's whip end cracked between their heads, missing their cheeks by a wind breath.

"Enough of your foolish chatter. I need to know what you can do so that I can train you, and I *will* train you, or I will give you pain Master Gregor could not hold a candle to. Now choose a weapon from the rack, and let's see what you can do."

The six of them gathered around the weapons rack, eyeing the swords, knives, and axes as closely as a merchant would a shipment of fruit. Lem was the first to take a weapon, and when he did, he took two, both long knives, perhaps a foot and a half in length. Everyone else followed shortly. One of the slaves Aiden hadn't met, another Champion now, picked a longsword while the other chose a double-edged battle axe. Rem took a longsword that seemed to dwarf him while Willem chose a shortsword that looked no larger than a long knife in the big musician's hand.

That left Aiden, standing, staring at the remaining cleavers and bashers, weapons made to maim and kill. He wasn't sure he could do that, not just to please a crowd. A bow and arrows would have been preferable if he had to pick. He had found long ago that being small meant he needed to either get up close in a fight, inside of his opponent's reach, or he needed to stay as far back as possible and not let that reach gather him in. No bows sat propped neatly among the rest of the weapons, though. These were all tools of melee, weapons for the Sands, and Aiden needed to pick. He felt the eyes of the others and of Sevion on his back. Fighting through the nerves, he made his decision, reached out, and grabbed a spear, perhaps six feet in length, with a steel head. Then, as an afterthought, he took a short knife as well and stuck it through his belt.

Turning, he met eyes with Sevion, who held his gaze for a moment, looked from him to his weapon choices, met his eyes again, and nodded before turning to Willem and Rem.

"No, no," Sevion said, shaking his head. "A Champion must choose a weapon fitting to him. You," he said, pointing at Rem, "are too thin of wrist and arm to use that sword for long. You will tire and drop your defense. When a Champion drops his defense, he dies. Do you want to die, lad?"

Rem shook his head, but for once said nothing. "Okay then," Sevion said and took the sword from Rem's grasp. "And you, my big, blond Champion, you have the strength to carry something larger to maximize your reach and the power of your swing. Why do you choose that needle instead?"

"Well, umm," Willem stuttered before clearing his throat, "you see, I've always carried a short sword. It was easier to carry when I had my guitar on my back, and I guess I'm just used to it."

"So you were a minstrel lad? Oh, but it makes no difference. You have no guitar now, and you will get *used to* this." Sevion took Willem's shortsword from him and placed the hilt of the longsword he had taken from Rem into Willem's hand in its stead. The short sword he handed to the smaller Rem before turning and looking over the other weaponry choices. After a moment he shrugged and nodded.

Turning, Sevion walked back toward the weapons rack. When his back was turned, the big slave with the battle axe, who Aiden had yet to properly meet, let out a scream, stepping forward and swinging his axe at Sevion's retreating form. Quick as a cougar, Sevion whirled back to face the oncoming blow. Yanking a knife from his belt, the trainer deflected the much larger axe when it was only inches from cleaving him in two. Sevion's opposite fist shot out and caught the other man in the throat, forcing him to drop his axe and stagger back. Bending in half as if there would be more air closer to the ground, the man clutched at his windpipe. Without haste or apparent pleasure, Sevion stepped forward and neatly kicked the man in the forehead, dropping him to the ground.

"There is always one," Sevion said, his breath coming evenly as though he had not come within inches of death a moment before. "Always one fool who thinks that having a weapon is the same as having his freedom. He has but to kill the gatekeeper," here he motioned to himself with his still drawn knife, "and he can be on his way, free as a Geldoran Hawk." Sevion shook his head much as a disappointed father would.

"Let me explain something to all of you. You are Champions of the Tournament now. The Death Games can do odd things to a person's sense of self-preservation. Some turn in on themselves, hardening until they are like a single diamond, sharp as a knife and armored against all who would attack. This is good until the right tool is used to cut and break them. Then they fall like anyone else. Others turn outward, having only the thought for flight. I assure you, every form of plot and scheme toward escape has been tried and has failed. You may waste your energies in this way, but I tell you now, you will die all the faster when the Games begin."

Sevion paused for a moment, looking into the distance, his eyes unfocused. Then he said, a hushed firmness in his voice, "There is a third way to react to the Tournament, a third way to conduct yourself and *live* in the Death Games. It is the way Marzin, the only Champion Slave to have been freed since Master Gregor reopened the Tournament, lived. But you will have to find that path yourself if you want to tread it."

The trainer's eyes refocused on them, and the thinnest of smiles touched his broad face. "Now, let us begin, and we will see if we can make fighters out of you dogs."

Chapter 10

...and know to you personally, if I do not return, I am sorry for my failure.

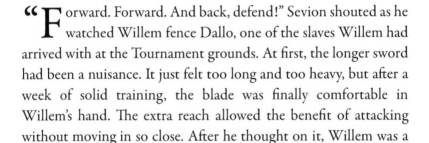

"Forward. Forward. And back, defend!" Sevion shouted as he watched Willem fence Dallo, one of the slaves Willem had arrived with at the Tournament grounds. At first, the longer sword had been a nuisance. It just felt too long and too heavy, but after a week of solid training, the blade was finally comfortable in Willem's hand. The extra reach allowed the benefit of attacking without moving in so close. After he thought on it, Willem was a big fan of not getting any closer than he had to when someone wanted to cut him open.

"Now back, Dallo, back," Sevion shouted, but it was too late. Dallo had overextended on a lunge and Willem had him. With a deft parry of his own blade, Willem knocked Dallo's sword from his hand. Then he swept the sword around, bringing it to within an inch of Dallo's throat.

"Yield. I yield," the ruddy-skinned slave said, standing back to his full height, hands raised in surrender. Willem and Dallo shared a brief smirk. It had been a good fight, but Dallo was not the swordsman Willem was turning out to be. Still, there was something a bit freeing about single combat. The power of fencing made Willem feel his own master, if only for a few minutes.

A whip cracked in between the two of them, vanquishing their smiles and returning the two of them to slavery.

"This game is not a joke," Sevion, or 'the Boulder' as Willem had heard him called by other Champions on the grounds, said in a quiet voice pregnant with warning. "Our training time is nearly over, and then it is to the Sands with you. If you lose your sword, Dallo, you will be cut down and gone to seek your forefather's halls or the grace of the Twin Angels." Dallo's head bowed slightly in acceptance of the chastisement.

"As for you, Willem," the Boulder said, "there are no friendly bouts in the Tournament. These are the Death Games, and they are a bloody, messy place. Do not expect anyone to yield to you when you best them. Until they are dead or Master Gregor holds up one of his six-ringed hands for stop, you have not won. You have time yet, but not enough, never enough."

Sevion's stare was intent and purposeful as Willem stared back into his gray eyes and nodded. "I understand," Willem said. "I have to be ready to kill." His heart was sinking, though, and his stomach felt sick. He wasn't at all sure he could kill someone else, not like this. He couldn't have cut Dallo's head off after he had disarmed him. He just couldn't. He would have to learn, though. That was the only way Willem was going to survive, so he just took a deep breath and nodded again.

Later, in the mess hall, he sat next to Aiden, trying to choke down the turnip, cabbage, and mystery meat stew. The hall was pretty well divided into groupings of Champion Pennants eating together at smaller tables or in truncated groups at the two great tables. The Tournament Champions were divided into roughly ten groups called Pennants, each comprised of five or six slave Champions. They all had patches sewn onto their shirt chests to show who they belonged to. Willem's Pennant bore the symbol of a three-peaked mountain and was called Boulder, after Sevion. Boulder was made up of himself and the five others he arrived with: Aiden, Rem, Lem, Dallo, and Hentor, the big man who had attacked Sevion on the first day.

Each Pennant was claimed and held by one of the grounds trainers and there was little interaction between Champions of different Pennants—that is until the Death Games began and battle commenced. Sevion, the Boulder, claimed Willem's Pennant a week ago, the trainer's final Champion from his previous Pennant having died in an extremely unfair bout on the Square Sands the week prior. Master Gregor, Twelve Rings, held a savvy business mind. He understood that people liked to watch the fights and would pay to see them, pay to bet on them, and pay to have a good time while there. He also understood that good fights meant better money for himself and the Tournament backers. Great fights meant excellent money for them instead. It couldn't be cheap to keep ten weapons masters on hand to train slaves that would eventually just be killed anyway. Still, the money must have been good enough, because Willem could already tell the gain. His skill with a blade had at least doubled, as had his battle readiness. He could see things on the sand, anticipate and counter them in a way that would have been lost to him just a week ago. All of that did little to cheer him, though, when he thought of how he would have to use that skill to kill or be killed.

"How went things for you?" Willem asked, pushing the disgusting stew away and turning to Aiden. Sevion had been training them separately or in pairs for everyone's second session of the day. When Aiden didn't answer, Willem nudged him with his elbow and asked, "Aiden?"

"Shh," came the smaller man's reply, "listen." Aiden nodded his head toward the table next to them where several Champions from another Pennant were sitting. Aiden wasn't looking at them, however. His head was down and he was slowly, methodically eating the nasty turnip stew.

After a perfunctory glance, Willem pulled his own stew back toward him and assumed the same position, listening all the while to pick up the conversation.

"No, that's what I'm saying," a Champion from the table was saying in a deep voice. The man wasn't whispering, but he was speaking quietly enough that Willem had to strain to make out the words. "Cett said he heard Gregor himself when Brey was delivering the post. He's supposed to announce tomorrow. The Game's back on. The new sheep are ready, or at least ready enough to put on a good show before they die."

"Nah," said another voice, this one high and nasally. "Old Twelve Rings always gives them new blood at least a month. We may be fighting, but they won't be. It's not going to be no grand affair, there's too few of us after that last bloodbath Gregor dreamed up, with the lions and all. Sevion just got his Pen a week ago, with Dennan's coming two days after and Qurell's and Yoh's a day later still. That's over half of us, Theq. Ain't no way, just no way."

A pause fell on the air, and Willem could almost hear the first man shaking his head. "Now, that's just the thing. I'm tellin' you like I heard it. There's some fancy lord coming to see this week, and Gregor wants to put on a show. Ready or not, Game's on."

The conversation turned from there to a discussion of what the Tournament might hold. Some had discussions of tactical battles between Pennants, and others thought there'd be more exterior forces, like the lions from last time.

Willem turned back to Aiden with raised eyebrows. From what Sevion had said, Willem had been of opinion with the second man. He thought they'd have more time, more training, but apparently, time had run out. "Well, I guess that's that," Willem said.

Aiden nodded and let his spoon slide into the rest of the Stew. "You ready?" Aiden asked.

Willem shrugged. "I better be. Come on; let's get in a quick round before everyone else gets to third training."

That night, as he lay on his bunk in the Champions' barracks, Willem fought back tears born of helplessness. His throat tight and raw, he tried to focus on breathing slowly. He didn't know if he could go through with this. Willem had been in plenty of scrapes. Life on the road invited nearly constant potential for a fight with bandits or even tavern patrons who had overly-indulged in a local brew. Drawing steel to protect one's self or one's friends from those who would rob you was one thing, but killing a chained man for another's entertainment, well, that was something else entirely. At least, it felt different. Even fighting the Swaar raider in Bellcross had been self-defense.

Kill or be killed, could those truly be his only options? Willem ran a freshly calloused hand through his hair, tugging against his scalp in frustration. He had to find a way out. That's what it came down to. Sevion had been right, though. The walls were patrolled by soldiers with swords and crossbows, lots of soldiers. The Champions were monitored with strict schedules at all times. Even his communication was limited with anyone but Sevion and the others of Boulder Pennant.

Willem didn't know how, but the fact remained, he had to find a way out.

Chapter 11

Do not be fooled by the appearance of things.

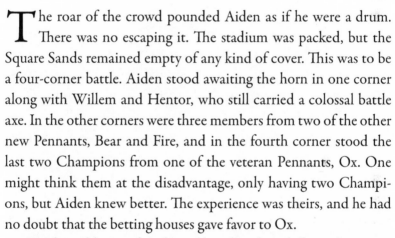

The roar of the crowd pounded Aiden as if he were a drum. There was no escaping it. The stadium was packed, but the Square Sands remained empty of any kind of cover. This was to be a four-corner battle. Aiden stood awaiting the horn in one corner along with Willem and Hentor, who still carried a colossal battle axe. In the other corners were three members from two of the other new Pennants, Bear and Fire, and in the fourth corner stood the last two Champions from one of the veteran Pennants, Ox. One might think them at the disadvantage, only having two Champions, but Aiden knew better. The experience was theirs, and he had no doubt that the betting houses gave favor to Ox.

The horn blew, and Aiden stole a deep breath from the unseasonably warm, humid air. *Wait.* That had been Sevion's advice and command. "Wait and see how the others begin—watch and you may learn—learn and you may survive." The prevailing wisdom of the untrained in the Tournament was that he who strikes first wins. That may be true for single combat, but not in a battle with more than two Pennants.

Aiden saw Fire and Bear charge toward the center Sand to meet each other as soon as the horn sounded, but Ox moved forward only slowly, giving themselves a little space from the corner and the walls. Aiden did the same, taking only a few steps toward the center. At his movement, Hentor's nerves and anticipation won over his better judgment. With a battle cry not unlike the one he had offered on the first day when he had attacked Sevion, Hentor raised his axe and charged for the center where Fire and Bear were converging.

"No!" Aiden shouted, but it was too late. "Dregs and drought, you twice-cursed fool," he yelled, making sure Willem wasn't about to bolt as well. Willem offered a reassuring nod and rolled his shoulders to loosen them. The one-time musician wore a black leather jerkin with the Boulder insignia patch on the chest. He also had leather leg plates, gloves, and bracers. A round buckler lay strapped to his left arm, while the grip of a long sword rested in his hand. His head was bare, however, as were the heads of all the Champions. Master Gregor believed the crowd should see and know their Champions by sight. It wasn't overly safe for the fighters, but then, these were the Death Games, after all. Willem looked every bit the warrior—quite a different image than the one presented to Aiden that first chilly day in the woods. For his part, Aiden was dressed in the same padded leather, but he doubted very much that he struck such an imposing figure. He didn't bear a sword, however. Instead, Aiden carried a spear, steel-headed and guarded, with the metal wrap running a full foot down from the sharp tip. His small shield, he wore strapped onto his back just in case, but he preferred using both hands to wield the spear. At his belt was a knife, too large for great throwing, but could come in handy if quarters became close or if his spear shaft cracked.

Spinning the spear from hand to hand, he jabbed forward with it before whirling the shaft back behind him, snapping the tip up above his head. Sevion had called this a katar, a kind of weaponized dance meant to loosen the muscles and gain control over one's spear. The katar always calmed Aiden, and this time was no different. Some of the tension fled from him. He was as ready as he was going to be. Still, he wished the big, lumbering Hentor would have held his peace a moment longer.

Aiden turned his attention back to the charging man in time to see him collide with Bear and Fire. Hentor slammed his axe into one of the Bear Champions, throwing the man to the ground in a spray of blood. With a scream of triumph, he yanked his axe free and whipped it around at another man who slid away just a little too slowly. Hentor's axe cut cleanly through the man's forearm. By then Hentor had turned his back on the rest of the champions battling in the center of the Square. Aiden took a half step forward as if to intercede, as he watched a sword plunge into Hentor's back and drive out the front of his chest. A look of astonishment swept Hentor's face—then he fell.

"Twice-cursed fool," Aiden muttered again as he caught himself from moving forward.

Then, movement from the far end of the Square caught his eye. Ox was moving: skirting the Square and staying close to the wall. Aiden traced the path in front of them and found their destination, or perhaps merely their target. One of the Fire Champions had slipped back away from the rest of the battle still being fought by one of Bear and one of Fire. The man was maybe thirty yards out, but even from that distance, he looked scared. The Fire Champion's eyes flitted between the two still raging in the center and the bloody men on the ground, one of which was groaning and thrashing. He didn't see Ox. He didn't know his turn for painting the sand red was near at hand.

With a grunt, Aiden turned in the direction of the Fire Champion and grabbing Willem's shoulder, started that direction. He wasn't about to let this man get cut down from behind for the simple crime of cowardice. There were plenty of cowards in the world—it shouldn't be a death sentence. Besides, with the way this battle was progressing, it was about to be two on two—Willem and him against the Ox Champions. He'd take an extra sword, even in a weak hand, if it could help level the odds that easily favored the more experienced Ox Pennant at the moment.

Aiden and Willem's starting position was closer to the Fire Champion, but Ox had a head start. It would be a near thing on who reached the man first. The Fire Champion, for his part, remained oblivious to being charged by four well-armed men. There was little enough he could do at this point, not knowing the intention of either side, but he could at least look around once to see the peril he was in.

"Hey!" Willem shouted when they were only fifteen yards away. The man looked over with a start and brought his sword up to defend.

"No!" Aiden yelled. "Look! Look back! We're here to help!" But Willem and he still had to slow their pace. This man's sword could cut them as easily as it could cut Ox. "Look," Aiden said again, stopping entirely and gesturing with his spear. They were only five yards from the Fire Champion now, with Ox only fifteen yards the other way and closing quickly.

The Fire Champion was having none of it, though. He didn't turn. He didn't look. He just stood staring at Willem and Aiden until the sword decapitated him from behind. *So much for evening the odds*, Aiden thought.

Then Ox was upon them. Willem parried blows from a tall, thick man, while an equally tall but lanky man came at Aiden. These Champions were about business, here to kill or maim as quickly as possible. Apparently, they weren't concerned with a good show—just survival and victory, which Aiden supposed were the same thing in the Death Games.

Aiden moved to his right, giving himself a bit more space away from Willem to wield his spear. Sevion had discussed the choice of a spear with Aiden at some length during their first singles train-ing session. Aiden had explained his decision based on his shorter reach and what he had found about fighting in the past. Sevion had nodded but added, "You must be very careful, boy. You are right about reach, but a long sword is hard to best with a spear if you are unwise with it. You give them a wrong step or overextend with a jab—you let them inside your reach—you'll die quick as a scream."

Aiden would have to be sure not to make that mistake. As the Ox Champion approached him, Aiden feinted with two quick thrusts of his spear, keeping the man at bay. Aiden pulled back then and the lanky man followed, swinging his sword down in an over-handed cut. Whirling his spear around as Sevion had taught him, Aiden smashed the sword away and down, forcing the man's mo-mentum to carry him on, staggering slightly. He brought the spear point back up to thrust, but the man was already too close. The point missed the throat he was aiming for, instead tearing a gash across the muscle of the lanky man's neck.

The man cursed as blood spattered from the wound. He stum-bled on toward Aiden, allowing his momentum to carry him on into a tackle rather than making him fall. The Ox Champion wouldn't be able to swing his sword at this rate, but it held more promise for him than falling and letting Aiden stick him to the sand. As it was, there was no time for Aiden to pull his spear back to fend the man off, and no space to use it if he could. The spear was his safety, his life in the Tournament, and it was gone. Still, he had to do something.

Letting the spear drop, he slipped his fingers around the hilt of his knife. Just as the lanky man barreled into him, Aiden slipped the knife free of its sheath and let it slide into the man's abdomen, beneath his ribs, as they both went down to the sand. For a sicken-ing moment his knife wasn't buried in this Ox Champion's stom-ach, but in Semlie's, and he wasn't himself, but the bald man,

Branke. He saw the light snuffed from Semlie's eyes as the color drained from her face—death sliding its veil over her features. Then Aiden came back to himself, and that was worse yet.

"No," Aiden whispered, returning to Semlie, "Antice, no." Blood was covering his hand and forearm in a warm pulse. "No...no...please no."

Then the lanky man, who still lay on top of Aiden, groaned as he tried to pull himself up far enough to hit Aiden with a fist. The punch landed but without any true force behind it. Still, it had enough effect to snap Aiden back to himself and the reality of his surroundings once again.

He pushed the Ox Champion off of him, rolling him up and onto his side. The man tried to hit him again, but he was weakening quickly. With a last push, Aiden threw the man the rest of the way over to the sand and scrambled to his feet. Then he grabbed his spear from the ground and drove it through the man's neck, completing the spear's original purpose.

The fight had only lasted a few moments, but during that time Aiden's focus had narrowed, encompassing only himself and the man who lay dead at his feet. Now the rest of the Square crashed down on him like a flooding wave. The crowd was screaming in so many unintelligible voices, a single man stood, seeming dumbfounded in the center of the Sands, the apparent victor of the Bear and Fire clash, and just to Aiden's left, Willem still crossed swords with the broad Ox Champion. A trickle of blood ran down Willem's shield arm from a wound near the shoulder. He cradled his shield close to his chest and was giving ground to the Ox Champion's assault. Willem wasn't out of the fight yet, matching the man's swordplay blow for blow, but most of his action was defensive.

Aiden needed to act. The Ox Champion drove forward time after time. With Willem's shield arm wounded, it would only take a single missed parry to seal his death. Aiden didn't know how to approach. They hadn't had time for training in how to engage two on one. In the moment he hesitated, trying to decide, his decision was made for him. The Ox Champion parried Willem's thrust and lunged forward for the killing blow. Willem wrenched his arm up just in time to collect the death strike on his shield, but the power of the impact forced him backward, stumbling until he finally tripped and fell.

Time was up. Aiden flipped his spear around, reared back, and threw it with all his force at the man before the Ox Champion could take the final step of driving his sword down to kill Willem where he lay sprawled on his back. Willem's opponent apparently didn't have the same narrowing of vision during combat that Aiden had. The man whipped his shield up, accepting the concussion of the spear's force without gaining so much as a scratch.

Aiden stood, out-matched and now with his best chance of survival quivering, tip buried in the Ox Champion's shield. His knife would be of little use against the long sword in the other man's hand or the skill with which that hand could wield it. Still, there were two Boulders and only one Ox. As the man's attention shifted to Aiden, Willem stabbed upward with his sword. The Ox Champion tried to pull his shield in tight, but Aiden's lodged spear added weight and awkwardness to the man's defense. Willem's sword bit through the man's light armor and into his abdomen. The man howled, trying to pull back his sword arm for a blow, but Willem pushed all the harder, driving the man back a step.

They paused there for a moment, frozen, with Willem propped up on one elbow, swordarm extended, the Ox Champion leaning back, trying to pull his sword back up for another swing. Finally, like a candle being blown out by a puff of wind, the Ox Champion fell backward onto the sand. Willem's sword pulled free of the falling man's stomach with a sickening suction sound that Aiden could somehow hear even over the roar of the crowd. Willem got to his feet, stepped forward, and finished his opponent much as Aiden had finished his own moments before.

Approaching slowly, Aiden resheathed the knife he had pulled from his belt. His spear still clung to the dead Ox Champion's shield, and he pulled it out, placing his foot against the splintering wood for leverage. For a moment, Aiden's and Willem's eyes met. Then they turned toward the center of the Square, locking onto the last opponent on the Sands.

They didn't get more than a step toward the center before the trumpet sounded, though. Aiden looked to the stands and found Master Gregor standing at the edge of his stone terrace with one of his six-ringed hands raised, the sun shimmering off his gold cloak. The battle was over, and points would now be tallied.

As if the horn were a signal, Willem bent double and offered his day's lunch back up and into the welcoming sands.

They had both just killed men, Aiden realized. He remembered the wash of warm blood pumping out, slicking his hand. *Semlie,* he thought but willed it away. "No," he whispered. "No."

Moving back toward their starting corner as directed at the game's onset, Aiden and Willem watched the giant scoreboard near Master Gregor's terrace. Gregor, along with a group of three judges, scored each round. The Champions were given individual points which also counted toward a total Pennant score. Sevion said they were judged on several factors including but not limited to: kills, assists, injuries sustained, opponents battled, strength of opponent, style, survival, and the ever-important, win. The points were accumulated and placed on the scoreboard, starting with the dead Champions. Their points did them little good, but the cumulative still counted toward their Pennant.

Aiden knew his points could buy him and Boulder Pennant small favors in the complex: better food, a second blanket, weapon sharpening or repair, but the true purpose of the points was not for the champions at all. The betting houses used the scores for odds at each battle, and betting houses meant money—money for Gregor—money for entertainment. What seemed ridiculous to Aiden was that many of the Champions acted as if the scores mattered to them as well—vanity taking root, even here in the Death Games.

A short, thick man dressed in gold and red stepped forward and, speaking into a megaphone, cried out the scores in a booming voice. "Tanton, Fire Pennant: one assist, one opponent battled; three points. Jaxworl, Bear Pennant: one kill, two opponents battled; seven points." As the announcer called out the scores, a group of four men pulled levers and flipped signs, arranging the scores next to each Champion's name and next to the name of each Pennant.

The Boulder Pennant gained eleven points for Hentor's berserk attack. Then it was Willem's turn. "Willem, Boulder Pennant," cried the announcer, "one kill, one opponent battled, survival, injured without loss, and the win; forty-two points." The crowd's cheers drowned out all else for a moment as if they had known all along, that Willem, whom they'd never seen fight before, had it in him the whole time.

The crowd quieted after a moment. Aiden was the last to be scored. Raising his megaphone back to his lips, the announcer called, "Aiden, Boulder Pennant: one kill, one double assist, two opponents battled, survival, and the win; forty-six points." The crowd exploded again, the cheers cascading down to wash the Sands.

Boulder had destroyed the rest of the Pennants in the standings. Both Willem and Aiden had received points for survival and the win, which made up over half their total. It made sense. The Champions who battled and came out victorious should be compensated for that victory. Aiden could think of a million things he

would rather have than points on a giant board, but points were all
they were giving out today. He somehow doubted the dead Champions were finding much use for them in the beyond.

Chapter 12

They are so rarely as they seem in this.

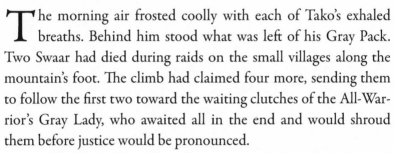

The morning air frosted coolly with each of Tako's exhaled breaths. Behind him stood what was left of his Gray Pack. Two Swaar had died during raids on the small villages along the mountain's foot. The climb had claimed four more, sending them to follow the first two toward the waiting clutches of the All-Warrior's Gray Lady, who awaited all in the end and would shroud them before justice would be pronounced.

Six dead and all worth it, for a tower of white stone loomed up out of the mountainside in front of him. Tako smiled despite himself. He had started to doubt the existence of this tower, spoken of only in the mythical description of an ancient script. More than that, he had become sure that his choice of paths had been wrong and wrong and wrong more times than he could count.

"We found it," Dante said from behind him. Tako grunted something in the affirmative as he turned back to the closest thing he had to a friend in this world. Small icicles clung to Dante's beard and mustache making a jingling "clink clank" when they struck each other as he spoke. His little band was looking awfully ragged and half-frozen. He hoped there was some dry wood for a fire in that keep, but he was fairly sure no one was home to offer any hospitality. No inviting smoke issued out the chimney of the tower at any rate.

"Aye, we found it," Tako said, "but we're not knocking at the gates just yet. We have a ways to go if we're planning to make it by dark, All-Warrior help us."

"All-Warrior help us," the other's intoned after him in unison. With nothing else said, they trudged on. A slippery climb up a steep rock face still lay before them and that was only after a more treacherous downward slope. If a path lay hidden somewhere amongst the snowy landscape of this rocky tundra, Tako hadn't found it. Nor had he known exactly what "around the star of Mountain Bright" meant, but here they were anyway.

Tako had continued north as best he could, guided by the Captain's Spear and Dragon's Head in the night sky. Finally, they had come to the mountains, stretching on east and west in a resolute blockade against Tako's path. Huge and menacing they stood, with sheer icy cliffs rising jagged from a cold, rocky soil. He could almost sense the mountains' disdain for Tako and his little group's plans. *"Be gone,"* the mountains seemed to call out in a chorus of whispered wind. *"Be gone and do not tempt these fates, you mortals."*

But Tako had tempted the fates and a good portion of his pack had paid for that choice. In truth, though, there had been no choice. Dal Tek had said to go, and they would find no comfort in returning empty-handed. The Dal's cold rage was enough to force Ren Tako on, even if he had stood alone against the mountainside. Still, the fear of Dal Tek was not all that drove the group of Swaar on.

The first night, Tako had called a halt and for camp to be set while they still lingered in the grasp of the foothills with the mountains an hour or more to the north. Once the sun had dropped in its return to the All-Warrior's forge, and once twilight too had run its course, just as the stars claimed the sky in full again for the night, it happened. The mountain nearest them, due north of their camp, lit as if a star's white light lay trapped inside, burning its brilliance in a desperate need to rejoin its sisters in the sky. The mountain shone white, glittering just as the stars above glittered.

"Rider," Dante Whisper, had said as quietly as his name, "it's beautiful." And Tako couldn't disagree with that statement. *"Around the star of Mountain Bright,"* Brother Terriase had written, and apparently the man had known something of this path after all. Surely, that was what they now beheld. What else could hold such a name but this star mountain? The glimmer continued for about an hour longer, offering an eerie lightness to the night.

The horses would be useless with the mountain ahead of them. More than likely, there would be places too steep or too narrow for them to make the passage. Still, they would want them, if they returned this way, if they returned at all. Tako had decided to send off only a couple of his pack to deal with the horses. Two armed strangers are less threatening than a dozen, he had reasoned. Tako chose Whisper and a smaller woman named Eleena, whom the men called Mass, short for Massive—only half a joke at the woman's size. Eleena was fierce and huge in battle with her incredible speed and quick thinking, truly a massive force to come up against. She was only one woman of two that Tako had chosen for this mission. The other lay dead from an axe blow in one of the villages they had fought their way through along their path. Tako would trust Mass in battle before nearly any man he had with him. He had seen her fight. There were few enough who could match her.

Besides, Whisper and Mass both looked close enough to low dwellers that they could pass as dirty travelers instead of Swaar raiders. They were to find an inn or farm where they could board the horses in wait for their return journey. Dal Tek had given Tako a small purse of gold and a larger one of silver, "For anything you cannot kill or steal to get," the Dal had said. The coin he entrusted to Dante, instructing him to pay well, but fair so as not to raise suspicion.

They waited a day, camped now nearly at the base of the glowing mountain. The two Swaar had been back from boarding the horses just in time to see the twilight die and the false light of the mountain take hold.

"Done as the Rider commanded," Whisper had said in his low, gentle voice.

"Rider," Mass had murmured in agreement, offering a nod in respect to Tako.

The next day they climbed, and when night fell two men already lay dead at this glimmering mountain's feet. The rest of his Gray Pack had tucked themselves into a shallow outcropping of rock. Tako had expected the same miracle of a sparkling landscape to appear. He had waited for it, watched as twilight gave in to night, and waited, spinning the ring on his finger and thinking of his mother's words, *as dark as night and bright as liquid starlight.* But waiting was all he could do. The soft star glow never returned to the rocks under his feet. Had the All-Warrior sent them a sign in their moment of need? Perhaps Tako could only see it from beyond the mountain.

He had laughed that night as he considered. For all he knew, some other traveler was staring up at this looming rock face and seeing Ren Tako, the Wolf Rider, glitter along with all else on the mountain.

From there the climb had only grown more gruesome, more grueling. It was a long time since Tako had felt warm, a long time since any amount of comfort had been his, and more men had died to top off the climbing experience. But it was all worth it now, or it would be by nightfall when they stood at the doors of that stone tower—The Keep of the White Tower.

A man named Sunto, a huge brute of a man who preferred a massive war hammer in battle, nearly fell twice on the descent down the short, slippery slope that lay before the final climb. He was saved, though, by the safety line they had hammered into the icy stone further up the slope. The ascent went better, and with an hour to go before sundown, their dwindled group stood before a rusted iron gate leading to a short bridge and finally, a solid-looking oak door.

The gate would not move. It was rusted shut, and Tako wondered when anyone had last used this tower. A rusty gate was not something to hold back the great Wolf Rider, however. Hands numb, he shrugged his great axe easily from his back and whipped its honed edge around and down onto the hinge of one side of the gate. The metal let out a terrible shriek as it found itself peeled away from where it was once joined. One more stroke and the right side of the gate hung loosely where rust had bound it to the rock face. Sunto, perhaps frustrated by his earlier falls, struck out with a boot and sent the broken side of the gate screeching in a hand's span before it jarred to a halt against a slightly raised chunk of stone or ice—not big enough for a man to slip through, but not a bad start to entry either.

Sunto's boot lashed out again, but when the gate refused to budge any further, Dante slipped over, silent as ever. He slid one of the spikes they had used for securing lines during the climb free from his belt and placed it deftly between bars at the base of the upraised blockage. The small fighting hammer with the hatchet blade formed on the back dropped easily into the quiet man's hand. As silent as a flickering flame, so that Tako couldn't even hear the strikes over the wind, Dante drove the spike into the chunk's base. Ren Tako watched as a dusting of ice and stone chipped away under the three swift strokes. Then all at once, the top three-quarters of the blockage lost its grip on the rest of the mountainside and slipped free to go tumbling down into the abyss beneath the narrow bridge.

Dante Whisper bowed swiftly and silently to Sunto and motioned him to go ahead. The big Swaar stepped forward and offered the gate a thundering blow from his boot yet again. This time the gate shuddered as it jumped the short remainder of the stone still blocking its way. The rusted iron screeched to a halt again, but this time the opening was easily large enough to allow a man to slip through if he held his pack out in front of him with one arm. It was enough. Luckily, the bridge widened out into a small platform at the gate, giving the group just enough room to slide through and regroup before crossing.

The bridge stood staggered and arching between two mountain slopes with a vertigo-inducing drop beneath. No sides or rails had been constructed, just a narrow stretch of stone. More than that, the bridge was narrow enough to let only one person cross at a time. Whoever the builders of this place had been, must have assumed no mount would ever make it so high, for they left no room for even the smallest of horses to cross. To make matters worse, the wind whipped up out of the chasm beneath and over the bridge with a seditious will bent on murder.

Decision time, Tako thought—but then, when was it not decision time on this slippery mountain? It came down to this: Did he link everyone with a rope, tying everyone's fate to each other's dexterity? Or was it every man for himself? The first option gave them the best chance to get everyone across the bridge, but also the best chance to send all that was left of their pack screaming down to their deaths. They were a pack, though—the Gray Pack. Tako smiled. All-Warrior protect them, but packs ran together, didn't they?

Before Tako could give the order, Dante beat him to the decision. The man removed a coil of rope from around his shoulder and slid his way back in the group to where Tako assumed he would secure the rope around Mass, who stood last in line. Instead, Whisper wrapped the rope around the edge of the gate still attached to the stone. After triple knotting to one end of the rope, he made his way to the near side of the bridge, slowly uncoiling the rope behind him.

Dante Whisper glanced at Tako for a moment before stepping out onto the bridge itself. A question lingered in his eyes. Tako offered the barest hint of a smile and gave the man a brief nod. Dante stepped out onto the bridge, the wind whipping at his clothes and hair, making the icicles in his short beard rattle. Slowly, oh so very slowly he edged across the narrow, slippery stone. At first, it seemed as if he would make the trip to the far side without incident, but just as he reached the zenith of the short, humped bridge, a huge gust surged through the unprotected air and nearly tore Whisper wholly from his perch.

Dante ripped his hammer from his belt and slammed it down into the stone, blade point first. The stone sparked and he was within a breath of still falling. At the last moment, the point of his hammer caught and Dante weathered the last of the gust in shaky silence. When the wind calmed back to something resembling a safe level, he worked his way up to his feet and shuffled more than walked the rest of the way to the waiting platform at the far side.

After a needed moment of composure collection, Dante drove a spike into the far wall of the mountain and secured the rope to it, offering a tight hand rail to the narrow bridge. Tako's grin grew a little wider, both with relief at his friend's safety and at the sheer audacity it took for Dante to carry out such a plan with no more than a moment's planning. So, perhaps some packs could have more than one leader in times of trial.

"And there you have Whisper, my lads," Tako growled at the others. "Never cross him, for this day he may have saved all of our lives."

"Whisper," the others intoned in voices much louder than the man's name.

Good, Tako thought, *it was about time these men started looking at someone other than himself with a bit of that awe.*

With the help of the rope line, it didn't take terribly long for the rest of them to cross the bridge to safety. It wasn't a fun crossing, nor an easy one. It was manageable, however, and manageable was far more than Tako and his Gray Pack had any right to hope for.

Tako hadn't planned on leaving a rope behind, but he didn't much care for the idea of going back to untie the far end from the rusty gate. Besides, if all went well, they would be needing that rope to cross back the other way. That all hinged on finishing their business with this White Tower.

The oak door was the last, but perhaps the most substantial, opponent left to their entry. Tako assumed it would be locked and barred, but Tako still had his honed axe if it came to it. He was the first to the door, a massive, bound, wooden construction with both latch and keyhole. He peered into the keyhole but couldn't tell if the key was in the other side or not, since all that lay beyond was darkness. *Well, not that it mattered anyway*, he thought. It would most likely come to the same end regardless. Still, he thought he would try the latch.

If it opened, he was sure it would be on similarly rusted and ill-kept hinges as those of the gate. To his surprise but happy acceptance, the latch rose with the barest of pressure and the door swung open without a sound.

Without so much as a glance back, Tako moved forward into the room. *"Do not show fear, not ever,"* his father had told him, *"else *wise men will find you fearful, and there is nothing to be gained by that reputation. Far better to be feared, Tako, than to be known to fear others. Far, far better."* Tako thought that counted double for command. He had built much of his persona on being both feared and fearless; no point in counteracting that now.

The room inside the open door was dark and cool, the only light flowing in through the door Tako had just opened. In their current state, however, cool was a vast improvement to freezing. The air lay still about them, and dust sat thick and stubborn on the stone of the floor. After the constant, penetrating wind of outside, the silence within these walls seemed eerie and fragile.

Tako called for torches and Whisper made his way swiftly forward, dousing the oil, striking the flint. Within moments a warm, red glow cast the shadows back from their long-held fortress perch. The room they stood in was not large but opened into three archways, two with doors and one without. Even from where Tako stood, still near the door, he could see the archway without a door opened onto a flight of stairs. Presumably, they led to the second floor of this Keep of the White Tower. What they were after—this word for the Shield of Ammereth and the defender would almost certainly lie further up, but it was best to be thorough—and better yet, to make sure that no unwelcoming host lay waiting to entrap them with some calamity or another.

Tako moved to one of the unopened doors, signaling Whisper toward the other. Each door had a lock, but each also had a key resting beneath its latch. More than that, the doors weren't even locked and swung open on their hinges as easily and silently as the front door had. Casks and crates filled the room in front of Tako. Dried sausages were strung densely along one wall, and rows of bottles filled a gigantic wine rack on the opposite side—a food cellar, or as close an approximation as one could find in a tower without a subterranean level, and fully stocked as well. Every piece of evidence pointed to an inhabitant or inhabitants of this tower. How they had hauled all these supplies up from somewhere in the valley was beyond Tako. It made no sense, but here it was nonetheless. Something was out of place here, but they hadn't seen all there was to see yet.

Tako left the supply room for now. They could always inventory later if time and circumstance allowed. He took only a step toward the other room before reconsidering and sending Mass back to cut a few sausages from the supply on the wall. Tako's unease was growing and he would curse himself later if he missed this opportunity for a bit of sustenance on their return trip if things went sour in the rest of the tower.

Whisper, Sunto, and White Zemin—a gray beard with a fierce reputation (and Tako could attest to the truth of that reputation)—stood inside the room when Tako entered through the open door. Five chests lay open on the floor. Two were filled with gold coins, two with silver, and the last sat brimming with precious stones of every color, glittering and shining in the reflected light of the torches.

"Well now, that is quite a sight for a poor old man's eyes," White Zemin said in his weathered, gruff voice.

"Aye," agreed Sunto. Whisper remained characteristically silent.

Tako gritted his teeth and narrowed his eyes as he peered at one treasure chest after another, giving each their due time as if secret clues lay buried within the glitter. It made no sense. None of this made any sense. But still, decisions were demanding to be made, and Ren Tako was never one to shy from doing what needed doing.

"We'll leave this for now," Tako said. "There'll be time to collect what treasure we can carry once we've found what we came for."

Dante nodded his immediate acceptance, but it took Sunto and White Zemin a moment to follow. It was never easy for men who had been raiding for any amount of time to leave treasure behind them. More often than not, some other Swaar would have claimed it for himself before you could get back to it.

Tako sighed inwardly. *It is always thus—the quick and strong take what they will and the rest learn only to guard what they stumble upon.*

"Very well," he said in a gravelly voice that broached no argument. "Each man may take one fist full of gold, one of silver, and one full of the jewels for their packs. The rest we will deal with after." Sunto and White Zemin both smiled and even Dante allowed a hint of enjoyment to brush at the corners of his mouth. Tako didn't know if Whisper's smirk was for the treasure or simply an acknowledgment of a well-played maneuver by Tako to keep his men happy.

Whether to spite Dante's smirk or to spur on the man's opinion, Tako wasn't sure, but he announced, "And Mass, cut a few more of those sausages and break out a couple bottles of whatever looks good from that rack." He glanced at Dante, eyebrows raised ever so slightly, daring the man to say something. Whisper's expression didn't change in the least, denying Tako the victory. Tako narrowed his eyes in mock irritation.

"Might as well help ourselves to some supper if we're going to pilfer the treasure anyway," he said more quietly, for Whisper's ears alone, after the other two had left to claim their portion of the meal. Whisper nodded, saying nothing, his tiny smirk remaining firm in its determination.

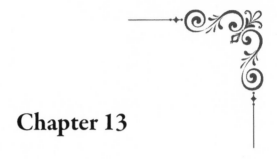

Chapter 13

These may be my final words to you and to those who come after.

Willem rubbed absently at his shield arm. Funny—when had it become his shield arm instead of his left? Regardless, the shoulder itched. They had brought in a surgeon who had examined the cut, declared the muscle intact, and then poured a nasty-smelling liquid over the wound. It burned like white fire and Willem howled.

"Oh yes, it will sting a bit," the surgeon chuckled with a slight lisp. "But you'll thank me for it when you have full use back in a day or two."

A tugging sensation drew Willem's attention back to his shoulder. The liquid had run down, off the wound and onto his side. The cut itself, though, was now left with what looked like some kind of webbing gapping the space. New skin pulled at each side of the wound, and even as Willem watched, the two halves pulled together, leaving nothing but a fresh pink scar and slight itching sensation.

"Marvelous stuff isn't it!" the surgeon stated more than asked. "Vellen, they call it—some far southern word for 'liquid skin'. Tremendous what one can find if one just looks, eh?" With that, the surgeon had turned and walked out whistling. He paused and looked back over his shoulder at the door. "Oh, and it will itch, my good man, so don't be worried about that. It'll fade in time."

But it hadn't faded, not yet at any rate. Willem supposed it could be worse. The cut could have been on his back where he would have a harder time reaching it. At least this way he could rub at it with enough ease. He also could be dead, he supposed, which would have taken care of the itching, but still might not have been the preferred route.

That had been over a week ago now, but if it hadn't been for the itching, Willem could believe it had been a season. Today Willem would fight in his third tournament on the Sands. Along with him would stand the other remaining members of Boulder Pennant—Aiden, and the twins, Lem and Rem. Hentor had died in the first tournament during the four corner battle he and Aiden had won.

Dallo, Boulder's fifth member, had died a few days later in the second tournament. After showing good promise with a blade in his first triples battle alongside the twins, which all three of them had amazingly survived, claiming another win for Boulder, Dallo had been forced into single combat with Gaw of Eagle Pennant. Gaw was a giant of a man who had survived the Death Games for over a year and a half now—quite a feat, with the average falling somewhere closer to a month after training, and plenty dying long before that. The huge man fought with a double-edged, two-handed sword at least five feet in length. Gaw had killed more men on the Sands than anyone other than Marzin the Champion.

Against this killing machine, Gregor sent Dallo. Willem had heard Sevion ranting at the Master that it was ridiculous to expect a man less than two weeks from the street to fight such an accomplished swordsman.

"It is not for the Champions that the Tournament is held, my good Boulder, but for the crowds," Master Gregor, Twelve Rings, had responded in his usual icy voice, and that was the end of it.

Dallo had fought well, giving Gaw one more scar on his hardened body. In the end, Dallo's smaller build and short experience were his undoing. Gaw knocked his sword away before cleaving Dallo near in half with a mighty wood-cutting swing from his great sword. Dallo's last act in the Death Games was offering his life blood to the Sands.

Now it was just the four of them, and after today's battle, Willem had no doubt there would be fewer still.

He entered the Boulder Pennant's small meeting room and nodded to the others already sitting there. Rem and Lem smiled up at him, but Aiden offered something closer to a grimace.

Dregs and draught, Willem hated it here. He wasn't made to be a Champion, slave, or warrior. He was a musician, and by Dentar's golden strings, a fine one at that. He shouldn't be coming into a room to discuss battle strategy or how best to kill someone. He should be onstage in a pub or inn on the outside of these walls, singing and playing, spending his time consorting with serving girls with a mug of ale in one hand.

Willem sighed and did his best to return the others' smiles. As usual, the twins were arguing about some ridiculous statement or another, finishing each other's statement before returning with their own argument and smiling all the time. Sometimes, Willem wondered if the two of them were completely sane—if they understood that at least some, if not all of the four people in this room would most likely be dead before day's end. There was nothing to do about it though. If they wanted to argue and laugh until Antice took them, then who was he to say they shouldn't? He even envied the twins their levity, but it would never work for him, not here not inside these Maker-forsaken walls.

The door opened again, and this time Sevion entered, his face grim and a folded paper clutched in his hand. He looked them all over for a silent moment. Even Lem and Rem had quit their incessant babble to look up at him.

"How bad is it?" Aiden asked when Sevion remained silent.

The Boulder sighed. "It's bad enough," he said. "The good news is the four of you will be together. The bad news is you are facing three Pennants."

Rem laughed. "Well, that's not so bad."

"Not any worse than normal at any rate," Lem answered. "So who else is in the four corners battle?"

Sevion just shook his head. "No, you," and he pointed at each of them in turn with a thick finger, "will be facing three Pennants."

The twins' laughter died as what Sevion was saying struck home. Willem watched the color drain from Aiden's face as his own stomach turned over, threatening a rejection of that morning's breakfast.

"Which Pennants?" he heard himself ask after a moment.

"Eagle, Horn, and Wolf," Sevion said. They were three of the most experienced Pennants. Gaw represented Eagle solely, but the giant was an army unto himself. Horn had four members, all of which had been there for the better part of three seasons—a tough, close-knit group. Then there was Wolf. Three men, all who fought with double curved knives. Willem had heard they fought their way in close, then used their feet as much as their blades to defeat their opponents. If it wasn't for Gaw, Wolf Pennant would hold the most seniority in the Tournament.

Boulder would be outclassed against any one of these Pennants but might have a chance if they were very lucky. Facing two at once would be almost certain death. Three to one, though...Willem thought he might throw up again.

"Why?" Aiden asked, obviously unable to hide the Quaver in his voice. "Why us?"

Again, Sevion shook his head. "Gregor says it is for the crowds, but the fact of the matter is, the lot of you have done too well for such a young Pennant. Other trainers have a closer place to the Master's ear than I do, and they are not happy to have their effort offered to the Sands by a group still fresh and pink from the street. They want your blood, and to hold to their veterans. In truth, I doubt Gregor cares for anything but feeding the Sands until they are bloated on blood.

"Angels and All-Warrior take that man! You lads have done all I've asked of you, and now you'll have to do more."

For all his blustering and rock exterior, Sevion seemed a decent man to Willem. He wondered what had brought the weapons master to this life of Champion training. That question would probably earn him a slap to the head, though. Besides, they had bigger problems than Sevion's past to deal with.

Sevion held up the paper in his hand. "In any case, today is to be a special occasion. Prince Greenlea is visiting Perry, and both the Prince and Grand Duke Bentrial will be in attendance. It is my understanding that Master Gregor has been planning for this event for some time. We must be prepared for the unexpected here." Sevion paused again and looked each man in the eye.

"I'll not lie to you," he said. "The odds are not in our favor today. The dice are weighted and the house is throwing, as they say. You have only been with me for a few short weeks—not enough time to truly know a man, train him or trust him. Still, here we are—knowing all we will of each other, training all that can be trained, and we must decide to trust if there is to be a tomorrow."

A heavy moment hung in the air, thick enough to cut. Then Willem forced himself through the despair of what they were to face and asked, "What do we do?"

Sevion smiled and clapped him on his good shoulder. "I will tell you, and if you fight well, perhaps we will talk again tomorrow."

Willem shifted in his armor, trying to appease the ever-present itch of his shoulder. The Sands lay in front of him, but they were different than they had been. Pillars of various sizes had been set all through the Square. Some sat short and squat, no more than two feet high. Others loomed up fifteen feet, standing with a wide four-foot stance. The pillars twisted this way and that, giving the Sands an odd, maze-like feel.

The change was good, Willem supposed. The Boulder Pennant wouldn't last long on flat Sands against eight opponents, all of whom outstripped the four of them put together in experience.

One other change had settled on the Square as well. Master Gregor had informed all of the Champions only moments before that the center of the pillar maze held a cache of weapons and supplies. He even hinted that longer-range weapons like bows and throwing knives may lay hidden there. It was clear enough that the center held the Boulder Pennant's best chance at survival, but it also told the other Pennants where they were going. The possibilities of so many different horrible deaths flashed before Willem, and he shuddered.

"Nothing for it boys," he heard Aiden saying, apparently following his own train of thought. "Stay close enough to help each other and we may have a shot."

The other Pennants were set on the opposite corner of the Square where Willem couldn't see them and where they couldn't see him. He didn't know if that was a good thing or not. He was glad they wouldn't be rushing his Pennant immediately, but he didn't like the idea of them sneaking up on him either.

He rolled his shoulders again, trying to satisfy the maddening itch. Then he saw Master Gregor step out to the edge of his dais. A six-ringed hand came up and a trumpet sounded. It had begun.

The four of them sprinted into the looming pillars. Willem looked this way and that, but Gregor had done his job with the pillars well. No matter how he looked, he couldn't see anything of the other Pennants. Only towering marble and squat, wall-like stone met his eyes. Still, nothing for it, they had to gain the center.

"Angels curse it," Rem snapped as he stumbled against a lower, wall-like pillar. Their path was anything but straightforward, and the four of them were forced to keep swerving back and forth, right then left, in order to make their way deeper into the maze. The Sands weren't that big, but when you could only take a few steps before having to turn, they could take a long time to traverse.

"Just keep moving," Willem heard Aiden say. "The center can't be that far." The roar of the crowd was only slightly muted by the surrounding pillars. The stands must have been situated in such a way as to allow the Champions to be visible, or mostly so, to all the onlookers.

"I know," came Rem's reply. "But what if—ah!" Rem didn't get to finish his thought because just then three forms rushed, barreling out from behind a group of pillars to their right. The three men each swung curved knives that tapered from a narrow base to a wide blade before sharpening back to a deadly point. Wolf had reached them.

"Keep them at a distance," Willem ordered, without pause and more to himself than to anyone else in particular. It was the advice Sevion had given them for Wolf that morning. *Easier said than done*, Willem thought. Rem was fending off one attacker with the short sword he carried while Lem, wielding his own two long knives, was having a harder time going toe-to-toe with one of the Wolf Champions. The third member of Wolf was sliding to Rem's left, trying to get around and past his shield.

They want to eliminate our advantage of numbers, Willem realized. Wolf, true to their name, was like a pack of hounds, attacking their prey in numbers. But this prey had a pack of its own. Just as the third Wolf Champion slipped around Rem's shield side, the man's curved knife swung down. The blow would have cut a deep gash in Rem's unprotected arm and shoulder, but Willem lunged forward, catching the attack on the blade of his long sword. The Wolf showed no disappointment or frustration. Rather, he continued his attack on Rem, dropping his right fist, still clutched around the hilt of his curved blade, to the ground and using his momentum to lift his left foot up and quick as a blur, bury his boot in Rem's side.

Rem staggered to the side, his defense crumbling into flailing arms as he tried to right his balance and stay on his feet. The second Wolf Champion, a small balding man who had been engaging Rem's main efforts, didn't hesitate. He stepped in close as he swung with his knife. Again, Rem was nearly sliced dearly with a curved blade. This time it was Aiden who came to Rem's defense. Willem saw the smaller man's spear whip through the air and slap the man's knife aside before opening a gash across the balding Wolf's cheek. The Wolf staggered back as Aiden pressed his advantage.

Then Willem was forced to back behind a wide pillar and lost sight of the others. The Wolf Champion whose knife he had blocked was lean-faced and quick as a wild cat. Willem swung desperately with his sword, but each step he took was backward. With as fast as the blows fell on his shield and sword, he would have sworn the man had four hands, all wielding curved blades. All Willem could do was parry and block, hoping the man wouldn't press beyond his defenses. Every moment that passed, he expected to feel the hot bite of one of those knives.

Frantically avoiding the Wolf Champion, he dropped behind a pillar to his left. Crouching behind his shield to guard against as many blows as possible, Willem waited the half moment it took for the lean-faced Wolf to follow him. Then he lunged forward with his sword, hoping to skewer the man before he could renew his volley of attacks. But again, the man's speed proved the better. The Wolf fell back, dropping his weight to his hand as Willem's blade drove harmlessly above him. Then both the Wolf's feet shot out in a mighty kick. His boots connected only with Willem's shield, but Willem was over-extended from his lunge and the blow was more than enough to send him sprawling to the ground.

Spitting sand from his mouth, Willem rolled to his back just in time to see the curved blade of a knife descending toward his heart. He yanked his shield up to cover himself, the thought of death skirting the tip of his mind. There was a *thunk* as the knife impaled the wooden shield, sliding two inches out the back side and scratching at Willem's leather armor.

The Wolf released his blade and swung his fist around the shield and into Willem's unprotected side twice. Willem kicked out with his left leg, trying to knock his attacker back, but again his opponent was too quick. He leapt back out of range, and Willem's foot found nothing but empty air. Still, the man had fallen backward, and that gave Willem a moment's repose. He made it all the way to his knees before the Wolf Champion was on him again. Willem swung his long sword, but the lean-faced man blocked it down with his remaining knife and jumped into Willem leading with his knee.

The impact knocked Willem back flat on the ground and drove the air from his lungs. The Wolf flipped over Willem, landed in a squat, and leapt at him again, this time leading with the knife in both hands.

This was it—death's merry tune come to play him beyond. He couldn't breathe, and his muscles refused his order. His shield lay over his chest but remained completely impotent at blocking the blade descending toward his face.

Then a knife flew in from the opposite side of the Sands, the side Willem and the Wolf Champion had come from. The knife soared past Willem's face and thudded sideways into the lean face of the Wolf. It hadn't been a perfect throw. Indeed, it hadn't even stabbed Willem's attacker, but several pounds of metal flying through the air and connecting with a person's face is enough to drop most men.

The Wolf's curved blade missed Willem altogether—its edge actually slicing into the man's owner's leg. The Wolf Champion let out a howl and tried to scramble away, but Willem's breath was coming back now and he too was on his feet.

Limping, the Wolf tried to slash at Willem, but Willem accepted the blow onto his shield and swung out with his longsword. The man was too slow to evade this time and Willem's blade took him just above the foot.

He cried out and dropped. "No! Stop!" the Wolf Champion yelled, but Willem didn't stop. He plunged his sword down into the man's chest once, twice, three times. The man screamed, gurgled, and then fell silent.

Panting, Willem looked behind him and saw Lem collecting the long knife he had thrown to save Willem's life.

"Thanks," Willem said, still breathing hard. "I think I finally have a strategy for this madness. I just need to fall down and let someone else throw something at whoever I'm fighting. Then, I can stab 'em."

Lem grunted and nodded and the two of them made their way back to the others after Lem had collected the Wolf's fallen curved knife and tucked it into his belt.

Apparently, Aiden's reach with the spear had allowed him to skewer the balding Wolf Champion who had attacked Rem. With one partner missing and the other dead, the third Wolf had decided not to risk a three-on-one battle and had fled.

"Two down," Rem said, his ever-present smile playing across his lips.

"Only six left," Aiden answered. His eyes were still hard. Willem understood his thoughts. Six on four were still terrible odds when not one of the four of them could take any one of the six of the others in single combat. If the other Pennants thought things through, they would combine their efforts and swarm Boulder. Nothing for it.

"We have to get to the center," Willem said. He knew it was still their best chance. It may be their only chance.

Aiden's head swiveled left, right, left, right, as they moved with as much care and as much speed as they could muster toward the center of the Sands. It was almost to the point of making him feel sick from the motion, but he refused to be taken unawares. If one of the other Pennants was going to kill him today, he at least wanted to see it coming.

It had been a solid couple of minutes since they had ended the fight with Wolf, and the center of the Square had to be nearly upon them. He was just starting to think the promise of long-range weapons was just another toying by Master Gregor when they came around a bend to find a stack of wooden crates lying inside a blank square of sand. He took in the area, a canteen of water lying on one of the crates, a stack of throwing knives on another, before his eye caught on a short bow with a quiver of arrows next to it on one of the crates. Normally, Aiden would have preferred something a bit longer for the range it offered, but inside Tournament Sands, the short bow would be perfect.

Hope rekindled inside of Aiden as he rushed forward to grab the bow. Then, the freshly-born flame died as an arrow whistled past his face and struck the canteen clean through. It was a trap. He had abandoned all precaution upon seeing what he thought would save them. "Fool!" he spat at himself. "Draught riddled fool!" Wolf had probably been sent for no other purpose but to engage them and slow them down so the rest could get here and set the trap. This square was supposed to be their salvation. Now, it would be all of their deaths.

He reached the crates and dove over. There was no time to grab the bow or arrows. He had only just slid over and down to the Sands when he heard the next arrow slam into the opposite side of the crate he had just dived over. Rem and Lem had seemingly lost any sense of wariness along with Aiden, for a moment after he landed in the Sands on the far side of the crates, they slid over next to him.

It seemed that Willem alone had remained watchful, and even as Aiden tried to decide what to do, he heard steel on steel as Willem began to battle with someone still in the pillars. He had just decided to take the risk of reaching up to get the short bow when figures appeared in the spaces between pillars in front of him.

"Oh, by the Angels," Aiden heard one of the twins swear.

Before them stood Gaw, his giant double-edged sword leaned nonchalantly against his shoulder. Beside him stood one of the Horn Champions, a big man in his own right, though not as big as Gaw. The Horn Champion had a curved scimitar in one hand and a round buckler shield strapped to his opposite arm.

Three on two, they may have had the very outside end of a chance, but with an archer behind them and more still unaccounted for...this was a bad spot. If they charged, at least one of them would almost certainly die with an arrow in the back. If they stayed, their chances weren't much better. If only they could get back into the pillars and out of this open square.

Slowly, Aiden inched his hand up to grab the bow—it was still his best chance. Gaw reacted without pause, however, and charged straight for them. Aiden acted with all the speed he could muster. Dropping his left back down to his belt, he whipped his knife free and hurled it at the oncoming giant.

Gaw didn't even pause. He slapped the thrown blade from the air with his sword as easily as a child swatting a lobbed rock with a stick and just kept coming. A mingling of anger and joy danced in Gaw's eyes, and Aiden wondered for just a moment if Gaw had always been crazy or if the Death Games had cracked him. Then the giant was on him.

Aiden waited until Gaw was in range of his spear before he got to his feet to attack. He'd just have to hope that the archer behind him wouldn't fire into the melee for risk of hitting his teammates in this soon-to-be massacre. He swung his spear low, trying to catch Gaw in the leg before he was close enough to use his huge cleaver. Again, Gaw knocked away his attempted attack, contempt plain in his stance. Pulling the spear back, Aiden tried several quick jabs, but to no avail. It was truly astounding how quickly the big man could maneuver his heavy sword. Try as he might, Aiden couldn't score a single hit against him. He was beginning to feel as if Gaw was just playing with him, a cat who knew the mouse had nowhere to go.

The twins seemed to be doing slightly better two-on-one against the Horn Champion. They had forced the man back several steps as he struggled to defend two opponents and three blades. Then, another man charged in from the far pillars—Tellos, Aiden had heard him called. He was squat and thick, but no slower for it—not in this maze of pillars. In one thick-fingered hand, Tellos held a short, slim-looking blade, more a long knife than a sword, and in the other he held similar steel but longer and slightly thicker.

Rem pulled off from his attack against the first Horn man and refocused on this second. The new assailant battered a few blows against Rem's shield and sword. Then, with apparent practiced ease, the squat Horn Champion engaged Rem's sword with his long steel before darting out with his shorter blade, driving it into Rem's sword arm, just above the elbow joint. Rem screamed and dropped his short sword as he instinctively staggered back from the sharp metal that would almost certainly be his death.

Aiden took an involuntary step toward the twins, his body betraying his desire to help. Then, Gaw claimed another foot of sand. Aiden whirled his spear above his head, trying to gain the speed he needed to finally land a blow on this inhuman mountain of a man. He whipped the tip around, praying that it might find Gaw's throat, but again he was thwarted.

Gaw flashed his huge sword up, then brought it down on the speeding spear. The sound of a *crack* filled Aiden's entire world for a moment as he saw the top third of his only defense break clean away from his spear. Aiden swung what remained of his spear at the tree trunk leg in front of him, but Gaw caught the blow in one meaty palm. The giant pulled the spear shaft free of Aiden's grip as easily as a father taking a stick from his toddler. Gaw threw the broken spear over his shoulder with no apparent effort, as if dismissing it from the fight. Then he reached out with his free hand and tried to grab Aiden by the throat. Aiden slid just out of range of the grasping fingers, bending his body back like a drawn bow.

Gaw's victory was not to be denied, however, and a moment later the flat of his huge sword smashed into Aiden, sending him half-flying, half-stumbling, crashing down on top of the crate behind him. Aiden heaved, rolling his body to the far side and away from Gaw, landing with a notable lack of agility. He sprawled in the sand, trying to fight his way back to his feet as he gasped for breath. Gaw stole a step backward and roared with laughter. He was playing with him, moving at an incredibly slow pace for one who meant to kill him. Aiden couldn't understand why Gaw hadn't cut him in half just now.

He's just putting on a show, Aiden decided, *trying to win favor from Gregor and the crowd.* Perhaps Gaw even had delusions of becoming the next Marzin—being set free to the cries of people's adoration. And Aiden was just his next step toward glory.

Aiden humphed as he pushed himself to his knees. He had no intention of becoming an easy step on this giant's path. Pulling his right leg up in front of him, Aiden reached into his boot and grasped the handle of the small falcon knife. He pulled it free in a flourish as he stood the rest of the way up.

A triumphant war cry sounded from the wall of pillars. Then, Willem backed quickly into the square, coming to stand beside Aiden. Blood ran unchecked from a cut along Willem's forehead, and his hand held tight around a sword broken a few inches above the hilt. A moment later, two men emerged from the opening in the pillars where Willem had exited. One was the Wolf Champion who had fled from their first encounter. The other bore the badge of Horn and sported what appeared to be the rest of Willem's sword in his shoulder.

A *thump* from behind him stole Aiden's attention. Rem had taken one too many blows to his shield—giving ground all the while—and now had been knocked against the crates. He slid down slowly, his legs refusing to hold his weight any longer. Lem leapt to his brother's aid, but now he was fighting two opponents at once, where he had been doing little more than staying alive against one.

Aiden felt so helpless. The feeling raged in him like a stormy sea. He couldn't decide between staying to help Willem with these two oncoming or attempting to save Lem and Rem from almost certain death.

"And the archer," he muttered, counting opponents. The archer made six.

"Killed him," Willem said, breathing heavily.

Aiden's eyebrows rose. Well, that explained the missing arrows in his chest. He was just going to comment on it when out of the corner of his eye he caught the flash of movement. Gaw. Curse him. The big man had reached over the wide crates, swinging a mighty blow meant to cut Aiden in half.

Aiden jumped back, but just a little too slowly and the sword point caught him across the hip, tearing a ragged gash in the flesh. He stumbled and fell.

So much for heroic plans of saving at least some of his companions. Aiden felt death's slow approach, and like a rabbit in its den, had nowhere left to flee. Willem's two opponents were still approaching, and all Aiden had to defend himself with was this small knife—a little memento of a life fading like a dream, broken and thinning.

He could still hear the clash of swords on the other side of the crates. Lem was still fighting then. He'd have to win out on his own if he was going to. Aiden couldn't help him. Aiden couldn't help himself for that matter, and their attackers were almost upon them. Along with the last Wolf Champion and the bleeding one from Horn, he now saw the huge form of Gaw out of the corner of his eye coming up from the left. He had worked his way around the crates and would reach them almost as soon as the other two.

"Willem, you have to run. Yes! Listen to me," he barked as Willem started shaking his head in denial. "Get to the bow of the archer you killed. Hide in the pillars and pick them off as they hunt for you."

"I'm not leaving. It wouldn't work anyway. I'd never make it halfway to the archer before one of these others caught up to me." He hesitated a moment, looking at the gaps in the pillars. "No, I'm staying. By the golden strings let's do what we can."

"No, listen..." Aiden started again.

But Willem cut him off with a fervent head shake. "I'm staying."

Aiden sighed but nodded. "Help me up then."

With Willem's support, Aiden stood. The pain in his hip was like fire, but if he stood with his weight on his left, it was bearable.

Their attackers were on them within another breath. Gaw's sword danced out, cutting the air and driving to finish its work in Aiden. Aiden's arm shot up, and he accepted the blow on his small falcon knife. Miraculously, the knife held. He forced Gaw's blade up and back with all his strength. The giant put his weight behind the sword, however, and his strength seemed ceaseless. Aiden tried to take a step back to better support himself, but putting his full weight on his bad leg was too much. He crumpled back to the sand as Gaw smiled.

Willem was somehow managing to stay alive for the moment, his back pressed against a tall crate, shield up, and broken sword still parrying blows. Behind the crates, Aiden could still hear the ring of metal. How Lem was surviving against two opponents, Aiden didn't know, but silently he wished him well. There was no one left to help, and he was all out of tricks.

Gaw took a slow step forward, the tip of his sword lowering as if all he would do is tap Aiden's chest to gain a point in a fencing duel. And, in a sickening way, Aiden supposed that was exactly what he was doing. This point would steal Aiden's life, however, and that would be game over.

The huge sword in Gaw's hand went up over the giant's head and linked with his other hand. This would be a two-handed cleave, a chop on the butcher's block, and Aiden was the roast. Gaw opened himself up wide as he bowed his body back in preparation, like a man driving a post into the ground with a hammer. Aiden raged inside as the big man's size and reach allowed him to stand clear of any kick Aiden could lay into his now unprotected middle.

He watched the sword fall in slow motion like it was pushing through a heavy stream. Wind rose up around Aiden. It ruffled his clothes and set his hair to dancing. *The wings of the angels come to take me beyond*, he thought. Then something landed with splintering force onto the crate at Aiden's side.

Aiden turned his head from the descending blade to look at his angel, but he looked remarkably like a man—no shimmer of stars about him or even outstretched wings, just a man in gray and black with sandy blond hair and pale blue eyes. *Just a man*, Aiden had time to think.

Then the man's arm shot out toward Gaw. Aiden felt the air tear through the space above him. Gaw let out a yowl as his sword clattered free of his grip and he was thrown backward into a pillar.

Tellos, the squat Horn Champion, slipped from his attack against the twins and came at the man on the crates. His swords darted out and Aiden was sure this newcomer was about to be skewered. Then, the blades stopped moving toward the man's chest as if they had been grabbed by invisible hands. Wind rose up again as the sandy blond man on the crates lashed out once more with his arm. Tellos flew backward just as Gaw had seconds before. His swords, however, stayed just where they were for a moment as if suspended in a puppet show.

Then the puppeteer moved again, and the two swords flew in opposite directions. One caught the thigh of the remaining Horn Champion attacking Lem and Rem. He fell backward with a squawk. The other sword thudded neatly into the throat of the Horn Champion fighting Willem, finishing the man with a blade to match the one protruding from his shoulder.

The final Wolf Champion hesitated only a moment before scampering back for the cover of the pillars.

Aiden stared up at the man on the crates, now less sure of his status of man instead of angel. The man pushed his sandy hair back out of his face and then, muttering to himself, whirled his arms around him, looking much like Aiden wielding his spear, but with no weapon. Then the man's arms shot down toward the ground and Aiden felt himself wrenched from the sand and high into the air.

All he could think as they flew over the seating and walls of the Square of Champions was, *Maybe an angel after all.*

Chapter 14

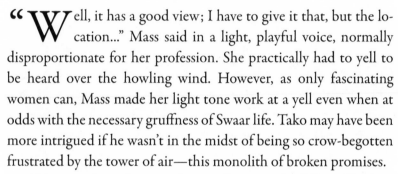

Still, I will not stop now...

"**W**ell, it has a good view; I have to give it that, but the location..." Mass said in a light, playful voice, normally disproportionate for her profession. She practically had to yell to be heard over the howling wind. However, as only fascinating women can, Mass made her light tone work at a yell even when at odds with the necessary gruffness of Swaar life. Tako may have been more intrigued if he wasn't in the midst of being so crow-begotten frustrated by the tower of air—this monolith of broken promises.

Tako stood on the top of seven floors in the White Tower, a wide circular room with pillars rounding the circumference to hold up the roof. Between the pillars, thick stone banisters were strung, offering the only protection from a sudden, intimate relationship with the stone of the mountain below. The open-air floor held nothing more than the rooms beneath it and in great part much less in as far as their search for this: *word for the Shield of Ammereth and the defender.*

On the first floor, following a brief meal and with the raised spirits from being out of the wind and accompanying a meal in their stomachs, Tako had again loosened his axe and led the way to the stairs. Sunto had argued for a bit of rest after supper—that the upper floors would still be there in the morning. Tako was fairly

certain that the man's composure was more rattled from his two
near falls only a couple of hours past than Sunto would ever admit.
Tako had shaken his head, though. If there was anyone home, he
had reasoned, he would rather know it presently than when a bit of
steel was pressed to his throat during the night.

"I would know who and what this tower holds before I lay my
head against my pack for the night," he had said, and that would be
enough for his Gray Pack. He led. They followed. That was the way
of things.

So, axe in hand, Tako had been the first to mount the steps and
gain the second floor. It had held a kitchen and more store rooms
again stocked with provisions for many days of feasting or enough
to feed a small garrison for quite some time. Tako thought it would
have been better to put the kitchens on the base floor so that the
heat could make its way up to the others, but he was no architect,
no builder. He would not argue with a man holding paper and ink
or stone and chisel as long as they left him to his axe work when the
time for battle came. Besides, the kitchen held no more heat than
the entry hall had. Its hearth was cold—its ovens clean and vacant
of use.

The third floor held servant quarters, small, sectioned-off
rooms with a privy to the back wall. The fourth had only a few larger rooms, presumably for officers or lords depending on who inhab-
ited the space. They had still seen no sign of such life, however, and
Tako's unease had only grown.

The fifth floor had a few smaller rooms, perhaps offices or guard
rooms for on-duty soldiers, as well as an armory. This, again, had
been well-stocked. Swords, spears, crossbows with quarrels, shields,
mainly smaller buckler-style for indoor fighting, but with the occasional larger siege shield thrown in, as well as knives, maces, and
pikes lined the walls and racks in an orderly fashion. All the tower
seemed to be missing was hands to wield the weapons.

The sixth floor was broken only into a large bedroom and a so-lar study, both of which sprawled spaciously and would have been comfortable for the ficklest of lords if only one had deigned to re-main there.

The final flight had brought them now to the seventh and final floor of the tower, this open-aired platform.

Tako walked to the railing, his hand trailing over his unkempt beard before it found a perch on the cold, spindled stone before him. *Nothing*, he thought, though of course, he would never say it aloud to his men. *There's nothing here, nothing but supplies and arms for a Delrethi Quarter Legion to rest comfortably for a half year.* He was missing something. He had to be.

On the entry floor, Tako had entertained the thought that per-haps the last of the people living here had died, but they found no bodies anywhere in the tower—no bones either. They couldn't even have fallen out on Whisper's bridge, for the tower was pristine in its appearance. No one would put the entirety of the tower in or-der before going out to check the front gate. With the exception of that front gate, every hinge remained well oiled, as did the weapons in the armory. And the food in the store rooms couldn't have been too old, for no rot had set in.

Tako gripped the railing harder. This whole issue was baffling; no it was more than that. It was the very essence of bafflement flaunting its baffling nature.

He stared out at the landscape surrounding them. Snow-cov-ered peaks punctured the sky all around. If he couldn't figure this out, he would have no choice but to return to Dal Tek empty-hand-ed. It wasn't his fault—Tako knew that. He hadn't asked to wander out north or go searching in the far northern mountains for some nursery tale's magic shield. Still, he doubted the Dal would see it that way. The Rock Giant was a hard man, ruling through fear and discipline as the All-Warrior directed. He might let Tako live, but he might just as easily claim his head. Failure was not readily accepted amongst the Swaar—not by soldiers and not by dals. Failure was weakness and only the strong survived in the East.

A tiny light blinked into existence on the slope beneath Tako, stealing him from his brooding thoughts. It was as if the shutter had been pulled from a window, allowing a hearth's fire to emanate out into the cold night. Someone must be down there, another climber perhaps. *Maybe they're looking for the hidden, unutterable, unreadable, inaudible word for the Shield of Ammereth. Best of luck friend. You'll find nothing but too—clean floors and unguarded treasures here.*

Tako offered a brief smile of frustration to the night. Then, the light blinked back out on the slope below as surely as if the window had been shuttered once more. For him to have seen the fire at all from his height it must have been burning well. What could have put it out so quickly? An avalanche would, certainly, but Tako would have heard the crashing snow if that light was just a campfire. He wouldn't have even seen the glow of it if the fire had been far enough away for an avalanche to extinguish it unheard.

When peering into the darkness offered no more of an explanation, he shook his head in disgust. *Just one more thing wrong with this place.*

"Let's go," Tako ordered, walking back toward the stairs. He raised his voice just enough to be heard, but not to the point of a yelling submission to the wind. *"Every man must bow to the wind, boy,"* his father's voice said in his memory. *"That is the way of things, for only a fool thinks to stand like a mountain against the wrath of a storm."* Maybe he was right, but Tako would not bow this day, not to the wind and certainly not in front of his men.

"Go where, Wolf Rider?" Sunto asked, his voice rising to the level of a yell in an attempt to assert dominance over the wind and showing only submission. He was probably frustrated that they were standing up here in the cold for so long without apparent purpose.

Tako decided not to rise to the bait of the man's tone and said, "Down; we'll make our way to the kitchens and see if we can coax a fire with some heat out of that wood." This idea seemed to appease everyone who had been standing atop the tower with him.

They didn't know what this little expedition was after, of course. Tako had told Dante the truth, but everyone else just knew they were on the hunt at the will of the Rock Giant. That had been enough to get them here. It stood as standard procedure for missions like this—that way if a man was taken he could betray only what he knew, which was never the mission's end. But Tako didn't know how long that explanation would hold if frustrations grew with lack of progress.

The fire kindled easily in the kitchens, and with a nod of approval from Tako, White Zemin set to making some kind of stew. Zemin fancied himself a cook, and in actuality the food he produced was passable. Besides, a meal of more substance than the sausages they had consumed before their climb would help spirits as well.

White Zemin had enlisted the help of Haru, a thin, lanky man barely out of boyhood. Tako had chosen Haru for this mission after he had seen him beat two men who thought him easy prey in a street fight. He had naught but his hands, but they had moved swiftly enough, and his mind had moved even faster. Haru had feinted a step away as if to flee and had then spun back, offering the first man a quick jab to the throat before rounding on the second with the full speed of a spinning body behind his elbow. The man had surely been unconscious before the dirt embraced his falling body. Tako had laughed when it was done, and now the young man was here.

Haru spoke little, but that was fine with Tako, and the others of his Gray Pack seemed to take to him easily enough. Still, there were always initiation periods for the young, which left little doubt who would be running to find ingredients for the new head cook of White Tower.

Everyone found their second supper far preferable to their first. It consisted mainly of White Zemin's stew: a combination of salted beef, carrots, onions, and whatever spices Haru could dig up that the old man found acceptable. Some dried flatbread and a few more bottles of the first floor's wine supply finished off what turned out to be a most satisfying meal. That, combined with the newly-found comfort of the kitchen fire, seemed to have set everyone at ease. Even Sunto's growing frustration had abated with the gathering warmth from both inside and out.

Finally, Tako set a watch, and the whole Pack made their way into different corners to sleep. The next morning, Tako and his Gray Pack did a second search of the tower. Unfortunately, the search turned up nothing the first hadn't revealed.

It was with frustration in their hearts that the group sat down to a late lunch of Zemin's cooking. As before, a hearty meal and a couple of bottles of wine went a long way toward easing their minds.

Deciding it was worth the further pilferage to finish the job of lifting spirits while he and Dante tried to figure out what to do from here, Tako sent Haru on a trip to the first floor storage to bring up another two bottles off the rack. After all, who lived here that would complain about an extra couple bottles?

Mass, perhaps a bit further into her cup, broke into a bawdy version of "Sir Menster's Boots" singing, "...and the man, the man, with the outstretched hand never thought she would resist. But the man, the man, found his face in the sand when he decided to persist."

Tako had just signaled to Dante, thinking this might be a good time for a private chat about the day's findings and future plans, when Haru appeared back at the top of the spiral stairs, his face flushed with excitement.

"A door!" he shouted, breathing heavily, cutting Mass off in the middle of the fourth verse. "Ren Tako...a door, a passage...come see, come see." Even in the boy's excitement he still used the honorific title of Ren, but then, what else was he supposed to call him? None of that mattered at the moment. Haru had found something, and something at this point was just what they needed.

All thought of merriment passed in the space of an eye blink. It was time for business and this Gray Pack of Tako's knew how to get to it without trouble. Their belongings quickly re-gathered and their weapons loosened in their sheaths, if not blatantly out in their hands, the group allowed Haru to lead them back down the stairs and to the same storage room that held the food preserves.

The change spoke so clearly for itself that Haru didn't need to point it out. Of course, in the man's excitement, he couldn't help himself.

"There. Look there," Haru said, pointing at the wall just to the side of the wine rack, or rather at the space the wall had occupied the last time Tako was in this room. From where Tako stood, he could see the first few steps of a downward spiraling staircase. *Well now, this is promising.* He turned to Haru, who answered the unasked question.

"You see that kind of blue bottle tipped up at the end of the rack?" he asked in a higher squeak of a voice than Tako was sure the man wanted to use. His excitement betrayed his youth, and there was no harm in that.

Tako simply nodded and Haru went on. "Well, my grandda had always told me about this blue mendalain drink that was supposed to be the sweetest he had ever tasted, and even that had only been a single glass poured from an old bottle they had found in the cellar of some mansion in the west. Anyway, I saw that the bottle was old and kind of blue, so I thought, All-Warrior willing, maybe I'll have a taste of this mendalain to tell him about when we get home. When we're done, I mean. But when I moved these crates here, worked myself over to it, and tried to grab it off the rack, it only lifted up like this. It must be a latch because when I grabbed it, this part of the wall swung in, silent as breeze over desert sand, to show off these stairs here. I nearly fell over the crates in my excitement, and I raced back up to find you, and well...I guess here it is..."

Haru trailed off a bit as he realized his headlong plunge of a story was coming to an end just a fraction too late. Tako smiled at him all the same and clapped the young man on the shoulder, revealing a hint of his actual relief and excitement at Haru's discovery.

"Good man," he said, gripping the axe his father had passed to him on his first bloodletting day and moving to peer down into the dimly-lit, winding stairway. "Now, let's see what might be hiding down here."

Chapter 15

...not after coming so far and gaining such a close purchase.

———⟨∿⟩———

Thump. *Roll. Groan.* Landing was the same each time, and each time sent fire lacing through Aiden's torn hip. Upon their first landing, which had been on a hill top just outside of the main city wall of Perry, he had sheathed the falcon knife that he had held clutched in one white-knuckled fist.

Aiden had stared at the sandy-haired man for a minute as the man knelt, breathing heavily. Then, his eyes wandered to Willem, lying a few feet next to him and to the twins who mirrored Willem and Aiden's position on the opposite side of the dark-cloaked man. Finally, Aiden's eyes drifted to the blade placed perilously close to his own chest. That's when he had slipped the knife carefully into his boot before returning his focus to the man in the middle.

Things were strangely quiet after the roar of the Champion Sands. He had just worked up the courage to say something when their mysterious savior got to his feet, muttered something that Aiden didn't catch, and again whirled his arms before slashing them back to the ground and launching himself into the air.

Once again, Aiden felt the tug of a rope, as if an invisible net had been cast over him and tethered to this flying man. The five of them shot up and out, away from Perry, staying airborne for minutes at a time.

After each landing, the man's breath grew more haggard, but his breaks did not grow longer. Aiden stopped counting the jumps, after a half dozen slipped by, and instead spent his time agonizing over the pain that was sure to come of the next landing.

Thump. Roll. Groan. And they were down again.

"That's it," the sandy-haired man said between gasps. "We walk from here."

The four of them lay sprawled in a clearing surrounded by pines and patchy grass. Ages of needles covered most of the ground, and the sound of flowing water drifted in from somewhere.

"That was quite the final leap there, Jumper. A bit risky don't you think, especially hauling a load of four others?" said a deep voice.

Aiden's eyes darted this way and that until he found a big bald man with a large mustache surrounded by dark stubble leaning against the trunk of one of the pines whose high branches allowed him to get so close.

I'll weigh risk versus reward, Thun," said the sandy-haired man. "We were fine. Plus it was better than landing in the open and having some farmer spread stories of how he saw a flying man land with four people dangling beneath him."

"Ah. Well, I'm sure you know best," said the big man, Thun. "I trust your theatrics went well?"

"Well enough. I think I only had to kill one, though the others may be scarred for life." This last he said with a grin starting to tug at the corners of his mouth.

Thun matched the sandy-haired man's smile. "And what of these others? Any of them survive the mighty show of Jumper?"

The man's eyes moved around the circle taking in the blood, mostly dried now, and the wary faces of Aiden, Willem, and the twins. "Barely, I'd say, to venture a guess. But come on let's get 'em inside if they can move, and we'll have a look."

Thun took several steps toward Aiden, putting him level with the sandy-haired man whose name, if Aiden had caught it correctly, was Jumper. Something triggered in Aiden's mind. He'd seen these two before. He couldn't place them, but he was sure he knew them from somewhere.

"On your feet, lad," Thun said, offering his hand down to Aiden, who only hesitated for a moment. The big man hauled him to his feet where Aiden struggled desperately not to put any weight on his bad leg.

"You hurt, boy?" Thun asked before turning to Willem. "How about you?"

"I'm okay," Willem said, standing himself without help. The dried blood covering his face seemed to contradict him, but he remained steady enough on his feet.

"Good," Thun said. "Then you can help this one." He pointed at Aiden. "We have a little ways to go before we can see to your hurts, and he may need your legs." Willem nodded, and Thun started for the twins who were still lying in the spread of grass and needles. With Willem's help, Aiden followed.

Rem had lost a lot of blood from the wound in his arm and was having a hard time not spilling over onto the ground. Thun pulled several white strips from a pocket inside his cloak and tied them around the wound to staunch the blood that still wept slowly out, dripping down to his dangling fingers.

Meanwhile, Lem still lay in the grass and needles, basking in the shade of a mighty pine. Dozens of tiny cuts paved this way and that across the chest of his leather jerkin. Some of the cuts continued on, slicing out across arms and down across legs. One particularly painful-looking cut ran up his left cheek, refusing to finish before it had claimed the upper third of Lem's ear.

The craziest part of the whole picture was the big grin that lay on Lem's face like an immovable sleeping cat. Then, all at once, the man started laughing. He laughed hard and deep as if he had just heard the greatest joke of his life. It was a drunken barroom laugh and just as contagious.

Aiden and Willem couldn't help but grin. And Rem added to the scene as he took a staggering step and fell over laughing as well.

"We're...alive," Lem chortled between gasps of breath. "I can't...believe...we're alive." It took several minutes before Lem had laughed out his merriment and lay still again, gasping for his exhausted breath.

"Alright now," Thun said, lifting Lem under the armpits and setting him standing on firm ground. "On your feet now, lad." The big, mustached man watched Lem for a minute before nodding his head, seemingly satisfied that he wasn't going to fall over like his brother. Then he moved back over to Rem, lifted him with apparent ease, and carried him like a sleeping child toward the far edge of the clearing.

"Bring that lot with, won't you, Jumper," Thun called over his shoulder, "and we'll all have a meal and a little talk."

A cabin lay five minutes' walk into the trees. Smoke curled from a small stone chimney and the front door stood open as if the occupant had just stepped out. The clearing that held the little cabin was even smaller than the one they had landed in. Perhaps three feet of needles and bare earth stretched from each wall before shrubs and pines choked the earth back out, covering the ground and sky in their presence.

"Here we are lads," Jumper announced, apparently having regained some of his fervor during the short walk. "Nothing like a home away from home after a long day's work. Anything in the pot yet, Thun, or are we at scratch?"

"Oh," the big man smiled, "there may be a bowl of broth and a touch of carrots stewing. There may even be a tiny surprise of wild game adding some flavor."

Now it was Jumper's turn to smile, and his smile only grew as they entered the cabin and the tantalizing smell of stewing deer invaded his senses. "You're the best, Thunder, my friend, the very best."

The cabin was small but built all as one room, so the cramped feeling with all six of them inside was really very slight. The mustached man laid Rem on a cot at the far end of the room, and Willem helped Aiden to another. All was fairly subdued as Thun made his rounds, seeing first to Rem's wounds, dabbing ointment from a small bag at his feet before wrapping the arm in a fresh bandage. Then he came for Aiden's hip. He dabbed a stinging salve on the cut, then ran a wet cloth around and over the wound. Finally, he reached into his bag and pulled out a small bottle, undid the stopper, and poured a liquid over Aiden's hip that smelled horribly of wet burning leaves. The ragged skin burned and then started to pull together.

"Vellen," Willem muttered under his breath while reaching subconsciously to itch at his shoulder.

Thun's head snapped around to look at him. "Well, a learned man. Can't say I was expecting that. Yes, they call it Vellen in the south or Poulter in the far north. If prepared and used properly it can be a miraculous concoction—if not, it can have some rather unsavory side effects."

Aiden winced and looked down at his hip, hoping this Vellen had been prepared properly. Trying not to think about what the side effects might be, he looked up at Thun, but the big man had already stepped away. With a tiny grin Thun moved to check on the slice across Willem's scalp, and then finally moved to Lem's many tiny cuts. He tsked and muttered, "It's too bad we don't have the rest of that ear. We could reattach. But, life is what it is."

His job of bandages and ointments finished, Thun stepped away and looked at the four of them for a moment with obvious satisfaction. Then, he turned and walked to a tall cabinet opposite the fire. Placing his hand against it, he slid a key from around his neck and into the keyhole. A muttered word later, Aiden felt something shift as if the ground were resettling itself in sleep. The lock clicked, and the door opened.

Thun slipped his hand inside and retrieved two muskets and two small shoulder bags. Aiden couldn't believe what he was seeing. Mist Falcons. He supposed it made sense what with Jumper pulling them all through the air like a giant bird. He had heard stories about the Falcons' extra abilities, their magic, as the children call it. But he had always assumed they were just stories created around the prowess of the most celebrated group of mercenaries and heroes in all of the Nine Cities. He had experienced more than just stories though, hadn't he?

Pulling off his cloak, Thun slipped one bag over his shoulder and secured it to a clasp at his hip. He then slipped the musket lengthways across his back with practiced ease so that the metal and wood huddled snugly against his body. A gleaming falcon brooch clung to the front of the black leather jerkin he wore over a dark gray shirt, confirming Aiden's assumption of his character.

By this point, Jumper had joined Thun in front of the cabinet and accepted his bag and musket, securing them in his turn just as the big man had. Then, Jumper reached inside the cabinet and retrieved his own silver brooch from a shelf near the top.

"I know you," Aiden heard himself saying as the final puzzle pieces fell into place. "I saw you in Oustenbasch a..." His mind tried and failed to figure the passing of time since the fateful night that Semlie had been stolen from him. "...a while back," he finished a little lamely. "It was the two of you at The Pearl. I knew I recognized you from somewhere."

Thun and Jumper shared a brief but knowing look, and then Thun smiled. "Aye, we were in Oustenbasch a while back, as you put it. I reckon that means you're the one, then. But I get ahead of myself a bit, forgive me. Proper introductions are in order. I am Jak 'Thunder' Klapp, go by Thunder mostly or Thun for short. And this here willowy fellow is Tobin 'Jumper' Carnes. He goes by Jumper for the most part."

Aiden and the others each took their turn for introductions, to which Thun smiled and nodded amiably.

When they had all been introduced Thun nodded again, "Well, there we have it. Jumper and I are part of a group, a band of brothers if you like..."

"You're Mist Falcons," Rem said from his cot.

"That's plain enough," added Lem, "with those death throwers sprouting from your backs."

"Not to mention that our new best friend, Jumper, yanked us from death and flew us here like some kind of leaping bird," Rem finished.

Thun pushed out his lips beneath his mustache and nodded. "Well, that's fair deduction, lads." He smiled again. "Not that we were trying to hide it from you, mind, but good for you nonetheless."

Aiden couldn't decide if the four of them were being mocked or not. It was hard to tell with these men.

"What do you know of the Mist Falcons?" Thunder asked.

"They're...I mean, you're mercenaries," Rem said.

"Powerful soldiers for hire," Lem said, smiling. "I've heard you can call on the power of the Angels for your employers, but that you cost a king's ransom to pay."

"Ha," Jumper laughed. "They have a point there, Thunder."

Thunder nodded slowly, thoughtfully. "It is true that the Falcons occasionally hire out our services to a just cause, but we are by no means your run-of-the-mill swordarms. We do not simply work for any upstart lordling with coin to spare. We are not intimidators, thugs, or secondhand soldiers. Our goals at times align with another's, and I'll admit our services do not come without cost, but we are first and foremost a brotherhood of seekers. But, enough said about the Mist Falcons. We are who we are, and more importantly, we saved your lives." Here Thun smiled to show there were no hard feelings on this score—simply stating the facts.

"Now, you may be wondering why the Mist Falcons would so publicly drop from the heavens to snatch you out of that splendid Champion Square."

"Well, semi-publicly at any rate," Willem broke in. "Not that I'm not grateful, but I did notice that you didn't wear your falcon pin or your musket, Jumper, which's got to be the number one sign of the Mist Falcons to the rest of us."

"Fair enough, fair enough," Thun said, holding up his hands in surrender. "Quite the observant lot you've brought with you, Jumper. Very well. It is true we made some small allowances to avoid a blatant showing of our activity. But, back to the point, you may be wondering why we grabbed you from your deaths at all. The simple answer is him," and Thun raised a thick finger to point accusingly at Aiden.

"Me..." Aiden spluttered, grasping for something else to say and failing.

"Yes, you, my boy. You and what you carry."

"Let's see it then, and we can be off," Jumper said. "Sitting still gives me the jitters. You drew it at the end of the battle, right? Come on, let's see the blade."

Aiden reached cautiously for his boot, wincing at the pull on the new skin of his hip. "This?" he asked, pulling the knife and sheath free of their hiding place, again struck by its lightness.

"All this for a knife?" Rem shot from the other side of the cabin.

"Ah, how much is it worth?" Lem added, a thief's grin tugging at one corner of his mouth.

Neither Thun nor Jumper looked away from the knife in Aiden's hand, but it was Thun who answered the twins. "That's it. All this for a knife. All this for *that* knife, actually. All this and more. It could win you a few gold eagles at most any pawner, I have no doubt, my young friend, but its value runs deeper than that. This is a Maker's Blade—or so we believe. We have been tracking it and you for a while now. Let's see, how to put this?" And he tugged lightly at his mustache, considering his word choice carefully. "An unsheathed Maker's Blade emits a kind of signal that can be heard by someone with ears to hear it, like a drumbeat in the distance." Thun smiled, falling silent and staring through the wall.

Jumper coughed, and when Thun didn't continue, he spoke instead. "The pulse of the knife was weak and brief but enough to give us a direction. We had been close to Oustenbasch on some other business anyway, so we made a detour in hopes that the blade would be drawn and reveal itself again. We searched there for some time, a tedious and fruitless task. Then, to our surprise, the knife pulse resurfaced. It wasn't in Oustenbasch anymore, though. This time it came from far in the north from the direction of Perry. We headed there immediately, though not as quickly as I would have liked." He glared over at Thun.

The big man smiled and shook his head. "Never have we traveled as fast as you would like, and we travel better as a team than apart. Remember that."

"At any rate," Jumper continued. "We went to Perry and found an auction house at the center of the pulse's origin. I assume you had been there in the days before." He nodded at Aiden before going on. "Well, at any rate, you weren't there then. A coin or two dropped in the right hand and I was able to get a list of slaves sold the weeks prior. Through some effort and investigation, we eliminated most of the candidates down to the group gone to the Champions' Tournament."

He smiled. "We hadn't planned on quite such a dramatic departure for you from the Sands. I was going to watch as part of the crowd and slip in later for an unobtrusive visit followed by a hushed departure. Then the lot of you worked so very hard at getting slaughtered in that ambush, and plans changed quickly. I was forced to a more drastic appearance and exit both. And you know the rest. Here we are."

Aiden thought through Jumper's story and tried to piece it together with the last weeks of his life. He had drawn the falcon knife that first day when he had found his costly treasure, then again sitting in the cell with the other new slaves before the auction, and then finally when Gaw had come within inches of killing him. He wasn't quite sure if he regretted drawing the blade at all or if he wished he never would have re-sheathed it. Regrets. Aiden supposed they would be his constant companion now.

Thun approached and Aiden's first reaction was to pull back as the big man reached for the falcon knife. It was, after all, the last remnant of the treasure he found and then paid so dearly for. He had traded Semlie for this piece of steel, and it was priceless to him for that if for no other reason.

The big man stopped mid-reach and said, "Forgive me my manners. I will return it, but we would like to test it. May I?" After a pause, Aiden nodded and allowed Thun's rough fingers to claim the knife. Jak 'Thunder' Klapp took the grip in one hand and the sheath in the other. Then he pulled as if to draw the blade. Nothing happened. Thun pulled harder, and Aiden felt the ground shift ever so slightly under the cabin floor. A vein pulsed in Thun's neck and ran up past his large mustache to where his forehead pulsed in unison. Still nothing. Finally, he relented and seemed to deflate as he let his arms fall back in front of him.

"Your turn," he said, handing the knife to Jumper. Jumper pulled but had no more success than Thun had. Thunder nodded and handed the knife back to Aiden. "If you please."

Aiden took hold of the grip and prepared himself to pull with all his might, wondering what he had done to damage the knife so badly, but the blade slid free as easily as ever.

Thun nodded as if he had expected Aiden's easy draw. He held out his hand, and Aiden gave him the knife a second time. Thun retrieved a heavily padded leather glove from the cabinet and tugged it onto one hand to protect it from the sharp edge. He then set to bending the blade, trying with all his might to break the steel clean in two.

The blade bent until Aiden was sure it would snap. Again, he felt the slight shift of the ground and Thun bore down further on the blade. Aiden's hand went up with a protective instinct as if to grab the knife back, but he had nothing to fear, for though the blade bent a hair's breadth further, still it refused to break.

After another moment, Thun gave up on brute strength and handed the blade to Jumper once more.

"You alright there, Thun? Jumper asked, a smile playing across his lips. The big man fluttered his walrus mustache with great exhales, breathing heavily.

"Fine...just fine. It's your turn," Thun said.

Jumper took the knife and placed it on a wood platter. After dousing the blade with water from a canteen, the sandy-haired man moved to the window and opened it. He then propped open the door with a chair and placed the platter on the ground. Jumper rolled his shoulders back before raising his arms theatrically like one going to deliver some great speech. The door rattled against the propped chair and the shutters banged back and forth outside as wind rushed into the cabin. It was like a storm had just been summoned into their midst.

"Show-off," Aiden just heard Thun mutter over the roar of the wind.

Air rushed in, compounding on itself as if Jumper was building a mountain of wind right here in the center of this small one-room cabin. The fire shuttered and guttered, too weak to stand against the might of the wind's fury. Just when Aiden thought the pressure would prove too much, Jumper dropped his arms—and with them, the rush of wind. Silence ruled for a moment as the roar receded. In that silence, frost glinted all around the falcon knife on the platter. The water now reflected the remaining firelight through shimmering ice.

"If you would there, Thunder Klapp," Jumper said, gesturing to the platter and the knife. The big man nodded and walked across the room to where a huge axe leaned against the wall. He picked it up, made his way back to the knife, and planted his feet to either side of the platter, giving himself plenty of room to swing. Thun lifted the axe high above his head. He blew out his mustache once and then brought down the axe with a mighty strike. Ice sprayed, and the platter shattered under the brutal attack, but the knife itself seemed unperturbed by the violence.

Thun leaned down and picked up the knife from the ground. He nodded slowly, then took the few steps and held the knife out to Aiden.

Aiden accepted the knife, expecting to feel a fierce cold emanating from the steel, but there was nothing. The blade was cool as any metal to the touch but no more than that. The blade should have broken from the cold and the axe blow. He had seen the ice with his own eyes, and now it wasn't even cold. He looked up and found Jumper staring at him with a big grin on his face.

"Well, looks like we got the right one then," he said, still smiling.

Thun nodded. "I'd say so. We had to test it you see...to be sure. A Maker's Blade is supposed to be unbreakable and impervious to the Elementals. We've just proven both, or at least close enough for me. You, Jumper?"

"I'd say we've got a keeper," the sandy-haired man agreed, his grin still plastered thickly to his pocked face. "And about time too."

Aiden was having a hard time keeping up. "So...it's a nice knife," he said after a moment of these two staring at him expectantly.

Thun boomed out a laugh. "That it is, my boy, that it is. A nice knife and more. But we'll have time for that on our way."

"On our way?" Rem asked.

"On whose way?" Lem added.

Thun smoothed out his mustache with forefinger and thumb, his forehead wrinkling in thought. After a moment his shoulders shrugged. "On all our way I suppose."

"They're all coming with us?" Jumper said, incredulity plain in his voice and on his face, washing away the toothy smile.

"Come now, Jumper," Thun said, "would you leave your new friends so soon? Not half a day ago you pulled the whole lot from the Death Sands, and already you're anxious to jump on. Not overly hospitable, now, is it?"

Jumper put his hands up before stuffing them in his pockets. "Whatever you like. Just wasn't expecting it is all, hospitality aside. Just wasn't expecting it."

"In truth, I hadn't thought about it much either, until now. But it's really all we can do. Our dear new Maker's Hand," and here he gestured at Aiden, "has to come for obvious reasons. As for the rest of them, well they can hardly be left behind can they? We can't expect them to live in this cabin for the rest of their days, and we're still too close to Perry for them to just go wandering off."

He turned his attention back to Willem and the twins. "Forgive me, but you must understand you are now fugitives of the city, escaped slaves and stolen property—valuable property at that, being Champions and all. No, you'll have to come with us, for your own safety and for ours."

Jumper's eyes were narrowed, and Aiden thought he looked much like a sculpture of a man figuring through a problem.

"We're not going to kill them, either, Jumper. It's not our way," Thun said before Jumper could speak.

"I never said we should kill 'em, now, did I?" Jumper said quickly, his ears reddening. "I was just thinking we could jump these other three out another ways from Perry. Then, they can be off, none the worse for wear."

"And do what exactly? It's not as simple as returning to their normal lives, Jumper. No, you saved them, and now they're your responsibility, at least until we can get them to Holmsguard and the lords can make a decision."

Jumper sighed and stuffed his hands back into the pockets they had come loose of in apparent acceptance of Thun's words. "Fine, but I get jittery standing around. Let's be off soon."

Thun turned back to the rest of them and said, "All of this is based on your acquiescence of course. You've been prisoners long enough, from my point of view. If you'd rather, we could follow Jumper's plan and jump you to within a day's walk of one of the other Nine Cities or at least a good-size town. If the three of you would come with us though, we could offer you something of a better start back into the world."

Aiden assumed he wasn't part of the three. So much for being a prisoner for long enough, not for this blade-carrying Maker's Hand. "I suppose I'll just stay in this quaint little cabin, until you move my cage along to my next cell, then."

Thun smiled something that Aiden was certain was meant to be reassuring and fatherly, but only seemed to make Aiden angry. "My apologies, of course. Forgive me, I have been too long looking, and now that it is in front of me I grasp at it like an urchin for a dropped crust. Of course, I should ask. Would you join us for a journey to Holmsguard on the Castle Isle?" His tone rang of formality but felt brittle somehow.

"And if I refuse?" Aiden asked.

The big man shrugged his muscular shoulders. "To be honest, you're probably coming with us whether you like it or not, but I would far rather have it be as a companion and not as a captive."

Aiden thought about it for a moment. He could feel Willem and the twins' eyes on him. Thun's stare never left his own for that matter, either. His face was hot with his anger. It exploded from his pores, washed down his neck and up to his ears. Anger wasn't going to get him anything here, though. A lot hung in the balance and even if the other three would fight alongside him and they were all well, which they weren't, he was fairly certain they couldn't take these two Mist Falcons. When options are limited, better to hold your counsel close, his father had told him once. Besides, these men had saved his life. He owed them something.

"Alright," he said. "I'll come, but I'm not making any promises after that."

Thun nodded, his smile returning to radiance beneath his setting mustache. "And you lot?"

Rem shrugged his shoulders and grinned. "Well, we can't go back to Perry. Besides, it could be fun. We're in."

"We're in," Lem echoed, matching his brother grin for grin.

Thun turned to look at Willem. The blond man scratched absently at his shoulder and stared off through the wall for a minute. He looked over at Aiden and then back to Thun. Then he said, "The Swaar took Bellcross a few weeks ago, though it seems a different life. Dal Tek The Rock Giant leads them himself, and I was fleeing them when I was taken into slavery. I had thought to warn someone, but then fate intervened."

He paused expectantly, and Thun said, "I knew the Swaar had descended on the Crossroads, but I hadn't known Dal Tek had come down from the high places himself. The lords will need to know this. You may tell the Council yourself if you would accompany us to Holmsguard."

Willem nodded. "Okay, I'm in."

Thun's smile broadened and he slapped Willem on the back as if they were old friends. "Then we will have something to eat and rest here for a night or so. After that, we're off to the Castle Isle."

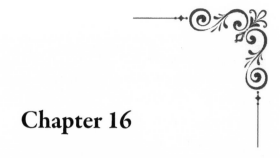

Chapter 16

Remember the teaching of the past...

Flicker, flicker, dance. Flicker, flicker, dance. The next wall torch offered the same promise as the one before it and the one before that and the one before that—civilization, life, something. All Ren Tako and his Gray Pack found at each, however, was a dingy, brass wall sconce with the promising flames, proven to be liars, and an ever-extending path for their feet. The only breaks in the monotony of dark stone were the colored veins racing the walls, ceiling, and floor and the occasional descending steps.

Tako had led his entire party down the steps from the storage room expecting to come upon whatever hidden chamber or keep lay beneath within a minute of descent. The steps had ended perhaps a story beneath, but they hadn't opened into some grand treasure trove—only a simple stone tunnel, perhaps seven feet high and five feet across. It was large enough that Tako didn't feel the need to hunch, but only just. They had trotted down this slithering path, the excitement still fresh and invigorating, sure their destination lay just around the next bend. When they dropped down the next set of steps only to find yet more tunnel, Tako had stopped and held up his hand.

"I've let my excitement drive us too far, too quickly," he had said. "We may need provisions, not to mention any weapons we left up top. None of us knows for sure what lies at the end of this basilisk hole. Come on, the path will not vanish if we collect our things."

They made their way back up and along the path, but they had reached the top of the second stair only to find a closed etched door blocking their return into the storage room and the tower above.

"All-Warrior's Blade," Sunto had growled in his gravelly voice. "Now we're stuck down here with who knows which of the Thirteen Terrors." Whisper had simply looked at the man and he stopped talking, giving the rest of them some air to breathe.

Tako had felt the etching of the door, but couldn't tell if it was stylized art or some kind of language. Either way, it told him nothing. He had groped along the top and edges of the door before finding what he was looking for on the far side of the doorframe: a latch. The builders of this secret tunnel had no reason to make it secret from both sides. What purpose would there be in keeping people above and keeping them below? At least, he hoped that was the case, and that the blue bottle wasn't meant to be stumbled upon by apparent accident leading them to a worse fate, imprisoned below. Only one way to find out.

He had tugged on the latch and it had given with surprising ease. A nearly inaudible click had sounded and the door had swung toward Tako on well-oiled hinges. The large Ren had to step back, forcing everyone to move down one step to allow the door its space.

Light from the storage room had flowed out to meet them, dispersing Tako's fears of imprisonment in a single warm wave.

They had spent half an hour gathering extra provisions as well as repacking their belongings for more convenient travel. A few of the Gray Pack even stole up to the armory to retrieve an extra short axe, stiletto, or knife—better for close-quarter fighting if it came to that in the tunnel.

So, weapons acquired and in place, packs provisioned and strapped tightly, they had gone back down into the tunnels again.

That had been several hours ago now, and Tako was beginning to think they may have to consider some short breaks along their path. If it was going to prove such an expedition, they may even have to sleep down here in the tunnels. Flicker, flicker, dance. Flicker, flicker, dance—the same broken promise—the same hinted lie.

Tako turned to Dante to ask his opinion on calling a brief halt, but he no more than turned his head to the man before Whisper raised a hand and pointed at the flame before them. It bobbed through the air at a regular gate and drew closer far faster than their pace would account for. It was coming toward them. It was coming *for* them.

The quiet song of blades being drawn from their sheaths rang gently in the stillness behind Tako, who in turn found a better grip on his axe. He had lain in plenty of ambushes before, but there was nothing to be gained by staying here. No cover offered itself for protection—no high ground set them apart with advantage. They stood in the center of a narrow tunnel with nothing else around. There seemed little to do but move toward what he assumed to be their long-awaited host, approaching at last.

Tako rolled his shoulders as he always did before a fight, and again started down the tunnel toward the oncoming light. The soft footfalls of his companions behind him fell comfortably on his ears, but he didn't need them. If they were to turn back now, to flee and leave him here alone, still he would march on. He was Ren Tako, the Wolf Rider—loved by few, but feared by all. And Tako would spread that fear to the owner of the bobbing light before him. He grew weary of slinking about, hoping to find something. His axe blade was thirsty for battle, and the muscles of his arms ached to quench that thirst.

Feeling his pace quicken, Tako had to check himself. Fearless-ness was one thing, but foolishness something else. Patience need-ed only hold reign a few moments longer. The light bearer slipped ever closer, and a slow creaking now accompanied the growing light.

A moment later, an odd contraption appeared, visible now from the lantern hanging from a bar that slowly dipped and rose, dipped and rose. Four large wheels ran along the bottom of the cart, supporting a narrow, rectangular platform that bowed slightly, rounding like a shallow bowl. A seat grew from the midst of that platform, surrounded by levers and knobs, and a constantly pivot-ing bar, one end of which clung to the lantern. Upon the seat rested a tiny, wizened man whose white hair and beard shone an orangey-red against the flickering flames. Tako would have thought him a child of no more than six or seven years if not for his wrinkled fea-tures. It left the little man caught somewhere between endearing and repulsive.

Just as the cart reached them it ground to a stop, and the man looked up with a smile. A gap lay dark between his front teeth, but other than that, the smile shone as brightly as his white hair.

"'Bout time you lot showed up," the man said in a raspy squeak. "Feels like I've been waiting forever, but then, maybe I have. Come on."

And with that, the man swiveled his seat to face the opposite direction, tugged on some kind of lever, and started off back down the tunnel from the way he had just come.

Tako looked at Whisper, knowing it might look like weakness to the others but not really caring. Dante just shrugged a *Whatever you think* back at him and Tako nodded. There wasn't a whole lot of choice at this point, follow or slink back up the stairs and down the mountain to explain to Dal Tek why he hadn't gone further down the tunnel. Knowing the Rock Giant's temper, that was no choice at all, so he led the way down the path after the little man and his cart.

The cart made a fine pace but didn't seem to pull ahead of the pace Tako himself set. He thought the first staircase they came to might prove problematic, but the little man proved him wrong. He reached out a small hand, turned a knob, and flipped some small lever. Short metal spokes extended from the wheels with a smaller wheel attached to each. These fit nicely into grooves just above the stairs that Tako hadn't noticed on the earlier flights. Whether that was because they weren't there or because he had no reason to look for them until now, he couldn't be sure. Either way, the cart slid smoothly down and around the spiral without making so much as a muffled screech on the stone.

Silence ruled the air, in fact. The little man's cart made next to no noise beyond its quiet creaking and none of Tako's Gray Pack would utter a word before he spoke, not in this, not before friend of foe had been established. So, the silence held as minutes turned into an hour or more.

Finally, the little man came to an abrupt halt, so abrupt in fact that Tako nearly ran into the now-stopped contraption. The little man scampered down off his perch and waddled his way a few steps further down the tunnel. Peering around to see what had instigated the holdup, Tako found the small man running some kind of metallic rod along the etchings of a door, not unlike the one that led back up into the storeroom. He pulled the rod free from time to time to move it into another trough of the etching. Within a few seconds of rapid movement, the little man finished and turned back to his cart and seat as the door swung open.

Light streamed out from the open door, bathing them with the first hint of a promised warm escape from the dreary tunnel. Without a word, the little man pushed a lever back into place. The chug-

ging rhythm of the contraption started up again, and the cart started forward through the door and into the light.

The choice was the same as before. So without pause, Tako led
his little group through the doorway and into the warmth of the
light. The room they entered sat sturdily built in a perfect rectan-
gle, as if someone had designed and built the mountain around
the room rather than hollowing out a space inside of the stone. As
it turned out, the light came from several torches planted in wall
mounts as well as three roaring fireplaces which rested in three of
the four corners.

The little, white-haired man parked his cart against the far wall
and clambered down from his seat again before making his way to
a table in the room's center. The table rested on four thick, stone
legs and patiently held up the weight of a sprawling feast. Roasted
lamb and sides of beef sat glistening next to fresh apples, pears, and
plumbs. To the side of several loaves of fresh bread, some kind of
stew steamed in a huge, porcelain serving bowl, ringed in sliced carrots, onions, and potatoes. At the far end of the table in a bucket of
ice rested several bottles of chilled wine, and beyond that, two kegs
sat, tapped and ready for mugs to be filled.

The man climbed on top of a stool, apparently placed there just
for him, and had served himself a steaming bowl of stew before he
even looked up at them. A puzzled look stole over his face as he
stared at the six Swaar standing just inside his doorway.

"Well, come on," he said, a note of irritation creeping into his
cracked and scratchy voice. "The food won't stay hot forever, which
is why I had to come looking for you lot in the first place. I was
tired of waiting, just sitting here smelling it all was about enough to
drive a man mad." At that, the man laughed as if he had just made
some hilarious joke. He laughed a raucous belly laugh that shook
him to his little core and brought tears to his wrinkled eyes. Tako
wondered if the food had succeeded in its quest to steal the man's

sanity, but just as suddenly as the laughter had started, it ended, and the man returned to his sullen nature.

"Now, get over here so we can eat. And for the sake of Antice's left foot, close that door—you're letting in a draft."

Tako looked over at Dante and nodded ever so slightly. Acting promptly, Whisper ushered Haru the rest of the way into the room and gently closed the door they had just entered through. Tako waited, listening, but there was no audible click of a lock, so he moved forward toward the table and the little, impatient man.

"Who are you?" the Wolf Rider asked.

The small man had once again been busy with the food, this time slicing himself a thick portion of the beef and several pieces of bread. He looked up, again seeming annoyed.

"I am the Keeper, Master of Keys and Watcher of Time." As if this should suffice, he grabbed a stein much too large for him off the table, hopped from his perch, and began filling it with a dark lager from one of the casks.

"Alright, Keeper. What..." Tako started again.

"Do you know how long it took to prepare all this?" the man said, his unkempt white hair swirling as he shot a look at Tako. "Now come on, the whole lot of you. Let's eat, then we can palaver of the prophecy and all that."

Tako considered for just a moment, but there was no point at pushing with this Keeper. He seemed the stubborn type, as likely to knife Tako for another question as he was to answer him. So again, Tako nodded to his Gray Pack while taking the seat opposite the Keeper. His men followed suit and they were all seated and waiting in a breath's passing. After watching the little man take a few bites from his own dishes, Tako served himself some stew, bread, and wine. Soon they were all enjoying the feast, albeit quietly. The food, for its part, was marvelous, putting White Zemin's fare to shame. It sent flavor dancing amongst Tako's taste buds and down his throat in welcoming warmth.

Distractions of food aside, Tako hadn't missed the Keeper's reference to "the prophecy." He wasn't sure exactly what this meant, but he assumed it must have something to do with the Shield of Ammereth. Dante exchanged a knowing glance with him, and Tako was sure the reference hadn't been lost on his friend either.

Tako allowed minutes to slip by, doing his best to relish in the good food. The only conversation was the occasional "mmm" or "That's good lamb" from his Pack. When the inhalation of food slowed and before any of Tako's Gray Pack dove too deeply into their cups, Tako decided it was time to move forward with what they had come to do.

Turning his gaze on the small, white-haired man, he said, "The food was delicious, Keeper. My compliments—your hospitality is too kind."

"Hmmph," the little man snorted. "Pleasantries and kind words. Blah, blah, blah, blah, blah. Of course the food was good. Do you expect an old man to eat gruel just because visitors are coming to call? Now, come on. Get to the point of this so we can get done, and I can be quits with this whole thing once and for all."

Tako offered the Keeper the hint of a smile—his dangerous smile, the one anyone who knew him or knew of him cowered from. "Very well. Do you have the Word—or better yet, the Shield?"

The Keeper raised one white eyebrow as he reached to his waist and pulled up an assortment of keys and rounded metal files on a ring which he shook, jingling them together. "An interesting start, but we both know that's not how it works. Now you say your bit, and I'll say mine. Then we can all get what we want and finally go our separate ways."

"Uh, say my bit?" Tako had no idea what the man was talking about.

The Keeper let out a powerful sigh that sounded a lot like a hiss. "You are the one, yes? The Stone Bearer? The Axe Wielder? The Wolf Rider?"

Taken aback, Tako paused, then cleared his throat and tried again. "I am known as the Wolf Rider and I do carry an axe which I have used on more than one occasion, but I don't know anything about a stone."

"No, no. That's no good," the little man said, his composure seeming to slip. "The stone, the stone, you must have the stone or the whole thing won't work. Why would you come all this way if you didn't have all the pieces? You can't play the game without all the pieces, you know." The man sighed his robust, hissing sigh yet again, a sound that Tako was beginning to find extremely annoying.

"I don't know about any game," Tako snapped back. "We came here to find the Shield of Ammereth or a Word for it, at least. I don't know anything about a prophecy beyond that. Now, if you know something, out with it. If not, then we'll do a search before taking our leave."

The Keeper was shaking his head, a look of disbelief spreading across his features. "You mean it, don't you? You're here, and you don't even know the prophecy." He leaned back and then climbed down off his stool altogether. Without another glance at Tako or his companions, he waddled over to one of the fires, squatted down, and started adding wood to the flames.

Tako narrowed his eyebrows in irritation and glanced at Dante. His friend opened his eyes wide and then cocked his head toward the little man and the fire as if to say, "I don't know any more than you do, but I bet that one does."

Fine, Tako could fake patience for a few more minutes if it got them some answers. He nodded to Dante, who stood to join him.

Making their way over to the fire, they squatted down by the Keeper and watched the flames as they licked up the new wood.

"Nine hundred years," the man muttered under his breath as he took a poker to the fire. "Nine hundred, and here I sit, forgotten. Dust and ash, all for nothing." He silently jabbed at the logs for a moment, then muttered, "When sour stars distill and fail and darkness glides in to prevail, bah."

"What was that?" Dante asked in his usual gentle whisper.

"Huh?" The man looked up as if surprised to find Tako and Dante squatting so close. "That's the prophecy, boy," he said, jabbing a stunted finger at Dante. "That's what you lot are supposed to be here for.

> "When sour stars distill and fail
> And darkness glides into prevail,
> Guard tight the secret that you keep
> Beneath the mountain of Gleneth's Sweep.
> Now master keys and watch the time,
> For nigh draws 'til Wolf Rider's climb.
> Wielding axe and bearing stone
> He'll come, the starlight to atone."

All this he said in a trance-like voice, his eyes becoming distant and unseeing. As soon as he had finished, his eyes snapped back into the present and glared at Dante.

"For nine hundred years I have followed the prophecy. For nine hundred years I have waited. And now you tell me that this is the Wolf Rider—this is the Axe Wielder..." The Keeper's voice which had been rising steadily with his temper trailed off as he sucked in a breath in an apparent attempt at self-control. "And he bears no stone? Ha. It might even be funny if it wasn't so cruel."

"Just what kind of stone am I supposed to have brought?" Tako asked in a harsher tone than he had meant. It was possible this little creature of a man was not entirely sane or stable. Just the same, they had come so far, and Ren Tako, the Wolf Rider was not about to be stopped by some forgotten pebble.

"A stone, a stone," the Keeper all but yelled, jumping twice to emphasize his point. "A tiny precious rock, as dark as night and bright as liquid starlight."

Without thought, Tako grabbed the tiny, wizened man by his slender shoulders, lifted him off the ground, and forced him up against the wall. "How do you know those words?" he snarled at the Keeper. Holding the man pinned with one hand, he cocked his other back in a fist so that the man could see it. "How do you know those words?"

Considering that he was held against a wall several feet above the floor, the man seemed nonplussed—excited, if anything. "Ha ha, the stone," he squeaked, his eyes focusing on the ring Tako's mother had given him. "And you said you didn't know anything about it. You're a liar and a mean one, but who cares. Come on. Now we can get things started."

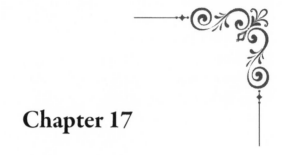

Chapter 17

...that two waterfalls may yet form one river...

Rocks loomed up on either side as the cliffs grew higher and higher out of the ground. The canyon gave Willem the uncomfortable feeling of being trapped. "One way in and one way out," he muttered to himself, thinking all the time of the Swaar.

Willem and his new merry band had left the cabin in the woods nearly a week past. They hadn't left the next morning after their arrival. Thun had decided the four of them and Rem, who had lost a lot of blood in particular, could use one more day's rest before attempting the trip. Jumper had not been pleased in the least for the delay, and even Thun only made the allowance grudgingly, but done was done.

That first day, Jumper had taken off after a noon meal of rabbit stew and bread. Willem had heard him and Thun muttering together about accommodations and provisions before Jumper had left, and sure enough, when he returned just before nightfall he had a bit more with him than when he had leapt into the sky hours before. He came riding a brown mare, leading three more horses behind. The beasts were laden with saddle bags filled with food and gear. Thun and Willem had helped unload the new horses and picket them with the Mist Falcons' other two horses in a grove behind the cabin.

When the next morning had finally come, it seemed Jumper would tear through his own skin for the need to be off. Willem had heard him mutter things like, "Today if possible," and "By the Maker and Angels both, let's just move."

They had moved, and it seemed to pacify the sandy-haired man, though they could never travel as quickly as Jumper would have liked. Willem supposed that was what came from the ability to leap huge distances through the air at will.

The first few days they had avoided towns, Thun saying they were still too close to Perry and that news and descriptions of the four Champions disappearing from the Sands and straight into the air may have lapped out a ways from the city. No one seemed to mind sleeping under the stars, however. They moved at an easy pace for those days and life in the fresh air seemed a gift to Willem, who had submitted himself to a life and death on the Sands.

On the morning of their third day out from the cabin, Thun had finally given in to Jumper's urgency. "Alright," he said, "you lot are strong enough for a real ride now, I reckon." They covered more ground that day than the two previous days combined. When they had pulled up in front of the inn of some small town, Willem barely had the energy to eat the stew and drink a glass of some warm ale before he found the comfort of a bed in the rooms Thun had booked for them. Rem hadn't even made it that far. Lem had taken some bread and cheese up to him, but Willem was pretty sure the man had been asleep before he could eat it.

The last few days had been similar to that day of hard riding. They had left the main road and come upon a small group of Swaar the evening before. The leader of the wild men had screamed something unintelligible and drawn his sword. That, apparently, had been enough for the Mist Falcons of their group. Thun and Jumper had both swung their muskets around before Willem even knew there was a fight at hand. A blast sounded, fierce and loud as the weapons exploded in unison. Two of the wild men dropped, still reaching for their swords. Another died as the wind rose, yanking Jumper from his saddle and sending him barreling into a Swaar, knife-tip first.

Thun caught the attack of a fourth man on his great axe, sent the Swaar's blade spinning away, and felled the man with a swift stroke across the throat before nearly cleaving another in two with an overhand blow. The final two Swaar died while trying to flee. Jumper's knives caught them quick as a spring storm, and they fell, beards and gangly hair flapping in the sudden wind.

And that had been that—seven dead in the space of moments. The four of them hadn't done anything but sit their horses. There hadn't been time. Thun and Jumper had fought so quickly and with such ferocity, there had been nothing for the rest of them to do. But still, the two Mist Falcons would not always be there, and apparently, they were riding through Swaar country. Thun had armed the four of them before they left the cabin, but Willem still remembered the last time he had gone to battle against the raiders from the east. He remembered Dal Tek and the terror that flowed from him like a royal robe.

One way in and one way out. He shook his head and tried not to imagine Swaar waiting in ambush. Flexing his fingers, he wished for the thousandth time that he had his guitar. By Dentar's golden strings, he missed the feeling of music flowing from the work of his hands. Ever since reclaiming his freedom, Willem had felt the nudge of need begin in his hands and his chest, but they had only stopped at the few small villages—no music shop and no tinker to be found. A secondhand flutist had played at one of the inns during supper, but Willem had never been much for the wind instruments. A sword's grip was comforting when a fight was upon you, but the polished neck of a guitar was the caress of a lover on a howling winter night. He would find a new guitar. He was free now. Until then he just had to breathe through the need.

A rush of wind, followed by a thump, forced a whinny and a slight buck from Willem's horse for perhaps the hundredth time. Willem sighed, trying to release a bit of the pressure from his pent-up frustration and fear. Following his landing from yet another scouting maneuver, Jumper walked forward and reclaimed his horse's reigns from Thun, mounting up. It seemed the slender Mist Falcon spent more time leaping to the top of the canon walls for a look around than he spent in the saddle.

"And?" Thun asked.

"Nothing that I could see, but you know how the Swaar like to hide themselves. *You won't see them till they're there*, old Hawk always told me, and isn't that the truth! Better at camouflage than anyone in the whole of the Nine Cities, those desert snakes."

He was in good spirits, but then he was always happy when he returned from his short jumping expeditions. He was the only one. Thun seemed serious as a stone and could have joined a club with Aiden for all the smaller man had said today. Even the twins rode quietly subdued, their jokes dwindling to silence.

"And why did we come this way, again?" Rem asked from behind Willem, though Willem wasn't sure he had meant it as a real question.

Thun answered nonetheless: "Because the king's highway runs us out and around another five days' ride and I am impatient to be home. Time is valuable, and I have none to squander on roundabout roads with no more reason than fear."

"Well, that settles that then. Doesn't it, Rem?" Lem whispered to his brother, a smile evident in his tone. "I've always said fear was a silly thing to be afraid of." So, perhaps the twins weren't completely subdued, but when were they ever?

Willem had no doubt that Thun had also heard Lem's quip, but he didn't deign to respond. He had pulled their short column to an all-stop and had his head tilted slightly as if listening for something.

"What is it, Thun?" Jumper whispered.

"Horses," Thunder said without moving from his listening position.

"At least a dozen, maybe closer to twenty." Willem looked around to see who had spoken. Aiden sat rigid in his saddle, his head tilted in a mirror image of Thun's and a slightly confused look painted across his face.

"How would you know?" Willem hissed without thinking. It came out more accusatory than questioning. *That's great, Will, beat on those around you 'cause you're scared and you lost your guitar.*

Jumper and Thun were looking back at Aiden as well. The smaller man just shrugged and shook his head. "I don't know. I can...feel them somehow. Like they're vibrating in my chest." He shook his head again. "Never mind. What do we do?"

Thun looked Aiden over for another long moment. Then he blinked and stirred himself. "We ride on. I'll not be scared off by desert raiders and their traps."

"Besides," put in Jumper, "there's just as likely to be Swaar waiting behind us now as in front."

"Well, there is that," Thun said with a conceding nod. "Let's be off before any of them catch up with us, and you may want to ready those weapons, lads." With that, he spurred his charger on, and the rest followed.

In truth, Aiden felt a little queasy from the drumming in his chest. And it was more than just that. Something was shifting in his eyesight. Things weren't blurry exactly, but they wouldn't seem to hold still, either, and the breeze kept whispering noises in his ears, things he shouldn't have been able to hear. They told him secrets of birds chirping far above and tiny stones tripping down the sheer sides of the canyon—unnecessary and disturbing. He felt overloaded, overwhelmed by it all.

Still, he had to ride. There was no getting around that. So he lowered his head, kept one grip on his bow and the other on the reigns.

Thump, boom. Thump, scrape, scrape, thump. Tat, boom, tat, tat. The drumming grew more and more constant. He could feel them—men and horses attacking the ground with their incessant movement. They were close now, more than he had thought. Two dozen, maybe thirty. They were close. They were here.

He opened his mouth to say something, but Thun beat him to it. "Weapons!" he bellowed as he pulled his horse up and flipped his musket around all in one motion. He was just in time. A man had sprung from behind a boulder, throwing axe at the ready. Thun's shot caught him in the chest and hauled him to the ground, the axe dropping uselessly to the stones.

Jumper's musket ball claimed a Swaar perched with an arrow knocked and drawn on a boulder further down the narrow valley. The wild man went down, but not before releasing his shot. The arrow flew true for an eye blink, but then Jumper's hand danced out and the wind shifted, throwing the shaft uselessly into the stone wall. As was his custom, Jumper leapt from the saddle and flew toward a group of Swaar waiting with weapons drawn.

Thun charged his horse forward, trampling a man who slipped from behind the same boulder as the man with the throwing axe. Willem put the spurs to his horse and followed, screaming and brandishing his sword.

The drumming was behind as well as in front now. Couldn't the beat just leave him alone? *Behind...wait.* He whirled his horse around and shouted at Lem, who had been bringing up the rear.

Lem turned at the last second. It was fortunate that Thun had called for ready weapons because Lem only just pulled his sword up in time to block the descending cleaver. Eight or ten riders had come from nowhere to sneak up from behind. Luckily they had been traveling quietly to gain the advantage of time and hadn't been charging, or they surely would have ridden Lem, Rem, and Aiden over.

Aiden didn't think. His first arrow plunged into the throat of the man attacking Lem. His second missed its mark on another man but caught in the flank of a third Swaar's horse. The beast screamed and bucked, throwing its rider and seeding chaos among the other mounts.

Lem slipped free of his saddle and attacked a man whose horse had thrown him while Rem struggled over an axe with one of the still-mounted Swaar.

Aiden shot another man in the chest, while his fourth arrow took an attacking Swaar in the shoulder. He reached for yet another arrow. The hand that closed on his arm broached no argument, though. He felt himself pulled, and down he went to crash into the crushed rock and dirt. Aiden let his bow slip from his grasp and reached out to catch his fall to little avail. He cried out as the tiny, sharp rocks of the canyon floor dug into the skin of his palm, slipped free, and tore at his face as well.

Ignoring the pain as best he could, he scrambled to his feet in time to avoid the arcing blade that flashed past and sent rocks showering from its impact. The brute of a man before him must have come from the other side of the canyon. Aiden was sure no Swaar had slipped by from the side he had been firing at. Much good that had done him, for here the man was anyway. The Swaar smiled as Aiden met his eye. He was big, could have been Gaw's bearded brother in fact, and Aiden felt he had about as much hope defeating him as he had had in the Sands against Gaw.

Aiden shuffled back over the rocks, trying to put some distance between himself and this hulking brute. The Swaar only smiled all the broader. Aiden glanced around him, but there was no help coming this time. Rem and Lem were both fighting for their lives and he couldn't even see Willem, Jumper, or Thun anymore. *Well now, doesn't this feel familiar? I wonder if there are any other flying men in the area waiting to swoop down and save the day?* Somehow, he doubted it.

It was just him then. He took in a deep breath and blew it out. The Swaar seemed in no hurry, redoubling the queer familiarity of the fight. Aiden felt the arrows left in his quiver after the fall, tickling at the back of his hair. If only he had held onto his bow. He could see it laying not two strides from the big Swaar in front of him, but Aiden somehow doubted the man would be so good as to let him retrieve it.

Aiden reached for his belt, but to his chagrin, found that he had left the short sword Thun had given him hanging from the saddlebags of his horse. The only weapon left to him was the falcon knife. He felt like a bit of an imposter carrying it, much more using it. And more than that—much good a knife would do him against this giant and his huge sword, but desperate times are not ones to broach argument in. You use the tools you are given, his father had told him. Very well; he would.

Grasping the knife handle, Aiden felt a kind of buzz—not a vibration exactly, more of a deep-seated hum. He drew it out of its sheath, but it seemed to grow as it slid free. When Aiden looked at it, it was not a knife but a sword, perhaps two feet in length and shimmering in the afternoon sun. A matching sheath hung from his side. Aiden looked from the sheath to the sword to the Swaar in front of him. The big man's smile had faded to a grimace. He had noticed it as well, then—Aiden wasn't crazy. You use the tools you are given.

Decidedly tired of waiting, the Swaar let out a war cry and charged like a maddened kaisasal bull. Sword or no sword, Aiden knew he was no match for this Swaar's crushing blow or his huge, two-handed sword. The wild man raised his sword high, and Aiden took a half step back, fear gripping relentlessly at his mind and snagging raggedly at the breath in his lungs.

Then, something solid seemed to dance up Aiden's legs. It was like the drumming from a few moments before, but steadier—more constant, sturdy, reassuring. He raised his new falcon sword and braced himself for the descending power of death. As the Swaar blade fell, the drumming surged up Aiden's body, pulsing through his arms and his mind. The huge man's blow struck Aiden's outstretched sword like that of a child with a stick. Aiden barely felt the impact, much less did it move him. The Swaar's eyes bulged in his head, the fear of the battle embracing him now instead of Aiden.

In truth, Aiden was no less surprised than the desert invader in front of him. Strength seemed to emanate from every pore in his body. He snapped the giant's blade away, which the man had apparently still been forcing down with all his might. The Gaw brother lookalike stumbled, and Aiden's sword caught him where the shoulder meets the neck and drove down through at a triumphant angle. If the man hadn't fallen the rest of the way to the ground, the falcon blade would have bitten clean through his torso, cutting him in two pieces diagonally to the hip. As it was, the man slid free of the blade with a few inches of that path yet unmarched. His death was no less real for that fact, however.

Aiden stared at the corpse for a moment, but then the rest of the battle came crashing back down on his senses. Steel screeched on steel as swords set to battering each other. There were no riders still mounted now, everyone having taken to foot and sword. Many of the horses had bolted back down the valley, while others milled restlessly, despondent and pathless without their riders. Rem was screaming. He had dropped to his knees, cradling his left hand which oozed blood from the stump of a missing finger. The Swaar who had apparently claimed that finger stepped forward, raising a cruel axe. Lem battled two Swaar at once, falling back all the time. He'd be of no help to his brother.

Aiden tapped the drumming strength of a moment before and leapt. There was no thought in it, only action. Rem knelt twenty paces further down the valley, but still Aiden's bound carried him smoothly there in time to plow, sword first into the Swaar attacker. He fell on top of the gasping man, his force smashing them both into the crushed rock of the canyon floor. The wild man grasped at Aiden's shirt but there was no strength in it, and Aiden pushed away easily enough.

He ripped his sword free of the man's ribs and the stony earth beneath. The Swaar let out a gurgling cry, but it too lacked conviction, soon fading to vacant silence. Aiden turned to find one of Lem's attackers sprinting toward him, a snarl twisting his bearded face. Aiden reached for the drumming strength of a moment before but found it absent—not ebbed or weakened—just gone. Fear sprang up as the Swaar's longsword came down. Sevion's training saved him in that moment of terror, for even as his mind refused to wade through the fear, his body acted of its own accord. Aiden's arm raised the falcon sword and absorbed the descending blow, sliding the wild man's sword over and down into the ground.

Coming back to himself, Aiden shot out his fist as the Swaar's momentum carried him a step further than he had probably meant to come. He felt pain lance up his fist as a nose crunched and a curse in an unknown language barked free of the man's clenched teeth. Aiden pulled back to hit him again. The man followed, tackling Aiden to the ground. The falcon sword slipped free of Aiden's grasp as the two of them fell backward. The Swaar man outweighed

Aiden by at least half, and he was on top to boot. Aiden grunted as the bleeding man's forehead smashed into his jaw. Pain blazed, blinding him for a moment. But there was something familiar about this kind of pain. Aiden had lived most of his life getting in Oustenbasch alley fights. A blunt hit to the face he could take.

Still, familiar and friendly were two different things entirely. Aiden squirmed and fought his hand free from the Swaar's embracing weight. He hit the man in the side twice, but his leverage was weak. The bigger man rose up, pinning Aiden down with his weight on one hand. His other hand came crashing down into Aiden's face and he felt his lip split as it recoiled into his teeth.

Aiden kicked out. He swung punches at the man's side. He squirmed and fought, but to no avail. His face exploded with pain as the large fist crashed into it twice more. Three times. Aiden saw lights dance before his eyes. This was not going at all well. The fourth blow struck like a smith's hammer and the dancing lights mixed with swirling blackness.

Then, all at once the man made a gasping noise and slumped over onto the ground and off of Aiden. As his vision cleared, Aiden saw Rem standing over him, a bloody knife in his uninjured hand.

"Thanks," Aiden croaked as the world started to level out again.

Rem nodded, his usual smile missing from his face. "You too," he said, "for that one," and he gestured over at the man Aiden had killed with his super-human leap. "How'd you do that?"

Aiden shrugged, "No idea. I just jumped." His answer fell lamely even on his own ears. But what was he supposed to say—that a drumming strength had filled him up like a cup to overflowing? No, that wouldn't do.

Instead, Aiden collected his falcon sword and turned to Lem in time to see him drive his short sword into his attacking Swaar's stomach, followed closely by a long knife into the man's throat. Aiden was just happy the other twin wouldn't be needing his assistance. The fight had drained out of him like a cracked wineskin. He was more than happy to wipe his blade on one of the dead Swaar's pant legs and sheath the falcon sword. Without much said, Aiden and the twins made their way slowly on foot toward the other side of the canyon where Thun, Jumper, and Willem had gone to fight the rest of the wild men.

The fighting had moved on down the valley and around a bend. Aiden would have bet all the eagles he could get a hold of that Thun and Jumper's powers in battle had driven the Swaar back at a good clip. Before Aiden and the twins could move past the bend they were assaulted by a great rumbling met shortly by a cascading cloud of dust that rolled back to encase them.

When the dust cleared, the three of them picked their way the final steps and finally rounded the corner far enough to see Jumper and Willem standing with blades out. Thun had dropped his axe and had both hands lifted as if in some strange benediction. Before the big man, climbed a pile of stones that appeared to have been torn from the canyon walls.

"Well, that explains the noise and the dust both," Lem said, a smile dancing along his lips. Rem nodded but remained silent.

"There were too many of them," Jumper said over his shoulder as if it were a throwaway statement, and Thun's ripping the very walls of the canyon down on their attackers was anything less than amazing and terrifying.

"Did you see?" Willem asked, turning to the others. His eyes were wide as a child listening to a grandfather's tale of grummels and wincels. "I've never...I mean, it was like...well, I can see why they named him Thunder Klapp. By the golden strings themselves, remind me not to make him angry."

"Ha," Rem barked, returning at last to his jovial self. "Speaking of things I've never, you should have seen Aiden's work on the other side of the canyon."

"Something new to share?" Willem laughed, turning a dust-streaked face to Aiden.

"Ah, it's nothing, "Aiden said. "I mean, I wasn't pulling down walls or anything. Just fighting, and winning in the end, I guess, thank the angels." He gestured to his face. "Barely though."

"Oh, come on," Rem persisted.

"That's not all, now, is it?" Lem added in the singsong way the twins had of offering the same speech through two mouths.

"Leaping a hundred paces and saving my life while he's at it—now that's more than just fighting. More than just winning too, I'd say."

"Yeah, well," Aiden started lamely, for some reason not liking the direction of the conversation. Then his eyes fell to Rem's still-cradled hand. "Hey," he said too loudly, the surprise of Rem, still bleeding into his shirt while laughing and smiling about Aiden's over-extended jump carrying him into excitement. "Your hand! Stones, man! You're bleeding!"

"Thun," he shouted over at the big man who had just let his arms fall from their benediction in apparent exhaustion. "Rem lost a finger and is bleeding all over himself. Can you help?"

Thun turned and made his slow way toward the group, his head bowed slightly as if trying to snatch a moment's sleep on the dozen-step trip. "Alright then, lad. Let's have a look." Rem held up his bloody hand and Thun studied it for a moment. "Hmm," the big man intoned. "Well, it's a clean cut for the most part, but the finger bone was crushed. There's no good way to reattach. We'll have to seal it up before infection can find a foothold. You may find a few things a bit harder to do, but all in all, if you have to lose something, a finger's not bad." Then as an afterthought, he added, "And you'll live, which is an added bonus free of charge."

Lem smiled, "And wait until you hear the stories he'll be telling in the next inn we find—twenty men, he'll have fought and lost only a finger for his trouble."

"Thirty men," Rem said, meeting his brother's smile, "and their pet bear, who bit the finger clean off 'fore I stabbed him through the heart."

Willem laughed something deep from his gut, and Aiden couldn't help himself; he laughed too. Rem could joke even after losing a piece of his body and bleeding himself a quarter of the way to death. Smiling, Aiden shook his head and started to sheath his sword.

"Wait," Thun's voice cracked like a whip in the tension-easing air.

"What?" Aiden asked, looking around for more attackers and finding none.

"The sword," Jumper said.

"Yes, the sword," Thun intoned. "How is it that the knife you carried now rests in your palm as a sword instead?"

"Well, umm," Aiden started as Willem and the twins looked more closely at the blade in his hand. The truth sounded insane, but he couldn't think of a believable lie. *I traded a wizened peddler my knife for this sword. Swords are so much more useful in a fight, you know. I'm pretty sure I got the better of the deal.* No, that wouldn't do at all. He supposed the truth would have to do then.

"I needed it," he said. "I was fighting this big guy over there. All I had left was the knife and he was big with a big sword to match, and well, I guess I needed something more. I drew the knife and out came the sword instead." He smiled, but Thun's face grew no less stern, so Aiden hurried on. "Look, I know it sounds crazy, but for Twin Angels' sake, you just pulled down a wall of stone to crush the Swaar. Is it really out of the realm of possibility that somehow I drew a sword from a knife's place?"

"'Course it's not out of the realm of possibility," Jumper said finding his smile again. "It's just unexpected's all."

"And don't forget your jump," Rem said. The eyes in Thun's unmoved face drifted to Rem and then back to Aiden. Aiden shot a brief look at Rem that he hoped conveyed the idea that Rem could try shutting his mouth for once. Rem's smile was just as impassive as Thun's stern frown, however.

With a sigh, Aiden told of how he had sensed the Swaar coming up from behind, how he had pulled on that same feeling to find strength to defeat the big Swaar who had pulled him from his saddle, and finally how he had seen Rem about to die and had leapt to save him. When Aiden was done, Thun nodded, finding life again at last.

"Hmm, I suppose that's that," Thun said, running his thick fingers over his mustache. "It's unusual for it to happen so soon, but then, life is filled with unusual, isn't it?"

"Oh, come on, Thunder Klapp," Jumper put in, evidently enjoying himself. "You'll never sail a ship with a frown. Everyone's still alive. We lost a finger, but no lives. And our new Maker's Hand tapped all by himself, drawing on the stone and manipulating the steel both. More proof, I call it. Now, let's stop with the storm clouds, have a look around, and figure out how we're going to get out of here, shall we?"

Thun sighed and nodded. He sent Willem and Lem to collect the horses and equipment. Thun's own horse was standing plaintively at the side of the canyon, nibbling at a bit of some plant that had forced its way through the stony ground. He went to it and pulled his healer's pouch from one of the saddlebags before returning to Rem, dabbing some ointment on the stump where his finger used to be and bandaging it. Thun then had Rem sit and rest against the canyon wall while he, Jumper, and Aiden walked to the opposite side.

Aiden's head and face ached from the pummeling they had received, but he tried his best to force that aside. He could be stronger than a beating. He had been before.

"Here it is," Jumper said, still as happy as a child with a bit of honey cake. Aiden was sure the good mood would fade before they had made it through the canyon. It seemed that if Jumper wasn't doing something exhilarating, moving at a headlong, storm-racing speed, then he simply couldn't stay content for long.

Jumper slipped out of Aiden's view for a moment, and then Aiden saw it: a narrow opening in the cliffside. The opening lay hidden behind an outcropping of rock, making it nearly impossible to spot before he was right at it. Thun disappeared into the opening after Jumper, leaving Aiden little choice but to follow.

All was dark inside. Then a flick of light, and a blaze seemed to ignite the entire world. Aiden blinked, and the world refocused, revealing Jumper's grinning face looming up out of the darkness. A torch flickered in the sandy-haired man's clenched fist.

"Take a gander at this, my young Hand," Jumper said, sweeping the torch around and along a lengthening strip of wall.

Normally, Aiden would have bridled at being called anyone's *young* anything, but his full attention was stolen by the gleam of steel raking the wall. In two neat rows were hung and stacked hundreds of swords, spears, and pikes. Square wooden shields were piled around a corner facing an open archway. A plain, cave-like room stood beyond with a few chairs sitting around an uneven round table in a far corner. The rest of the room sat naked, void of furniture or anything else recognizably man-made.

"What is this place?" Aiden asked.

"Swaar..." Jumper muttered, shaking his head.

"They must be preparing for a larger assault than we thought," Thun said. "Bellcross was bad enough, but all this in one lonely canyon and who knows what else they have here and in other little caches."

"Why couldn't it just be a group of Swaar getting ready for another raid?" Aiden asked

Thun shook his head slowly. "Our desert friends don't work like that. They don't work like *this,* for that matter. They don't stockpile weapons to equip their men in time of need or war. Each man carries his own weapon, shield, and armor, as far as armor goes with them. A Swaar would just as soon give up his life as leave his blade resting in some stockpile."

Again, Thun shook his head, his mustache waving a slightly different beat than the rest of him. "No, this smells too much of recruiting for my comfort, that and equipping themselves for something bigger than border raids. They're out of their element being this far west anyway. It doesn't make sense."

"Alright, alright," Jumper said, visibly twitchy again. We're not going to figure it all out standing here in the dark."

"Hmm," Thun nodded slowly, unperturbed by the lanky man's anxiety, "I suppose we're not at that." In the flickering torchlight, his eyes seemed to return from some distant place, refocusing as they found Aiden and then Jumper. "At least we know why you didn't spot our little band of awaiting hosts. Even your vision wouldn't have seen this tucked-away cave from very far away."

Back outside, Willem and Lem had gathered horses aplenty. Luckily, all their original mounts were still among the herd, and half a dozen others besides.

"There were lots more, but they bolted down the valley the other way before we could round them up," Willem said.

"Good thing, too," Lem said. "I feel like we're going to get trampled to death as it is." Then he laughed to show that his fear was anything but pressing. "What are we going to do with twelve horses and only six backsides to sit them."

Thunder smiled. "Well, we'll sell them of course. I thought it was you lot who accused us of being mercenaries. A good swordarm never leaves an opportunity for profit behind. Besides, something to sell gives us a more viable reason to chat up some answers when we come to the next town."

"And what about the weapons?" Aiden asked, nodding at the hidden cave entrance and wincing at the additional pain the movement offered his head.

"Those with the dead we will have our pick of, but remember we still have a distance to travel and the only one to carry what you take is you and your horse. Whatever we don't take, we'll throw in there," and Thun mirrored Aiden's head nod at the cave entrance. "I'll seal it before we're done.

"The dead, we leave for the crows. Let them be a warning against any who would attack the Mist Falcons."

Aiden couldn't help but think that the Mist Falcons hadn't done all the killing, at least not on his side of the canyon. *No, you fool, that blood is on your hands. Congratulations.*

His piece said, Thun rolled his shoulders and turned back toward the wall of stone he had dropped on the Swaar. The others drifted slowly away. Aiden found his bow, slightly scuffed among the rocks, but still whole and serviceable. He was able to scavenge a dozen fresh arrows from a dead Swaar's quiver. Surprisingly, there were good steelheads on the arrows. Bone or stone to tipped arrows from the Swaar seemed more likely to him, but that was little more than wild speculation. Tucking the arrows into his now full quiver, Aiden surveyed the other dead. He pulled a knife out of one man's belt and hauled a heavy axe up from the stones where another had dropped it. He couldn't bring himself to cut his arrows out of the men he had killed with them. *Keep them—my gift and the last you'll ever receive.*

Aiden tucked the knife into his belt, slung the axe over one shoulder, and made his way back to the cave entrance. Lem dropped an oversized sword just inside the doorway and then turned back to Aiden with a nonchalant smile. Aiden followed suit, leaving his axe only a step inside before turning back himself.

Willem was waiting for him as he emerged back into the bright sunshine. As Aiden approached, Willem held out a steel-headed spear. "I know Thun and Jumper didn't have one for you back at the cabin, and I thought you might want it."

"Oh... yeah, great," Aiden said, taking the proffered spear. The long handle was a bit thicker than he was used to and the weight a little more, but he had grown used to the extra reach in their short time on the Sands, and the wood grain felt right beneath his fingers. It'd be good to have a spear again. "Thanks," he added after a moment. Willem nodded and headed off to the cave to make his own offering of a long sword and a club.

A slow rumble set Aiden's chest to pounding. He whirled to find the stone Thun had collapsed on their foes shifting slowly out and up, opening a narrow canyon within the canyon they currently resided in. Thunder himself stood in front of the wall of stone, his arms raised again, orchestrating the slowly-shifting stone. Aiden knew his mouth was open, but he couldn't seem to force it closed. He had assumed they would have to go back the way they had come and take the longer journey around. He had had no notion that what Thun was doing was even possible.

"By the forgotten gods, and Twin Angels too," he heard Rem intone from where he still rested against the near canyon wall. "I've never...uh, I mean...well, that's slam tilt amazing, mate."

Aiden tore his eyes away from the shifting rock long enough to glance at the twin and nod, vaguely aware his mouth was still hanging open. With some effort, he finally snapped it closed before turning back to Thun's magic show.

After several solid minutes, the rock flow slowed and then stopped. Thun's arms dropped as if weights had just been attached to his hands. His shoulders slumped, and Aiden could see the big man's chest heaving in great, tired breaths.

Jumper strolled over to Thun with an easy gate and a smile. He offered him a canteen of water, which the big man grasped in a shaking hand and took several long pulls from.

"Are you getting old, my friend?" Jumper asked. "That's a lot less rock than you pulled down in the first place, but look at you—wheezing like you just ran the Great Race from Frantelin to Celtari."

"Humph," Thun snorted a great exhale through his nose. "As if you'd know. You could never run a dozen steps without leaping. Besides, shaping takes a lot more than brute force. When I collapsed it, I didn't much care how much rock I grabbed, other than that it was enough. But unless you wanted this nice hallway falling in on us partway through, I thought I'd place each stone a little more precisely."

Jumper nodded all through Thun's explanation, a sarcastic smile sketched across his face. "Touchy, isn't he?" Jumper said to the others.

Thun just smiled, still pulling in air in great gulps. "Not that I expect you to understand. Wind is Wind, after all. Not a whole lot of shaping there. Just leaping and tossing, leaping and tossing."

Jumper's smile fell like a mask. "You mean to tell me that Wind is easier than Stone? Are you kidding me? Try grabbing something as insubstantial as air and molding it to your will. Never jump too high or fall too fast. I make more calculations in an hour than most merchants do in their lives. No brute force. Never overshoot. Never undershoot. Always precise. Always precise. Always."

Thunder was laughing by this point as Jumper's words of defense continued to tumble over each other in their haste to find form. "Who's touchy now?" he chortled out in his booming laugh.

After a moment Jumper's tirade turned to a frown and then, slowly, into a smile. "You old camel eater. You think we can go now, or does your old man body need a nap?

"Almost," Thun said. "There is still the matter of the cave and about six inches worth of stone at the end of our path. I didn't want to open it all the way up, just in case someone is still waiting for us at the far end. But half a foot should be no problem with a little bit of, what did you call it, ah, brute force."

Thun smiled and made his way to the cave entrance. "What's left can stay. It's best we be on our way sooner rather than later and away from here before other Swaar start to wonder what became of their...uh...friends. This first, though." Thun raised his hands toward the entry much in the same manner as he had to the wall of stone before.

Aiden and the others waited in silent anticipation, Willem going as far as taking a step back from the entry. They expected something grand, something big, a crack and a whoosh, followed by a pile of rubble. What they got in payment for their silence was simply more silence.

At first, Aiden thought he had just misjudged how long it would take to manipulate the stone with Thun's ability, but time stretched on and on. Seconds turned to a minute, then to five, then to ten. Thun's arm, still outstretched, began to quiver and shake.

Aiden felt the almost familiar drumming and closed his eyes. The drumming was strong and came unsurprisingly from Thun's core, sending out waves toward the cave entrance. He let the beat carry his mind's eye on its current, and in a moment's time he, found himself with the stone of the entryway, but there was more than the single beat now. There was a chorus of drumming already in the stone and it rang out its beat at odds with this new beat of Thun's. Aiden didn't understand, but every time Thunder's drumming found a percussion to meet the stone, a counter beat would ring from somewhere in the stone, denying the beat's truth or dominance.

The beat countered and countered. There was always a beat low for a beat high, a beat soft for a beat hard, up for down, and down for up. It reminded Aiden of nothing so much as a well-fought duel. With that thought, he knew what he needed to do. Cheat the duel. When next Thun's beat struck low, Aiden struck high, but from without the stone and not within as the counter beat had been doing. He felt the other drumming waver, unable or uncertain of how to react to both low and high. The stone shook above the entry.

Thun beat hard and loud, a hammer on an anvil, and Aiden sent a gentle strum of whispered *titter tat tat* wafting toward the stone. Again the other beat wavered and the stone shook again, sliding slowly downward to Thun's will. Finally, Thun beat a drumming of insistent fire, like cedar burning in open flame. Aiden offered a few great booming arcs, and it was done. Thun did something inside the stone that Aiden didn't quite understand, and the rock around the entry crashed down, sending dust ballooning up and out.

Aiden opened his eyes, lost balance, and sat back, hard, with a thump. His head spun and he found his chest heaving as if he had just been underwater for minutes. As his eyes refocused, he saw Thunder on one knee, breathing heavily himself and staring intently at Aiden.

"How...how'd you know...whew...how'd you know what to do?" Thun asked, still sucking in air.

Aiden could feel everyone else's eyes on him as well, but he tried to focus on Thun. He shrugged. "Umm, I...I don't really know what I did, or how, I guess." Thun's eyes narrowed and his brow pulled together. "I don't know, I just...I guess I wanted to know what was going on, so I followed the drumming. That's all." Aiden didn't know what else to say. He didn't know how he had heard, felt, or followed the beat of Thun's work. Instead of fumbling through any more explanation, he just narrowed his eyes in a sullen match of Thun's stare and waited.

After a moment, the big man relented. He blew out his mustache with a great exhale and shook his head. "Well, I don't know what to make of you, my Maker's Hand, but perhaps I shouldn't be so surprised. At any rate, I'm glad you helped."

Glancing over at Jumper, he continued, "The Swaar might have a Stone Shaper, and if they do, who knows what else. Either that or they found a cave someone had strengthened before them. Someone had to have worked on this stone before us. There were already Elementals at work, and strong too. I don't know if I could have bested the craftsmanship of it alone, not tired as I am." He glanced sidelong at Aiden. "But then, I guess I didn't have to."

Aiden was still feeling woozy as he mounted his horse and fell into line with the others. Each rider had a spare horse tied to their saddle, and the path Thun had opened was only wide enough to allow a single-file line to traverse it. Thun took lead so that he could finish opening the end of the passage. Aiden came next, followed by Rem, Jumper, and the others in a strewn-out line.

As Thun came near to the sheer stone still blocking their path, he turned back to Aiden with a smile and said, "You've seen a bit of the intricacies of Stone Elementalogy. Now, let me show you some of the brute force Jumper was talking about." He raised one hand, and there was no waiting this time. As quick as a thought, the stone in front of them exploded outward as if a giant's fist had just slammed through it.

Thunder glanced back as he moved his horse into a walk again, and his smile stretched bigger yet. Aiden found himself smiling in return even as it pulled at his swollen and cut lips. As he fingered the pommel of his falcon blade, he thought, *This might prove an interesting journey after all.* Then he thought of Semlie bleeding out on the cobbles and the face of the bald man, Branke, drifted into his memory's vision and with him Baron Raz. He gripped the falcon pommel with a full fist now. *And if the power these Mist Falcons carry is real, maybe I'll make a few visits to Oustenbasch soon.*

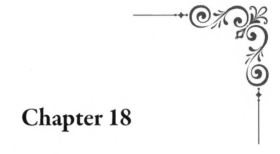

Chapter 18

...and even wide, swift rivers cease when swallowed by the ocean.

"The stone, the stone," the little man chanted as he continued to work keys loose from a ring that had hung hidden at his belt. Each key, he fit smoothly into an invisible key hole in the stonework surrounding the fireplace. "When sour stars distill and fail, hee hmmm," the Keeper muttered under his breath in a sing-song fashion as he worked another key into a lock that Tako couldn't see. "And darkness glides into prevail." Another key slid into place. "Guard tight the secret that you keep beneath the mountain of Gleneth's Sweep. Oh, I have. I have." He giggled, slipping another key free of the ring. "Now master keys and watch the time." Two more keys into their holes. "For nigh draws 'til Wolf Rider's climb," the Keeper hummed as he placed an ornate-looking key above a column of other keys and turned it. "Wielding axe and bearing stone." His voice grew more serious now. There was a "click, click" from inside the stone somewhere, and then a whirring noise began as if some great mechanism had just been engaged. "He'll come, the starlight to atone." And saying that, the Keeper placed his last key into the stone, turned it, and the world fell out from beneath Tako, Dante, and the little, wizened Keeper.

Down they plummeted. Darkness reigned the world as utter quiet silenced even Tako's own cry of surprise. Tako could feel a cool rush of air whip at his hair and beard, but its caress against his face was more of a gentle breeze than a torrential gust, prophesying his oncoming death. He was aware of Dante near him as they fell through the darkness. Tako couldn't see him, couldn't hear him, but he could feel his presence just the same. The Keeper was falling right alongside them, dropping toward whatever awaited them. Even without seeing his leathered, old face, Tako was sure the Keeper offered nothing but smiles of joy to the darkness.

Then, all at once, the three of them stopped. They didn't crash. They didn't break. The downward plummeting ride simply ended without slowing. Tako just stood for a moment. After the space of a few breaths, an illumination began creeping into his vision. The world was still thin and gray, but black no longer. He could make out Whisper standing a few paces away from him but the little Keeper was nowhere to be found. The light was just enough to reveal a small path leading straight ahead.

"Dante," Tako whispered, and though his voice had been little more than a hiss, the noise echoed up off of high arching walls and ceiling. Dante didn't turn, however. He didn't look. He didn't move. The man could have been a statue for all the response Tako got. "Dante," Tako said a little louder, hearing his voice redouble in echo.

"He can't hear you, I'm afraid," The Keeper said, appearing now from someplace behind Tako. "This place lives doubly out of time, Wolf Rider, very similar to how the Tower does above. But whereas the Tower acts as a buffer for its occupants, this place offers no buffer. Your friend cannot live here for he requires the movement of time to frame his actions. For the moment, however, time has skipped over him, forgotten him. He now waits for time to return to him and catch him up. Don't worry. He should be fine."

"Should be?"

The Keeper smiled something toothy that looked eerie in the dim light. "Nothing is certain, oh Wolf Rider, and no one knows all of time's wandering paths save he who made them. Still, your companion won't come to harm in the time of what we need to accomplish. I am the Watcher of such, remember."

"What about us, then, little man?" Tako asked, "being outside of time and all?"

"I am the Keeper, Master of Keys, and Watcher of Time. I am not chained by such laws. And you...well, you have the stone, now, don't you." The Keeper smiled again, but there was no warmth in it, no comfort for Ren Tako. Still, he was the Wolf Rider, fearless in battle, fearless in life. Tako refused to be cowed by a wrinkled little man in a cave, even if that man was a Keeper with keys and time on his side. Tako smiled right back and allowed nothing but chill to emanate from his expression.

Another moment passed in silence as the two stared at each other. Then the Keeper shrugged his slender shoulders, apparently willing to accept defeat in this little game. He stepped around Tako and started down the narrow, lit path.

"Come along, Wolf Rider," the tiny man said without turning back. "We still have some distance to cover."

Tako looked at Dante one more time, and then followed. He caught up to the little man's stunted strides within a few quick steps of his own, but then not wanting to pass or lose sight of this Keeper, he slowed his pace to match the slower walk. And the pace was slow. The Keeper did not have his automated cart down here, and so was left to only the power of his two, short legs.

The path grew narrow, offering only enough space for Tako to slip the bulk of his broad shoulders through. In places, he even had to turn so as not to wedge himself between the stony outcroppings of the forever-high walls. As they walked, Tako noted unexcavated, shimmering stones in the narrow walls as well as in the floor.

Apparently, these stones offered the dancing, shadowy light for the path, for no other light source presented itself.

After a while of watching the glittering stones, Tako noticed patterns taking shape. At first, they were only vague shapes dancing back and forth amongst the lighting, but as he watched, images began to leap forth. Tako had seen cave drawings of the ancients far to the east depicting history of the Swaar's earliest life—their dangers, foes, defeats, and victories. This, however, was only similar on the basest of levels. It was like comparing the ember glow of a nearly exhausted campfire with the radiance of the sun in high summer. All-Warrior help him, this was amazing.

The shapes leapt from stone to stone—from wall to wall and then to floor before returning again to the originating wall but to a different stone. Tako began to see the path, not as a dimly-lit, narrow way, but as an ever-dancing myriad of colors, shapes, and images. One figure came to the forefront of the dance, a man dressed in mail with a circular shield strapped to one arm. A helm claimed the man's head and a mask stole the vision of his face. Two new figures appeared in the glimmering lights, one a monster or demon with a cruel-looking scimitar raised for the kill, the other a cowering woman holding fast to something. As Tako watched, he saw that what the woman clung to was a small child, a boy of no more than two or three harvests. She was not cowering but protecting, offering her own body as a shield for the child. All at once, the demon with the scimitar hurled his blade downward for the kill. The first man, the armed one, leapt and just at the last moment caught and turned the blade with his shield. As quick as that he was back on his feet and dealt the attacker a crushing blow with the shield. The monster dissolved in a vapor of light.

"I'm sure you know the tale of the Shield of Ammereth," the Keeper said, his voice cutting through the scene of the shielded warrior. The Keeper never broke stride and never looked back at

Tako. He simply started telling his tale without waiting for a response.

"Many myths and legends have been created surrounding the Shield of Ammereth. Most cling to at least a piece of truth, but much is simply tale-telling. One man tells the story and another, hearing it, adds a bit in its retelling. And so on and so forth it goes down through the ages until little but the core remains and even that can be skewed and misinterpreted. This is the true story concerning the events surrounding the Shield and the man who wielded it—the man who became it.

"Centuries ago, in times nearly forgotten by today's world, when most Elementals still lay bound far beneath the earth, and before the breaking of the White Stone, dark powers walked freely, unchained by the universal laws that have bound such things since. To this world, a man was born." As the Keeper spoke the dancing lights began to form images of the scene he described. Great demon-like creatures rose up, portrayed more by their lack of light than any actual form.

"Now the Darkness hated humankind and destroyed them and their creations wherever it found them. Humans for their part had no real defense against the Darkness. Flame was of some use of course, but keeping fires burning during the daytime, ready and at hand, was wearisome and costly of time. Moreover, the Darkness did not attack any given tribe or settlement but rarely, reinforcing the need for but a sloppy defense. Humans are funny creatures. A demon attack would ravage a settlement, leaving dozens of dead. The survivors would be on top alert—spears to the ready and flames burning all the day round with torches wrapped and ready by them. They would remain like this for a week, a month, maybe two, but when their enemy failed to make a reappearance, everyday life began forcing precautions back to the outskirts of thought.

"Now the Darkness was sly and cunning. When a region's defenses were lowered once more, then it was safe for a renewed attack. And so it went with the human population dwindling ever smaller while the Darkness feasted on the fear and death of thousands."

The flickering lights danced out a dreadful scene before Tako, offering him the vision of the Keeper's feasting demons. Still, the small man didn't look back, but offered his tale as his short legs outstripped the path one step at a time.

"As I said, into this time a boy was born in what was then the small town of Ammereth. That boy was named Josimmian. Josimmian grew and grew. Ammereth was small in those days, and so the Darkness paid it heed only occasionally. Still, by the time Josimmian reached the cusp of manhood, he had survived nearly a dozen attacks. He hated the Darkness and the demons it sent to ravage the land. The older he grew, the more and more the notion of fighting back took hold of him. During one raid, he lit fire arrows and used them to hold back the demons from his home and the homes of his closest neighbors.

"He rallied what support he could from Ammereth and began organizing a watch and defense system, but before he could bring his plans to fruition, the Darkness attacked in strength. The demons hadn't much cared for Josimmian's defense, nor did they like him organizing others to defend. The battle that the demons brought nearly claimed Josimmian's life. It was only by luck or providence that when he was struck, he fell amongst a ring of burning torches that the demons dared not pass to finish him and claim their prize."

It was all Tako could do to keep from stumbling as he watched Josimmian get struck with a massive, clawed fist of black demon mail. He watched as the survivors pulled Josimmian's broken body from the ground and laid him on a bed of linens.

"Ammereth was all but destroyed by the Darkness in that battle. Only a few broken buildings were left to the survivors. It was to this mess of crumbling village that a wandering traveler arrived, a pack upon his back in the fashion of a peddler in those days. Now peddlers were not well respected, considered rogues and con artists by most. The survivors of Ammereth were anything but pleased at this intruder's presence. 'Just another mouth to feed,' one of the town elders said."

Tako saw the lights form the remaining farmers and craftsmen of the village grabbing pitchforks, shovels, and hammers as they began closing on the traveling peddler.

"Then the peddler spoke and his voice rang harmoniously, sweeter to hear than a dozen master musicians. 'Fair people of Ammereth,' he said. 'You have been through much and I mean to take nothing more from you. I have come to give and to see the man called Josimmian.' And with that, he let down his pack, and it fell open showing the contents of bread and blankets. Both were in short enough supply after the demon attack, and the people were grateful."

Now the scene changed again. Once more the dancing lights revealed Josimmian lying on a pallet. This time the peddler squatted next to him. The newcomer's hood was thrown back revealing an unremarkable face.

"Finding Josimmian still in anguish from his burns and breaks, the peddler laid a hand on the man's chest. 'Peace,' he said. A glow started in the peddler's hand where he touched Josimmian and then spread through the man's broken body."

Tako had to squint as the lights grew and then flashed around Josimmian and the peddler. The flash passed, and the scene revealed the change. Josimmian now stood, whole and unbroken. A man stood in front of him, but not the same peddler, for the dirty cloak had been replaced by one of shimmering silver and the man's features, now handsome and striking, glowed, lit from within by some hidden power.

"Josimmian was healed," the Keeper said, his stride still unbroken by the dancing lights. "He knelt before the now-shining stranger. 'My lord,' Josimmian said, his head bowed, 'who are you? For I was broken, in pain and dying, but you healed me, saved me from my torment. Tell me your name that I may know who I now serve.'

"The shining man bent and grasped Josimmian by his shoulders with both hands, pulling him to his feet. 'I am...' he smiled, his features even more radiant in his joy. 'You can call me The Maker, for that title fits as well as any other.'"

The Keeper stopped walking so abruptly that Tako nearly ran into him and had to grab the wall to keep himself from falling on top of the little man. The dancing lights didn't cease in their endless, flickering dance, but the scene froze as surely as water in a pond when a whipping winter storm breaks on a glade. "You may want to pay special attention to this part of the tale, Wolf Rider, for now we come to the heart of our story, and I think you may find it more than a bit interesting." The Keeper offered Tako a wink and a disconcerting smile that was all the more troublesome for the genuine glee behind it. If what the man claimed was true, Tako supposed he had been waiting a very long time for this little walk of theirs. So he guessed he couldn't blame him. Still, the impish man was not likable, and Tako couldn't help feeling that a trap lay at the end of this passage.

With nothing else said, the Keeper turned back to the path and began his slow pace and story once more. As he restarted, so did the images of the dancing lights. "'I have heard the cries of the children,' The Maker told Josimmian, 'the cries and the gnashing of teeth. But nowhere have I heard the trumpet of defense, nowhere but in Ammereth and by no voice but yours. You stand alone, Josimmian, a tiny flickering candle in a sea of darkness and though the Darkness has tried, it has not overcome you.'

"'It's come fairly close,' Josimmian said, trying at a smile.

"'Quite,' The Maker responded. 'But I have come now to answer the cries and to guard the light you kindle, for you are to be a shield unto all the people of this land, bearing my Stone and offering the protection of the light to all.' Saying this, he took the ring from his glowing hand and placed it onto Josimmian's finger. With a wink and a whistle, the peddler—The Maker—vanished in a tiny flash of song.

"That very day, Josimmian set to rebuilding the defenses of Ammereth, for as he said to the other survivors who were awed at his recovery, 'What good is rebuilding Ammereth if we cannot defend it when next the demons come?' He and those who followed his lead dug down and built short walls in a layer fashion around the city to stop the demons from sliding beneath the earth and leaping out mere paces from their victims. In this way, they would have some warning when the inevitable attack came, for it was commonly known that demons cannot travel far beneath the surface soil, nor can they pass through stone. He then went about reinstigating the watches with spears, torches, and fire at hand in any of six guard posts surrounding Ammereth, as well as two posts centralized in the heart of the square.

"The Darkness left them to their work for no more than a week, for it had noticed the renewed efforts toward defense. This time, not a stone would be left on another in the village, and not a man, woman, or child left alive, for the Darkness knew that hope was a terrible human disease, easily contagious. It could not be allowed to spread.

"The demons came in force, and though stymied by Ammereth's new walls, soon made their way into the village to begin their hideous work on its people. The demons had not counted on

Josimmian, however. The very first victim that the lead demon tried to take, Josimmian leapt in front of, jabbing a spear at the creature's chest. The demon dodged and swept a clawed fist down at the man. Josimmian held up his free hand, the one bearing The Maker's ring. Light flared into the darkness and the ring spread into a circular shield of light large enough to cover Josimmian's whole arm. The demon's attack fell onto the shield and its fist shattered against it."

Tako saw the clawed fist descending on the unprotected Josimmian. He watched as the shield of light spread from the man's hand, and inwardly cheered as the demon's stroke could not break it—indeed could not even withstand it.

"That night was the very first victory against the Darkness by humankind—the first victory and the beginning of hope and a new age.

"As the news of the victory spread, people flocked from the land all around the village, seeking protection and a chance to meet Josimmian, the Shield of Ammereth. More willing hands meant larger defenses, and faster. Josimmian doubled his efforts, architecting higher, more sweeping, connected walls further out in order to accommodate all the new arrivals and space for more yet to come. He placed more torches, spears, and a new basin of hot coals to light torches at each outpost, which now numbered more than a score around the wall and centralized in the village. He also set a newly-arrived huntsman to making bows and fletching arrows.

"A few came, simply to meet Josimmian, to see the ring and Shield of Ammereth, and to see what he was doing with the defenses of this growing village. They soon returned to their cities, though, unwilling or unable to abandon other interests and settle in Ammereth.

"The Darkness was not idle, however. The Lord of Darkness had noted the threat and sent a call for all his roaming army to rise to his banner. In but a short time, the demons came again, this time in far greater numbers, all that the Darkness could gather to himself, and he whose name will not be spoken, the Nameless One of Old, came at their head. Ammereth's defenses were improved, but not ready, not in such a short time and not for the falling of the blackest of evils. Newly built walls shattered under the pounding of fists of night. Fires were squelched, shafts broken. Torches flared, spears flung, and flaming arrows lit the sky, but though demons fell, none could stand before the Lord of Darkness and live. The tiny flames of man could do little but irritate him in his wrath, and the best-forged steel spearheads dulled and turned against his black, armored flesh.

Still, the Shield of Ammereth remained to be contended with. They found each other, Josimmian and the Lord of Darkness. With much of Ammereth burning around them, walls broken, people dead, injured, and dying, the two of them finally met in the square of town. A few moments they spent circling one another, watching, taking account, and then the Nameless One of Old leapt forth, a huge blade growing from his hand, and the battle began."

Entranced, Tako watched as a fully-armored Josimmian accepted the first blow of the demon lord on his shield. The devil blade did not shatter as others had, but nor did Josimmian fall, crushed beneath the blow. Deflecting the first strike, Josimmian attacked with the axe he held in his other hand, swinging with such force that even the thick, armored hide of the demon lord could not fully repel it. The huge beast let out a roar as the armory flesh of his thigh splintered, emitting dark, oozing blood.

The wrath of his returned volley was immense. Horrorstruck, Tako watched as blow after massive blow crashed into Josimmian, driving the figure further and further toward the outskirts. No one could survive such a barrage, but somehow, amazingly, Josimmian remained on his feet, shield upraised and axe at the ready.

"The two of them battled long, ever-moving further from the defense walls and up into the mountains," the Keeper said. "At long last, when dawn sat poised less than an hour from breaking the horizon, the two of them stopped. They stood now on the precipice of one of the lower slopes. Rendruse, that place was called—the Lonely Lookout.

"'Are you ready to die now, human?' the Nameless One asked. 'You have come too far from your walls and your fires; you are alone, small, and weak.' Looking around, Josimmian saw that other demons had gathered, closing a large ring around him and their lord. 'Noticed, have you?' the Lord of Darkness barked, offering a burst of chilling, horrible laughter to the night. His evil joy resounded from the lips of the ever-tightening circle of demons.

"Josimmian was a mortal man and the laughter and circumstance frightened him, but he refused to be paralyzed by them. He had only to wait for the swiftly approaching dawn, for it was known that demons could not stand the blaring eye of sunlight.

"As if sensing his thoughts, the Nameless One said, 'We have more than enough time to deal with you this night, little human, and with you gone, tomorrow night will be a joyous occasion in your sweet Ammereth. Can you hear the people crying as they burn and die, oh defenseless Shield of Ammereth?' Again the Lord of Darkness laughed, and as if his laughter were a sign, demons leapt toward Josimmian from every side.

"He deflected the first blow, allowing the demon to shatter itself against his shield. The second, he cleaved the head from and sent sprawling down the mountainside. But the third blow came from behind and sent Josimmian sprawling on his face, sparks flying as his armor skidded across the stone. Looking up, he found himself at the feet of the Nameless at the very edge of the precipice. Below was a thousand-foot drop into rocky abyss. There was no escape, no fleeing, no stalling for time. This was it. He knew it. This was the end.

"The Lord of Darkness offered Josimmian a gruesome smile, long fangs glinting in the last rays of moonlight, as the Shield of Ammereth pushed himself partway onto his feet. The Nameless lifted his massive, dark blade for the crushing stroke, but Josimmian never tried to stand. Instead, he leapt forward with all the energy he yet possessed. Thrusting his shield before him, Josimmian crashed into the chest of the Lord of Darkness, the Nameless One of Old, and together they went over the edge. Down they plummeted, Josimmian smashing his shield into the prone Dark Lord over and over until together they crashed into the waiting rocks below. The force of their fall was like thunder from heaven striking the earth. Down through the stones they battered as rocks filled in a tomb behind and around them."

Tako blinked as the Keeper stopped talking and the flickering lights ended their continuous dance of images at the same time. He looked up at the Keeper and then at the walls with their glittering stones. "And then what?" he said

"Then what?" the Keeper said. "Then nothing. Josimmian, the Shield of Ammereth, gave his life to end the tyranny of the Nameless, Lord of Darkness."

"What about the rest of the demons, though? What about the people of Ammereth?"

"Many of the demons went mad at the loss of their master. They couldn't live without his guidance, without his control. Most died outright or killed each other in their grief and madness. Those that survived were but a shadow of their former power and were beaten back by the human population as it expanded throughout the land.

"The people of Ammereth mourned the loss of their hero and protector of course, but they rejoiced at the victory and ease of their new lives."

Silence filled the space between Tako and the Keeper. "And that's it?" Tako asked. "That's the whole story of the Shield of Ammereth, the greatest Champion to have ever lived?"

Tako could hear the smile in the Keeper's voice as the little man said, "Well, it is and it isn't. Time is ever flowing, young Wolf Rider, and lives are ever being lived in its current. Believe me in this, for I am ever watching. Josimmian died that day upon Rendruse, but he was merely a single actor on a larger stage. One might say all of human history has been a side effect only made possible by Josimmian's sacrifice."

"It's not that. It's just..." Tako started but didn't know quite how to finish. He didn't usually begin speaking before he knew what he was going to say, nor did he hold qualms about offending those around him. The Keeper's tale had offset him somehow—drawn him in and then left him with a feeling of loss at its closing. He wasn't sure if that loss was for Josimmian, or the lights, or the story itself. And he didn't know how to explain that to this little man who Tako couldn't decide if he liked or not.

"It's just, I've heard a lot more stories about the great Shield of Ammereth and his exploits," Tako said, after failing to wrestle his thoughts into words and still feeling that he needed to say something.

"Of course," the Keeper said. "Human nature, that's all. A man in a tavern overhears part of a story told by strangers one table over. The next night, mug in hand, he tells the overheard tale. Let's say it was of some great escapade—a lion is killed, ripped apart with nothing but the hero's bare hands, especially if it was done in the defense of another, preferably a woman or child. Then, since the eavesdropping man didn't get all the details, it is easier for the teller to tack on the deed to a hero he knows. And who better to award the hero's badge than to the Shield of Ammereth, defender of mankind? Multiply that by a thousand taverns or campfires, a

thousand thousand, and you have yourself a legend. But that is neither here nor there. For I told you at the start I would tell you the
true story, the core of the legend, and there you have it."

The Keeper stopped walking and turned back to him so quickly
that again, Tako had to catch himself to avoid bowling over the
impish man.

When he spoke this time, the Keeper's voice came out softly,
not quite a whisper, but hushed and solemn. "But the tale of the
Shield of Ammereth is not over, for as I said, time continues on.
Even now, the story moves, and perhaps, if you don't die, it will
move in a greater fashion than it has moved for a thousand years."

Offering Tako a tiny wink, the Keeper turned back and ushered
them through a narrow archway. A large room lay nestled on the
other side of that doorway. Curved walls and ceiling gave the room
an odd, spherical feeling. At the room's heart lay a stone sculpture.
Tako had never taken much time for art—neither the making of,
nor the appreciation in—but even he could feel the aura surrounding the stone carving before him. Power rested here somehow and
in some form that Tako couldn't wrestle into understanding.

He couldn't make out what the sculpture depicted at first—too
many branching pieces and sprawling limbs. Then it struck him,
not physically but with enough force that Ren Tako, the Wolf Rider, staggered back. It was all true: the Keeper's tale, the Shield
of Ammereth, all of it, for before him lay the petrified, mingled,
remains of two broken forms, one much larger than the other—Josimmian and the Nameless.

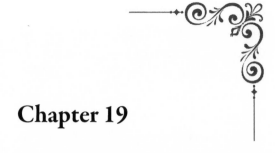

Chapter 19

Do not be fooled by the appearance of things. They are so rarely as they seem in this.

Willem ran a hand gently over the neck of his new guitar, a faint smile playing on his face. The extra dirk and two knives he had claimed from the dead Swaar had gotten him a golden eagle, three silver pennies, and a handful of drabs. He had the distinct feeling the smith merchant would turn a triple profit on what he had paid Willem. With the added fear riffling through the households of, Terrel Bay, he may even have had them sold yet that day. Still, Willem hadn't had time or know where to look for those who might pay more.

Either way, Willem would have traded all his worldly possessions for the guitar he found in the secondhand store. It was worn with a missing guard and scratches running down from all the strumming following the guard's departure. The strings were old and in need of tuning. The guitar was nowhere near as fine as the beautiful instrument he had lost to the slavers, and Willem had never seen anything as gorgeous in his whole life.

They hadn't stayed in Terrel Bay for long. One night in a bed at the small inn was all Thun had allowed. That had been long enough to hear all the gossip there was to be had. All the talk was of the Swaar. One old man claimed his brother's family had been murdered by a passing army further east. A frumpy middle-aged woman remained emphatic that the Swaar had already moved further south and west, burning fields and taking captives as slaves. Yet another man told them that his brother returned from a trading route into the northern hills still loaded down with all the goods he had gone to trade. He had arrived at the hill village to find it empty of everyone and everything of value. The buildings still stood, but only ghosts were left to greet the trader.

Those stories and more they heard as well as that from one weathered traveler, well into his tankard, who claimed that Sansol and Antice themselves descended from their lunar thrones to drive the Swaar back across the eastern border. All of the conflicting talk told Willem little enough. Thun and Jumper, on the other hand, seemed all the more determined to press on, and their group had left at first light.

Luckily, that had given Willem enough time to sell the weapons and buy the secondhand guitar. It cost him all but a few drabs of his new coin along with two golden eagles that Aiden had dug from his boot, apparently a treasure that had walked with him since Oustenbasch.

"I know how much it means to you, Will," Aiden had said simply, his voice sad but with a smile forced on his face as he had placed the coins on the shop's counter as an opening bid before walking back out to wait in the street. It may have been the greatest gift anyone had ever given him—his music's return.

Willem let his hand fall back down to the strings of his new prize and plucked a few short notes simply for their company. Playing while riding had never been his specialty. He was no courtier minstrel, riding along on some hunt or day in the country. When it had come time to mount up, though, he simply couldn't bring himself to let the guitar ride any place but in his hands.

They rode with the North Gulf on their left and rocky shore stretching before them in an endless parade.

"Only a few days now, lads," Thun said as they pulled up by a small grouping of trees to make camp for the night. Something was different about the man, and it took Willem a moment to place it. A smile lay on Thun's face and creased the corners of his eyes. The big Mist Falcon had grown more sullen as their trip had progressed. Willem hadn't seen him smile even in pretense for days, but his jovial attitude seemed to have returned now and the man's tension had leaked from his muscles.

He's almost home, Willem realized. There must be something more going on than his new companions had been letting on—more danger, more risk. He clenched his fist to keep his hand from shaking. That something could trouble these two powerful men to such a great level did not bode well. Almost home now, though. Thun's smile had to be a good sign.

The hope of that smile and the joy of having his new, worn instrument in his hands was more than enough to keep the fear of newly-realized danger at bay.

That night around the fire, the twins called for a song. "We're tired of seeing you cradle that box of kindling like a baby in arms, mate," Lem said.

"And never playing the crow-begotten thing," Rem followed in their usual way of completing each other's thoughts. "Give us a song, man, and show us what a minstrel trouper can do."

Though he had been tuning it a little at a time all day long, Willem was unsure of actually playing the guitar. Since he had first started on his uncle's guitar at the age of six, Willem had never gone this long without playing. Not that he had been without a blade or foreign to the occasional fight before the Swaar and slavers had unwittingly conspired to steal that life from him, but a sword now seemed to fit his hand as well as the guitar.

Forcing his troubled thoughts aside, Willem stared into the fire, fingered the strings, and struck a chord, driving silence from the air. A slow sad Dala Ballad was the first song to come to him and so he set into it, finding its slow, powerful notes as a balm to his haggard soul. Willem only got as far as the first chorus of,

"So come dine with me, my sweet, my love.
Come dine with me and know—
that none will come here e're again
as long as north winds blow."

Then, a ragged croak escaped Aiden's throat. "Enough," he gasped, tears streaking his pained face. "Not that. Anything but her song. Something different, please."

"Alright," Willem managed to mumble. "Sure." He stared into the fire again, but no song came to him—no barroom ditty, no forlorn love ballad. Still, his fingers found their strings as the flames filled his vision, and music pranced forth in a cacophony of notes. The flames danced and the notes found each flicker in partnership. The world faded. Willem faded. There was fire, fingers, and music—each moving for the others' delight. Willem played his songless music, his fingers racing this way and that of their own accord. He played the truth of their fire, the truth of the flames. He played their comfort and warmth, their heat and danger. Willem played their dance. As he played, the flames grew in his vision. They grew and grew until they surrounded his shrunken self. The music grew. The flames grew. And Willem shrunk.

He felt himself fade, felt himself slip away from himself, as if he were only a shadow, breaking free from his body and slipping into and between the huge flames of their tiny campfire. Then, for a moment, he was freefalling, a headlong dive through nothingness. The music still surrounded him and the flames held fast as if by a tether. Holding his fingers to their work was the only thing that mattered, but somehow they continued to move without his conscious effort.

Voices drifted to him from somewhere beyond the music, beyond the heat. Vague outlines began forming in the space in front
of and below him. People, their faces obscured, slipped free of the
haze. The flames were all but gone now, leaving smoke and haze
licking from the embers.

A voice wafted out from one of the slowly-forming people beyond the fire. His music was still with him but somehow did not
obscure Willem's hearing. "...And you say they will be here in two
days?" Willem couldn't hear the response of the second figure, but
he hadn't liked the tone of the first at all. Something cold and dangerous lay in that deep voice. "Then we will have to prepare something for them, won't we, Tee? You'll need to check the nets and..."

The face of the speaker was nearly visible now, the light almost
catching his features. Willem tried to lean forward, not really
knowing how to move his shadowy form. By trying to move,
though, he fumbled his fingering and the notes clattered off each
other in a jarring jumble.

All at once, Willem felt himself torn backward and up, revers-
ing his freefall in one gasping breath. Then he sat before the fire
again, dizziness swirling over his vision for a moment.

When his eyes refocused, the others were staring at him. Both
the twins had tears in their eyes, Jumper's mouth was open and
Aiden's face was pale, even in the firelight, his jaw tight and lips
pressed together.

"Why did you stop?" Thun asked, slightly breathless.

It took Willem a minute to find his voice. "I...um...I fumbled
the fingering. I guess, ah...I guess it's been a while. I mean...did you,
ah...did you see anything?"

"At first it was the best thing in the world," Rem said, his voice
distant and dreamy, "like the promise of gifts on Reaping Day. But
then..."

"Then it turned into the saddest thing I've ever heard," Lem said, "like back a year when Old Lord Renke took Lanni from Lommy Tapwood at Bridge End, just 'cause Lommy was winning at Queen, Nucks, and Gallant, and Lord Renke could take what he wanted."

Silence held for a minute as Willem met each man's eye in turn—all but Aiden's, who had returned his gaze to the fire, something painful still etched on his face. Willem tried to reason this through, tried to figure out what had happened and what was happening. Had he lost his mind? Was it still missing, stolen someplace away from him?

Without lifting his eyes from the flames, Aiden said, "It was destruction and death, wrapped in the promise of hope—a meal given to and then snatched away from a starving man." He looked up and met Willem's eyes. Blowing out a huge exhale, he shook his head and said, "By the Twin Angels, Will, you can play that thing."

"Yeah," said Jumper, "just warn us next time that you're playing that—whatever that was, and not *Mind Me Once and Mind Me Twice*. Maybe we can prepare our hearts for the race."

Willem did his best to smile and offer lame apologies. He didn't know what to make of the whole thing. They all acted like he had just played a heart-wrenching piece, moving, but not transporting, not literally ripping any of them from their bodies and into the flames to hear a man speak of plans to be made. No, that was just for Willem. Perhaps he had simply moved himself, the way he had moved the others. It had been a while after all. He hadn't played guitar in weeks, maybe longer. Time was hard to track since the Swaar had attacked Bellcross. But his vision had been so real...so insistent.

He did his best to smile and politely refused when the others asked him to play more. "I fear my fingers have lost their customary hold," he said. "I'll need a bit of time to regain my practice."

No, none of them had seen anything beyond the visions of a moving song. None of their shadows had leapt through the flames and found a world beyond, and either he had or he was losing his mind. He didn't think he was ready to discuss either possibility just yet.

Chapter 20

The Traitor stands before me...

"Yᴏu'll take us across tonight, Hammond, or you and I are going to see how long you can hold your breath under these waves you're so happy to dance across during the day." Thun's voice was little more than a growl, and Aiden couldn't imagine anyone denying the big man anything at the moment.

It had rained the last two days of their trip toward Holmsguard, and outlooks had fallen steadily with the rain.

Hammond was a slim man, maybe as young as Aiden, and he didn't seem like he much liked the prospect of telling Jak "Thunder" Klapp, no.

"Ok," he stammered out after a moment, obviously still a bit upset at being pulled from his bed hours before the sun would rise. "Fine, but crows take you, Thunder, if we get over there and I get put on probation for bringing you before the sun rises."

Thun smiled a smile holding something close to warmth, as close to warmth as Hammond was going to get after two days in the freezing rain. "That's a good lad. Don't you worry about the other side. I'll take care of that when we get there."

As it happened, it took Hammond nearly another hour to wake enough men to man the longboat and prep it for departure.

Holmsguard sat on an island called Castle Isle, just off the coast where the North Gulf met the ocean. It was only accessible by boat, hence the need for the town of North Port which housed, amongst other things, long boats crewed by men like Hammond. They, for a price, spent much of their time ferrying goods and personnel back and forth to the Isle.

Finally, all was ready. They and what supplies they had were loaded, and Hammond gave the order to push off. The horses, Thun had stabled at the large complex just off the coast by the docks. "We won't need these for a while at least," he had said. "Besides, these poor beasts have earned a rest as much as we have."

Whether Hammond had gone purposely slow or it simply took extra long to ready a boat and crew in the middle of the night, Aiden didn't know. However, with the delay, their longboat was only halfway across the gulf before the sun sent its first rays clawing up off the horizon and into the waiting sky, scattering the last stars, lurking darkness, and the final shadow of the twin moons. The fresh sunshine highlighted only one thing for Aiden's sight—Holmsguard. The castle itself rose like a kraken from the sea, thick turrets raising this way and that out of dense stone walls that glittered, jewel-like, in the rising sun. It looked as if small, precious stones had been fitted here and there all over the walls, making the sun dance in shades of blue, red, and green.

For a moment the glittering was all he saw. When he finally pulled his sight away from the sparkling promise of treasure, Aiden saw that the castle's main high wall gave way to a lower one that encircled stables and a great yard dotted with smaller buildings. Beyond this wall on one side lay a sweeping forest and on the other, the bay and docks, with a tall lighthouse rising from the sloping, stony ground that appeared to be built more as a guard tower with thick stone and regular murder holes for archers. The stone of the lighthouse was worked in much the same way as the castle itself and it shone back the rising sun.

"Wow," he heard the twins say in unison. For once there was no joking to their tone, just awe. And Aiden had to agree. Holmsguard struck home an understanding of woven beauty, power, and steadfastness all in a single glance. In comparison, the mansions of Oustenbasch and lords' halls of Perry were beggars' hovels.

"Welcome to our home, gentlemen," Thun said over the sound of the waves as a giant grin seized hold of his face. Still, there was something tight to his eyes. He was clearly glad to be home, but Aiden thought the man's tension remained palpable—like a disobedient child coming back to his parents to accept his punishment.

"Well," Jumper said, standing, as they were only six or seven hundred yards from shore.

"Must you?" Thun asked.

"Don't be jealous, big man. Of course I must, thank you very much, and we both know you would too if you could. Now," Jumper said, turning to Aiden and the others, "if you will excuse me, I have a pressing appointment with a bath, my very own bed, and perhaps a glass of aged Celtarian Canta." And with that, the man hoisted his pack and leapt into the air. The boat rocked a bit with his departure, but only slightly more than if he had dived into the dark water beneath them.

Aiden shook his head as he watched Jumper soar through the early morning air and land on the far awaiting shore. The sight of a man in near flight still sent a shock of excited energy down his spine.

"You have a wistful look in your eye, Master Aiden," Thun said.

"Can you blame him?" asked Rem.

"Yeah," said Lem, "that Jumper bloke said he had a bath, a bed, and wine waiting for him on the other side."

"And look at that," Rem continued. "He's on the other side just like that."

Thun smiled and offered Aiden a knowing wink. "Well, we'll all be on the other side soon enough, and I'd wager there'll be bath, bed, and wine enough for all. There may even be a decent meal at hand if we are willing to wait for breakfast to bless the tables."

Aiden offered a half-hearted smile in return and nodded, feeling his partially-healed face complain at the extra motion. The rest and food would be enough for now, but if he could learn to leap as Jumper did... Aiden could not force away the memory of Gaw's huge blade being thrown back by the raised hand of Aiden's sandy-haired savior, of Gaw himself yielding to the smaller man's will, of blades twisting of their own accord in the air. Nor could he forget his battle with the Swaar—his unaccounted-for strength and speed and his work with Thun on the stone doorway. He wanted to know more—needed to know more.

Sand engulfed the bottom of the bow of their longboat and Aiden's thoughts were not of the beauty of the island or of Holmsguard itself. *Semlie,* was all he could think, and of two men waiting in Oustenbasch for his unexpected return.

Thun did indeed take care of the watch from the harbor as he had promised Hammond. In a matter of minutes, the longboat was heading back for the far shore and Thun was leading the four of them up a slope toward the front gates of Holmsguard. From up close, the walls were even higher than Aiden had thought in the bay, and this was the lower of the two walls. As they entered the gate they had a long, shaded walk before they reached the main yard. The walls must have been two or three times thicker than any castle or palace Aiden had ever seen.

"'Impenetrable' is the word your mind is searching for," Thun said, acknowledging Aiden's awe. "Since our brotherhood took up residence here, hundreds of years ago, Holmsguard has never fallen, never been taken, never even been breached. Remember the stone in the canyon, my boy, then think of what years of work with many hands, many minds and souls, could do." The big man forced another wink before his mouth went tight with strain. It was entirely possible that Thun held some reservations about returning home. Then they were through the gateway tunnel and into the sunlight of the main courtyard. A large stable lay just to the right inside the courtyard and the sound of men at work within found chorus with the neighing of the horses themselves.

A blacksmith hammered at his anvil in a nearby building. Dogs barked in their kennels, and several men worked at a rather large vegetable garden. Everything was alive with movement as people raced to achieve their individual tasks, even at this early hour.

Something nibbled at Aiden's mind, something out of place or something missing. It took him the distance of half the courtyard to put his finger on what it was.

"They're all in black and gray, and that man there," he pointed to one of the garden workers, "he has the silver falcon brooch. Do you dress all your servants as yourselves?"

"Ha," Thun let out a great booming laugh and much of his stress seemed to drain away. "Well, yes and no, lad. We dress our servants as ourselves because we serve each other in the Mist Falcons. Each man has his own gifts. When a man is too proud to help his brother, he has lost a piece of what it means to steward the gift he holds. The man you point at is Cleos, and among other things, he is one of the best gardeners you could meet if you traveled all of the Nine Cities. The smith you heard at work on the anvil—his name is Tao, Heavy Hand. Any warrior would be hard-pressed to beat him in a fight, but Tao also forges better steel than any smithy in Perry. You will grow to understand if you stay with us for any amount of time, but for now know that above all else, we use our gifts to serve each other and not only our own purposes."

Aiden smiled and nodded, but grimaced inside. Thun's words struck a little close to an opposition of Aiden's own thoughts and motives.

A little further into the yard, they came upon a clashing of metal that forced Aiden's feet to set down roots. He had seen men spar before, even seen a warrior of some renown train against three opponents at once. He had whirled, blocked, and struck with the ferocity of a Delrethi Cobra, his attacks seeming to flow from his defense without pause or hesitation. That great warrior was as a boy with a wooden sword next to the men training before Aiden now.

He saw two men nearly as big as Thun circling each other, both wielding twin great axes. Then all at once, they met and the ground shook from their opposite blows as if the Thirteen Terrors were finally clawing their way back to the surface of the world from their long imprisonment by the Lord of the Twin Angels.

Not forty yards from these axe-wielding giants, two men fought with bow staffs, but the game was a bit more complicated than simple blocks and parries. Each man was leaping from ground to air in great arcs, occasionally changing direction mid-jump to fly right at or away from their opponent's flying staff.

As their small party moved through the courtyard of training Mist Falcons, Aiden caught occasional murmurs of "That's Jak Thunder Klapp," and "Thunder—is that really him?" Awe soaked the voices as Thunder was recognized. Some of the older men and women amongst the Mist Falcons nodded to Thun or even greeted him by name as Aiden's party moved through the small crowd, but many Falcons just stared or murmured in excitement at Thun's arrival.

"Thun's quite the celebrity around here," Willem whispered as they came to yet another small circle arena in which two men with long swords faced off. Aiden nodded his agreement. He supposed that Thun might be gone to all parts of the Nine Cities for long periods. It still seemed odd that so many people would look on his quiet return as if it were a spectacle. Aiden glanced over at Thun before returning his attention to the combatants in the training circle.

The two Falcons stood still as stone, and then all at once, they were at each other. Swords dashed this way and that in such a whir that Aiden could make out little but the sparks leaping from their repeated contact. He had never seen anyone move a blade so quickly or precisely, and to have two masters at it here...well, Aiden thought he should watch all day so as not to miss this opportunity. When Thun tried to move them along, a smile evident not only on his face but in his eyes as well, Aiden explained his desire to watch the masters.

Thun laughed heartily at that. "These two are in their third year here, and getting quite good to be sure, but masters—no, my boy, not masters. Be patient and you may yet see masters at their work."

And that was that. Thun guided them past the training yards and through a massive open gate leading into the main castle of Holmsguard. These walls were higher and thicker still, incredibly so.

Willem was shaking his head as they walked. "A fleet of a thousand ships would be hard-pressed to take this island," he said.

"Dandel the Corsair tried a hundred years ago," Thun said, "and he had nearly twice that many. It was a near thing. The lower yard was almost breached, but in the end, the might of the Mist Falcons prevailed."

"Better think twice before you take a bunch of boats to attack somebody who controls the wind," mused Rem.

"Not to mention strikes like lighting and shifts mountains at will," added Lem.

"There's definite benefits."

"I'd say," laughed Lem. "Especially in a fight."

The castle yard stretched out smaller than the lower yard, but far from small just the same. Another group trained here. These seemed to be playing a game of push with a ball lit on fire. How they controlled it remained a mystery to Aiden, but it was amazing nonetheless to watch as the opponents' arms moved this way and that in an attempt to push the fireball past each other into a waiting pail of water.

"Beginners," Thun said, turning to Aiden as they passed, "but they are getting better with some of the basics.

Aiden nodded again as if he knew anything about forcing a fireball past an opponent.

At last, they reached the castle itself, entering through huge oaken doors that stood open on great bronze hinges. It was only as he crossed the threshold into the main castle that Aiden realized—no one had checked their weapons. They were walking, fully armed, into the heart of the Mist Falcons, and no one batted a concerned eye in their direction. What if they were here to kill all the leaders of these mercenary kings—assassins forcing Thun to lead them here under threat of...of what?

Then full realization struck as surely as thunder follows lightning. The idea of the four of them coercing Thun to do anything through force was laughable. The big man would take them apart. He'd end them as easily as he would a pestering fly. They weren't sliding in because someone forgot to check their weapons. The simple truth was these Mist Falcons did not fear them, and it was more work than it was worth to disarm four men that would die so easily—armed or not.

Aiden let out something between a cough and a chuckle but walked on without mentioning his realization to the others. This place was daunting enough without having delusions of safety shattered.

A man approached dressed in the gray, wide-sleeved shirt of a sailor with a vest of black, emblazoned with a silver falcon. "Lord Klapp, you have returned to us at last," the man said before glancing at the faces of each man trailing behind Thun. "And where is Master Carnes? He is well, I hope."

"I'm sure Jumper is doing just fine, Nathaniel. You know him, though, hardly has the grace to say hello. You'll have to forgive him. My guess is, he found an easier perch further up and is already enjoying the comfort of a pillow or two." Thun smiled and Nathaniel returned his smile, showing that no offense was taken.

"Is the Council in session?"

"Yes m' lord. The rest of the lords have just convened following breakfast and are meeting in the Council chambers, not in the lounge."

"An audience?"

"Not that I know of, not unless you count yourselves, now. But then I didn't know you were returning today, so perhaps just a happy coincidence. I assume you remember the way."

Thun nodded. "Now, I have not been gone so long as that, Nate." He made a show of straightening his travel-stained shirt and cloak. "If you wouldn't mind preparing places for our four guests, good steward, I believe I will announce them."

"Of course, Lord Klapp," and with that, the steward moved to the far end of the room where he offered a few whispered commands to two men standing by an open door.

As Thun led their small party up a central stairway, Aiden caught his eye and raised his eyebrows in question. Thun looked at him, perplexed for a moment, but when Aiden glanced back at Nathaniel, the big man laughed.

"Yes, even old Nathaniel, a gray brother through and through. The man played steward for the Talessie family of Taalmor for many years. He saved my life during an expedition that claimed

Lord Talessie's own life. There was little enough for Nathaniel to return to, so I brought him home with me. He was accepted into the Mist Falcons shortly thereafter. Another stranger turned family." Jak "Thunder" Klapp smiled and it was clear enough he had nothing but warmth for him and the others.

Then something hard stole over his face and Thun said, "Now come; not all of my brothers are as pleased when I bring home new friends. Just the same, when you stand before them, you must speak only the truth to their questions. Can we agree on this, lads?"

"Oh, alright," Lem said, blandly.

"But you should know, we only have one agreement in us each day, and this will fill the quota," said Rem.

Thunder smiled again. "Fair enough, it's right this way." He pushed open a large set of double doors and ushered them through.

Beyond lay a wide room that fell away in a three-sided amphitheater. Down a long flight of steps lay a raised platform with a large, narrow, stone table at its center. Gathered around the table were the room's only inhabitants. Nearly a dozen men and two women, ranging from mid-thirties to upper seventies, sat encircling the table. Two chairs sat empty, leaving a gap in the otherwise encompassing oval. One or two attendants sat just behind each of the Mist Falcons at the table, creating an odd oblong ring to their appearance from above.

Aiden was surprised to find women sitting amongst what he assumed to be the Council of the Mist Falcons. He had seen a few women out in the yards but had assumed them to be group followers, servants, or maybe wives of some of the Falcons. Maybe not though. Thun had said that there were no formal servants—that they served each other. Was it really such a stretch to believe a woman could be a Mist Falcon, and if so, why would they not sit on the Council as well?

He tried his best to absorb his new revelation in stride and focus on the goings-on of the inner circle of the Mist Falcons. After all, how many people had ever gotten to stand where he was standing now, in the hall of the heroes of old? For all he knew, the Shadow Knight and the Emerald Blade had both walked down these very steps. A small grin tugged at the corners of his mouth despite his best efforts.

At the sound of the opening doors, several attendants glanced up, but the men and women at the table continued on without pause.

"And what of Nyrn?" an ebony-skinned man of perhaps fifty with close-cropped gray hair was asking. A faint accent played about his voice, but only slightly. *An islander,* Aiden thought, *from off the west coast.*

"Nyrn cares only for Nyrn," one of the oldest men at the table responded as Thun ushered them into a slow descent. "It has always been so and will always be so. Brothers, let us not make this more complicated than it already is. Nyrn will care nothing for this conflict one way or the other."

"But how will we know unless we ask?" responded the first man.

"And waste two months of envoys and pleasantries? No, please Skip, let us move past this."

The dark-skinned man, Skip apparently, hesitated a moment, grinding down on his teeth. Then releasing a sigh, he said, "Very well, I will not push the point, but do not blame me if we make few friends in Nyrn simply by ignoring them."

A man at the head of the table with a golden medallion around his neck nodded. "Very well. What other business?"

"Forgive me, Lord Commander," a thin, sallow-faced man said on the opposite side of the table from the one Thun led the companions down. "But I believe our long-lost brother has returned and brought with him the business of some stray dogs."

Aiden's eyes narrowed at that. He didn't know what he had expected exactly, but he was fairly certain he had just been called a stray dog—not the warm welcome he had hoped. He thought of Semlie, her blood coating his hands and the cobblestones. Aiden exhaled slowly through his nose. He had been treated like a stray before, and he would weather the abuse again if it brought him another step closer to possessing the power of his vengeance.

The substantial muscles in Thun's neck flexed for a moment. Apparently, Thun hadn't liked their welcome either, but when he spoke, it was apparent from his voice that a smile had found his lips even though Aiden couldn't see Thun's actual expression.

"It's good to see you as well, Jabren, and the rest of you brothers. It's good to be home for that matter."

A broad-shouldered man who had been facing away from them during their descent whirled at the sound of Thun's voice. "Jak," he bellowed as he rose from his seat and started for the stairs. "Jak, you old scoundrel, welcome back." The man was as wide as a tree trunk with a fierce, weather-beaten face beneath hair more gray than black, but there was true merriment in his voice and in his eyes.

"Bear," Thun rumbled as the two men embraced. Aiden felt small and insignificant next to these two giants. He was like a child waiting on the adults to move him along.

"It's good to see you as well, old man," Thun said as Bear released his grip and started to lead the way back to the table with a smile firmly planted on his face. Thun followed and soon stood behind one of the open chairs.

"Brother, please, come rejoin our Council. Your voice is ever welcome here," the Lord Commander said from the head of the table, his hand sliding once over his golden medallion.

"Thank you, Lord Commander Dellan," Thun said in more formal a tone than Aiden had heard him use before. "It is an honor to retake my Council seat and once again rejoin you." Aiden got the sense that this back-and-forth had been exchanged before and that it was more formality than necessity.

Thun reclaimed his seat before he spoke again. Not knowing what else to do, Aiden and the other surviving members of Boulder Pennant simply stood behind the big man's chair a few feet, trying not to feel like they were intruding.

"My lords, you will recall that I, along with Brother Tobin Carnes, left here nearly half a year ago in search of a hermit in the southern marshes. The man was rumored to possess both abilities and information the Mist Falcons might need."

"The man was also rumored to be a gray beard," the sallow-faced Jabren broke in. "Unless the hermit has learned the secret of age defiance or found a way to split himself into four men instead of just the one, I would say you and Jumper failed in your mission, Brother Klapp. Wouldn't you agree?" The man's tone dripped condescension. Aiden was half sure Thun would flip the table and tear this Jabren's throat out.

But all Thun did was exhale a breath through his nose and say, "How terribly observant of you, Jabren. No, none of the men standing behind me are the Hermit of Oxdale Marsh..."

"Well then, Brother Klapp..."

Thun's fist struck the stone table so swiftly and with such force, Aiden was shocked it didn't shatter. Jabren stopped talking, though he failed to shut his mouth all the way.

When Thun spoke, he did not raise his voice, but something dangerous laced his words all the same. "You may call me Thunder. You may call me Klapp or even Jak. If you must use the honorific you may call me *Lord* Klapp. Or maybe you have forgotten the circumstances propelling me to Lordship. I will be happy to remind you if you need the lesson. Now, perhaps the last year of sitting, scheming, offering little enough of service to the Falcons, has caused your brain to wither, so let me help you with your tasks over the next few minutes. Do not forget Taalmor, Jabren, for I have not. And do not interrupt me again or you and I will take a short trip out into the yard through a Challenge of Right and I will remind you why they named me Thunder."

Thun's gaze had not left Jabren's face for the entirety of his speech, and the man glared back but remained silent.

After a moment of thick tension, Thun dismissed Jabren's glare with a smile and returned his attention to the group as a whole.

"As I was saying, we went looking for the hermit, and after much searching—for the man had guarded his privacy dearly—we found him. I regret to tell you, The Hermit of Oxdale Marsh is dead. From best we could tell, he died as a result of one of his experiments. If you will allow me forbearance, I will hold the tale of it for once more pressing matters are resolved."

This last he said with a glance to the Lord Commander who nodded, apparently unconcerned by Thun's outburst at Jabren.

"Thank you," Thun said, offering a small nod of his own. "We were just finishing with the hermit when we felt the voice of an unsheathed Maker's Blade. It pulsed only for a moment and then went quiet. Still, remembering our mandate, Jumper and I left the hermit's almost at once, heading northwest toward Oustenbasch where, as best we could tell, the voice had pulsed." Everyone else in the room simply seemed to be accepting Thun's explanation of a Maker's Blade pulsing and such. In fact, they seemed enthralled by the discussion.

"We felt it here as well," Lord Skip said. "But it was faint and slow by the time it made its way here."

Thun nodded his acknowledgment before continuing. "We reasoned that if the blade had been drawn once, it almost certainly would be drawn again. We were sadly disappointed at the amount of time between the two draws, however, and our new Hand was well north of us in Perry by the time the second pulse came. So, after much fruitless searching through Oustenbasch and the surrounding country, we headed to Perry." Thun went on to tell of how he and Jumper had discovered the slaving house and from there made the connection with the Champions' Sands. A sharp intake of breath sounded from somewhere in the outer circle of attendants when he explained how Jumper had leapt into the middle of the square to pull the four Champions out from certain death.

"To be fair," Thun said, stroking a hand over his walrus mustache once, "Aiden had just proved himself to be a Maker's Hand by drawing the blade and deflecting a giant's sword strike. The blade pulsed and Jumper leapt in. We had planned on a more cautious entry, slipping in for a simple observe and extract, and took obvious precaution, but there was little else to be done. That is unless anyone here thinks it would have been best to allow the newly-found Maker's Hand to have been cleaved in two by the next two-handed blow of a three-hundred-pound man?" Thun allowed the statement to become a question, and let the question linger in the air above the table, inviting disagreement.

Aiden wondered if Thun was protecting Jumper as much as himself. It was after all Jumper who had made the judgment call to leap so dramatically into the heart of Perrian society and flaunt his power so egregiously.

No disagreement came. So, Thun continued his tale with their journey from Perry to Holmsguard. He told of the whispered rumors of Swaar activity and then of the canyon battle with the Swaar themselves.

"And when I struggled with crumbling the entry to the weapons cache, for there were strong Elementals at work already in the stone, Aiden here reached out by apparent instinct and battled alongside me as we crushed the entry." Thun paused, giving his words full time to set in the minds of his silent audience, for even Jabren was listening intently.

Then the big man turned to Aiden and said, "Alright, my friend, the time has come. Draw your blade."

Willem watched as Aiden drew his short sword without ceremony or flourish and handed it to Thun. The Council put it through all the same rigorous tests Thun and Jumper had done in that small cabin outside of Perry. All that and more they unleashed upon the blade as each Lord took his or her turn bending, heating, cooling, crushing, or striking it. One of the women went as far as a quarter of an hour of superheating and then freezing the area around the short sword. Willem felt the rush of air as the heat and cold intermediately pulsed—hot then cold, hot then cold. But when she moved aside and allowed the barrel-chested man Thun had called Bear to step over to the blade with a huge war hammer grasped in his hands, Willem thought this might actually do it. If anything could break this hero-story blade, this certainly would. He almost cringed as he watched the big man's huge arms, rippling with slabs of muscle, lift the war hammer high before ripping it down through the air, offering a deafening crack as it struck.

Well, that's that, Willem thought. *A broken blade.* What would they do with the four of them now? But when Bear reached down and picked up the short sword, it was completely unmarred.

The "crack" Willem had heard had been the stone of the floor beneath the blade. For a moment, he wondered if the other Lords would be angry with Bear, but without ever taking his eyes off of the blade in front of him, the older Lord swept a hand over the crack in an absent-minded fashion. The blemish in the stone vanished as surely as if it had never been there.

Still keeping his eyes on the blade, Bear then walked to the far wall and pressed the sword against it. In the space of a heartbeat, stone had flowed out of the wall like liquid in an attempt to wrap and grab Aiden's sword. Try as he might, however, the stone simply would not form around the blade, as if the steel itself was forcing back the stone, refusing its solidity. After another moment's effort, the man gave in and allowed the stone to flow back into the wall where it reclaimed its form as perfectly as the cracked floor had.

All told, Willem and the others stood in the Council chambers for the better part of two hours before every Lord had done their worst to the blade and still left it unscarred. They had even asked Aiden to re-sheath it so that each one of them could try to draw it just as Thun and Jumper had tried. The Council Lords had no better luck in this than the two of them had had in the cabin. Finally, Aiden had been allowed to slip the sword and sheath back onto his belt.

"Good enough for me," Bear rumbled when the blade had been returned. "If the lot of us can't break the thing, then it is what it is."

"Perhaps," Jabren said steepling his fingers while staring across the table past Thun and directly at Aiden with nothing but a winter's cold fury in his eyes. "But there are other tests one might perform—other ways to make sure this so-called Maker's Blade and the hand that wields it have not been tampered with by other...hmm...magical arts, if you will." The man was slippery as a fish in the stream but more dangerous than any stream fish had the right to be. Willem would have to remember that.

"By the heat and waves, Jabren," Skip nearly shouted in his melodic voice, "the blade has passed and if the boy can draw it, then he can wield it. That is the code. That is the law."

"Yes, Skip, I know the code," Jabren said in the voice of an understanding father to a child. "Still, better to be safe, better to know for sure than to let this pup slip in uncontested. No offense, Thunder, but if this boy has played you somehow, isn't it better to know for sure before he is set to the station of Maker's Hand?" He chuckled slightly at this as if the notion were ridiculous. No one joined in his laughter, but still, they stared at Aiden, uncertainty plain on their faces.

"Master Tohmen?" Lord Commander Dellan inquired, turning to the oldest man at the table. The Master's face was weathered, with blue veins standing out beneath his receding white hair. Tohmen seemed to consider, running a hand down his impressively thick beard that had been woven into three white braids with golden beads.

"The Code of Pelthos the Wise, First Master, Singer, and Poet," Tohmen began in the voice of a lecturing history scholar, "spoken in the trance of a waking flame to Kandar, Lion Slayer, the first Lord Commander of the Mist Falcons, saying, '*Behold, the darkness rises and flame can do but little to cast back the shadows. Hands will be drawn from the Falcons and they shall wield nine Blades forged by the Maker. Nine Blades for Nine Cities. Only the Hands may wield the Blades and no power of the earth, sky above, or depths of the sea will steal the strength from them. Blades of the Maker wielded by his Hands to be shield and light in the coming darkness.*'"

Finished, Master Tohmen reached forward, took his cup, and drank deeply of a sapphire wine that dripped down, leaving blue streaks in the old man's beard.

"And there you have my conundrum, brothers," Jabren whined, "for this boy is not of the Falcons. He comes here an outsider, a stranger to our order, our code, and our tradition. Are we to take him in so simply, he and his strays with him? Have we forgotten the other so quickly? Let them be tested—the Elementals Trial surely should prove little challenge if this boy is to be Hand."

Thun's fist smashed into the top of the table, and Jabren sat back into his chair, startled. "A Trial?" Thun growled in a low, ominous voice, allowing the word to linger in the air above the table. "An insult. This is a Maker's Blade, Jabren, and he is the Hand that wields it."

With obvious effort, he pulled his emotions back under control and then spoke to the group at large. "Surely, you see. Philosophizing aside, it is a Maker's Blade. Aiden wields it and thus is a Maker's Hand. It matters little that he wasn't one of us before. He is one of us now. Let us be grateful for what has been given and let us act with the grace that has been shown us."

All remained quiet in the hall for a moment before the Lord Commander spoke. "Perhaps your friends might wait outside for a moment while we deliberate, Lord Klapp." It was said with the utmost courtesy, but Willem could tell from Thun's tightening muscles the man felt as if he had just been slapped.

Silently, Thun stood and gathered the four of them, leading them to the top of the stair and out into the corridor once again. The steward Nathaniel waited there for them.

"Nathaniel will show you to your rooms," Thun croaked, strain still obvious in his voice. "I clearly have some work to do with the Council, but I will come to you when I can. Please, make yourselves at home, and I will resolve these misgivings shortly." He turned to go back into the Council chambers but then hesitated. Looking over his shoulder he said, "Perhaps it would be best for you to remain in the room Nathaniel takes you to, just until I come to fetch you." He winked at them before leaving, but even that felt forced.

So the four of them were taken to a suite of rooms, three flights of stairs up. Nathaniel had made sure a plentiful meal was waiting for them as well as hot baths, which was a true treat after their time on the road. Just the same, Willem felt like a prisoner all over again. Distractions or no—comfort or no—he couldn't leave this room.

It took Thun several hours to arrive, and the man looked worn and tired when he sat down at the big table with the remainder of their meal still strewn across it.

"It's to be a Trial," he told them. "All four of you. The Elementals Trial can be undertaken alone, but few are ever successful that way. Dregs and drought, Jabren wanted you tested individually, of course, but in that, at least the Council heard reason."

Thun sighed, shaking his head. "Still lads, you don't have to. The Trial I mean. You aren't slaves anymore, not here. I will see you put back to the mainland with provisions and horses. You will not starve and there is always work in the world for a man who would seek it. Wait a couple days to decide, though. Tomorrow you'll have more of an official tour, and the day after, some training will start. That will only be some physical tests and strengthening, though. You can leave at any point, but give it a full think through, and we'll talk further."

The four of them each nodded their agreement and Thun gave a tiny, tired smile beneath his big mustache.

"Good," Thun said. "I'll go then. I have work to do that will take me through the next few days, but I will be back to talk with you soon enough. Nathaniel will see you through a tour and make sure a trainer is sent to you. Sleep well, lads." With that, he left, and Willem was sure none of the rest of them had any better idea of what the Elementals Trial was than he did.

Still, he said he'd give it two days and he would. So he found an overstuffed chair and cuddled up with his guitar and what was left of a bottle of wine. No more strange incidences leapt from Willem's music, the room staying firmly planted where it was around him as he played into the night.

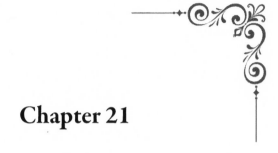

Chapter 21

...and I will not let him slip back into his shadows again.

"What is this, Keeper?" Tako whispered. "Where are we?" Staring at the stone forms of Josimmian and the Nameless Lord of Darkness, he already knew where they were—where they had to be—but he needed the Keeper to talk. He needed the clarification and the anchoring of another person's voice.

The Keeper leaned against a rounded wall, arms crossed, staring at Tako, an intense gleam in his beady eyes. "You see it, don't you?" the Keeper said. "You feel it, of course, everyone feels it, but you can actually *see* it—their forms mixed, tangled for all of eternity."

Tako took a backward step toward the archway, growing suddenly horrified. "What are we doing in this tomb, Keeper? How are we even here? They died, buried in rock a thousand years ago."

"Yes they did, but I told you time is ever-flowing. In truth, stories rarely end. Characters die off. Some protagonists and antagonists carry on, but more are extinguished and replaced. And always the grander story of time plays out. Don't be so prideful as to think your life is about you, Wolf Rider.

"After Josimmian's victory through his sacrifice and after the majority of the remaining demons had been killed or driven off, a society was formed. Knights of the Shield, they called themselves, or simply, the Shield. A bit grandiose, perhaps, but those days were filled with such, as hope bled away the nightmare humans had lived in for an age. In any case, the Knights of the Shield began a search for Josimmian's resting place and the resting place of the shield that had given him his power and title. You see, the demons were defeated, but there were plenty of other dangers now to be faced. And perhaps above that there was the power. The mere idea of the strength, influence, and power one could possess in the new world while wielding the Shield of Ammereth could be intoxicating.

"For whatever reason and for their own reasons, altruistic or self-serving, the men and women of the Knights of the Shield came together. These were some of the greatest minds and most driven individuals of their day. Together they delved deep beneath Rendruse and after much toil, they found this place, this preservation of a fallen age."

The Keeper made a circuit of the room until he stood on the opposite side of the statuesque forms. "Come here, Rider. This is for your eyes to see." Bolstering his courage, Tako forced his feet to make the same circuit around to the far side, all the time knowing that each step was one more step away from the archway.

Where the Keeper stood, a stone hand, a man's petrified hand, jutted out from the rest of the pile. It lay open but cupped as if to offer something. The hand held nothing, though, it's only offering air. A flattened stone grew next to the hand. Scratches lay across its surface in some language that Tako couldn't read.

"And now we come to the point," the Keeper began and then read:

"As dark as night and bright as liquid starlight,
Take and keep and pass along this stone of simple might
Your lives are short. To dust you'll sleep
Before he climbs to the Rendruse Keep.
When sour stars distill and fail
And darkness glides into prevail,

Guard tight the secret that you keep
Beneath the mountain of Gleneth's Sweep.
Now master keys and watch the time,
For nigh draws 'til Wolf Rider's climb.
Wielding axe and bearing stone
He'll come, the starlight to atone."

The Keeper looked up at Tako, a tiny smile playing about his lips. "And here you are," he said quietly, as much to himself as to Tako. "That hand," he gestured at the stone hand next to the plaque, "held a prize of immense value—immense value and immense power. Now, have you been following, Wolf Rider? My time is at a close, my task nearly completed. Soon, I will rest beneath the stone with my brethren, once again inside time but finally beyond its reach. But first I must be sure you understand. Tell me, Ren Tako, have you grasped it? What did the hand hold?"

Tako looked at the Keeper, their eyes fencing out a great contest of wills. At last, he spoke. "You were not always here," he said to the impish man. "You were one of the Knights of the Shield. And this plaque," he pointed at the scratched writing with one strong finger, "this stone mortuary and tomb are your mandates. You were one of the first. Were you the greatest of those who delved here or the least, that you would have this assignment?"

A tiny smile again split the Keeper's lips. "I am the Keeper, Master of Keys and Watcher of Time. But you see much, for I was not always as I am now. And soon I will pass from this blessing and this curse. Still, tell me, Tako—what lay in that hand?"

The Keeper's glare flared so intensely that Tako hesitated. But slowly he raised his fist, and on his finger rested a ring, and on that ring gleamed a fiery stone. When the stone was level with the open petrified palm, it flared a blinding white light that extinguished the room for a moment. As the light dimmed, Tako's vision cleared just in time to see the Keeper, fading into a misty nothing, a true smile brightening his face to the last.

"Keeper? Keeper!" Tako shouted, but there was no reply—no answering quip, no veiled insult. The Keeper was simply gone, faded, evaporated.

Tako stared at the spot where the little man had been. Then, slowly, his gaze slid back to the stone hand. It took him a moment to see the change, but somehow, with the discovery of this tomb and now with the disappearance of his only guide in this strange, timeless place, he had run out of shock.

A hole had grown in the palm of the outstretched hand. It wasn't a large hole, no bigger than a finger, no bigger than a small stone. Tako's gaze fell from the stone hand to his own fist, still upraised, with the ring glittering on his finger. "As dark as night and bright as liquid starlight," he recited, now only to himself. And with nothing else said, he reached out his curled fist and pressed the precious stone of his ring into the newly-found hole of the waiting hand.

The world sparked and spun as Tako was whirled off his feet and out of his control.

"Darkness grows," he heard a whispering voice boom. Then silence. "Defend the weak," the voice again rang out, gentle and yet firm as a bell toll.

"Defend the weak," he heard himself repeat.

"Cast off the oppressor," the voice spoke again, rich and true.

"Cast off the oppressor," Tako responded, his own voice sounding small and insignificant against the grander cacophony of the whisper.

"Shield the Light," the voice rose in benediction.

"Shield the Light," he repeated.

The world slowed. Tako again found himself standing alone in the tomb of Josimmian and the Nameless. Glinting in the soft light of the chamber, a round shield grew where the ring had once held only a stone. The shield was not all; Tako's entire body shimmered in armor as tight and light as his skin, casting off tiny dancing lights like those that had so entranced him on the path to this chamber. Tako laughed. He didn't know the next step, didn't know the way out of here, but he couldn't help himself. This was the Shield of Ammereth—he was the Shield of Ammereth. So, he laughed. He laughed, and he laughed, and he laughed.

Chapter 22

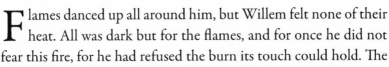

Trace the heat and ride the waves, my friend.

Flames danced up all around him, but Willem felt none of their heat. All was dark but for the flames, and for once he did not fear this fire, for he had refused the burn its touch could hold. The flames swirled around him then, through him and within him. The exhilaration swarmed up his veins as he felt the fire consume him and yet bend to his will.

But something was wrong. The flames began to bore down on him—through him, pulling him against his will. *I've lost the music,* he thought, knowing it was true but not knowing why or even what tune he should be holding to. The heat grew. Willem screamed as he felt himself start to cook from both inside and out. This was it: the promised death for the unwary.

He woke just as the fire flared too hot to live through. His blankets were tangled around him in gagging, twisted bondage, and sweat coated him in a thin, glistening sheen. Willem kicked at the blankets, desperate to be free of their groping hold. The cold air of morning was so refreshing as he stood that he shivered and smiled despite the nightmare of the flames. Willem stretched his aching body, trying not to grimace at the twinge of his muscles and knowing that the second day of training would probably be harder than the first.

Aiden had drawn his Maker's Blade three days ago now at the prompting of the Council of Lords. That had of course been followed by Thun informing them that they would be put to an Elementals trial, whatever that was.

Nathaniel had come for Willem, Aiden, and the twins the day after their audience before the Lords. Following a late brunch, he offered, "If it would please the young masters, Lord Thunder has instructed me to provide you with a tour."

The old steward had proved himself more than competent as a guide around Holmsguard. He led them through many of the upper floors of the main, enormous structure, pointing out offices and residence wings. Then he brought them up a winding stairway that ended on a flat rooftop, open to the sky. "The astronomy tower," Nathaniel announced. "At night it offers an unrivaled view of the stars and twin moons in their promenade through the sky. Even now, I believe you will find it offers a rather astounding view of the surrounding area."

Looking around, Willem had seen that Nathaniel had not overstated in the least. To the south, he could just make out the town of North Port across the waves. To the North, those same waves lapped out for a forever span. Drawing his eye back to Castle Isle, he could see the minuscule forms of Mist Falcons on the training yards below. Beyond the great walls of Holmsguard, spread a landscape of trees and hills, shaded in greens of every hue. All in all, the view was breathtaking.

From there, Nathaniel had led them down into some kind of underground bunker. A dozen men and women occupied the space, intent upon whatever it was they were working on. "Welcome to Research and Development, young masters," Nathaniel had said, "or as most call it, the Lab. Inside this hall and a few others like it around the complex, the Mist Falcons create the scientific wonders that have been a piece of our calling card for years. Cannons and muskets, for instance, were developed within these walls."

As if on cue, one of the Falcons working in the Lab, a squat, thick-set man with a dark complexion, hurled a small metal ball that he had been working on to the far end of the chamber where it exploded in a massive bang that shook the tables and chairs. The force of the blast threatened to knock Willem from his feet. Immediately, two Falcons standing near the squat man who had thrown the ball raised their hands, ushering in wind from somewhere. The wind sent the smoke created from the blast racing up and through a vent in the ceiling, apparently designed for just this purpose.

"Wow," one of the twins muttered from behind Willem.

"Precisely," Nathaniel agreed. He had led them on a short circuit of the rest of the room where Willem had seen glimpses of a handful of different projects. One group had a fire coming from a tube, boiling a pink-colored liquid in a glass jar above it. Another group was performing some kind of metal casting with a shiny liquid that formed perfectly around its subject, a leather gauntlet, and then released into a neatly folded sheet.

Willem had a hard time guessing at the purpose of most of the projects going on in the room, much less at the means of the research. In several cases, Elementalogy was obviously at use in the creation of whatever research was being done, but Willem found the workings of the Elementals just as elusive as the research being performed.

Finally, Nathaniel had led them through the training yards and then back to their chambers. After seeing to a supper being brought up to them, he had bid them to get a good night's sleep.

The following morning Nathaniel had shown up with breakfast—early this time. A few minutes later, as Thun had promised, he returned, ushering in a man named Zekkel who was to be their trainer. Zekkel seemed a hard man, tall and thin, but muscular. A pair of thin swords crossed his back and a third, shorter sword lay sheathed at his hip. Zekkel seemed neither pleased nor displeased to be there, working with them, but when training started, Willem had felt punished all the same.

Zekkel had led them down to a different training yard than the one they had walked through on their way into Holmsguard. This yard was laid out as an obstacle course with ropes and structures to climb or slide beneath strewn across the dirt and patchy grass.

Willem found himself grateful for the sheer amount of physical training the Champion Sands—and then travel mixed with battle—had required of him because, over the next several hours, their new trainer put them through a horrendous amount of work. They had been set to complex climbs up rope ladders, cliffs of rock, and a ridiculous metal rod that Willem had to snap up and into groove after groove in order to gain enough height to reach the next platform. They were forced to run through obstacles, which they soon learned moved to intercept their paths forcing them to lurch and spin to avoid collision. At several points, Willem had been certain the twins were going to walk out, but they rallied each time and moved on to the next exercise with Aiden and Willem.

By the time the sun had climbed to noon, Willem was ready to drop. Zekkel gave them a brief break along with a small meal of nuts, fruit, cheese, and wine so watered it was barely a light pink, much less red. The trainer wasn't done with them yet though. After they ate, he led them on a short hike out through a far gate of the castle and to the sea. They spent the next few hours leaping off of platforms and simply swimming long stretches of buoyed course.

When the end of their day's training had finally come, the four of them had been so exhausted that they ate their meal in silence, washed briefly in the baths and all found their beds early.

Those few days were behind them, and now that Willem was out of bed and thinking on what might lay ahead for this day, he wasn't entirely sure he wanted to be out of bed at all. Still, awake was awake, and he had never been much good at going back to bed after stretching and fully waking up.

Wandering to the main room, Willem found Thun already sitting at a table laid out for breakfast. The big Mist Falcon held a mug with something steaming inside in one hand and absently pulled at his mustache with the other.

When Thun saw Willem, he offered him a small nod and a tired smile. "Morning time generally ends when the sun reaches its peak in the sky, or so I've heard. I thought you four might end up missing it altogether." Willem bent to look further out the window and saw that the morning may be well underway, but he was still shy of noon by a solid two or three hours.

"Just made it," Willem said, sliding out a chair and sitting across from the big man. "Or at least I did. I can't speak for the other three." Filling a plate full of eggs and lathering a roll with honey butter, he added, "I can't blame them either. Zekkel put us through the twice cursed ringer yesterday. Even with all we've done in the last few months, I can barely move today. I hurt everywhere."

Thun smiled a little bigger smile. "That was only the first day, Will."

"That's what I'm afraid of," Aiden said appearing in the doorway, stifling a yawn behind his hand. Shortly after Aiden joined them at the table, the twins moved into the main room, walking stiffly and complaining as if the world might end.

"This just isn't how life is supposed to be for a simple thief, mate" Rem whined.

"We never asked the world for much—just a little bit here and a little bit there," Lem added. "But by Sansol's left hand, we got more than we wanted from that string bean yesterday. What'd you give us to him for anyway?"

"Zekkel was simply doing his job, and a job that I could not have enforced because you know me too well and would probably have found a way to weasel out of the last hour or something. Even if you didn't, people would assume I had gone easy on you, since I brought you here and all. But the first day is always the hardest, or at least the most purposefully hard, from the physical aspect. You see, many men cannot force their bodies through pain. Call it weakness if you like, but they simply shut down when forced into a situation beyond them. Mist Falcons are forced beyond their abilities and endurance regularly so we can't allow a brother to join that can't master their strength to push through."

"So it was a test," Willem stated rather than asked.

"Of a sort, yes. And you will be happy to know you all passed. Not one of you broke. The twins complained a bit I'm sure, but then nothing would keep them from their moaning on a sunshiny picnic—there'd be trundle bugs buzzing or those little black ones that sting, so that can hardly be helped." Thun smiled and took a sip from his steaming mug. "So, yes you all passed this first test, which brings us to our next—the Elementals Trial. There are three ways to enter into the brotherhood of the Mist Falcons, three ways to claim one's seat inside Holmsguard. The first is Trial by Battle, the second, Trial of Lord, and lastly is the Elementals Trial.

"Trial by Battle is perhaps the simplest of the three, and though it is not used very often now, it was once much more common. In this trial, an initiate hopeful presents himself at the front gate, what is known as the Poet's Gate for future reference, and calls out their name with a challenge for a Trial by Battle. This is to say, an invitation for a one-on-one battle with a brother or sister of the Mist Falcons. The catch is, and this is probably a big part of why few try this route, the challenger does not choose his opponent. It is left to the Falcons to decide on their Champion. This is for obvious reasons. Though every man and woman of the Falcons is valuable beyond measure, not all are great warriors. You could not, say, present yourself at the gate and demand a trial by battle with old Nathaniel. Though the steward is trained and may even fare well against many attackers, his primary strength is not in battle. So, why trade him for some fourth son of an up-jumped count or baron?

"In the handful of times I have seen a challenger attempt a Trial by Battle, it has always ended swiftly and badly for the would-be Falcon. I'm sure you can understand why. Would any of you really want to fight me, or even one of the trainees you saw in the yard on our way in? No, I doubt it. Still, there have been plenty of cases, well, I shouldn't say plenty, but a few notable ones who have joined us like this throughout our history. Traey, the Giant Slayer, for one, and Gento, who men called Silent, for another. He had to have a companion call out his name and challenge for him since he swore himself to silence. You can imagine this caused quite the stir since he hadn't issued the challenge from his own lips, but that's beside the point.

"Anyway, that is Trial by Battle. You challenge. You fight. You win, and you're in. But usually, you lose instead."

Thun exhaled, blowing his mustache out, then tested his mug with another sip and, deciding it was ready, took a longer drink. "That brings us to the Trial of Lord. There is nothing an individual can do to earn entry through this trial on their own, that is apart from impressing one of the ruling Lords. Including the Lord Commander, there are thirteen Lords of Holmsguard and the Mist Falcons at any given time. A possible initiate must be sponsored by at least one Lord and approved by a two-thirds majority, which comes to nine votes in assent or eight if the Lord Commander is among the yea votes. Some of the thirteen Lords have no interest in adding members to our brotherhood, which shrinks the possibility of an individual being found, considered, and sponsored, much less approved.

"Just the same, the Trial of Lord is the most common way to gain entry as a Mist Falcon."

Taking another drink, Thun looked at the four men sitting around the table. For once, not even the twins had some clever comment to insert. They all waited, knowing the third Trial held the bearing on their lives.

"By the White Stone, lads, I had planned, hoped, and assumed we would be dealing with a simple Trial of Lord, but Jabren has always been sly and he played the game too well. Before I even realized the dice were rolled, that path had been stolen from beneath our boots.

"So here we are, and an Elementals Trial lies before us. It makes no matter that Aiden has already proven himself to be a Maker's Hand. Jabren has stirred his cup and squelched the Council's hope with fear from the past. They're afraid it will happen again, by heat and waves, and so we are left with the most dangerous of the Trials."

Willem considered breaking in there, wondering what past fear Thun was talking about, but the big man had hesitated when he said that last, and Willem decided to wait for now.

"Centuries ago," Thun went on, "in the early days of the Falcons, a common belief gripped our body of Mist Falcons—the belief that only the Elementals could choose a Falcon, or at least a true Falcon. This was propagated by a man named Roe, who followed in succession from Pentalanius Stone Finder and Pelthos the Wise, as First Master and Poet of Holmsguard. Master Roe had undergone the Elementals Trial and emerged triumphant to gain entry into the Mist Falcons, so his view was understandable, if flawed.

"You know already that much of the *magic* the Mist Falcons are acclaimed to have is, in actuality, a practice in the art of Elementalogy. There are dozens of ways that the use of Elementals can be combined—dozens of dialects, if you will. But there are only six main Elemental practices: Stone, Heat, Wind, Steel, Water, and Wood." These last Thun ticked off on his fingers as he spoke.

"Every Mist Falcon has at least some ability in at least one of the Elemental studies, but not all are gifted in the same way or to the same extent. Some are gifted only a very little in one Elemental. For instance, old Nathaniel can manipulate heat, but only in small ways and when the energy of heat is at a high point. He could relight a fire from partially cooled embers or coax a fire into life a little faster than it might have taken by itself, but that is about the extent of his abilities. This makes him no less a Falcon, so don't misunderstand me. I'm just telling you how it works. Some are Poets and some are Warriors, but all are needed and valuable regardless of what Master Roe thought hundreds of years ago or what that sniveling Jabren thinks today."

Thun tightened his grip around his mug and the twins used the moment to jump in. "So, not to interrupt your hatred of this Jabren fellow, mate," Rem started.

"But you keep talking about Poets," Lem followed.

"And somehow, we were thinking maybe you weren't talking about the ink-fingered Nettle who would stand on a barstool at the Vacant Oak after having one too many and offer a verse to the room at large."

"Ah, no, I'm not," Thun said. "The title of Poet has nothing to do with the writer of verse save for the concept of a learned man. Perhaps, your friend, Nettle aside." He smiled.

"A Poet of the Mist Falcons holds ability in all six Elemental disciplines. Now, these may vary in strength and for the most part, they are not overly strong in any one line of study. Warriors stride the opposite line of Elemental studies. They are strong, uncommonly so, in a single Elemental but often possess little other ability in the art. There are even a few Twin Warriors, which means a Falcon has strong abilities in two of the six, but there are only a few of these in the history of our order and only three living Falcons can claim this title.

"Now, I'm just a Ranger, lads. I'm no Master and no Poet—no true teacher of the art, so I don't know everything there is to know about every Elemental, but I have been doing this for quite some time. I think I can give you a quick overview and tell you something of each at any rate so you can have an idea of what to expect. Stone, as I'm sure you have guessed, is my discipline. I'm a Stone Warrior. I've also got a light dusting of Steel and Wood, but barely enough to be of any use.

"Stone Elementalogy deals with the earth and the rock under our feet. More accurately, it deals with the manipulation of this stone. All Elementalogy for that matter is the manipulation and use of the Elementals in the world around us. Heat is the manipulation of temperature, usually through flame. Wind—well, you've seen what Jumper can do. I can't describe it better than that. Steel is the use of all metals, its name aside. Some of the best swordsmen in the world dwell within these walls and that is in no small part due to their Elemental art of Steel. Water—now, Water is tricky, but it deals with movement and sense, buoyancy and weight. You'll learn more as we go, but for now, understand that the Water Elemental deals with far more than calling up a cold draft on a hot day. That brings us to Wood, which lives inside the world of forest and trees, manipulating things that grow or once grew.

"And that's that." Thun set down his now-empty mug and dusted off his hands as if he had finished some grueling task.

"What about the Trial?" Willem asked. "The Elementals Trial that we've been so kindly signed up for?"

Thun sucked on his teeth before exhaling, blowing out his mustache in his usual nervous twitch. "In an Elementals Trial, a potential initiate, or in some instances, as in yours, a group of potentials, are led to the Crags of Telsair. There they are lowered down into the cavernous network beneath this island where wild Elementals run unbound and dangerous. At times one can feel the ground shake beneath the Crags, and the wind will screech up through the entry with such ferocity that it can knock a person from their feet. A man will descend a potential. If he rises back to the surface alive, he will be an initiate. It's that simple...or at least the concept is.

"I say none of this to scare you. But you lads need to know what you're up against if you want to continue down this path. The fatality rate of the Elementals Trial is over eighty percent. Brave men and women, fighters with years of battle experience, have gone down and never come out again. Sometimes they just vanish. At others, you can hear the screaming from above. The simple fact is, it is impossible for anyone to go down into the pits beneath the Crags and survive without the art of Elementalogy as his tool, weapon, guide, and friend."

"But we can't do the things you do," Rem protested.

"Well, maybe Aiden can, but the rest of us...we'll be swallowed in darkness faster than a rat's fart in a cellar," Lem said.

"And we're not huge fans of the disappearing and even less so of the screaming bit," his brother followed in their usual back-and-forth.

Willem remained silent, his fingers aching for his guitar and his thoughts drawn inexplicably to the night at the campfire.

Thun was nodding profusely, and he raised his hands, stealing Willem's attention back. "Yes, yes. I know you can't control the art yet. But remember what I told you, most people can control the Elementals in some fashion. We humans are linked to them some-how—most just don't realize it or have such a small link that it is quite nearly absent. At any rate, boys, here on Castle Isle control-ling the Elementals is easier than anywhere in the Nine Cites or anywhere else that we know. The Elementals are so thick, you see, so strong—it's easier to grab hold. And there's training to be had, fine training by people far more skilled at teaching than I am. If you lads accept the invitation to Trial, you'll be given a full moons' turn of the best training the Mist Falcons can offer newcomers."

Again he paused and ran a nervous hand over his large mustache. "But—and of course there's a 'but'—if you accept the invitation, if you say you'll go beneath the Crags of Telsair, then you're locked in. Once the Falcons begin training you in the art of Elementalogy, you go into the pits. If you come out, you're a Falcon. If not, well.... This is important, though; there are no cold feet, no last-minute jitters. If you say yes and then run, we'll hunt you. The Mist Falcons allow no man, woman, or child to steal our secrets and leave. I know this sounds harsh, but this is why you need to think carefully. If you run after starting, the Falcons will kill you."

Chapter 23

Know that I have left the item we discussed.

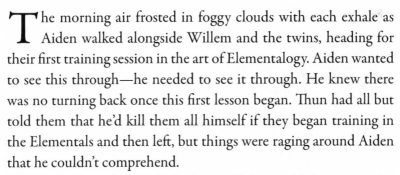

The morning air frosted in foggy clouds with each exhale as Aiden walked alongside Willem and the twins, heading for their first training session in the art of Elementalogy. Aiden wanted to see this through—he needed to see it through. He knew there was no turning back once this first lesson began. Thun had all but told them that he'd kill them all himself if they began training in the Elementals and then left, but things were raging around Aiden that he couldn't comprehend.

He didn't understand why he could draw a blade no one else could or how he had leapt a superhuman distance to kill the Swaar. He didn't know why he had heard and understood the stones in that canyon with Thun or why he could hear the cobbles whispering under his feet even now. But he needed to know. Power played at his fingertips, coming close before darting away. Aiden longed to grasp it.

The memory of Semlie drifted unbidden to the forefront of his waking thoughts. He could still see her easy smile, but even more vividly, he could see the bald man's knife and the blood blossoming from around Semlie's sprawled body. He could see the stupid grin spread across Branke's face just as quickly, and fresh rage boiled up inside Aiden.

Since his father's death, Aiden had lived his whole life in the shadows, dancing from one to the next, scavenging what he could and selling it to whoever would buy before running for cover again. No one could hurt you in a solitary life, but Aiden was tired of hiding from people. He was tired of being afraid. He would learn all he could from the Falcons and then Branke and his leash-holding Baron would learn what real fear could be.

Offering yet another long, misty exhale, Aiden tried to calm himself. Training would be of no use if he didn't clear his mind.

He still couldn't understand why the others were going along with this. The probability of death clung to the fairly high range. "You know, you don't have to do this," he said for probably the hundredth time.

"'Course we do," Lem laughed. "Didn't you have any of that onion and meat pie Old Nate brought up last night? Mmm, best thing I ever tasted."

"Yeah," Rem chimed in. "If you think we are going to miss out on one single morsel that comes out of that kitchen for us, mate, then you've lost a bit of that wit of yours." Rem winked at him before diving into a discussion with Lem on the variety of beers, ciders, and wines the two of them had sampled in some out-of-the-way cellar the night before.

The four of them walked in silence for a few strides. Then Willem said in a low, whispery voice, "We're not going to leave you, Aiden. That blade of yours and whatever it makes you is the only reason we're still alive anyway. You have to see this through—we all see that, and Antice can take us before we let you walk into this Trial alone."

Aiden opened his mouth to argue, but Willem continued before he could phrase a rebuttal. "Besides, the rest of us may have questions we want answered as well." Aiden raised an eyebrow at this and would have questioned him further, but at that moment they rounded a corner to find a short woman standing, hands on hips. Dark hair fell gracefully partway down her back and her eyes danced with a playful light, but a stern expression held her lips tight.

"Good, you're here," she said. "We have a lot to cover and very little time to cover it. Tomorrow, please arrive with the sun if you hold any desire to remain alive past the next month."

Taken aback, the four of them simply nodded their agreement. "Good." The woman smiled and realization struck home for Aiden. He knew this woman. He knew that smile.

"You," Aiden said.

"Me," the woman agreed.

"But you were in Perry, at the auction I mean. You bid on me at the slaver's auction." He didn't know if he meant this as an accusation or a statement, but there it was.

"I was, I was, and I did," the woman agreed again. "To be honest, I wish I'd bid another eagle or two now that I know more about you, but there's rarely enough time in selecting a purchase to truly get to know the merchandise." Again, she offered her impish smile and Aiden found it hard to decide if he liked the woman or not.

"But here we are, and I'll be training you for the next few weeks. Oh, and by the way, if at any point during our time together you wish to refer to me as something more than the ever-charming '*you*,' then you may call me Threll."

With that, Threll turned and marched more than walked through an archway and onto the training field. Not knowing if this first interaction had already been a colossal failure or not, Aiden led the way after her.

The shadows lay sprawled over the wide grassy area, high castle walls refusing entry to the rising sun's rays. Frosty grass crunched beneath each step of their little party, and the air seemed colder on the field as a gentle breeze sought any exposed skin to caress with chilly fingers.

Threll stopped them in the center of the training grounds at a small section of paved stones surrounded by grass. A few small stands of training weapons waited absently for combatants, but besides those, only the five of them were present and the large field seemed ominously absent of life, hollow and discarded in the cool morning air. She turned to Aiden and the others, looking at each for a moment before speaking.

"Well, you're all here, and I understand that Thun has already talked to you about ramifications and such. So I should be able to assume you all know—or at least think you know—what you're getting into. Still, a lot is riding on this for you, so I'll give you one last chance to walk away. This is the line in the sand, boys—the moment of no return. The probability is that you will all die in a few weeks if you stay. If you are here through coercion, or you fear loss of face if you turn away, understand it is your life you are gambling. The Crags give no quarter and show no mercy. You go down the Crags, then you win or you die. Last chance. Supplies and a boat are waiting to take you to the mainland. Anyone feel like putting this nonsense behind you and taking a little trip back into life?"

She waited, and Aiden gritted his teeth, sure the other three would leave now for certain. Everyone always left, and in this instance, he couldn't blame them one bit. The moment passed though, and all four of them remained standing in front of Threll. She offered her impish smile again and said, "Okay then. Let's get started."

Threll led them further across the field to where an old stone building stood, aged but no less solid for that fact. A thick stone door stood sentinel, denying any who would enter. Here she stopped.

"Look around you." Threll said. "If you have eyes to see and ears to hear, you can perceive the art of Elementalogy all around you. The door is locked. How would you force entry if you needed to?"

Aiden and the others hesitated, but when she raised one thin eyebrow, Aiden knew their first test was upon them. Moving to the door, he tried the huge latch; not only was the door locked, but the latch wouldn't so much as jiggle. Willem pushed against the door. Then they both did. The bigger man went as far as to draw his sword and strike the latch, but the door rewarded him only with an unmoving clank and jarring arms.

At this point, the twins slipped in. "Thieves, remember," Rem said with a smile as Lem slipped a lock pick set out from somewhere and began to work the lock. Soon Rem's smile faded, though, and he replaced his brother at the lock, twisting this pick here, replacing that one there. No matter how he twisted and fiddled, however, nothing seemed to work. Finally, with a huff, Lem grabbed up his picks and forced them unceremoniously back into their small kit.

With nothing else said, the four of them looked up at Threll, who offered another impish smile. "Eyes and ears, gentlemen." Her eyes unfocused for a moment, and then the wind came up—not a gentle breeze strolling across the lawn, but a roaring lion of a wind that staggered the four men as it buffeted against them.

The wind lifted Threll off the ground and several feet into the air. There she snatched a wooden bow staff from where the gale carried it as easily as a leaf. Still in the air, she twisted the thick wood several times until it formed a multilayered, perfect circle. Within a heartbeat, the wood burst into fire while Threll still held it tightly in one fist. The fire grew from campfire orange to white as snow. A look of supreme concentration etched onto her face, she hurled the fiery ring at the door. It encircled the latch, slowly boring through the door. The stone seemed to absorb the blaze, accepting it as an old friend.

Threll landed softly back on the ground as the wind ebbed and ceased. Before them, the door swung lazily in on what must have been well-oiled hinges inside. Now that it was open, Aiden could see that the stone of the door was at least eight inches thick, and a wide hole now gaped where the latch used to be.

"The Elementals are a Mist Falcon's greatest ally and support," Threll said in a quiet voice that still seemed to carry in the sudden silence left in the roaring wind's wake. "Our training, of course, goes far beyond just the art. We train diligently in marksmanship, swordplay, and hand-to-hand combat, along with numerous less-battle-focused disciplines. But," and here she held up one finger as if to forestall argument as she looked around at each of them, "Elementalogy is always the heart, the core of our study. It compels us, surrounds us, and sets us apart.

"An impenetrable door stands before you, or at least impenetrable by anything less than a battering ram. The stone is reinforced with steel rods and plating, and Elementals have been set to strengthen the rock. The latch is dipped in a jeweled alloy, and Steel Elementals offer a rotating lock to counteract anyone trying to pick it. You could have taken turns beating at it with war hammers for hours—you would go away sweaty and sore, but there the door would stand, firm and resolute."

Again she looked at them with her silent, impish smile playing about her lips. "So, how did a little thing like me penetrate that impenetrable door? Anyone? The art of Elementalogy. Focusing my feeling, sight, and will, I tapped Water, lightening my own personal weight, making me more buoyant for what was to come. Then, summoning the Wind and tapping the Elemental of Wood, I pulled the bow staff from its place on the rack across the field, and lifted myself up for a better vantage point, not to mention created an ambiance of power around me. Never underestimate the strength of ambience. If someone fears you, they may hesitate—they may make a mistake. If nothing else, it will usually buy you time, and never was there a more precious commodity in battle than time. In the situation that the four of you had been trying to stop me from opening this door, the extra ambience time may well have been the difference between success and failure.

"Again, still tapping Wood, I manipulated the staff into the spiral ring, and with Heat I torched it. You'll find it easier to control Heat, especially in the form of fire, if you have a burnable subject—like a ring of wood for instance. Then I had only the matter of weakening the iron latch and the stone surrounding it, countering the Elementals already at work around the latch, before super-heating my torched spiral ring. Melding the Heat and Wind at the end to create a strong enough projectile to pass through the weakened stone was a bit trickier than the rest, but there you have it. That's how a hundred and ten-pound girl can knock a hole in a door four men can't dent."

"So you're a Poet," Aiden said. It wasn't a question.

"Forgive us our naiveté, Threll," Willem said with one of his flattering smiles. Aiden had no doubt that a thousand women had fallen for that smile.

"Ah, yes," Threll said, "Willem Silver Tongue, Golden Voice." Willem brightened further at this. "I saw you once, playing at a little roadside inn near Celtari. You can sing, and you can play. I'll grant you that. Unfortunately, I don't think either one will gain you much here or in the Crags."

Willem flushed and bowed his head slightly. "Be that as it may, I was wondering: how is it that you can accomplish so much? We were led to understand that Poets had a rather wide use of Elementals but perhaps not a very deep one."

Threll smiled. "Suave as ever. And for the most part, you're right. My ability in most of the Elemental studies is rather limited; however, as well as being a Poet I am also considered a Warrior, a Twin Warrior if you want to get technical. I have a good understanding of all six, plenty to instruct you for the next couple of weeks, but I specialize in Heat and Wind. Notice that what I just performed on the door was aided by all the Elementals but focused on those two."

"So you're a Warrior Poet then," Rem quipped.

"Kinda has a nice ring, don't it, mate?" added Lem.

"No," Threll said, cutting the air with her hand. "No, I am no Warrior Poet, only a Poet and a Warrior. Warrior Poets hold power in all six disciplines, but it's more than that. They master all six, gripping strength enough to make the world tremble, or at least they did. Warrior Poets are little more than a legend now, a memory of what once was."

She took a breath, shook her head as if to clear it, and then offered another impish smile. Just like that, her stoic demeanor flipped back to playful disdain.

"Right," she said. "I guess it's time to see what you're made of."

Chapter 24

Offer my apologies to the rest of the council, and know to you person-
ally, if I do not return, I am sorry for my failure.

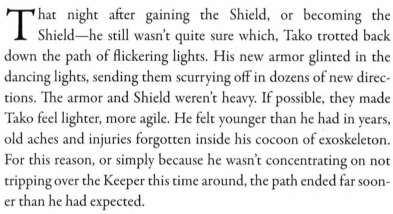

That night after gaining the Shield, or becoming the Shield—he still wasn't quite sure which, Tako trotted back down the path of flickering lights. His new armor glinted in the dancing lights, sending them scurrying off in dozens of new directions. The armor and Shield weren't heavy. If possible, they made Tako feel lighter, more agile. He felt younger than he had in years, old aches and injuries forgotten inside his cocoon of exoskeleton. For this reason, or simply because he wasn't concentrating on not tripping over the Keeper this time around, the path ended far sooner than he had expected.

He found Dante, still frozen in time, but somehow this didn't seem insurmountable or even delaying. He knew the way now, could see the way now. "Time for Time," he commanded before touching Dante's shoulder with one hand and then grabbing a stone outcropping with the other. The two of them raced upward, propelled by a silent, touchless breath of wind until the hatch they had fallen through snapped shut beneath their feet once more.

Ren Tako's Gray Pack blinked and stared at Tako and Dante, who once again found time's current. "Da...Dante, what?" Mass all but squeaked. "You fell. We saw you fall. Just now. Gone. Wolf Rider? All three of you down the hatch, and us, not even enough time to scramble to the hole."

Seeing that they were caught somewhere between dumbstruck and terrified, Tako decided to take it easy on them. Instinctively, he pulled back on the Shield, forcing it back inside himself—through himself. The mask of the helmet went first, revealing his face. Tako felt as it slid around his face and into the rest of the helmet before the helmet itself drained into the rest of the armor. Within a few seconds, all that remained visible was the Shield growing from the ring on his hand. Finally, the stone of his ring drank that as well, returning Tako's appearance back to what his companions were used to seeing.

"And now we're back," Tako announced with a wolfish grin. He gave them a brief description and explanation of the events below, choosing to trust them with more than he normally may have but still holding some of the details back. Once Tako got them to understand that their mission had been achieved, they gathered supplies from around the Keeper's large chamber in preparation for the return journey.

Fittingly, Haru found the door by accident. Tripping while rummaging through a pile of roughly woven sacks, he reached out a hand and grabbed a torch sconce to steady himself. The sconce twisted and a previously seamless wall split open and swung inward. A narrow path wound out from the open doorway, leading down the mountain at a gentle slope.

Tako stepped out on the path first. A large stack of firewood nestled against the mountainside where two sheer cliff edges came together. Looking up, he could just make out the Keep of the White Tower standing proudly a long way up the mountain. He hadn't realized how far down they had come through the secret door in the wine cellar. The light he had seen from the keep's top floor balcony now made a lot more sense. The Keeper must have opened this door to gather some wood and the light of the fires inside had blazed out for any who were looking to see. As Tako looked around at the little glade outside the Keeper's room, he realized it had been well crafted, hidden from view. In retrospect, no one, except someone in the tower itself, could have looked down and seen the fire inside the open door. The walls were too high and the stone seemed to lean in, forming a protective umbrella. No one would have seen, and Tako supposed that was the point.

Their supplies gathered, they started down this new path rather than making their way back up to the Keep through the tunnels. Being so much lower down the mountain, their return trip proved far easier.

About a quarter-mile into their trip they found a wall of stone blocking their path. The wall stood, daunting and unbroken, with no apparent door. Groping this way and that, however, they soon found an outcropping stone, that when pressed set yet another hidden door to swinging inward.

A far rougher path waited for them on the other side—returning them to the same mountainside they had climbed not long before. Closing the hidden door behind them, it was no wonder they had missed it on their way up. Given a three-night camp in the exact spot, Tako doubted that even Whisper would have found the entry. Tako had no doubt there was a similar opening mechanism on this side of the door, but its chief defense was its perfectly-blended camouflage.

"Dante," Tako said. The man nodded, already moving. He skirted a circuit along the wall, out to a cliffside, and then back, his eyes capturing every detail of stone, shrub, or path. Now they'd be able to find their way back if ever they had the need. The man was truly a wonder.

From there it was a simple matter of the final descent and retrieving their horses from the inn. They all went this time and found the innkeeper polishing half-clean glasses with a grubby rag. Shock battled fear across his round face as so many armed Swaar stepped into the common room of the inn, The Laughing Princess, the sign over the door had read. Finally, the man's eyes fell on Whisper and clung to him like a man dangling off a cliff clings to a lowered rope.

"Good master," the innkeeper began, "welcome back. To tell it true, I wasn't at all sure you was comin' back at all."

Dante Whisper, put on his most disarming smile as he drifted to the counter and started counting out coins. "And why's that?" he asked as if the answer didn't matter one way or the other.

"Well," the innkeeper chuckled, nearly jovial now that a bit of coin was falling his way, "don't get me wrong, now, but you lot have just been gone longer 'an expected, see. In truth, I'm just glad I didn't sell your beasts and all. The mountain's not for everyone, you know, and you lot were gone long enough for me to assume that the old shimmering stone had claimed the bunch of ya. Not cheap feeding horses, brushing 'em down and the like."

"How long?" Dante asked, offering another disarming smile. "Time in the wild can be so deceiving."

The innkeeper smiled as Dante added several more silver coins to their payment pile for the additional time. "Oh, I'd have to double check," he said, "but it was a moons' turn if it was a day."

Tako left without argument, just turned and walked out, leaving the payment in Dante's capable hands. Still, he was sure they had left the horses closer to twelve days ago. The Keeper had referred to this time difference when he and Tako had fallen below. Tako just hadn't understood the ramifications.

Regardless, there was nothing to do but move on, and they spent the next several days re-crossing the lands that led to Bellcross.

They camped not far outside of Bellcross, and Tako sent Dante in for a closer look at how things now stood. "The Swaar have abandoned Bellcross," Whisper said immediately upon returning to their camp, a couple of hours later, another man in tow. "Tuvry Quick Fist was left behind to wait for us," Dante said gesturing at the new man.

The man stepped forward and inclined his head. "Wolf Rider, Dal Tek left me to await your return. He bid me say that they had gleaned all they could from Bellcross and that you were quite right. The Rock Giant rode south with much of the Swaar forces over ten days past. They have gone to seize Taalmor. I was told you would understand his purpose there and that upon your return, you were to make all haste to join him with any tidings you bear."

Tako narrowed his eyes and stared at Tuvry Quick Fist, for a moment. He had found that most men grew uncomfortable under such a stare and would begin backtracking from any lies or half-truths they had offered him. Tuvry simply stood, enduring the gaze silently.

"Very well, Quick Fist," Tako growled. "I trust you have sup-plies ready for this leg of the journey?"

Tuvry nodded, unperturbed. "Dal Tek had me see to it before he left, Ren Tako." Tuvry's use of the honorary "Ren" did not have the desired effect of making Tako warm to the man—quite the op-posite in fact. The man was slippery with an easy, offsetting smile that seemed to make people like him. Tako had seen Tuvry cheat too many times at cards, dice, and wheels to ever really trust him, however.

The sun was only reaching its zenith, and there was no need for delay. So they started their trip south from Bellcross to Taalmor as soon as camp could be broken. Tuvry had a horse for himself, along with enough food and gear to outfit Tako and his original Gray

Pack of twelve. To that end, there was more than enough to stuff the saddlebags of their smaller party.

Having grown tired of what they could glean from the Keeper's table and supplies, Tako's Gray Pack warmed to the thought of something fresh, especially if that something came in large quantities.

By the time they stopped to make camp for the night, Mass and Haru were practically salivating. White Zemin had promised a potato and bacon stew to go with some of the fresh bread and wine Tuvry Quick Fist had provided.

As Zemin was setting to his task, once again ordering Haru here and there for the different ingredients, Tuvry came to sit across from Tako at the fire.

"So, Wolf Rider," he said, "what lies in the north that could force the Rock Giant to send forth the great Ren Tako to fetch it? What did you find there?"

His tone, as ever, remained a perfect compromise between honorific posturing and polite conversation. That was a skill Tako had failed to learn. He had half a mind to simply not answer, but he had heard Tuvry trying to cajole news of their mission out of the others as they traveled. So far, his Pack had remained mute on the subject, doing a good job of laughing off Quick Fist's intrigues. Still, it was only a matter of time until someone slipped up, or more likely just got lax after Tuvry's presence became commonplace. He would get it out of them if Tako stayed silent on the matter.

He waited just long enough for the pause to be awkward for conversation and thus ensure all of his companions were listening. Then Tako said, "Our task was our own. I will inform Dal Tek of our findings, and I believe that will suffice for reports."

Tuvry's smile didn't fall so much as a half penny's worth. "Fair enough. Fair enough," he chortled, holding up his hands in surrender. "I meant only to make conversation. You can't blame a man for his curiosity."

His words rang with practiced sincerity, but the man's furtive glance toward Tako's ring shouted that Tuvry knew more than he was letting on.

Tako pondered that glance as they rode the next day. Night followed day, and day, night. On the third night, all thoughts were forced from him. Just after the sun had finished setting and darkness began its reign, Tako saw the brightness in the southern sky. He could make out the ebb and flow of the dancing flames, lighting the whole sky like a beacon. They traveled another solid mile before he even saw the eight towers of Taalmor, backlit by those flames. He knew the distance of a huge city, especially one alight with flame at night, could be deceivingly far away. There was no point in stopping now, though. Battle was at hand, and the Swaar were laying siege to one of the nine great cities of the West.

Tako kept their pace steady, refusing the desire to spur his horse into a gallop—to race to the battle and his people's aid. Riding an exhausted horse into battle could be a death sentence for rider and horse alike. They would ride quickly, but he wouldn't turn his Gray Pack or even Tuvry Quick Fist, into easy targets for the Taalmorians.

They came upon the rearguard of Dal Tek's Swaar less than a half-mile outside of Taalmor's main gate. A man named Ghein recognized Tako and took their group straight to Gray Riller, who was receiving and relaying messages and orders in an attempt to coordinate the Swaar's efforts.

"No, I don't care, Crones take you," Grenat Riller yelled at a messenger. "Tell them to fall back from there and head west toward the Queens' Gate to reinforce Taune. The fire will do its work in time. Now go." The man nearly fell over himself in an attempt to bow and leave Riller running at the same time.

When Gray Riller turned and saw Tako his lips pressed together in a mask of sternness. Then the façade broke, and the man
smiled. "All-Warrior, it's good to see you, Ren Tako. We have need
of you this night like we never have before." His face grew serious
again. "Mist Falcons were visiting Taalmor when we attacked.
We're not sure how many, a handful I'd guess. They laid down a
blanket of wind and fire when we first attacked the main gates. The
Dal has gone into battle himself to try and counter them. Storm
Eater went with him, but even so, these Mist Falcons and their
magics...well, it's good you're back."

"Grenat," Tako intoned, inclining his head. "I'm here to serve,
of course. Where is the Dal?"

Riller pointed east and said, "We've been assaulting the Beggars' Way, which is now in flame as well as the Queens' Gate. The
latter should fall to us within the hour. We have men inside the city,
but they are focused mainly on sabotage and chaos, disrupting order for Taalmorian troops, and are of little use in actually opening
the outer gates for us.

"Tek and Olivat took two score men and went around west to
the Garden Gate. We splintered the gates there early on and scattered the defenders. The breach was too small to let us all pour in,
though. Besides, Taalmor is set up more like eight interconnected
cities than one big one, so we needed multiple access points if we
were to take and hold the city as a whole. Still, the Garden Gate was
more than sufficient for their small group. Dal Tek wanted to slip
in and then focus his energies on finding the Mist Falcons. Once
they were dealt with, he was going to work his way back toward the
Queens' Gate to attempt an opening from within."

Gray Riller sighed, and for the first time, the big man seemed
old and tired to Tako's eyes. This icon aging, frightened Tako as
if water had just become dry. *He's been warring all his life,* Tako
thought, *one battle to the next.* The thought that came next terrified

him even more. *And what have you been doing, oh Wolf Rider?* He snuffed that thought like a flickering candle—no time for that fire at the moment. He had work to do.

"But?" Tako prompted Riller.

Gray Riller lowered his voice for Tako's ears alone. "But there's been no sign of him. No signal. No word. I sent in another score of men led by Shau, Long Axe, but it's a big city. There's been no word from Shau either, and I can't spare the men from the Queens' Gate to seek out the Rock Giant. We should be through the Queens' Gate within the hour regardless, but without the Dal..." He let the thought trail off as if voicing it aloud would give it more credence.

Riller seemed scared, actually scared. He had always been so strong, so unbreakable. He was Dal Tek's strong right arm—a crutch the Rock Giant could lean on in any difficulty, knowing it would never break. Tako had never thought of how meaningless a crutch was without someone to lean on it. Without Tek, what was Gray Riller? Tako didn't know, and neither, it seemed, did Riller.

"We'll find him," Tako promised before turning to give orders to his Pack.

An hour later, Tako led a group of nine Swaar through the splintered Garden Gate. Behind him came his five remaining Gray Pack along with Tuvry Quick Fist and two of Gray Riller's personal guards—Ghein and Zon. They had taken their horses as far as they could, but from their side of approach, the last two hundred yards were sheer and rocky, too rough for any but the nimblest of beasts to climb. Tako didn't want to take the longer route around to a clearer path. Time was too precious at this point for that, so he had brought whatever other men Riller could spare and had them take the horses back from there.

As it turned out, the streets inside the Garden Gate were too narrow and winding for the horses to have been of use anyway. They would have had to dismount and cut the horses loose to run back the way they had come. At least this way they would have the chance to reclaim their mounts—that is, if they made it out alive.

The area inside of the gate sprawled just as lifelessly as the stretch outside. Any inhabitants had apparently fled to other parts of the city after the Swaar broke down this gate. Tako paused and let the others regroup closer to him so he wouldn't have to shout.

"Whisper, you take the lead," Tako said. "Zemin, you're his shadow. Bow in hand, right? Mass, you have the rear. Let's stay out of sight if we can and keep our eyes open for Dal Tek and Storm Eater or any other Swaar you recognize. Weapons out, but remember, we're not here to win this battle with the nine of us. We're here for the Dal. Let's move."

The others nodded, and they were off.

They trotted several blocks with nothing. Then, Dante's hand shot into the air and gestured right. They moved into the shadows of the right-hand building and waited. After a minute, Whisper and Zemin made their way back to Tako.

"Trap," Dante mouthed and gestured back further down the road. They crept back a block and into a side alley before Dante spoke. "The next corner has a convenient double twist—convenient, at least, for those who know the area. If someone approached unwarily, they would run into the waiting roadblock before they knew they were in trouble. We have company. Two archers on the roof of the north building, three on the south. Four, maybe five soldiers with spears and swords behind what is supposed to look like an unintentionally tipped wagon, and at least that many crossbowmen hidden for crossfire inside a storefront with broken-out windows in the north building. We walk in there like this, we're all dead."

"Good eyes," Tako said.

"How'd you see all that?" Tuvry asked, suspicion thick in his voice. "I mean, you stood there for no more than a minute. There's no way."

"He saw because he can," Tako announced. "That is enough for me. We'll take this alley around and hope to double back to the main way somewhere past the bottleneck."

Tuvry Quick Fist, gaped at Tako as if he had lost his mind. He looked down the alley, tightly built in the first place, now crowded with junk and debris, some of which looked a little too deliberately placed to have happened from the first attack through here or the flight of the Taalmorian citizens. It would be anything but quick going to get past it. The previous alleys had looked much the same. This was deliberate, Tako was sure.

"Wolf Rider," Tuvry started again, frustration showing in his voice. "In case you have forgotten, we are in something of a hurry. Dal Tek may be in desperate need of our aid right now. We don't have time for digging our way through this rubbish. The main road will be much swifter. If there are defenders, we kill them and move on."

"No, we go this way," Tako barked. Hopefully, it will only be a few blocks before we can get back to a cleared road."

"Tako," Tuvry pleaded before they could start down the alley, "don't do this. Just because your gentle Whisper thinks he may have seen something... You're supposed to be..." The man hesitated, glancing again at Tako's ring and then back at Tako. "Ahh, come now."

Tako's axe was up, the keen edge at Tuvry's throat before the man could blink. "I'm not certain what you think you know, Tuvry Quick Fist, but you're an idiot who would risk all our lives. The Taalmorians have piled things in these alleys to herd us on along the main road and right into the trap that Dante caught for us. I will not play into their hands simply because you think it is faster.

If Shau, Long Axe, didn't catch it, then I'm sure he walked right into that trap. If he couldn't plow through with twenty men, what makes you think the nine of us will do it?

"Now, you can either shut your mouth and follow my orders, or I will kill you myself and leave you for the rats. Clear?"

Tuvry blinked and swallowed, but didn't dare do more with Tako's axe blade at his throat.

"Good," Tako growled. "Now, let's go."

Chapter 25

It is hidden safely six days shy of a month...

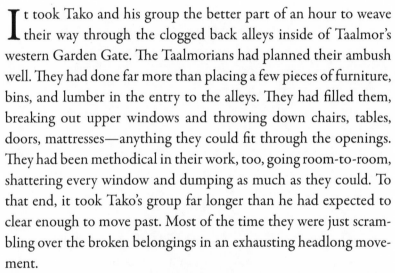

It took Tako and his group the better part of an hour to weave their way through the clogged back alleys inside of Taalmor's western Garden Gate. The Taalmorians had planned their ambush well. They had done far more than placing a few pieces of furniture, bins, and lumber in the entry to the alleys. They had filled them, breaking out upper windows and throwing down chairs, tables, doors, mattresses—anything they could fit through the openings. They had been methodical in their work, too, going room-to-room, shattering every window and dumping as much as they could. To that end, it took Tako's group far longer than he had expected to clear enough to move past. Most of the time they were just scrambling over the broken belongings in an exhausting headlong movement.

Tuvry, for his part, seemed to be pouting as they moved along. He had said no more after Tako's threat and helped out just enough in moving the rubbish to fend off Tako's wrath. Still, Tako wasn't overly excited about having the man at his back. They had avoided the Taalmorian trap, but they were still almost certainly headed into battle. And in battle, a man who couldn't trust his companions may very well end up dead. There was nothing for it, though. He could kill the man, but Tuvry had done nothing further to provoke it, and doing so would damage the others' trust in him. That trust could be the difference between action and hesitation, which in turn could be the difference between living and dying.

Tako couldn't send him back to Gray Riller, though. Tuvry knew too much to be sent off alone. If he was taken, he could jeopardize all they were seeking to accomplish. One man was too vulnerable alone in this city, and Tako couldn't spare anyone else to go back with him. Even if he got back to Riller's camp, Tako couldn't trust that Tuvry would deliver the message of their findings accurately. "A blind man can't tell what he sees," Tako's father used to say.

There was little else he could do. Tuvry had to stay. Tako would just have to hope he didn't regret it when things heated up.

Once they finally reached an unclogged road again, it felt like they were flying, so unhindered were their steps. They traveled down four or five more back alleys before coming to the main road. Dante led them well, and soon they reached what was supposed to be the closest gate out of the Garden Sector and into the Queens'. The gates were closed, chained, and barricaded. Sentries with crossbows stood on top of the smooth stone wall.

"Well, that couldn't be less inviting," White Zemin said to general agreement. Most of Tako's Swaar would surely die in any attempt at scaling this wall. They would have as much luck going back to help Gray Riller's troops batter down the main gates as getting through here.

Whisper led them back through some alleyways, onto a road for a short time, and then back through alleys again. He brought them up short at the second gate, which offered the same tale as the first.

"There're troops on this side of the closed gates," Mass said. "I can't imagine the Taalmorians would just seal them in here. There has to be a way into the other sectors."

"The Tower," Tako said. "The courtyard would be big enough to move troops through, and it's probably the only defensible location in the sector. Dante."

With nothing else said, Whisper plunged them back into the alleys. They wove their way through the roads and alleys until they could see the Tower looming up in the skyline.

At the next main road, Dante's hand came up, and they all stopped as he examined the path ahead. He waited a moment and then moved out into the road. At the next corner, he hesitated again, went a little further, and then moved them into another alley. They zigzagged their way along for a couple of unhindered blocks, and then reappeared on a second major roadway.

As they made their way through the alley, Tako fell back to find out if Mass had seen anything from her post as rear guard. He paused and turned when Dante stopped yet again, swiveling his head back and forth as if looking for something illusive. It looked as if Dante would lead them on. Then he turned back toward Tako and started running. "Falcon! Run! Tako, Fal..." he hissed in something a bit louder than his normal whisper. That was all he got out before something invisible hit him from behind and sent him tumbling down the alley past Tako.

White Zemin, slower to act than Dante, held his ground and loosed an arrow at an opponent on the road that the buildings just blocked from Tako's vision. Tako watched as the arrow leapt from the string, straight and true, only to turn back mid-flight and plunge into Zemin's own chest. The older Swaar cried out as he fell, his white hair and beard blown about as if in a storm.

Then their attacker rounded the corner and Tako understood. A young man with receding red-blonde hair walked toward them slowly, his silver brooch glittering reflected sunrays from inside the dark silhouette of his black and gray garb. In his hands, Tako had no doubt, the man gripped a musket. Tako had seen one once, but only from a distance. Still, the Mist Falcons were renowned for their deep learning and innovation. The musket that each of them carried reigned as the most visible sign of this.

The Falcon had no more than appeared before the end of his leveled musket let off a tiny explosion. It seemed at the same instant Tako heard one of his men cry out.

With an easy motion, the Mist Falcon looped his musket around onto his back and tightened the strap down to snug. It seemed in the same breath the man had drawn a short sword from a scabbard at his hip and continued his approach, unrushed.

Tako was only part way back to his usual place at the lead behind the scouting Dante and White Zemin when the Falcon attacked. That meant Riller's personal guards, Ghein and Zon, were the next in line to meet their attacker.

Zon's sword strike was parried as the man charged and at the same time the Mist Falcon's off hand shot out toward Ghein, who was just nearing for a swing with his axe. Ghein flew to the side as if struck by a charging Kaisasal bull. He hit the wall of the alley a half-dozen yards away at a strange angle, rotated once, and crumpled in a broken heap.

The Falcon didn't spare a second glance for Ghein after he launched him. He wasted several seconds trading sword thrusts and parries with Zon, but when Sunto and Tako approached, the Falcon leapt amazingly high into the air, performing a single, perfect back flip and landing ten paces further back down the alley, his cloak fluttering in its own breeze.

With a flourish of his free hand, the blonde man let loose several small throwing knives. They flew astoundingly fast, and only Tako's hard-won experience forced his axe up, anticipating the throw. A resounding gong emanated from the axe head as the knife struck perfectly on tip, but Tako suffered no damage. Zon and Sunto were not so lucky. Both dropped instantly, a knife protruding from Zon's throat and a second lodged in Sunto's eye socket.

Mass let an arrow fly from somewhere behind Tako. The arrow flew true, but in the last moment, it shot sideways, clattering uselessly against the alley wall as if slapped away by an invisible hand.

Tako charged. He was far bigger than the Mist Falcon, and magic or no he was fairly certain one good axe blow could finish this. The man's hand came up and Tako felt the wind hammer into him, knocking him backward. He stumbled and nearly fell, but then he righted himself and drove forward again. He was ready for the wind when it hammered into his chest this time. It slowed him, stopped him, and then started pushing him backward. Feeling his feet sliding back across the pebble-beaten ground of the alley, Tako cried out. The resemblance to his dream was too close. He heard his cloak rip free as it whipped in the wind. His feet gave more ground regardless of how Tako tried to brace himself. "Not like this," he growled through clenched teeth and jerked his free hand around.

There, without knowing he had willed it, blossomed the shield from the stone of his ring. The wind struck the shield but could not overcome it. Tako felt the wind being cut off as if someone had closed a door on it. It wasn't like the shield was buffeting the wind from him, but rather as if it refused the wind its place.

Tako rushed the baffled-looking Mist Falcon again. The blonde man tried to raise his sword in defense, but it was already too late. Tako's axe bit deep into the man's chest and it was over. The Mist Falcon lay dead at his feet.

Tako checked his vitals to be sure, but unless Falcons' hearts beat differently than other men's, the man was dead. Turning back to what remained of his party, he found Dante approaching. When Tako had seen his friend blown past him, he had feared the worst. Whisper's hands and face were scuffed and bloody from scraping along the ground, but he seemed well and whole beyond that.

"Ghein's neck is broken," Whisper said. "The Mist Falcon's musket blew a hole the size of my fist through Haru's chest. Zon and Sunto are both dead from the knives, and Zemin..." He trailed off as he looked meaningfully over to where the older man lay, his own arrow still lodged in his chest. Zemin's eyes were open, but they stared out at the world, unblinking and unseeing, blind in death.

In any normal battle, five lives in exchange for one Mist Falcon would be a bargain, regardless of the skill of the lost warriors. At the moment though, Tako couldn't help but feel crippled by their losses. Nine down to four, and they hadn't even found Dal Tek yet. They may not survive a second encounter if there were more Falcons in Taalmor.

"I knew it," Tuvry said, too loudly and too excitedly as he rushed forward. "Wolf Rider, I knew it. You're it. You're him—the Shield of Ammereth. You're the Shield Bearer." He pointed at the shield still on Tako's arm and grinned.

Tako didn't hesitate. His shield arm shot out and crashed into Tuvry's grinning face. Quick Fist staggered backward into the wall and slid down it, blood streaming down from his freshly-twisted nose.

"Five good men lay dead here—five companions and brother Swaar, and you," Tako ground his teeth, "you come to me with your crone-begotten grin calling out things you don't understand. By the All-Warrior himself, I should kill you here, but you are not worthy to lay down with these."

Tako turned away in disgust, but Tuvry couldn't leave it. "But you're him. You defeated the Mist Falcon. I saw—you broke him even as he was tapping. That's unbelievable, Wolf Rider. Don't you see?"

There was so much unbridled joy in Tuvry's voice, and it grated horribly in Tako's ears. Men lay dead and the fool couldn't be silent for a moment's peace?

Tako turned back to Tuvry, his anger flaring hotter by the breath. He thought he might kill the man then, but Whisper was there, sensing the flow of their current path and wanting to dam it before more blood was spilled.

"You have said more than your fair share of words at present," Dante said to Tuvry in his normal, soft demeanor. "Now you will shut your mouth, or I will show you the danger of a gentle whisper."

Tuvry's joy turned to exasperation. He fumed but said nothing. Whisper always had the ability to unsettle the most brazen of opponents.

Seeing that Tuvry was well cowed, at least for the moment, Dante turned to Tako. "We can't linger, Rider. Not even for these. We need to move or let whatever ground we've gained with the Mist Falcon's death slip from beneath us."

Tako nodded, silently promising himself he would come back to see to his fallen companions. He had seen hundreds of men die, both in battle and out. Half the team he had led out of Bellcross had died before his Gray Pack had even reached the White Keep. By the All-Warrior, Tako didn't know why the deaths of these men resounded inside his chest so much, but they did. He would come back. That was all he could do.

Concentrating on what he had done to bring the shield out, he willed it to shrink back into the stone. Then forcing thoughts of the deaths aside as best he could, he started forward again, Dante keeping pace with him. Regardless of what Tuvry thought he knew, Tako would rather not announce his Shield Bearing to the world just yet, and certainly not before he had told Tek of their findings in the north—that is, if they could find the Dal.

The four of them moved together through the streets and alleys, their party now too small to bother with scouts or rear guards. Once they fell back into the shadows in an alley to avoid an onrushing group of Taalmorian soldiers, but there was no sign of more Mist Falcons. Even so, it took them a quarter of an hour to reach the courtyard of the Garden Tower. Tako had reasoned this would be the only place that Dal Tek could take enough control to force his way in and open the Queens' Gate. If he could control the Tower, he would control the access, both ways. Seeing what the other gates had offered, Tako knew this was the Rock Giant's only way in from this side, but even so, the odds of taking the courtyard and Tower were slim at best. If the Taalmorians had left the Tower Gate open between the two sectors, they would also have left it well guarded.

There were half a dozen entries into the courtyard. Dante led them around until they found one he thought least likely to be guarded. It was a side servants' entrance, wide enough for a servant, arms piled high with firewood, to walk through unhindered, but not large enough for a horse and definitely not a rider. Still, for their group, it would work just fine.

The sound of fighting rang from inside the courtyard, and Tako knew his assumption of the Dal's movements had been correct. Abandoning their crouched concealment, they hurried from the alley and tried the door to the servants' entrance. The latch moved easily. Dante swung the wooden door inward just enough to allow the four of them to slip inside and behind an empty barrel cart.

The courtyard was a whirlwind of destruction. Scores of Taalmorian soldiers lay dead and dying, their bodies mingled with a smattering of fallen Swaar. It looked as if the Taalmorians had prepared for a strike against the Tower. They had known the Garden Gate was vulnerable, and so, unwilling to abandon the sector altogether, they had barricaded all the gates but one, set up at least the one trap that Whisper had saved them from, and set to defending the Garden Tower.

Apparently, no ballistae or other heavy weaponry could be spared from the outer walls, but still, they had placed plenty of personnel to make sure the Swaar could not complete any mission similar to the one Dal Tek had set out to accomplish.

Judging by the number of dead and the sheer amount of destruction, the battle must have been raging in the courtyard for some time. Tek himself still stood, missing only the helmet to his great stone armor, an island of wholeness in a sea of destruction. He, along with a few men still left with him, crashed through Taalmorians as they tried to overwhelm the Swaar with numbers. Tek had aged since his prime, but here in this courtyard was proving again how he had claimed the name of Rock Giant. His war hammer whirled, crushing any Taalmorian foolish enough to step in his way. As Tako watched, Dal Tek blocked a falling axe, side-stepped a spear thrust, and then crumpled both opponents with a single swipe of his war hammer.

Tek had lost most of his men in this assault, but he was nearing the Tower Gate now. The defending soldiers had been thinned, and Tako doubted they could withstand the Rock Giant as he barreled into their midst.

As impressive as Dal Tek's giant strength and fighting style were, the truly amazing sight moved on the other end of the courtyard where Olivat Storm Eater, battled in a fight the likes of which Tako had never seen. Fire bathed that entire side of the courtyard, leaping from burning source to source in a whirlwind of flying debris. The wind gusted and howled as if a sea storm had centralized on this tiny bubble inside Taalmor. Inside that storm, three figures stood—Olivat, as well as a darkly-clad man and woman. Mist Falcons, or so Tako assumed. The three of them sent discarded shields, weaponry, and armor, along with flaming barrels, splintered wood, and clothing hurling back and forth at each other in an ever swirling game of Crown Me. Olivat had his hands full trying to keep both of these magic hurlers in check, but he was holding his own, raining down as much fire as was rained on him.

As Tako watched, one of the Mist Falcons—the woman, he thought, but it was hard to tell inside all of the chaos—launched a spear at Olivat. Storm Eater leapt aside, and the spear went clattering harmlessly past. By leaping, though, he lost a bit of his footing and the endless cacophony of wind forced him to stagger. The other Mist Falcon had been ready and sent a torched barrel hurtling at Olivat. He tried to dodge again, but couldn't find his footing in time. The barrel caught him in the side and sent him to the ground.

Rather than exploiting Olivat's fall, the first Mist Falcon took off across the courtyard, heading for Dal Tek, her auburn hair whipping out behind her and a knife flashing in her hand.

Tako didn't pause, didn't think. He leapt out from behind the barrel cart and sprinted for the Dal, feeling the Shield expanding from the stone in his ring, this time flowing over his whole body like water. It enveloped him in a cocoon of perfectly-fitting, diamond-hard exoskeleton. As before, the armor didn't slow him. Rather, it was like a strengthening drug shot directly into his muscles. Fire burned in them, pumping pure strength, pure speed.

The Mist Falcon flew forward as if launched from a catapult, the windstorm of the battle forming ranks to aid her lunge. She was fast. Still, Tako was faster. Just as the Falcon reached the Dal, who still fought toward the gate, his back turned and oblivious to the danger hurtling toward him, Tako crashed into her. His outstretched Shield sent the Falcon's knife spinning out of her hand, and the concussion of his huge form at full sprint was enough to send both of them cartwheeling past Dal Tek and into the middle of the courtyard.

Tako allowed his inertia to roll him several times, not fighting the inevitable, until he was finally slowed enough to use it to pop up onto his feet again. He had left his axe by the barrel cart, but yanked his knife from his belt which his Shield armor had intuitively grown around while leaving the blade accessible, and turned to where the Mist Falcon had fallen. The ground had failed to hold her either. She stood a few paces from him, gulping in huge breaths, but apparently unwilling to stay down even after getting hit by a charging Tako. She had lost her blade to Tako's Shield, but that was not her only weapon. She raised one hand and fire blossomed in her palm. A moment later she lofted the flame, then brought her other hand forward, apparently striking the fireball with a force of wind because it shot toward Tako with the speed of a diving Geldoran hawk.

Tako didn't even have enough time to raise his Shield. The onrushing fireball struck him squarely in the breastplate of his exoskeleton. And...nothing—no explosion, no burning, not so much as a warm sensation. Nothing. The fire hit and dissipated like a shadow found out by the sun.

The Mist Falcon tried to ready another fireball but was too late to even attempt the attack. She couldn't do more than widen her eyes in surprise as Tako's hurled knife buried itself in her chest. She dropped, and Tako turned back to where Olivat had been fighting the other Falcon. Before Tako could take so much as a step to help, Olivat, no longer hampered by fighting two opponents at once, finished the Mist Falcon with the thrust of a flying sword.

Returning his gaze to Dal Tek, he found that the remaining Taalmorian defenders had perished in the Rock Giant's onslaught. The Dal turned to Tako then, fury still fresh in his eyes and his bloody war hammer ready in his hands. Dante and the others rushed to Tako's side, Mass handing Tako his axe. Tek's gaze flicked to the others and then back to Tako, a confusion misting over the fury. The Shield, Tako realized. His armor covered him completely, including a masked helmet that hid his features.

Concentrating, he willed the helmet to recede back into the armor, revealing his face. Dal Tek's expression of confusion split with a wide grin.

"Ren Tako," Tek thundered as he came forward to greet Tako. "You have returned to us in our dark hour of need. And successful, it would seem," he added with a glance at the Shield on Tako's arm and the armor that embraced him. "You must have lived one great fire-serpent of a story, Wolf Rider. But come, there is yet work to be done before our victory. Our talk will have to wait until it is done."

Tako nodded and together they went forward through the open gate into the Queens' Sector.

Chapter 26

...and a month past a day's worth of counter spin.

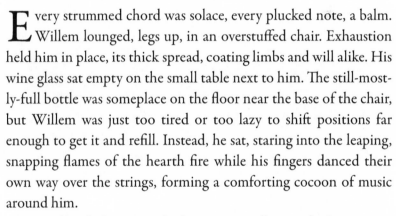

E very strummed chord was solace, every plucked note, a balm. Willem lounged, legs up, in an overstuffed chair. Exhaustion held him in place, its thick spread, coating limbs and will alike. His wine glass sat empty on the small table next to him. The still-mostly-full bottle was someplace on the floor near the base of the chair, but Willem was just too tired or too lazy to shift positions far enough to get it and refill. Instead, he sat, staring into the leaping, snapping flames of the hearth fire while his fingers danced their own way over the strings, forming a comforting cocoon of music around him.

Another day's training had not gone well—not for him, at any rate. But then, the day's training never went well for Willem, not here. More than two weeks had passed and still he struggled, grasping at strands of nothing as he tried to catch light with his bare hands. He kept coming close, but it was like trying to grab hold of the wind. Aiden, of course, had done fine almost immediately as Threll had explained some of the most common ways to connect with the Elementals and begin one's manipulation of the art, starting with Wind.

"Listen for the wind," she had said. "It whispers. It roars. Even a calm day echoes of a voice unheard. Your ears will know better than your eyes. Use them." Willem had listened, but though he heard the gentle song of breeze rummaging through the leaves and over the grass, it did nothing for him. No tingling beneath the skin. No rumble in his chest, heart, or mind.

Aiden, on the other hand, must have felt something. He described all of those sensations, actually, right before he raised one hand slowly, with his eyes closed, and summoned a gust strong enough to knock the twins from their feet.

"Dregs and draught," he had sworn, smiling apologetically at Rem and Lem as they got back to their feet. "That was something."

Threll had left Aiden to his new discovery that day while the rest of them moved on. The breeze had fluctuated for the rest of their time on the training grounds.

After a few days, Lem showed some promise with steel, forcing a latch open without ever touching it, while Rem was able to keep a rock floating in a cup of water. Willem had felt something with the latch, but he remained fairly certain that something had only been desire. "Your feeling, your sight, your will," Threll kept on saying, but Willem couldn't grasp how to put the saying into practice. He just didn't have any place to start from. By the time they had discussed theory and basic practices for all six of the primary disciplines, and yet another afternoon was fading toward evening, the only thing Willem had been able to summon was a headache.

Perhaps this was all a mistake. He hadn't wanted Aiden to go into the pits by himself. He still didn't want him to go by himself, for that matter. But what good would Willem do down there if he had nothing to offer but a pleasant tune?

"Well, that's something, at any rate," he said and allowed his absent strumming to turn into a low, chanting song he had heard his grandfather sing before the fire when Willem was still a boy. It seemed to fit his mood at present, and so he sang:

"In caverns dark and dungeons deep—down, down, down.

In caverns dark and dungeons deep—down, down, down.

You'll find the treasure that you seek, but down, down, down.

You'll find the treasure that you seek, but down, down, down.

Through open doors of solid stone, go down, down, down.

Through open doors of solid stone, go down, down, down.

And there you'll find your rest alone—down, down, down.

And there you'll find your rest alone—down, down, down.

In caverns dark and dungeons deep, yes, there's the treasure that you seek,

Through open doors of solid stone, for there you'll find your rest alone...

Down, down, down.

Down, down, down.

In caverns dark and dungeons deep, yes, there's the treasure that you seek,

Through open doors of solid stone, for there you'll find your rest alone...

Down, down, down.

Down, down, down.

Down, down, down."

Willem let the words trail off but his fingers still kept their own counsel with the strings, offering their constant solace as he stared at the dancing flames. He played—he didn't know for how long. The fire reminded him of their last night on the road before Holmsguard. The flames beckoned, licking out slowly. So entrancing. So addicting. He felt his fingers find rhythm in the dance of the flames as they lulled him in, pulled him in.

"...and you're sure they'll all be in place before the Trial? It could be quite the embarrassment if your traps are off by even a day..."

The flames rolled all around him, welcoming him in an unquestioned embrace. He was back, just like the night on the trail, and the shaded voice fell oh-so-familiar in this place. He didn't try to move this time, didn't strain against the flames. He allowed them to move him and matched his music to their flickering whim.

"The traps are well in hand, my Lord. The Hand Pretender will not survive his trial even if the Elementals welcome him with open arms. They are quite ingenious if I do say so myself, which I fear I must."

"Yes, yes, Tee. I am well aware of your gifted nature, but we can have no mistakes in this. The plan can't afford this kind of road-block. If he slips through...well, one hand is bad enough, but a second."

"If he slips through, he will be dealt with the same as Spirit. But he won't. As I said, I'm seeing to the traps myself, and they'll be...wait! What's that? In the flames just there?" The shadowy form of Tee moved forward, closer. "There, do you hear it? Did you heat guard this room?"

Willem could almost make out real features now. Just a little further. But again his fear took hold and his fingers missed just one flicker of the flames, and he was back in his overstuffed chair, sweating and breathing hard.

The Hand. The shadowed figures had been clear on that point, by the Golden Strings. Aiden, he had to get to him, to warn him. But what could Aiden do? Thun, then, or Jumper. But Willem had to tell somebody. The Trial couldn't go on. He had to stop it.

Willem, still holding his guitar, moved to the door, pulled it open, and took off down the hallway. He was already up a flight of steps, heading for Thunder's quarters when he realized he still clutched his guitar in one hand and had failed to put his boots back on. Cursing himself for an idiot, he continued on regardless, not wanting to waste the time going back for them. He reached Thun's door, knocked, and then let himself in. Presumptive, perhaps, but this was important, for Angels' sake.

All that greeted Willem, however, was a cold hearth, an unlit lamp, and the normal tidy nature of Thun's bottled herbs and medicines. In the next room, Thun's bed sat squat and neat, obviously unruffled by use, much less sleep. Willem sighed and turned to go. No sooner had he stepped back into the corridor than Old Nathaniel appeared to his left.

"Ah, Master Willem?" Nathaniel intoned one eyebrow raised at Willem's huffing sweating form. "Exercising are we? Good for you. Lord Thunder helping you with the Trial training? I've been sent to see if he needs anything further this evening."

"Oh, well, he's not here," Willem said, not caring for the moment how he looked. "I need to find him though. Do you know where else he might be?"

"Hmm, yes. Follow me, Master Willem."

"Ok, great." Willem sighed, slinging his guitar over one shoulder and onto his back. He was more embarrassed that he had forgotten his boots than by the fact he was randomly carrying around a guitar. He was a musician, after all.

Nathaniel led him down five or six flights of stairs until Willem was sure they were below ground. He followed that with several corridors and a smattering of left and right turns. Nathaniel quickly became both Willem's anchor and his beacon. Holmsguard was huge and he had no idea where they were at this point. It would take him hours to wander his way back to a part of the castle he recognized.

Finally, they stopped in front of a door, and Nathaniel knocked. By this point, Willem's sweat had cooled, and he was all too aware of the cold wicking into his bootless feet. After a moment of waiting, he heard a muffled voice, definitely not Thun's, say, "Come in."

Nathaniel opened the door and ushered Willem inside before closing the door again. The room rang out all too familiarly. His sight from the fire had been shadowed and hazy, but there was no mistaking it. Willem had seen this room twice before, both times from the fireplace opposite him now. Two men still sat in the room, neither of which were Thun.

Dellan, the Lord Commander of the Mist Falcons sat behind a large mahogany desk in a stuffed leather chair. On the opposite side of the room stood a man in the grays and blacks of Falcon traveling gear. Though his features were familiar from his time in the flames, Willem didn't think he had seen the man around Holmsguard.

"Steward Nathaniel?" the Lord Commander asked.

Nathaniel cleared his throat nervously before speaking. "I went to Lord Thunder's quarters as you bid me, Lord Commander, but he was not there. However, our guest, Willem, was just leaving the chambers. You had said to bring everyone there, and I thought that would hold even if Lord Thunder was not among their company."

"Yes, very well," Lord Commander Dellan humphed. "You may go. I will see that Master Willem is cared for."

Nathaniel offered a shallow bow and left, closing the door again behind him. Willem watched him leave, his gut tightening as his mind raced to find something to say, some way out. When the latch clicked into place, he turned back to face the desk, one eyebrow raised in question and then waited. The Lord Commander seemed unconcerned and yet inquisitive as he leaned back in his stuffed chair, fingers steepled over his mouth.

"So, Willem," Dellan began after a too-long pause. "Willem Silver Tongue, Golden Voice. I've heard tell you are quite the musician, up and coming in the world of entertainment. That is, you were until you decided to turn to a life of gladiatorial tournaments—an odd choice it would seem, don't you think?"

"Not as much of a choice as one might think," Willem said.

"Yes, of course, the wrongful imprisonment and slavery. Bad business, that. But all roads lead somewhere, and yours has brought you to our door. I trust you've been treated well, fair accommodations and the like?"

"You have been more than kind, thank you." Willem had the feeling the Lord Commander was circling him with words, trying to get him to talk, and through talk to find a chink in his armor. Willem was sure that if Dellan found the chink, there'd be a knife in it faster than he could blink. Less words, less chance to get stabbed then, that's simple enough—simple enough to survive a few more minutes, perhaps not enough to win.

"Good, good. I'm glad to hear it," Dellan said, and then apparently decided he had had enough circling. After all, when a cat had a mouse under its paw, it really didn't have to play games anymore. "And tell me, Willem, what were you doing in Lord Thunder's chambers alone this evening?"

His brain too slow to come up with an all-inclusive lie that might hold up to scrutiny, Willem decided to go with the truth, or at least a part of it. "I was looking for Thun, actually."

"At this late hour? Really? And what pressing business did you have with him that couldn't hold 'til morning?"

"Well, it sounds a bit foolish now, and I didn't mean to cause any trouble by it. Thun had heard a song one time and could only remember a few of the words. At the time, I had one of those instances where the music is on the tip of my brain, but I just couldn't remember the whole thing. I was playing my guitar tonight, trying to relax my brain, and the tune hit me.

"Threll wants us on the training grounds first thing in the morning—before first thing, really. And, well, I didn't know if I'd have a chance to play it for Thun." Willem forced a smile onto his face. "It sounds juvenile now that I say it aloud, running around barefoot in the middle of the night going to most likely wake somebody up just to play them a song. I don't know, I guess I was just excited, and I let that excitement run away with me. I'm sure sorry for any inconvenience this causes. Twin angels, I'm embarrassed now."

The Lord Commander raised his hands as if to wave the offense away. "It's fine. It's fine. Don't be embarrassed, my boy," he said forcing out a fake chuckle. "Did you get to play your song for Lord Thunder?"

"Ah, no, actually. He wasn't there, like Nathaniel said. I was so excited to get there and then Thun was off somewhere else. Kind of a letdown, but that's life. I'll have to catch up with him later, I guess." Willem sighed and shrugged his shoulders. Offering a half-smile as he took a half step toward the door he said, "Anyway, please do forgive my late night running around, but I'll not waste any more of your time, Lord Commander."

Willem bowed his head slightly and had just gotten a hand on the door handle when Dellan spoke again, as if in afterthought. "Oh, Willem, what was the song? The one you remembered and were going to play for Lord Thunder?"

"Oh, um," Willem's mind blanked, swept clean like a towel over a chalkboard. "I...uh...well, I don't actually know the title." There didn't seem to be a lie in sight, so he went with the first thing he thought of. "I just kind of hummed the tune and the words came back to me. *Down, Down, Down* is the only thing I've ever thought of it as. It really isn't anything too thrilling, just a basic chant-style oldie."

Dellan smiled fatherly. "I hope I'm not imposing, but I see you have your instrument with you. Would you do us the honor of a short rendition?"

"Well, I'm really not rehearsed. Plus it's late and training begins so early."

"Yes, yes. I won't hold you long," Dellan assured him. "I've just heard so much about your extraordinary musical talent. Give me three minutes of your night and then you can be off to bed."

Willem had no desire to play here in front of the Lord Commander and his silent companion, but there was no way around it without being terribly rude. So he nodded his head and swung his guitar around from his back.

"In caverns dark and dungeons deep—down, down, down.

In caverns dark and dungeons deep—down, down, down," he began, and sang the song he had played not long ago in his rooms before the world grew so complicated.

When Willem finished, Dellan offered him a strained smile and thanked him for playing, assuring him that the gossip about musical talent had not misled him. "Quite the gift you have," he said. "Master Tanbuary will see you safely out. It can be quite the maze down here, you know. One could get lost for days on end if he wasn't careful."

Willem nodded and allowed Tanbuary to usher him out. He didn't have much desire for this man to be leading him anywhere, but in truth, Willem didn't know the way back to his rooms. He didn't begin to grow worried until, after several blind corners, Tanbuary led him down a flight of stairs. He was positive Nathaniel had only led downward on their trip to see the Lord Commander. There would be no reason to go down further.

Seeing his discomfort, Tanbuary said, "It's a shortcut, lad. Don't worry, we'll have you in your quarters before you know it." The man smiled then, but Willem found no solace in his glinting smile. Tanbuary stood an inch or two taller than Willem, at least a barefoot Willem, and he was a good deal broader, with a thick black cape draping from one shoulder. He was not as big as Thun, but he was still bigger than most men Willem could think of. A sword with a jeweled, bone-white handle clanked at his side with every other step as he walked, and the light cast by the torch he carried glinted off of several jewel-laden rings on each hand. An ostentatious man, Willem thought, or simply confident.

Willem stopped at the second downward stair and looked quizzically at Tanbuary, who only offered his greasy, glinting smile again. "Come on. I told you it was a shortcut, we're almost there now." Willem didn't like it, but what choice did he have? So he followed as Tanbuary went down. He followed as they twisted this way and that down a few more corridors. And he obeyed as Tanbuary opened a door and motioned Willem inside.

Only when the door slammed shut from the other side did Willem fully realize his mistake. He groped for the door handle but heard a key snap home a deadbolt before he could so much as push.

A small panel slid open from the other side, again offering Tanbuary's torch light to his vision. "Now, did you really think I wouldn't recognize you in the flame? Especially after you played that merry tune of yours? Regardless, you just sit tight, my little eavesdropper, until Tanbuary sniffs out the truth of your Thunder friend. If you cooperate, you may even live to see the sun again." With a chuckle the panel slid closed, extinguishing the light. Willem was left alone in the dark listening to the receding, step, clank, step, clank, as Tanbuary left him imprisoned.

Chapter 27

You'll remember the spot, I have no doubt.

"He didn't run," Aiden spat. His anger raged like a storm blazing inside him. Threll just looked at him, that sickening, patronizing half-grin of hers offering nothing but more fuel for the flames. The twins, for their part, just stood there silently, offering no defense—having to know the truth, having to see it, but saying nothing. Their cowardice enraged him all the more.

"I'm sorry, Aiden. These things happen. You know he wasn't finding it. Sometimes something just breaks in a person and they can't take the stress, the thought of things to come. They run."

"Will didn't run. He's smarter than that, has more courage than that. More courage than you two and you're still here," he shot at the twins, who still said nothing. It wasn't a fair jab, but Aiden didn't care about being fair right now. They were going to hunt Willem down. The Falcons would kill him and bury him rather than bring him back. No trial, no chance for explanation, just hunted like a beast in the wild. But something was wrong with all this. Willem just disappeared during the night. He was gone and his guitar with him, but that was it. His pack still lay in the corner—even his boots still lay by the fire, burning off the damp.

To add to all the chaos, Aiden couldn't find Thun. He'd gone off on some errand or was buried away doing something in some forgotten room of Holmsguard. The castle was huge, after all, and the catacombs stretched on and on, running deeper than the towers stood above ground, like the roots of some enormous tree. Thun would do something about this. He'd see what Aiden was seeing. Aiden didn't know where Willem was, but he wouldn't have just taken off without his things, without supplies.

"How'd he get off the island, then, or even out of the castle for that matter?" Aiden snarled. "We are sitting in the middle of Holmsguard, for Angels' sake, the most impregnable fortress in the Nine Cities and beyond. The main land is miles off. How did a musician without any notable ability in Elementalogy make such a grand escape?"

"I don't know," Threll said, her patient tone infuriating, "but I am not investigating, either. That task is being left to others. I heard something of a small boat sighting, but that is not my job. My task is here, training you."

"And what if I go after him? Dregs and draught, If you Falcons find him, you'll kill him. You're going to kill Willem, Threll. Don't look at me with your condescending smirk. I get it. The secrets can't get out. But this is Will. You really think he left to sell what he knows of Elementals to the highest bidder? I can bring him back. We can figure out whatever's going on."

"Aiden, stop," Threll said raising her voice for the first time. "I liked Willem too, but all of you were warned. You made your choice. Willem made his. Remember the line in the sand? There's no deserting now—no leaving for that matter, not until you've passed through the Crags and come back. This is too big, too important."

"Important enough to kill over—to murder a man who has done nothing to harm you?"

Threll sighed. "There are powers at play in this world that you know nothing about—dark powers that would rather see the world burnt to sunders than for people to flourish in anything like free-dom. The darkness would love nothing so much as squeezing our secrets from a half-trained student. So yes, it's important enough to kill over. If you leave now, you'll be in no position to help Willem. The best you could hope for is joining him in a short existence of running for your lives."

"And you'd kill me, Threll, you and the rest of the Falcons, re-gardless of the Blade I carry? Regardless of the Hand that draws it from the sheath?"

Threll hesitated for a moment, very unlike her. When she spoke, it was in a quieter voice. Aiden couldn't tell if she was trying to be calming or just didn't want to be overheard. "You are not a Maker's Hand yet, Aiden."

"Says who?" It was an incredibly arrogant question and he knew it, but at that moment he really didn't care. He would push this as far as he could, as far as he had to. Willem was probably dead unless he did something.

"Says the Council, at least for now."

"And it is up to the Council to decide when the code applies?" Aiden was in way over his head and he knew it, but this was impor-tant and his anger boiled.

"Tradition dictates that you must first be a Mist Falcon to be a Maker's Hand. You have to come through the Crags first."

"Fine. Then let's do the trial now. Why wait?" She raised her hands, trying to cut him off, but he plowed on heedless of her protest. "I go in. I come out. I find Willem, wherever he is, and we get to the bottom of this."

Right now, Aiden might be throwing away all his plans for the future—for revenge on Semlie's murders. He may well be throwing away his life, but he couldn't just do nothing. He wouldn't. "Is there any rule against me going into the Crags before my weeks of train-ing are up?"

"It is traditional to wait the moons' turn, to glean as much as possible from one's trainers, and there is a ceremony before an initiate goes down. But no, there are no rules that I know of that say you can't begin sooner. But Aiden, this is no game. The Crags of Telsair are a kind of danger you've never encountered. People die in Trial. Good, strong, people die in the Crags. You're learning fast, and you're not without skill in the art, but you're still new to the study. You can use as much training as you can get if you want to survive."

"Training takes time and people can die when I'm not ready. Now will have to do. If you could get whatever ceremony ready, I'd appreciate doing this as soon as we can."

Aiden turned and started to walk back toward the castle from the training yard. After a half-dozen paces, he turned. She was still watching him. "And Threll," he said in a loud enough voice to carry not just to her but to other Falcons practicing in the yard. He gripped the sword at his belt and pulled the Maker's Blade free from its scabbard with what he hoped was a flourish. "If you could remind your friends and the Council what blade I carry for not being a Maker's Hand. And also let them know that I will kill anyone who harms Willem."

With that he sheathed his blade, turned again, and strode to the castle, willing himself not to look back at what effect his words had had. He had no doubt that most of the people here could utterly destroy him in a fight, but he carried a Maker's Blade. To these people, if not in reality, that made him special—that made him powerful. He would use that power, imagined or not, to save Willem's life if he could. If not, then he would avenge him because Threll was right—he was learning fast.

Chapter 28

Avoid my errors and do not follow in my footsteps, save in greater
preparation and wisdom than I have shown.

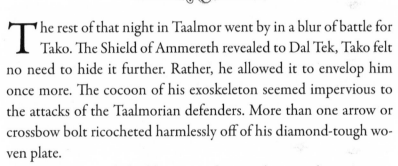

The rest of that night in Taalmor went by in a blur of battle for Tako. The Shield of Ammereth revealed to Dal Tek, Tako felt no need to hide it further. Rather, he allowed it to envelop him once more. The cocoon of his exoskeleton seemed impervious to the attacks of the Taalmorian defenders. More than one arrow or crossbow bolt ricocheted harmlessly off of his diamond-tough woven plate.

His armor and shield protected more than just his person as well. The shield coupled with Tako's muscles and own intuition, seeming to sense oncoming danger to any of his companions and move instinctively in their defense. Once, his arm shot out, only half beckoned, reaching for the block, and only when he felt the arrowhead ricochet, turned from Mass's back, did he realize he had acted. He had laughed aloud at that, and again when his Shield had blocked the blade of a diving assassin that would have claimed the Dal's chest. There was joy in his ability to defend, his invulnerability, pure and intoxicating.

It hadn't taken long for their small party, made up of Dal Tek, the Dal's two remaining guards, Olivat, Tako, Dante, Mass, and Quick Fist, to cleave their way through to the outer Queens' Gate.

Gray Riller had had more trouble than he had planned on in getting the gate open. Tako felt unstoppable as he broke the defense and led their group through to open the outer gate.

In a matter of hours, the Swaar had swarmed Taalmor, and broken down the doors of the Central Tower. Dal Tek had crushed the begging Lord Regent with a single blow of his war hammer as he strode to claim the ruling seat. He had declared a feast in honor of the freeing of Taalmor, to be put on courtesy of their new hosting city.

Now, as Gray Riller organized the efforts of securing the city, Tako sat again at table with Dal Tek and Olivat Storm Eater, as a familiar tapping could be heard beneath the floor of the main hall in the Central Tower.

He couldn't help but wonder what they could be looking for now. What they found in the crypt beneath the Bellcross temple had spoken of two words for the Shield of Ammereth—one in the north where Tako went and one here in Taalmor. But Tako had found—had become—the Shield of Ammereth. Something else was going on, but Tako couldn't bring it to terms in his mind.

Tek, for his part, was all smiles on the night. And why not? The Swaar had just conquered one of the strongest cities in the west.

"Ren Tako," the Dal said. "Help me win a wager with our good Grenat, would you?" Tako raised his eyebrows listening but said nothing.

"The stone is in the ring, is it not?" Dal Tek asked, and Tako nodded. "May I see it?" Tako rose and stretched out his hand so that Tek could have a closer inspection of the stone. The Dal laughed and shook his head, though. "Off your hand, if you would."

Tako hesitated but could think of no way of refusing that wouldn't be a straight insult to the Rock Giant. New Shield Bearer or no, that just wasn't something a man did and got to walk away from the table at the end of the night. So, instincts at war inside him, he slipped the ring he had gotten from his mother off of his finger and held it out to his Dal.

"Ha," Tek laughed, snatching it from Tako's open palm. "I told you he'd let me see it if I asked, Storm Eater." Then the Dal turned to one of the door guards. "Renez, come here, man. Put this on." He held out Tako's ring to the guard as he approached, and Tako shot to his feet, his chair crashing backward from his haste. It was as if Tek had just offered Tako's lover to another man. It was wrong. Every part of him screamed to fight for his ring.

"Relax, Wolf Rider," Tek said, holding his joking tone, but something dark and cold had crept into the Dal's eyes. "You'll have it back. Now put it on, Renez, and let us see."

Without so much as an apologetic look to Tako, Renez pulled his glove off and slid the ring onto his own finger. For a moment nothing happened. Then Renez began screaming. The ring and stone glowed white-hot. It pulsed once, twice, three times as Renez tried to pull it off to no avail. Then, a fourth searing flash bathed the room, momentarily blinding everyone.

When Tako could see again, he found a burnt husk of a corpse lying where Renez had been standing. He took the two strides between himself and the dead man without thinking. Reaching down, he pulled the ring from the skeletal finger. It slid eagerly off the corpse, clean and bright as ever. Not waiting for permission, Tako slipped the ring back on and rounded on Tek.

"And what was that supposed to prove?" Tako boomed.

Tek only smiled. "That no one else should put on your ring, of course. Now come sit down. We need to talk." Tako did as he was bid, reclaiming his seat from the ground, but he couldn't seem to pull the scowl all the way off of his face.

"Now, Wolf Rider, let me tell you a story," Tek began, setting his cup back onto the table and steepling his fingers. "When the original Shield of Ammereth began turning his little village into a stronghold to withstand all of demonkind, many flocked to him and his protection. However," and here Dal Tek raised a single finger for emphasis, "not all of those who journeyed to see the Shield stayed in Ammereth."

"I know," Tako said, doing his best not to look at the charred remains of Renez and wondering how Tek knew even that much of the true story of Jossimian and the Shield's origins. Tako certainly hadn't told of the timeless cave or the tale of the dancing lights. "Some came just to see the ring and the Shield, to study it or something, but then went back home," he continued warily.

"Precisely," Tek said. "Back home to Kantavollie—back home to Taalmor. Here a man named Tenlin led an effort of scholars, using what they had learned to try and recreate the Shield. He wanted the entire world to share in this Maker's gift and not just one small village. Why not have all of mankind safe from the demons and their darkness?

"Tenlin philosophized that the Maker had focused energy of the Elementals into the stone of the ring—an art related to that of our good Storm Eater here, and to that of the black birds of Holmsguard. Tenlin, of course, was not the Maker and failed time and time again in his attempts. I'm sure you understand that this was long before the Mist Falcons and their toying with the world. So, there was nowhere else to go for answers on his hypothesizing.

"Then one day he had an epiphany." Dal Tek stood suddenly, pushing back his chair. "Do you want to know what he realized, Ren Tako? Do you want to know what he found?" The Dal smiled, but Tako could see the dangerous, dark smolder of his eyes. "Come with me, and I will show you precisely what he found."

Tako got to his feet, hesitant to follow, but with little choice.

Dal Tek led the way to a downward-spiraling stair. There, Tako and Olivat followed him down to a familiar scene. At first, the walls were smooth-cut with doorframes and well-fitted doors on greased hinges. Then they came to a rough opening where an old door had obviously been forced open. Beyond it lay cracked and broken stone walls with old paving stones underfoot. Footprints in inch-thick dust and broken, splayed cobwebs showed an old, and until recently, forgotten hall in disarray.

At the end of the hall, a huge stone door sat in a rolling track of some kind. It was chiseled and mostly fractured now, but when it was whole, Tako imagined it weighed several tons.

"We've had men working on it since we arrived," Olivat confided to Tako. "The door was meant to roll in the track, but it had been sealed somehow. Still, hammers and chisels always seem to prevail against stubborn stone." Olivat smiled, and Tako was reminded of how he disliked this man.

Several men and women were still busy pulling broken stone pieces out from the doorway and piling them in the corner, but they had cleared more than an ample path into the room beyond, as long as one didn't mind ducking.

"This was to be cleared away by now," Dal Tek snarled in a cold voice to a woman supervising the excavation. "This is unacceptable." Without hesitation, and yet without undue hurry, the Rock Giant slid a dagger from his belt and across the woman's throat. The supervisor choked on whatever excuse she was about to offer and, eyes bulging, fell dead to the floor. Tek bent, wiped his bloody blade on the dead woman's sleeve, sheathed it again, and continued on.

Tako had to force his outrage back down as he stepped over the dead woman to follow the Dal through the now-open doorway. Losing soldiers in a battle or to a cause was one thing. Stealing their lives to abate your own fury—that was something else entirely.

Entering the freshly excavated chamber, all other thought was forced from Tako's mind. A large machine, made entirely of some kind of translucent, shimmering metal, squatted propped on a raised dais like a bird of prey waiting to spring. Four metal pillars propped the body of the machine off of the stone floor. In the center of the pillars, chains of the same translucent metal crisscrossed over beams, and at each corner, manacles gleamed, hanging open and ready. Above the pillars, a shimmering dome stood with tiny inlaid gems connected by a carved script that Tako couldn't read covering the surface. And behind it all lay a woven mesh of cogs and gears, again made of—and woven together by—the translucent metal.

"By the All-Warrior," Tako whispered, the warning bells of his mind going off. Tako just stood still, though, failing to place what exactly he needed to defend against.

"This is it," Olivat all but crowed as he rushed past Tako to a stone stand just beneath the dais. There, sat a thin stone slab, similar to the one beneath the Bellcross temple, strange writing chiseled into its surface. Olivat's eyes darted back and forth across the slab, absorbing whatever the alien text had to share. His face was all concentration for a moment. Then it lit up, a smile tugging at his cracked, weathered features.

Olivat looked up to where Dal Tek stood examining the apparatus on the dais. "It is just as the tome spoke of in Allisii. We've done it. This is it."

"Yes," Tek agreed, nodding. "And all the pieces are finally at our disposal." He said this glancing at Tako who felt notably disquieted by it.

"And now, Wolf Rider," the Rock Giant said, "I will tell you what Tenlin found in all his studies of the Shield of Ammereth. He found several truths—first, that the power of the ring and of the stone it held could answer only to its one true Bearer; second, that power and craftsmanship could be duplicated by none save the Maker himself; and third, and perhaps the most fascinating of the discoveries, that the Shield's power could be amplified and spread to surroundings further than the Bearer's own person."

Here Tek stopped and offered Tako a tight, cold grin. "The first one I think poor, dead Renez can attest to, or at least we can attest to it in his absence. The second, we will have to take Tenlin's word for in his writings, though I have no doubt *we* would have little luck in the Shield's recreation at any rate. And as for the third, well, if you recall our battle to the Queens' Gate and then to this very tower, I think you will find the truth of the third point in your own actions."

Tako looked back at the hulking Rock Giant, trying to trace the lines between the Dal's words and his purpose. *What are you and your magician after here, Tek? What do you want from me?* Tek's smile didn't fade with Tako's hesitancy, but that didn't mean anything—the man was nothing if not controlled in his own self.

"Tell me, Ren Tako," Dal Tek said. "Tenlin speaks of the Shield *prompting* the Bearer in defense of those around him. I confess my curiosity. Tell me, what was the battle like for you?"

Tako thought of the arrow meant for Mass's back. He knew how it would have planted itself between the ribs—could imagine the pain and instant shortness of breath, could almost hear Mass gasp. He thought of how his shield arm had moved as if by subconscious need, hearing the arrow's call with invisible ears and reacting.

That had been craziness, though—wild imaginings. The Shield couldn't hear anything, couldn't want anything. Yes, but neither could the stone of a ring turn into a Shield that bathed his whole body in armor. Yet it did.

Something of the realization must have shown in his eyes, for Dal Tek's smile grew broader. "Yes, you know of what I speak. It's true, then. You felt the Shield's power to protect those around you. You felt it, Wolf Rider. You used it."

The excitement in Tek's voice was almost worse than his usual cold indifference. What could drive the Rock Giant to something so near giddiness?

"And the power of protection was meant for mankind, not just Josimmian, the first Bearer," Olivat intoned from the stone slab at the dais's foot. "Thus, the Maker, in his wisdom, created the Shield of Ammereth to expand at the Bearer's touch and guard the Maker's children."

Tako looked at Olivat and then at Dal Tek, back and forth several times. "Fascinating," he said after a moment had passed. "It's all truly fascinating, but—forgive my density—why do you care? Why do you care, Storm Eater? The intellectual challenge? And you, my Dal? This matters to you personally? To the Swaar and our survival?" All of the information seemed to pertain to Tako as the new Shield Bearer, but not to Tek or Olivat. Still, the intensity of the stares of the other men spoke of vested interest, and though having the new Shield of Ammereth on your side in battle had obvious advantages, Tako would not believe their interest was only in helping him to understand his new abilities.

"Ah," Tek said. "That is the part of the story that we know, and you don't. Come up here a moment, Wolf Rider."

Tako refused to show fear. So, stepping further into the room, he climbed the steps to the round stone dais. Standing close to the machine, he was struck more fervently both by how beautiful the glistening surface was and how terrifyingly the waiting manacles hung.

Tek smiled at him again, a blustery, frozen smile. "The truth, Ren Tako, is that Tenlin took his findings about the Shield of Ammereth and he came here to build. To build this." He laid a caressing hand along one of the machine's shimmering pillars.

"I am strong, Ren Tako. I doubt very much if there is a man living who could beat me in single combat with sword, axe, or hammer. The Swaar are also strong—strong enough even to come all the way here and take Taalmor, barred gates or no.

"Still, there are others, Tako—others who could kill me faster than the words it would take to describe it could be told. I don't mean crossbowmen or ballista crews. This has nothing to do with range, but rather with power. There are men who can control the wind and call the flames, releasing them from their chains in short spurts of destruction before binding them again. There are women who can pull the very strength from the earth beneath us and use it to crush any who stand against her. Or she may whisper with the trees and plants, and regardless of a farmer's prowess with the plow and irrigation, wither entire fields of crops at a whim." Dal Tek shook his head slowly as if saddened by the very thought. What was worse, he seemed so fervent that Tako couldn't help but believe he was telling the truth—or at least what Tek believed to be the truth.

"Power has come to man, Ren Tako, which man was never meant to have—power to crush and destroy and hold fast only what it fancies in any given moment. Think. The Swaar are strong. I am strong. We came here to conquer this city of towers, and if not for you and Olivat Storm Eater, we would have failed. We would have failed because of two men and one woman—three people, no more. And who were these people? Great leaders, who inspired their troops to the defense of their homes? Strategists who could have outmaneuvered us in a huge game of Angel's Gambit? No, they were three Mist Falcons, gorged on power stolen from their ancient stronghold. Three people would have defeated the Rock Giant and the Swaar."

Tek shook his head again, and Tako was struck once more by just how big the man before him was. The Dal stroked his beard and slowly raised a finger. "I see the doubt still kindled in your eyes, Tako. Do not look away. I am Dal because of my strong arm, but also because I can read other men better than most. I will not fault you for your doubt—for your wariness.

"And yet, you must look at the grander picture and see the world as it truly lies, for this is the duty of every leader." Tako was aware of how Tek tried to pull him into his confidence—speaking to him as an equal and inferring his status as a leader. Even so, he enjoyed the Dal's acceptance, even if it was a sham for his benefit alone.

"Let's talk history for a moment, Wolf Rider. Nine great cities stand here in the West, the last witnesses of a fallen kingdom, a fallen greatness. When Jarish the Bold died, leaving Tais and Vallen to squabble over an already-corroded nation, the last seeds of death were planted for the Renillion royal line. The brothers had been born a mere eleven months apart and had been rivals from the moment the younger Vallen learned to chase after his older brother. You know of how the Princes' War raged between them after Jarish's death, how the cities were ripped apart by supporters on both sides. What you may not know is how the two princes died, ending the line of Renillion.

"Tais died in battle against an overwhelming force. The older prince claimed that none would take him from the hill he stood upon, for the Twin Angels themselves would hold his line. Either the Angels failed, Prince Tais saw only what he wanted around him, or something else altogether was going on.

"Vallen Renillion fell mere hours after his brother when a sinkhole swallowed him whole while crossing the Benatine Reach in an attempt to circle around Tais's forces. His companions later pulled the prince's body from the sinkhole, but it was too late. Vallen was dead."

Dal Tek stopped again and stared intently into Tako's eyes, holding his gaze for a long silent moment. Then Tek said, "As I'm sure you know, this ushered in the end of the original Princes' War.

The different factions fizzled out when left without a monarch to back. From there it was a swift descent for the West as the land degenerated into nine squabbling cities and a plethora of squabbling leaders. All of this, you may have known. What I'm sure you don't know is that Prince Tais and Prince Vallen were murdered—Tais by those he trusted, Vallen by those he refused to trust.

"You will have to bear with me, for this requires a bit of explaining. Vallen's murder is easier to see. Think of what we know of the situation. The scholar Yenalies writes about the Princes' War, saying that there was a fairly public scene of one kind or another in which Prince Vallen refused the Mist Falcons' backing supposedly due to the Falcons' demands. Vallen proclaimed loudly that he would 'not surrender the throne simply to sit upon it'. Then, mere months later, the gallant prince, renowned as a hunter and outdoorsman, walks blindly into a sinkhole? His friends and followers lived in bafflement. Never before had Vallen blundered so, but what were they to say? Was not his body enough evidence that he had indeed failed in this event?

"History can choose to believe Vallen's death an accident if it wants, but I think I will see through the inked-in lies. A Mist Falcon, or perhaps several, murdered Prince Vallen for his refusal and chastisement. They opened the ground beneath him and swallowed him whole. Think of the stories you've heard. Think of their power in the battle just passed. This is well within their ability, and Vallen's refusal of them more than suffices for a motive.

"The history and murder of Vallen is easy to read between the lines of if one has eyes to see. Tais's murder, on the other hand, requires a bit more delving. At first glance, young Prince Tais is killed in a valiant effort to hold his position against a force far outnumbering him. Nothing suspicious floats to the surface of the tale. That is, until you look a bit closer. Tais had openly welcomed support by the Mist Falcons, though actual military assistance seemed very slight. In truth, we have found reference for only two Falcons ever actually fighting for Tais or in the Princes' War at all. There was a woman named Darise, Wing Fall, and a man only referred to as Hammer Stone.

"These two Falcons are mentioned being present at three of Prince Tais's battles. The first two were Tais's ringing achievements of the War; the third ended in Tais's untimely demise. Look again at the prince's claim before the battle. He claimed that none would take him from the hill he stood upon for the Twin Angels themselves would hold his line. The Twin Angels themselves... Maybe, Tais was a pious man. Maybe he believed his right to rule was divinely given. Or maybe, the Twin Angels he spoke of were none other than Darise, Wing Fall, and Hammer Stone.

"He had won two huge battles with his Mist Falcon allies at the lead, why would he fear a larger force when *Angels* walked beside him, defending him.

"Here our story takes its twist, though. Tais's Angels failed to defend him. In fact, the prince's entire company was slain at Weeping Hill. Not only that, but three battalions of Vallen's supporting troops, the entire attacking force led by General Astapor in Vallen's absence, were slain as well. There were but two survivors, two solitary soldiers left at the end with two thousand dead troops lying all around: Darise, Wing Fall, and Hammer Stone."

Dal Tek smiled. It was not a friendly smile, exactly. It was too cold for that, but it was a conspiratorial smile as if Tek and Tako were sharing in some grand secret.

"Now you could believe, as it appears Yenalies does, that the Mist Falcon duo was so stricken by Tais's death, and by their failure to protect him, that they raged against their foes, slaying every last one. This doesn't quite fit, however. Tell me, Ren Tako: you are a warrior, no alien to battle; why does this account ring false?"

Tako didn't have to think about it. His mind had held pace with the Dal's. "Survivors among Tais's troops, if not among Vallen's."

Tek smiled again. "Precisely. If Darise, Wing Fall, and Hammer Stone had rallied at some point to such a degree as to kill all of Vallen's remaining soldiers at Weeping Hill, it is incredibly unlikely that none of the rest of Tais's force would have survived. Two survivors in a battle of two thousand is unheard of. People would be injured enough to take them out of the battle, maybe left lame but not slain. Others would have run when the fighting grew too hot. Some may even have thrown down arms in fear. We are a fickle race who fears death. Rarely does a group truly stand to the last man, regardless of what the singers would have us believe, and never do both sides stand thus.

"We are left with the only alternative, then—that the two Mist Falcons were the only survivors because they were designed to be the only survivors. Whether they killed Prince Tais themselves along with the rest of the soldiers on that hill, or whether they allowed General Astapor's forces to do their damage and then slew everyone that remained alive, matters little. The Mist Falcons murdered Tais either through their purposeful apathy or their deliberate sword thrust. In this, murder is murder."

Dal Tek The Rock Giant, fell silent. Tako had always seen Tek as a capable leader, inspiring through fear and violence, but strong, and his prowess in battle was unmatched. He had never known the Dal's interests lay so strongly in history, and though this was a fascinating theory of the past—important, Tako supposed, to the history of the Nine Cities—he didn't understand why Tek was telling the tale to Tako in this moment.

He decided to play along, at least until he could figure out what was going on. "So the Mist Falcons killed Prince Tais and Prince Vallen, thus ending the Renillion line and leaving the Nine Cities in a broken, kingless state." Tako felt an almost uncaring shrug lift his shoulders. "Why? The Falcons kill them, throw the world into turmoil, and then what? They go back to their island and sit there as decades build on decades and time drifts slowly into history? Not exactly a master plan. Why would they bother with any of it? What do they gain?"

Dal Tek tapped a raised finger against his own temple. "You are a sharp man, Wolf Rider. Why, indeed? Why does the serpent strike or the tiger devour? Falcons betray. It is what they do. Their purpose could be any of a dozen reasons, or more likely, all of a dozen reasons wound together. Perhaps old King Jarish had offended them somehow. Perhaps a united kingdom posed too much of a threat to Mist Falcon supremacy. Or perhaps they simply acted because they could and there was no one to stop them.

"The fact remains *that* they acted—that they used their unnatural power to sway the world for no one's benefit but their own. The Mist Falcon order is too strong, too fearsome, and too threatening to be allowed to survive. The simple truth is, Ren Tako, they have to be stopped, and now with you and with the fruit of Tenlin's research at hand, we have the ability to do so."

Tako's mind still held grudgingly to its confusion. Tek's face was all smiles, strained at the corners, but fervent nonetheless. "My Dal will have to forgive his slow-witted servant," Tako said, "but why do we care? The Swaar, I mean. We are of the Endumaar that flows swiftly beyond the Sands, of Allisii and Quae in their mountain fortresses, of the Vale and its hidden green pastures. Ours is the East. What do we care for the West, for the Nine Cities or of tyrants who would manipulate its people?"

The Rock Giant's smile faltered and he seemed to deflate ever so slightly for a moment, but then he nodded his head. "Fair enough, Tako; you are wise and level-headed, but I have not told you all. We must look even further back in history than the tale of

Tais and Vallen to find the answer you seek. You know, I am sure, that the Swaar were not always nomadic, nor are we in our entirety born of the East. What I am sure you don't know, what very few are privy to, is that Penaux, Stone Crown, his three Champions, and his orphan followers did not originate in Allisii in the way we are taught as children. Penaux, who bound the early tribes together with fire, sword, and victory, forming the Swaar as we know it, came from the West. He was born in a village named South Darry, the second son of the local blacksmith, and given the name Penaux Renlyn. His older brother was none other than Teldarios Renlyn, or Teldarios Renillion, the Magnificent, as he was known after forging the Nine Cites into one nation and changing his family name to promote a bit more grandeur.

"Penaux rode at his brother's side for nigh on fifteen years as they settled one dispute after another, winning allegiance from group after group and conquering those who would not kneel. Then, one day not long after Teldarios had been crowned on the steps of the Great Angels' Cathedral, a group of farmers and craftsmen in the Eastern Reach beyond the Forest of Hale rebelled. The Renlyn brothers had spent little time in the region, touching only a few of the larger estates on their way north to conquer Frantelin and Perry. The rebels saw no need to bow before the new High King nor pay his taxes. They strung up the first tax collector and drove off the small retinue of soldiers he had with him.

"When Teldarios came himself and his brother, Penaux with him, as well as a huge portion of his army, the king decided to make an example of the people of the Eastern Reach—and in particular those of a small village named Hearthstone from which most of the rebels had arisen. None would think to rebel, not after Teldarios was done here. He killed the men, every last one, be they old or young, rebel or not. Most of the younger women, he enslaved. The older women and the children he ordered to be locked into

Hearthstone's meeting hall, in which the rebels had met to plan their activities.

"Teldarios ordered the doors and windows barred, and then took a torch in his own hand and moved forward to light the thatched roof. Penaux caught his brother by the arm before he could hurl the flame and murder the hundred children and grand-mothers inside. 'It is not worth this, brother. Your point has been proven.' Teldarios raged against his brother's grip, but Penaux had always been the physically stronger of the two.

"When at last King Teldarios threw down the torch to burn out in the dust, Penaux released him. 'Then you may have your swaar,' Teldarios spat at his brother, for that was a slur name given to war orphans in those days. 'But, you shall have naught else from me, Penaux, for you are my brother no more.' This was quite a blow, for Teldarios had always promised his brother half the realm to rule when they came into their own.

"Penaux did not argue, though. Instead, he went to Hearth-stone's meeting hall, unbarred the front door, and led the children and old women out and into the East beyond his brother's sway. His three best friends went with him into exile—Gallen, Hintu, and Bektin. Somehow, Penaux kept those orphans alive across the long leagues to Allisii, and from there he began his work in uniting the tribes and forming the Swaar.

"So, you see," Dal Tek said, "we are not only of the East, but also of the West, for we are Penaux's Orphans, and it is the first king of the Nine Cities who named us. We are the Swaar, and the Renlyn bloodline remains in our midst—the bloodline and a story, guard-ed and passed down from father to son, from Penaux Renlyn, Stone Crown, down to Tek Renlyn, the Rock Giant.

"We care, Ren Tako, because the Nine Cities belong to the last heir of Renlyn as surely as Endumaar, Allisii, Quae, or the Vale do.

We care, for this is my inheritance, our inheritance. And I mean for us to claim it."

Tek took a deep breath and tugged once again at his beard. All of this was new to Tako. Everything he had ever known had been of the East. They raided here beyond the river, sure, but never had thoughts of moving here or claiming it as their own. All he could do was stand, dumbfounded, and stare at Tek.

The Dal seemed to find himself again and pushed on. "To claim what is ours, though, we must first deal with the Falcons, and for that, I need you. I said before, the Swaar would have lost here if not for you, if not for the Shield of Ammereth. The Mist Falcons are too strong, their power too unimaginable for us to find victory. I need you to help me stop them."

Tako shook his head slowly. "I don't mean to disappoint, but you overestimate my ability. I won against a Mist Falcon in an alley and again against a tired one in the courtyard, and that only with Olivat's help. I can't hope to conquer their entire order."

Dal Tek smiled again. "I know, Ren Tako. I know you cannot beat the Falcons."

"But then—" Tako broke in.

Tek bulled over Tako's objection. "You cannot beat them as you are and without help, but that is where Tenlin comes in." Again, Tek caressed the nearly-glowing machine. "Surely, you noticed that the Mist Falcons', shall we say, *extra powers,* had no effect on you during the battle. Stripped of their unnatural powers, they were left only with their skill and true abilities. They froze—dead in the water. Dead on land too, for that matter. Somehow the power of the Shield dampens a Falcon's abilities. Still, the effect has a limited range. Olivat and the other Mist Falcon were still in combat while you were facing down my assassin. Whether due to range or concentration, their powers were not inhibited.

"Tenlin's machine, here, will fix that issue of range. He used some kind of shimmering, dancing dust, he writes, that he found in a cave that once held the stone you now bear." Tako thought of the Keeper and the dancing lights that played out the scenes of the little man's tale. They had been so alive in their dance. It seemed wrong for them to be frozen, wrought into this shimmering monstrosity. Looking at the machine again, the sight of the manacles caught his eye with new meaning.

"And how exactly will this machine *fix* the issue?" Tako asked. "How is this going to work?"

Dal Tek's eyes were hard—not with the icy fury that sometimes lingered there, but something akin to it. "I will not lie to you, Tako. This will require some sacrifice on your part—some giving up of the personal for the greater good. I don't know exactly how it will work beyond what Tenlin writes. But somehow, the machine will take the power of the Shield of Ammereth and you as its Bearer and expand it, fire it in some kind of great array.

"We need this. The Swaar need this, Tako; don't you see? This is our path to victory. This is our chance."

"And what happens to me?" Tako asked.

Tek shook his head. "I don't know. Tenlin didn't know. He writes that, in theory, the Shield Bearer will be surrendering his control of the stone, but I don't know how permanent that will be. It may be only as long as you are in the machine."

Tako considered for a moment, staring into Tek's cold eyes. "Let's say I do this. Let's say all goes to plan. The Mist Falcons are destroyed, the Swaar conquest of the Nine Cities complete. Then what? What of these Nine Cities? What of home in the East?"

"When we are victorious," Tek said in a low, quiet voice, "then we, the orphans, will come home, and these Nine Cities, these descendants of Teldarios, will know the wrath and vengeance of the heir of Penaux and his Swaar." The Dal's voice barely rose above a whisper, and yet the sheer, frosty, ferocity with which he offered the statement could make even the stoutest of men quake. Tako forced himself not to take a step back from the venom in Tek's voice and the fury in his eyes.

"Come, Tako," the Rock Giant said, holding out his hand for Tako to grasp in a hold of friendship. "Serve me in this and you can have whatever you please. You want Allisii and Quae as your strongholds? Take them. You want this towered city? It's yours. Name your prize, Wolf Rider, up to half the kingdom that will be mine, and you can have it for your own."

Tako looked at Tek's proffered hand and then at the glimmering machine with manacles, cogs, and gears. He thought of how the Keeper had relinquished his knowledge to Tako—how at peace the man had seemed as he faded out of existence. He thought of the gentle, booming voice in the darkness: *Defend the weak. Cast off the oppressor. Shield the Light.* But who was weak here and who was strong? Were the Falcons the oppressors, or did the man standing in front of him now get to claim that title? *Shield the Light.* What did that even mean? Tako stood frozen, torn by his loyalty to Tek and the feeling of what was right in his gut. Then, slowly, so very slowly, he began shaking his head.

"No," Tako whispered, and then with more strength, "No. No, Dal Tek, I can't step into this machine of Tenlin's. The Shield of Ammereth has come to me. I said the words, and I must be the one to live them out. If the Maker had wished for the Shield to dampen all of the other magics in the world, I am sure he would have bestowed the gift upon it, upon me. But it is not my place to surrender my strength solely to another. Not even to you."

With a tightening of his jaw, sad anger blossomed across Tek's face. He nodded his head slightly and said, "I understand, Wolf Rider. It saddens me, but I understand." Then, louder, he called, "Bring them in," his voice a cracking thunder.

Through the excavated opening, Gray Riller with Tuvry Quick Fist, and a dozen other Swaar at his side marched a bound Dante and Mass. There had obviously been a struggle. Mass's lip was split and the side of her face was bruised badly. Tako wondered if the hand that had struck her was still attached to its owner. Knowing Mass, he doubted it. Dante had fared no better. His left eye was nearly swollen shut and the hair on the back of his head was matted down with dried blood. It was clear they hadn't been asked here nicely to wait upon Tako's decision. Just another self-satisfying decision by Tek—always have a plan to win, regardless of who it hurts. The man was terribly efficient—brutal, but efficient. That did nothing to lessen Tako's anger. If Tako had agreed to the Dal's plans, his companions probably would have been released, but only after Tako had been strapped into Tenlin's glittering contraption, his power stolen away and his rage echoing deafly around the chamber.

He met both Dante and Mass's eyes, finding that neither of their spirits had been broken. Then, Tako turned a cold gaze on Gray Riller and Tuvry Quick Fist. Riller had the decency to look away after a moment—not proud of what he's done, then—but Tuvry was grinning broadly. Tako could have killed him for that, would have killed him if the rest of the situation wasn't so pressing.

Finally, Tako turned back to Dal Tek. "This is how it is, then?"

Tek nodded. "I told you that I needed you. You should have known I don't allow people to turn me down. You should have made my bargain. This could have been so much better for you—for all of us.

"Is that so?"

Tek nodded again. "I would have been true to my word—up to half my kingdom. But you refuse me?" Riller climbed the steps to the dais and took up a position directly behind Tako.

"And now, things are different between us," Dal Tek continued.

"Things were different when Riller and his boys went after two of your loyal warriors who just traipsed hundreds of leagues across the Nine Cities at your request, and then returned with me, just in time to storm this cursed cesspool of towers and save your life from the Mist Falcons. When you bruised their faces, things became very different between us." Tako was having a hard time holding in his anger, and he knew his voice betrayed him even if his hands were steady.

"Well," Tek said, "if it is their faces that have offended, we can always have them removed along with their heads." At that, two of the Swaar brought knives up around Dante and Mass's necks and rested them at the prisoners' throats. It all felt rehearsed, which stoked Tako's anger further.

Tako glanced at the prisoners before turning back to Tek, choosing his words as he spun. When his back was fully turned, Gray Riller struck out low, trying to drop Tako in a single strike behind the knees. Some part of Tako reacted instinctively. He whirled, his shield forming on his arm. Riller's spear cracked against the Shield's hard metal. Less than a moment later, Tako felt as a giant fist struck the back of his head. The blow should have been enough to knock him to the ground, if not knock him out altogether. As it was, his body, or the ring, or some combination of the two again acted through instinct, his armor rushing up his skin, forming a helmet before the blow could land. The hit rocked him forward onto the balled feet of his crouching position, but no more—none of the pain, not even the jolt of a heavy blow hitting armor. He stood, spinning, and shot out his hand in time to catch Dal Tek's second punch in one armored hand of his own. Tako caught and held as Tek struggled to pull his hand free. There were a number of gasps from the Swaar soldiers. They hadn't meant to gasp, Tako was sure. Gasping could be a death sentence in this situation. But, to be fair, even Tako was astounded. He was certain no man had ever caught the Rock Giant in this way, not since Tek had been a small boy. Even then he had been bigger and stronger than boys three and four years older than him. This was something new entirely.

"If he doesn't release me by a count of three, kill the prisoners," Tek shouted down to his men, quite different from his normally cool demeanor. The men with knives pulled tighter on Dante and Mass while the two crossbowmen in front leveled their weapons at the prisoners. Tako may survive a battle in this, but his companions surely wouldn't.

"One," Tek all but squeaked, as Tako squeezed down on the Dal's caught fist. The Dal wouldn't be moved in this, Tako knew. The man would trade his life for those of Mass and Dante simply because he had decreed it. "Two." Tako let go and the Dal took a stagger step backward, visibly shaken by his strength's inadequacy.

"I go into your machine, and they go free," Tako said in a voice barely above a whisper.

Tek nodded, massaging his released hand, obviously hating having the terms dictated to him.

"Swear it," Tako growled. "Swear it by the All-Warrior, his crones, and the crown you would claim."

Dal Tek seemed to recover himself enough to answer strongly. "I swear it to you, Wolf Rider—yes, even by the All-Warrior, his crones, my crown, and my life. Submit to me in this and your friends will not be harmed."

"Say their names, Tek."

The Dal nodded, but his eyes grew hard and cold as if Tako had offended his honor by insinuating that he might betray and cheat Tako in this. Tako might have smiled at that if the situation wasn't so dire. The Dal was betraying and cheating him at this very moment.

"Neither Dante Whisper nor Eleena Mass, will come to any harm by my hand or those I command if you obey and chain into Tenlin's invention."

Slowly, Tako forced his exoskeleton armor to evaporate back down and into himself, into the ring. He had to fight the Shield's desperate desire to protect him, and for a moment, he wasn't sure he would win. Then the power of the Shield seemed to yield all at once, and his remaining armor washed away like a crashing wave.

Tako took two short strides into the space of Tenlin's machine, obviously built for him. Reaching out, he took hold of the first manacle and snapped it shut around his own wrist. It took a moment for Olivat to scramble up the steps and snap the other manacles into place before checking the one Tako had done himself to make sure it was fastened correctly.

Tako looked out and held Mass's gaze just as the first wave of pain racked his body.

Chapter 29

Perhaps, I will follow this message shortly myself...

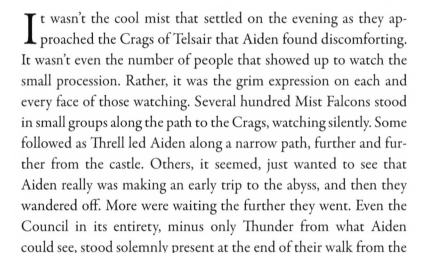

It wasn't the cool mist that settled on the evening as they approached the Crags of Telsair that Aiden found discomforting. It wasn't even the number of people that showed up to watch the small procession. Rather, it was the grim expression on each and every face of those watching. Several hundred Mist Falcons stood in small groups along the path to the Crags, watching silently. Some followed as Threll led Aiden along a narrow path, further and further from the castle. Others, it seemed, just wanted to see that Aiden really was making an early trip to the abyss, and then they wandered off. More were waiting the further they went. Even the Council in its entirety, minus only Thunder from what Aiden could see, stood solemnly present at the end of their walk from the castle.

"Quite the turn out for little old us," Rem whispered from behind Aiden.

"You'd think there was something important going on here tonight."

The twins had stayed with Aiden. They had found him in the main room of their attached suite a few minutes after he had stormed from the training yard.

"By the Angels, Aiden, that was some speech," Lem had opened for them.

"Threatening them, everyone, and moving our date up...gutsy. I hope we don't get killed, mate," Rem had added in his usual playful tone.

"You two don't have to come," Aiden said. "I didn't mean to volunteer all of us for an early Trial. I don't want to steal any of your training time. It's alright. You guys can wait. I just...I had to do something, you know? I had to act and this seemed to be both in the way of action and my only possible action that didn't involve immediate death by a score of angry, hunting, Mist Falcons."

"No; death by marauding, wild Elementals sounds far more comfortable."

"You could have left before, you know," Aiden had snapped. "I didn't ask you to stay for the training or to go into the Trial." He wasn't really angry with the twins. In truth, he didn't know who or what he was angry with—Willem for vanishing, Thun for his absence, the Falcons for their ridiculous secrecy, Branke and Baron Raz, himself for never being quick enough to save. He breathed out slowly. *Semlie.* Well, that thought would have to wait. He had a Trial to prepare for.

"It's fine, you can just wait. I'll go down now, and I'll let you know how it goes."

"Now, it's possible that is the worst plan I've ever heard," Rem had said.

"And we've heard some daisy pots," Lem had added. "Remember that idea Danlith had to swipe the Ruby necklace of Orshandts?" Lem had started to laugh, but Rem hadn't joined in.

"That was my idea, you git. And it would have worked if we had had enough rope." When Lem had laughed all the harder, Rem hit him hard in the shoulder. "Never mind," he had said as Lem rubbed at his arm and sucked in long breaths, trying to regain composure from his laughing. "The point is that we're goin' with you, Aiden. We know we don't have to go, and we probably wouldn't have volunteered to go early, but we probably wouldn't have thought of it either. Let's face it, mate—we wouldn't have much of a chance going in without you anyway. You're the Maker's Hand and all that, I mean."

"Do you think it'll work?" Lem had asked. "Saving Willem?"

Aiden had sighed. "I don't know, but this is all I could think of. If they think I'm important enough or if they're scared enough of me, then maybe. If not, well, I can't imagine Willem running very far with the Falcons after him."

That had brought him back to Willem, again. Aiden had glanced over at the overstuffed chair. Willem's boots still sat next to the chair, discarded and lonely. Who in their right mind would leave their boots behind if they were planning on running for it? Maybe someone who meant to swim. But no, it was way too far, and Willem was smart enough to know he couldn't swim it, smart enough to know he would need supplies and resources, smart enough not to leave after knowing what was at stake. Aiden had known Willem wasn't devouring Threll's lessons the way he was, but still, Aiden just couldn't see him taking off like this. It made no sense.

His detective analysis had been cut short by a knock at the door. Threll. "I've arranged the Trial for this evening," she had said, a hint of frost in her tone. "I also passed along your warning."

"And?"

She had shaken her head. Her face, so used to smiling, looked tight and sad. "I don't know, Aiden. This has no precedence. People are concerned. You wield a lot of sway in Holmsguard, and it seems you know it. Some feel that you should not have to go through an Elementals Trial, that the Blade is enough proof. They think you are acting now only to protect your friend from a situation that

should never have been forced upon you. Thun has a lot of supporters himself, and he has backed you from the first, which means you
have their support as well. Others are scared, and not without reason, that you are elevating yourself above the Mist Falcons. They
fear the standard that this sets for the future and the possibility of
past terrors being reborn."

Aiden hadn't had any idea what she was talking about, but before he could ask, Threll had said, "An hour before sunset is customary. Meet me at the North Gate. We'll have a short walk." After
a brief glance at the twins, she had looked back at Aiden, nodded,
and turned away.

"Wait," Aiden had called, his mind trying to fit the pieces together. Hadn't Thun said something like that? "What do you mean
'past terrors' and all that?"

Threll had stared at him for a moment, silent, considering.
Then she said, "There is much I am forbidden to speak of to anyone
who is not a full Falcon, and there is more yet that I don't know.
I can tell you this, though: you are not the only Maker's Hand to
have risen since the Fall, indeed even in the last decade." She had
shaken her head once more. "That might be saying too much already. Come through the crags and we will talk. Remember, an
hour before sunset." Then she had turned and walked off.

And that was that. The three of them had met Threll at the
gate and started their slow, solemn procession. The night was turning chill and Aiden tugged his cloak a little tighter around himself.
He had to adjust his weapons to get back to a comfortable equilib-
rium with the tighter cloak. A potential initiate was allowed two
weapons. Aiden had opted for a compact, short-range bow and arrows as well as his Maker's Blade. He would have liked to have a
spear, but he didn't want to give away the range of the bow and
didn't think it would be right to leave behind the Maker's Blade,
not with what was riding on this.

The twins had opted for a sword and a hatchet in Rem's case, and a pair of long knives for Lem. It felt oddly reminiscent of going onto the Champion Sands. Of course, they were missing Willem, who could have been a huge help in whatever was to come.

Aiden gritted his teeth. He couldn't afford to go down that line of thought. He had to focus on what was before him. They were doing this now for Willem anyway, and that would have to be enough.

As they came around the last corner, fleeing the cover of the few remaining trees, Aiden saw that even Jumper had come down to see them. Aiden hadn't seen their onetime savior since he had leapt from Hammond's little boat upon their arrival at Holmsguard. Aiden offered a tiny smirk, but Jumper's solemn face soon washed away any levity at his presence. Jumper's lack of his usual flippant, joking nature was more disturbing than all the other serious faces combined.

Well, at least he wasn't out hunting for Willem, Aiden thought. He had seen Jumper fight. It would be a predator descending on prey; Willem may not even know Jumper was on his scent before the singer was dead. Aiden had a hard time seeing Jumper taking up that particular duty, but then, Aiden was having a hard time with the whole situation. Too many betrayals in his life. Aiden knew firsthand he shouldn't take anything for granted.

Threll brought their little party to a halt in front of Lord Commander Dellan, who stood at the crest of a semicircle of the Council.

"From the beginning of our order," the man announced in a deep orator's voice, "Elementals have been at our heart. They set us apart from any and all other groups. Since Kandar, Lion Slayer, and Pelthos the Wise were first led to Castle Isle and tamed the first of the wild Elementals in the forging of the first Mist Falcons, we have ever sought the Elementals' counsel and their taming in making new Falcons.

"This night we offer these new initiates into the will that is beyond our own. We send them down into the earth—into the Elementals' lair to be tested and forged anew in the smelting fires. If these who go should return to us, let none among us naysay their presence amongst our ranks, for if they return, they return Mist Falcons."

"Mist Falcons," all those gathered except for Aiden and the twins intoned.

With that, the liturgy ended, and Threll again took the lead. The three of them followed her forward to the edge of a long, narrow gap in the earth, stopping to peer into the endless darkness below. The Crags of Telsair were true to their name. It wasn't a pit or a cave that Aiden stared into, but rather a thin, open mouth, ready to swallow him down into the bowels of the world.

Threll handed them each a small satchel that was to contain a few supplies. She then looked at them each in turn before holding Aiden's eyes and intoning, "Remember—Your Feeling, Your Sight, Your Will."

Aiden nodded and then hooked his foot into the loop at the end of his waiting rope. Threll had coached them on this part as well. They would be lowered into the pit slowly from above. Once down, the ropes would be pulled back to the top. They were to survive for at least the night and then find their way back to the surface—a vague goal, but who was Aiden to argue?

Slipping over the edge, Aiden allowed the rope loop to claim all of his weight as he felt his heart rate pick up to a trot. This was the real deal. 'Time to fly or fall,' his father would have said. Their descent started almost immediately, and soon the stars of the sky were only a narrow slit in a ceiling of blackness far above. The Crags were narrow, and occasionally Aiden had to push off one way or the other to keep from getting wedged between the two walls.

Finally, he felt his feet scrape onto a sandy, rock bottom, not a ledge this time, for he could feel the space had opened up. The other wall stood just a little further off. He stepped out of his loop and felt it almost instantly being drawn back up.

He heard a few loud *thwacks* to the side where the twins had been descending and immediately drew his sword, heart skipping over the canter and going straight to full gallop.

"See," one of the twins laughed. "I told you it would work."

"You told me?" the other responded. "It was my blooming idea, you git."

"Well, I'm the one who said it would work, ain't I?"

"What are you doing?" Aiden asked, his voice hinting at his raised stress level. "What are you two talking about?"

"Well, I had this idea, see," one of the twins said. Aiden was pretty sure it was Rem, but it was always hard to tell the two apart, especially in the dark. As he spoke, Aiden groped closer until he could make out the vaguest of shadows in the nearly-pitch dark. "Lem and I talked it over, and they were going to pull the rope back up. And that's fine—we get it. We have to find our own way out. Okay, but that don't mean we can't have a bit of rope for ourselves."

"Being thieves and all," Lem cut in, the twang of his street slang slipping in just slightly, "you never know when a bit of rope 'ill be just what you need."

"So, we cut it. When we got to the bottom, I mean. It's not a lot, just as high as we could reach, but here we have it."

Twin Angels, Aiden should have thought of that. Well, too late now—his rope had already slithered back to the surface. "Nice," he said. His turn to be useful.

He pulled the torch out of his small pack of supplies. It was dark enough that he really couldn't see the torch, so he looked up at the few stars he could make out through the tiny slit of sky. "Feeling. Sight. Will," he mumbled to himself, focusing on the light of those few stars. In his mind, he forced the light into heat—found the Elementals surrounding him, even in this cold cave, visualized his torch alight, and forced his will on it. The torch sparked and then lit.

Aiden smiled at the freshly-revealed faces of the twins. "Alright; should we see where we are?"

Chapter 30

...and we will laugh at all our extra caution.

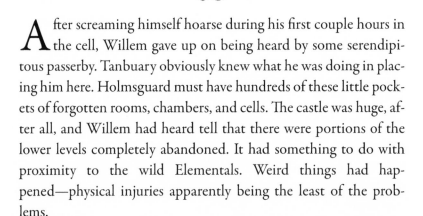

After screaming himself hoarse during his first couple hours in the cell, Willem gave up on being heard by some serendipitous passerby. Tanbuary obviously knew what he was doing in placing him here. Holmsguard must have hundreds of these little pockets of forgotten rooms, chambers, and cells. The castle was huge, after all, and Willem had heard tell that there were portions of the lower levels completely abandoned. It had something to do with proximity to the wild Elementals. Weird things had happened—physical injuries apparently being the least of the problems.

He tried not to focus on that. He was running out of things to focus on, though, and the thought of a monstrous, wild Elemental—whatever that was—crashing through the wall and gobbling him whole kept slipping in.

Aiden and the twins were out there somewhere, though, training, preparing for the Crags. And all the time, Lord Commander Dellan and Tanbuary were finishing plans on some trap to kill them during the Trial. Willem had to do something. He had to get out.

Willem had landed several solid kicks on his cell door after Tanbuary had left him, but the oak was thick and strong. Besides, kicking in the dark is harder than it sounds. There are just no points of reference. On Willem's third attempt, he had gotten too close to the door and knocked himself backward, landing hard. Missing his guitar, which was still strapped to his back, had been a near thing, and he had to roll onto his stomach to keep his momentum from carrying him onto his back. It had been mostly pointless anyway; Willem's bare feet couldn't take many more blows to the wood.

Now he sat slumped in the corner, trying not to think about the cold stones wicking away his warmth. He plucked noncommittally at the strings of his guitar, offering a tune to his melancholy as his mind wandered about, working on a way out and coming up with few options. Sleep had found him for a few hours earlier, but without any way to stay warm, he had woken up shivering and couldn't get back to sleep.

A *step, clank, step, clank,* invaded his solace and Willem got to his feet. A clicking sound scraped against the door, and then a light popped into existence on the door, but near the floor. There must be a panel, Willem thought as a bag was dropped inside the opening. Then the panel slid closed, and the light vanished. Just as quickly a small panel at head level opened, and the light leapt back into the cell.

"Tonight is the Elementals Trial for you and your friends. I thought you might want your satchel of supplies for going into the Crags," Tanbuary's voice said from beyond the light.

Willem's mind whirled with the implications. They weren't supposed to go into Trial for several days yet. Something must have happened to force things forward faster. His disappearance, he thought. But who was forcing the issue? Squinting at the light, Willem scowled and said, "I'm going into the Crags, then?"

"You're welcome to," Tanbuary said, and Willem got to his feet, surprised but hopeful. Still, something didn't seem to fit. "In fact, if you don't, the Falcons will have no choice but to label you a Trial deserter. I think we both know what that will mean for you, my friend."

Tanbuary leaned closer to the barred window, a broad, arrogant smile smothering his face. "Like I said, you're welcome to go to your Trial. I'm just not going to help you." Tanbuary laughed as he slid the panel closed once more, plunging Willem back into darkness.

Still on his feet in the dark cell, he ground his teeth as he listened to Tanbuary's receding *step, clank, step, clank*. Once silence had regained rule, he made his way cautiously forward and felt around until he found the bag that Tanbuary had left behind. Willem groped inside. He obviously wasn't going anywhere, and maybe this was just some sick way of Dellan and Tanbuary to cross their *T's* and seal their wax—but even so, he was going to take advantage of whatever the bag had to offer.

The first thing Willem's hand brushed was amazingly soft. Working by touch alone he pulled the item out and examined it. After a moment he felt the corners of his mouth tug upwards. It was a shoe—more of a slipper, really. He stuck his hand back into the satchel and immediately found its pair. His smile grew. The slippers were feathered and fluffy. He had no doubt that they were meant to be humiliating. Perhaps there was some bylaw that required initiates to be given proper attire for the Trial if they didn't already have it, and these were the worst shoes they could find for him. He didn't care in the least. His cold, bare feet welcomed the new warmth with thanks.

His new slippers in place on his feet, Willem reached back into the satchel, searching for whatever treasures still remained. The items proved elusive in the dark, but slowly he took inventory of his new stash of treasure. A rock, that he assumed was flint, was of little use since the only weapon they gave him was an overly-dull butter knife—checking off another item on the list, no doubt. Willem was fairly sure an initiate was supposed to choose their own weapons, and that they were supposed to get two of them. Dellan and Tanbuary must have been counting his guitar as one and perhaps just ignoring the choosing bit.

A small round of cheese, a hard loaf of bread, two apples, and a small canteen of water finished off the bag's contents. Having not eaten since supper of the night before, Willem helped himself to a bit of his rations. He tried not to overindulge. Dellan and Tanbuary's hands were tied into this feeding with the supplies satchel, but who knew when his jailers would see fit to feed him again?

After his few bites of cheese and bread along with one of the apples and a mouthful of water, he huddled back into his corner, trying to ignore the fact that any heat he had left there had been wicked away by the constantly chilling stone. He picked up his guitar and strummed a tune. There had to be a way out of this cell—had to be a way back to his friends. His "weapons" would be useless. A butter knife and a guitar weren't exactly the formula for a successful jailbreak.

Willem laughed at the thought, but then stopped. *The formula for a successful jailbreak.* What had Tanbuary said?

"Now, did you really think I wouldn't recognize you in the flame? Especially after you played that merry tune of yours?"

That merry tune...that merry tune. How would Tanbuary have recognized him from his song? His song in the flame. Twice Willem had done something with his music while staring into a fire. Twice he had moved himself, or at least sort of moved himself. Why not? It was worth a try.

He pulled the satchel strap over one shoulder, and trying to force himself into the right mindset, he played. Willem played, and he played. Nothing happened.

When his fingers started to hurt from the effort of playing, he stopped and slammed his fist into the stone next to him. This also did nothing other than make his hand ache. He didn't have fire, which he knew was probably key. He sighed. Dregs and draught, he didn't have any idea what he was doing, for that matter. That part might also come in handy.

Rubbing at his eyes in the dark, Willem tried to think. He didn't know what he was doing—that part was true. But he had done it twice before—that part was also true. He needed fire, or at least he had needed it the only times he had done anything like this before. That wasn't going to happen. Even if he could strike a spark off of the flint with his butter knife—and that was doubtful—he would still have to have something to burn. Unless these stones were flammable, he was out of luck for that.

Another memory came to him, more of Tanbuary's words: "Did you heat guard this room?" he had asked the Lord Commander while Willem had been eavesdropping in the flames. How long ago had that been? A night? A day? Two days? The incessant darkness was so disorienting. Willem was losing track.

"Focus," he said aloud, fully aware he was only talking to himself. Heat guard. The Elemental wasn't fire—it was heat. Obviously the two overlapped, one offering the other, but still, they weren't the same. If he was really tapping Elementalogy at all—and he really wasn't sure of that—maybe he could do something with it now.

Your feeling, your sight, your will—that had been Threll's mantra to them. Feeling...feeling. Heat. Body heat was the only thing he could think of, but that did nothing for him. Sight was a non-player in this blackness. He couldn't see anything, least of all his own body heat. This was pointless.

So Willem did the only thing that he knew he could do. He re-gripped his guitar and played. He played and played, forcing away thoughts of impossible escape and missed Trials. He played the dance of the wind over grass and the gallop of thunder amongst storm clouds. He played until all else was washed away. Hours passed and it was just him and the music—him *in* the music. He didn't even hear the approaching *step, clank, step, clank,* until it was nearly to his door. By then, Willem was so wrapped up in the melody that he couldn't stop. His fingers found their familiar places even as the upper panel slid open, revealing Tanbuary, torch in hand.

Smiling, Tanbuary sneered, "I just thought you should know, your friends just went into the Crags. They won't come out if that is any balm for your anger. Not that it will—hey. Hey!" Tanbuary was yelling by the end and frantically fitting a key into the lock, but it was too late.

Willem felt the song yank him bodily forward as soon as Tanbuary had unveiled the light. He felt as the notes of his song twined with the heat of the flame—changing, morphing, becoming one. And Willem was in the song. He was the song, and the song was the heat. He danced and flickered for a breath, and then the fully-heated song tore him deeper.

All was flickering between darkness and light. The darkness looked like stone, and after a moment he realized the only light came from himself, for he was the flame, the heat, the song. And then he was himself, still one with those but separate. In the space of another moment, he chose to step out away from the heat and toward the cold, dark stone.

Willem didn't leave his song, not at first. He had done that the last two times and had ended up back where he had started. This time he was sure that where he started was not where he wanted to be. He made sure he had stepped clean from the heat, and then he let the song slip. Willem stood in darkness, but reaching out his hand he felt rough, moist stone. This wasn't the worked stone of his cell. He didn't have any idea where he was, but he was out of his prison.

Chapter 31

The Traitor stands before me and I will not let him slip back into his
shadows again.

The whipping of the wind through the underground caves before them baffled Aiden. The twins and he were hundreds of
feet underground. The wind should have had no presence in this
trapped suffocation, and yet here it was, howling.

"Wild Elementals?" Lem asked.

"I can't imagine there's an inlet large enough to push through
this much air," Rem said, nodding.

Aiden just shrugged. It didn't matter if the wind was natural or
some kind of Elementalogy. Either way, the three of them needed
to move through the windy chamber, gust or no.

They had made their way along a narrow path with high rock
walls racing upward to either side. Then, without warning, the ceiling height had fallen to no more than six feet at its highest. There
were some places where even Aiden had to crouch to get through.
The path had wound this way and that but never had an offshoot
split from the narrow way, never a fork in the road. That path had
led them here to the howling caves where, finally, a choice lay before them. From what Aiden could see, two openings lay in the
walls of the larger cavern directly in front of them, with smaller
caves branching off from there.

In theory, the assignment had been simple enough—go into the Crags and survive long enough to find another way out. Initiates were forbidden from simply climbing back up and out from the crack they were lowered down. The climb would be a long, difficult, one—impossible for some. An experienced climber may have been able to do it, however, and the point wasn't simply to get out. The point was to survive the wild Elementals and thus prove your ability as a Mist Falcon.

There was nothing for it. They would have to move forward, and sitting, listening to the wind wail wasn't getting them any closer to out of here. Aiden handed his torch to Rem and stepped out from the opening that had been sheltering him. One step was all it took, and the cacophony of wind tore Aiden from his feet, scuffing his hand and plastering him back against a stone outcropping in the floor.

He thought he heard Rem and Lem calling after him, but he couldn't make out their words over the howl. He shut his eyes tight as tiny rocks and sand whipped past him, some striking his face and pelting against his clothes. Instinctively, Aiden tapped Wind, reaching for the Elemental as he had done with the Stone back in the valley after the Swaar battle. He could feel the Wind, its mood and temper. The trick was to let the Elemental in, but then to tame it to your will rather than being enveloped by it. It was all just a way of seeing the world of Elementalogy. The wind's Elemental wasn't sentient. It wasn't a he, she, or it. It wasn't really a separate thing from the wind. Instead, it was the essence of the wind. It was the wind, and the wind was it. Still, it was easier to separate the two—to see through the one and find the other.

While tapping Wind, Aiden let the Elemental fill him, just as Threll had taught him. He felt the Wind's anger, felt it pulse against the confines of the narrow cave, felt it rage at being shackled here instead of roaming free over green grass and budding trees. He felt the anger, absorbed it, and then wrapped it to his own purpose. Slowly, he stood. The wind still howled around him, but it could no more harm him than harm itself. He reached a hand out for focus and whispered, "Peace." Speaking really wasn't necessary, but Aiden found it easier to vocalize his desire. The wind hushed all at once, falling away as if great blowing lungs had just expelled their last breath.

"Angels, Aiden. That was amazing," Rem gasped as the twins stepped from behind the protection of the tunnel wall.

Aiden agreed, but wouldn't say so aloud. The power inside the art of Elementalogy was more than a little scary, and he couldn't imagine having to fight someone who had been training in it their whole life. Maybe he had been a little rash in threatening the whole of the Mist Falcons before coming down into the Crags. That was neither here nor there, though. He could worry about the Falcons once they were through here and out to the surface again.

Two options lay before them, two openings leading into more caves and tunnels. Rem and Lem just stood there as if planted, waiting for Aiden to decide their path as if Aiden had any better idea of where to go than they did. Fine; any decision was better than just standing here. So, he just took the path to the left for no other reason than it was closer than the right-hand path.

He stepped through the cave's gaping mouth with the twins a step behind him. They had barely traveled a handful of paces before a wailing sprouted in the air, followed closely by a fast *thrump, thrump* of the approaching feet of something heavy, moving fast. The twins readied their weapons as Aiden tore his bow from his back and yanked an arrow from his quiver. Another wail, and this time Aiden could make out the outline of a shadowy figure moving toward them quickly on four legs.

"Angels' blood," Lem cursed as a bright flash suddenly engulfed the running figure. Flames sprung to life as a beast that was somewhere between a wolf and a bear ignited with flames that seemed to burn from within.

Aiden staggered back as the beast hurtled toward him. He let his arrow fly, but he stumbled over a rock in his attempt to scramble away, and his shot went wide. He had nearly pulled himself to his feet when a massive paw crashed into his side, sending him careening into the wall. The twins yelled something and struck out with their blades.

The beast howled again, this time in pain. Its attention was fixed on Aiden, though, and it refused to be turned from that course. Aiden tried to focus on the flames burning from within the bear-hound. He tried to tap them as he had the Wind, but he had hit the wall hard and the sharp, snarling teeth were so close.

Your feeling, your sight, your will, Aiden tried to remind himself. *Your feeling, your sight, your will.* But they were just empty words. Any meaning they had once had fled when the beast came.

One more step and the fiery wolf-bear was on him again—all-encompassing, world-consuming. Aiden froze. He couldn't concentrate—couldn't act. So this is how death comes, he thought, as the beast opened its maw wide for the strike. Then, all at once, a blade sprouted from the creature's gaping mouth and grew out a full foot past the menacing teeth.

The wolf-bear let out a mixture of its previous howl and a gurgling whimper as it slumped forward, the blade tip only narrowly missing Aiden's leg. The flames dwindled before being snuffed out altogether. In the near darkness that followed, Aiden could make out Lem and Rem's forms, but could only tell them apart by their weaponry. Lem straddled the dead form, both long knives sunk deeply into the wolf-bear's flesh—one in the neck, the other entering just behind the skull and exiting through the now-slackened mouth. Rem's sword had dropped somewhere, but he must have struck the beast's side with a two-handed blow of his hatchet because the blade had sunk deep between two ribs.

"I couldn't," Aiden mumbled aloud, not sure if he was talking to anyone but himself. "He was so close...and the fire. He had those fangs, and I couldn't..." He trailed off, realizing he was just rambling. *I should have drawn my sword at least*, Aiden thought.

"It's okay, mate," Rem said.

"Yeah, don't worry about it," Lem added, yanking his first blade free of the dead beast's hold. "That's why we're here together. The two of us would have been right stuck without you stopping the wind. This time, it was our turn. That's just how it works, mate. A team, right?"

"Yeah, a team," Aiden said, trying to force some conviction into his dead voice. He knew the Wind had been different though. He had time to reach out and take control—to stop it. Granted, it was plenty unpleasant being pelted by the Wind, but he had time. The Wind hadn't been threatening to rip his face off with razor teeth. He would have to do better next time. If he froze again, it could mean all of their lives.

"Besides," Rem put in, apparently still wanting to cheer Aiden, "that monster thing only had eyes for you. Gave Lem and me a chance to attack from behind. You had to do the hard work o' gettin knocked about, mate. Not that I'm complaining about that part. As long as you're comfortable getting throttled a bit, well, I'm comfortable letting you. Some of us have our looks to consider, after all. The womenfolk for a hundred leagues would wail a flood and ruin the crops if my pretty face got mangled down here." Rem posed, grinning what Aiden assumed was meant to be his most dashing smile, turning his head slightly and throwing his hooked nose into sharp contrast in the dim light of their single torch.

Aiden shook his head, the fear retreating, removing his shackles. He pushed himself up and retrieved his torch from where he had dropped it to reach for an arrow. Fortunately, the flame hadn't guttered out; that was something, at least.

"Shall we see what else awaits?" Aiden said trying to force some levity into his voice as he stepped further into the chamber. He didn't go more than three steps, though, before the floor under his stepping foot sank beneath his weight. It didn't sink far, a couple of inches at most, and it was only a small square, barely large enough to pedestal his whole foot that sank. Looking down at it, Aiden could see that it was a different stone than the rest of the floor, lighter in color and smoother, though someone had tried to conceal it with scuff marks and dust.

You're getting sloppy, he told himself. There had been a time while scavenging around Oustenbasch that he watched every step, every movement. Not doing so could mean your death, and now it might. Teach him a few tricks with the Wind and all of a sudden he thought he could run around with his eyes closed. Fool.

He stood as still as he could, listening, but nothing seemed amiss. Death would come calling when he stepped off then, instead. Great.

"What is it?" Lem asked, coming up behind Aiden.

"Stop," Aiden barked, maybe a little too harshly, but to no avail. Lem was already around him, looking down at Aiden's planted foot, and the too-cleanly-cut stone beneath it.

"What is it?" Rem echoed his brother taking, a step toward Lem and Aiden.

"Pressure plate," Lem answered back. "The reverse kind, judging by the fact that we ain't dead right now."

"Fantastic," Rem said. "Can you see the wire?"

"Nah, more complex than that, I'm afraid, mate."

"Listen," Aiden cut in, taking a deep breath, "you two need to get out of this chamber, maybe try the other one back there, past of the wind tunnel. Once you're away, I'll step off of this and we can see what happens."

Lem shook his head. "Don't be a git, mate. How do we know this here pressure plate don't set off something terrible in that other cave, huh? Maybe we scurry in there, you step off, and then we die in a blaze of agonized screams. I think I'll pass on that if it's all the same to you. Rem?"

"Pass," the other twin echoed.

"Come on," Aiden said. "This plate was put here to kill whoever stepped on it, not to fry somebody two caves away. I'm the idiot who fell for it. So whoever put it here can win with me, but let's not all die for it."

"Ah, but whoever put that plate there wasn't counting on having the Pestelson twins down here when you stepped on it," Lem laughed.

"We're thieves, remember?" Rem added. "We've had to get out of all kinds of tight spaces, mate. Kinda comes with the job, you see."

As Aiden watched, Rem and Lem carefully squatted down until their faces were nearly touching the pressure plate Aiden stood upon. Slowly they scuttled back and forth, circling Aiden and his standing spot. They looked like nothing so much as squirrels cautiously examining a fallen apple along a footpath. Occasionally, they would chatter to each other. Aiden only caught pieces of their quiet, stunted banter.

"Two white stones," one of them said. "Could be a Dance and Flame."

"Excess dust," the other responded a moment later. "Maybe a bait and switch."

"Or a double slip."

"Yeah, but not with this lot—too clever by half."

And so their conversation continued as they got further and further from Aiden—first tracing one line and then abandoning it, coming back and tracing a new one.

After several minutes, Lem said, "Here's another one. Better too—more natural with the rest of the rock. I might have stepped on this one myself."

"What do you think?" Rem asked. "Double blow?"

"Nah, rooms too big. Single blow. Double switch, or multi-switch if there's more. And, large payload, big enough to take out a bloke on any and all of the switch plates."

Aiden narrowed his eyes trying to weave his way through Lem's words—the man's street slang growing thicker as he talked.

"Which would also mean a centralized location for the spring," Rem said as he and Lem made their way toward a large outcropping of stone growing from the cave floor near the center of the chamber and not fifteen paces from where Aiden stood.

The two of them made a full circuit around the stone twice before their heads disappeared down behind the far side, and Lem said, "Oh, now that's clever mate. Look here. Just big enough to hollow and pack."

"What is?" Aiden asked, growing frustrated. He didn't like having to just stand here.

Rem's head reappeared from behind the outcropping. "This stone is mostly just pretend, mate. Chocked full of enough musket powder to blow us all to meet Sansol and Antice in a charred, fiery mess."

"The stone won't even stop it," Lem's voice said, still from behind the rock. "Whoever did this, hollowed the thing down so finely that it will just blast apart in the explosion sending tiny shards of stone soaring as additional projectiles. A lethal construction, really. I have to give it to them. Effective, or at least it would be if there wasn't someone here who could detach the spring from the trigger."

Aiden took a moment absorbing all of that. "And can you? Detach the thing from the thing, I mean?"

"Of course, mate. The Mist Falcons have always assumed they were being so very careful with their fire powder, but at times they have sold off small quantities to some few special interest groups. At least one of those groups, The Touch, happens to be in Perry.

Aiden's breathe caught. The Touch. He hadn't known they functioned outside of Oustenbasch. Since his father's murder, they had always been a shadow of death in his mind—forcing action but never seen and never heard. He had to force his lungs to resume their even pace, doing his best to listen to the rest of what Lem was saying.

The Touch spent quite some time and more than a handful of golden eagles paying alchemists to recreate the fire compound. I don't know if they ever got the formula just right, but they certainly used the stuff to blow a few holes in doors and walls that, rather unfortunately, blocked their way."

"And you just happened to be part of this Perrian group," Aiden said trying to keep his voice from shaking with the emotions roiling inside of him.

"Us?" Lem asked. "No, no, we just had certain run-ins with them, if you take my meaning. We're thieves, remember?" Lem winked at Aiden before turning back to see what his brother was doing again.

"Anyway," Rem went on, his voice now muffled and echoy as if his head were inside of the stone outcropping, which, Aiden reflected, may be exactly where it was. "The Falcons think that their secret is their own, and that no one else could possibly be smart enough to figure it out. That kind of arrogance can make a bloke sloppy. And, when you're sloppy sometimes you take shortcuts and just...there."

The twins reemerged from behind the pitted stone all smiles. "Alright mate," Lem said. "You're free to go."

"I can just?"

"Yeah, step right off. We should be fine."

"Should be?" Aiden asked, but stepped off anyway. The stone he had depressed slid back to the surface without so much as a hiss or a click. Nothing happened. Aiden let out a sigh he didn't know he had been holding in. Then he smiled a huge, I just outran a charging bull, smile.

"Well, I can say truly and fully, I'm glad the two of you came down here with me. I would have been dead twice over. So, thanks, I guess."

"You're welcome," Lem said immediately offering a huge grin.

"Just doing our part, mate," Rem added slapping Aiden on the back. "We had to do something beyond being devilishly handsome."

Aiden smiled again, still just happy not to have been incinerated in some giant explosion.

Together the three of them made their way to the far end of the room and the open mouth of yet another chamber. As they walked, they watched each step, careful not to step on any more trigger plates. Who knew what other surprises lay hidden in this floor?

They had just crossed into the next chamber, rounding a corner and checking what may lie ahead, when the world behind them exploded in a brilliant cacophony of flames and debris.

Chapter 32

But if not, remember...

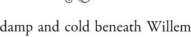

The stone was damp and cold beneath Willem's touch as he walked along the narrow passage. He couldn't see anything—hadn't been able to see anything since he had left his prison cell behind, somehow traveling through flame, heat, and song and finding himself here in the dark. He had been strangely tired after his remarkably odd transporting journey, as if he had run miles at full sprint.

Willem had slumped down right where he was in the dark and rested his sweat-slicked head back against the cool, damp stone. In truth, he had no idea how he had gotten here. The song of course, but how had he gotten here? He remembered a feeling, a pulling through the flames, like he was anchored, roped to something else that dragged him here. To what, though, he didn't have the faintest notion.

After some time had passed, and the shock wore off a bit, he had the presence of mind to check himself and the area around him. It seemed that everything he was wearing or holding when he leapt into Tanbuary's torch flame was still with him, including his guitar and the satchel Tanbuary had given him in mockery.

He had rummaged through the satchel, pulling out and helping himself to a bit more of the cheese and bread along with another mouthful of water. Willem had spent much of his life wandering the countryside, making the rounds from inn to inn where he and his troupe could perform. He had always been amazed by how much strength a few bites of food in one's stomach could lend. He found himself amazed once again on this night.

Holding to that newfound strength, Willem had climbed back to his feet and begun his creeping exploration through the caves.

Time had escaped his grasp here in the dark. Now Willem wasn't at all sure how long he had been creeping along this narrow stone hallway. An hour? A day? He didn't know. No turn-offs presented themselves and the passage seemed to continue on forever. He didn't know where he was or where he was trying to get to. What he did know was that a light had appeared ahead just now with a crash and a whoosh of air. It flickered and danced an invitation, a promise of something more beyond this narrow stone way.

Willem fought the urge to call out in an attempt to hold that light close and not let it slip. He had heard too many stories of grummels in the deep places of the world carrying off children to roast over underground bonfires. He was no child, of course, but still, he held his tongue.

He approached the light as quickly as he could without stumbling, still in his darkness. As he approached, the flames split their flickering into several different promising dances. The space began to widen out from a tunnel into a stone chamber, and slowly Willem could make out images from the light cast by the flames. Charred rocks and small pieces of smoldering timber lay scattered carelessly across a smooth, stone floor. This lit timber offered the faint promising light that he had seen originally.

First things first, Willem pulled a torch from his pack and crossed to the slowly dying flames. Bending down, he lit the torch. With its light, he stepped back for a better look.

The chamber was more or less round with only two exits, one of which Willem had just entered through. The other lay almost exactly opposite from him across the chamber. It appeared that there had been a third passage, but this had been blocked by large piled stones bearing the same charred soot as the stones crowding the floor. All of this he took in at a glance, for just inside the now-blocked archway lay three unmoving forms that Willem knew well. Sprawled facedown lay Aiden, Rem, and Lem, blanketed by disheveled cloaks, with packs and weapons strewn around their unmoving forms.

Willem rushed forward, finding Aiden first, farthest from the door. Careful not to drop the torch, he used his free hand to turn Aiden's body over. The smaller man's chest still rose and fell slowly. Unconscious but not dead, then—good. A nasty-looking cut oozed blood from above his left eye, but it didn't look life-threatening.

Moving on to the twins, Willem found them both breathing as well. One of them—he thought it was Rem, but the twins were hard enough to tell apart not bloodied—had scrapes all along the right half of his face, and swelling had already started around that eye. Willem wondered if the ex-thief would even be able to open it by the time he woke up.

Worst of all was the second twin—Lem, he was fairly certain. The partially upturned half of Lem's face glistened in a streak of his own blood, and the man's leg was buried beneath the fallen rubble of the archway.

Willem stood, dumbfounded. They were all breathing. That was good, but he really had no idea of what to do next. He was no medic. He wasn't even a soldier to have seen and dealt with injuries before. He was just a musician, Angels help him, and his friends needed more than a song right now.

Rolling his shoulders, Willem took several deep breaths and blew them out slowly. He could do this. He could do something, at any rate. They were breathing, after all. He just had to help. He started with Aiden, deciding he looked the least injured and would therefore be the easiest to help. Rationalizations in times like this didn't have to make sense. They just had to keep a person moving.

Willem rolled Aiden onto his back and slowly slid him over to the wall. Before leaving him, he propped him up slightly, just in case he was to vomit or something and could choke on the bile. He had heard that head injuries could do that.

Next up was Rem, who got a similar treatment. Willem left him in turn propped next to Aiden and returned for Lem. This one would be a bit trickier. Lem's leg was fully wedged beneath the fallen stones. Willem tried lifting the large rock that seemed the primary culprit in Lem's captivity, but it was big and mostly buried beneath the rest of the rubble itself. *Won't get you out that way,* he thought. What he wouldn't give for some of Thun's ability with Stone Elementals right now. He could use both the strength and the art to force these rocks to abide by his will.

Stepping back, Willem scanned the room, looking for aid. After a moment, his eyes settled on a thick beam—a header for the doorway, he guessed. The beam was about five feet long and a full handbreadth wide. Whatever had caused the fire and collapse must have hit the beam like a wave washing it out from the doorway's stone embrace and discarding it into the chamber's center. Regardless of how it got free, Willem picked it up gratefully.

After dragging the beam over to where Lem lay with the rubble, he abandoned the wood for a moment to go in search of a rock that was free of the rubble's crushing weight. He had hoped to find a large stone that he could prop the beam against for leverage. All of the biggest stones, however, were buried as part of the immovable mass that now blocked the passage into the third room or tunnel. He searched for several minutes, prying at stones with fingers calloused from long hours on the strings, but in the end, he admitted defeat and settled for a medium-sized, charred rock that had presumably been blown into the chamber before the rubble could collect into its pile. It wasn't as big as he had hoped, but it would have to do.

Willem half lifted, half rolled the rock over into position next to the still-unconscious Lem. Maybe it was best he hadn't found a bigger stone. This rock proved to be about as heavy as he could handle. That fact offered little hope to his plan, but he would try anyway. It was all he could think of.

So, propping the beam on the rock he had found to use as a pivot and forcing the far end as far under the stone that held Lem captive as he could, Willem hauled back on his end of the beam. Just as he thought there might be motion—the rubble might be moving—the far end slipped from where he had wedged it and he went tumbling backward. As he fell, his fully-flexed arm muscles continued in their duty just a moment too long and he brought his end of the beam smashing down into his own stomach. He gasped for breath. The air betrayed him, however, abandoning his lungs and refusing to reenter, but for tiny, unsatisfying wisps.

For a few minutes, Willem just lay there, trying to breathe and gather his strength again. Slowly, his wind returned and his heart rate restored itself to normal. He looked over at where Lem lay. He sighed. He had enough breath to sigh again. "Yeah alright," he muttered. His stomach still hurt, but there was nothing for that. Willem got back to his feet, picked up the beam, and placed it again against his rock pivot and beneath the stone rubble.

He tested it but wasn't sure he had enough grip. He tried to force it further into the space between floor and pile, but it was no good. There was no more space. Willem looked around frantically. He didn't know why he felt such urgency—didn't know if Lem would really be that much better off against the wall rather than lying here. But it felt important. Willem *had* to get him out—get him moved.

Then his eye found it. Reflecting lightly in the torch's fiery dance, lay a discarded hatchet. The blade still held a finely-sharpened edge and Willem could only assume it belonged to one of his friends. Regardless, the hatchet was exactly what he needed at the moment. Picking it up, he started working on the far end of the beam with as powerful of strokes as he could muster. The blade was as good as it had appeared, and within a dozen blows Willem had trimmed the end of the beam down into a roughly hewn wedge.

"Okay, let's try this again," he said aloud to no one in particular as he replaced the beam again onto his rock and into the space beneath the rubble. It slid in a few inches further this time. Willem hoped it would be enough. For the second time, he threw his weight down against his end of the beam, muscles pulsing from the exertion of tugging the makeshift brace downward.

Just as he was sure it was hopeless, the stone that held Lem's ankle pinned shifted up just slightly. With a cry of exertion that echoed off the stone walls and ceiling, Willem let go of the beam with his left hand, reached out, grabbed Lem by the sleeve, and hauled with all his might. Willem had always been a big man and the training he had done first on the Champion's Sands and then with the Mist Falcons, had done nothing but tone his muscles. Now, he was grateful for every ounce of body and strength, for it took everything he had—more, really, than he had known he had—to move those stones and Lem's dead-weight body as well.

The previously-captured leg free, Willem released Lem and the beam both. The wooden beam clattered to the ground, luckily missing Willem this time, and the rubble shifted back lazily to where it had been a moment before.

Willem pulled off Lem's boot to check his ankle, but from what he could tell, it didn't look that bad. He had expected a crushed bone and a good amount of blood. Though the ankle looked swollen and was turning black and blue even in the flickering torchlight, it wasn't nearly as bad as Willem had expected. So, leaving the boot off, he pulled Lem over to where Aiden and Rem already sat perched against the wall. He then rolled his pivot rock over and put Lem's leg up on it. Thant had broken his ankle once while they were traveling. The healer woman from a local village had told them to keep him off it and keep it resting up. Willem figured it would be worth a try for Lem too. Angels knew there wasn't much else he could do for him.

Finally, he tore a few small sections from the bottom of his own shirt, and using a bit of the water in his canteen, Willem cleaned the blood away from the faces of the three men. He was sure they would have some monster headaches when they woke up, but none of the cuts looked terribly serious.

His meager abilities as a healer exhausted, Willem did the only thing he could think of to add something of value. It was cold in these caves; he wanted a fire. He gathered up the wood shavings from when he had hacked the beam into a wedge a few minutes before and piled them near his three friends. He then gathered up whatever bits of wood lay scattered on the floor or that could be pried from the rubble. Lastly, he dragged over his trusty beam. It wasn't a lot, but it should be enough to keep them warm for a few hours at least. Using his torch, it didn't take long to get the fire going.

Fire kindled and flaming, Willem put out his torch to save it for later, sat back with his guitar, and began to strum lightly. As he played, the thought finally struck him—if Aiden and the twins were here, then he had made it somehow. Willem had entered into the Crags of Telsair and thus into his Elemental Trial.

Chapter 33

...for one may yet come after

—⁂—

The first things Aiden was aware of as he woke were flickering light, a throbbing headache, and the sound of music. His vision was blurred, his memory more so. Someone strummed a guitar, occasionally picking out individual notes that hummed of a powerful deepness.

"Down, down, down," a voice sang, twining seamlessly with the guitar's music.

"In caverns dark and dungeons deep—down, down, down.
In caverns dark and dungeons deep—down, down, down.
You'll find the treasure that you seek, but down, down, down.
You'll find the treasure that you seek, but down, down, down.
Through open doors of solid stone, go down, down, down.
Through open doors of solid stone, go down, down, down.
And there you'll find your rest alone—down, down, down.
And there you'll find your rest alone—down, down, down.
In caverns dark and dungeons deep, yes, there's the treasure that you seek.
Through open doors of solid stone, for there you'll find your rest alone...
Down, down, down.
Down, down, down.

In caverns dark and dungeons deep, yes, there's the treasure that you seek.

Through open doors of solid stone, for there you'll find your rest alone...

Down, down, down.

Down, down, down.

Down, down, down.

In caverns dark and dungeons deep—down, down, down... "

The voice, one Aiden knew from somewhere, began its dark tune again. He had the feeling that voice had been singing this song over and over for some time.

Blinking his blurred vision away, Aiden looked for the source of the song. By the light of a dying fire, he could just make out the form and face of Willem sitting across from him, perched against a rock, legs outstretched. The musician stared, unseeing, into the flames as he offered his music to the near darkness.

Aiden's mind cleared as if the fog covering his thoughts had been blown free by an approaching wind. Everything came rushing back—Willem's disappearance, the Crags of Telsair, the wild Elementals, the pressure plate, and then the explosion. But then there was a gap until now, here, this song, and Willem.

"Willem," Aiden rasped through a dry throat. The man's song stopped, and he looked up, startled.

"Aiden, are you alright? How do you feel?"

"Like someone used my head for a drum." He sighed. "But I'm alright, I think. What happened?"

Willem shook his head. "There was a crash, and then I found you three in here, bits of flame still smoldering across the floor."

"But how..." Aiden's question was cut short by a moan to his right.

"Dregs and draught," Rem groaned, "what was that?" The man brought a hand up to rub at his face but pulled it away again, wincing as his fingers brushed against multiple cuts and scrapes. "Willem?" Rem asked, looking up and squinting across the dying flames.

"Of course it's Willem, you git," Lem answered from Rem's right side, eyes still closed and voice muffled. Who did you think was serenading us?" It was hard to tell in the dim light, but Aiden was pretty sure Lem offered a half-smile, still keeping his eyes closed.

Aiden waited a moment and then started his questions again. "Willem, how did you get here? Where have you been? And, what in the Maker's name are you wearing?"

Willem gave the barest hint of a smile. Raising one foot and shaking it slightly, he said, "These were a gift and a wonder for my poor cold feet. As for the rest, I don't know exactly, but what I can tell you is that we may all be in for an unwelcome surprise when we reach the surface. It would appear that our dear Lord Commander has plans that we all fit into better dead than alive." From there, Willem went on to explain how he had first moved into and through the flames of their campfire the night before they got to Holmsguard, how he had overheard two men talking before returning to himself. He told of how, on the night he supposedly disappeared, he had done something similar in their common room, hearing an important discussion clearly not meant for his ears. Willem explained how he had raced off barefoot to find Thun but had found only Nathaniel, who had, in turn, led him to Lord Commander Dellan and the man Tanbuary who had tricked and imprisoned him.

"And then I started playing my guitar, just to calm myself and take my mind off of it, you know," Willem said. "Well, I kind of fell into a trance, and then when Tanbuary came back again with his torch, I sort of leapt into the flame and ended up down here. Well, I ended up down there, actually," Willem gestured to one of the doorways that led from the room. "Not that it matters, though. There's nothing down there—just a long, low tunnel leading to a dead end of stone."

Aiden tried to wrap his mind around the different impossibilities of Willem's story. Willem had traveled, jumped through flame. How? How had Aiden calmed the torrent of wind two chambers over, though? It seemed crazy, but crazy was quickly becoming life.

"Well, sounds like we found this Tanbuary's traps," Rem said, resting his head back against the wall. "There must have been a secondary timer on the fuse that we missed. We're lucky it took as long as it did."

"Hold on," Willem said. "What happened to you lot?"

And so it was their turn for a tale. Neither of the twins moved to answer, so it fell to Aiden to relate all that had happened after Willem had been taken. He told him of the assumption that Willem must have fled and of his own threat against anyone who harmed Willem.

"It was brilliant," Lem chimed in from where he still sat, leg up, head back, eyes closed. "You should've heard him, Will."

"Better yet," Rem agreed, "you should have seen everyone else wet themselves when Aiden drew his Maker's Blade and held it up, daring anyone to defy him. It was amazing."

"It was stupid," Aiden said. "Any one of them could have killed me where I stood, but I had to do something, and moving up our Trial along with the bravado was all I could think of. Plus, I was mad."

"Oh, Aiden being mad," Rem mocked with a grin.

"Shocking, isn't it?" Lem added, completely deadpan.

Aiden didn't have enough energy for more than an unseen glare of disapproval. So with a sigh, he finished his story of entering the Crags and of their journey up through the explosion that had left them in this room.

"It's a bit comforting to know that Tanbuary's traps are already taken care of," Willem said. "I mean, I'm sure you three hurt and all, but nobody's dead. Tanbuary failed, regardless of his bold words to the Lord Commander."

"Thanks to these two," Aiden said, nodding his head toward the twins. "I don't think he planned on having anyone with knowledge of their explosives down here."

"I don't know that we can rule out traps, though," Lem mused, opening his eyes for the first time and sitting up a bit. He winced as he moved his leg down from its perch on the rock. "We made it through one room, barely, but who's to say that git didn't put explosives all over the place down here."

"That's a possibility, and we should keep a lookout for it," Willem conceded, "but I don't know. You didn't hear Dellan and Tanbuary talking. It just didn't seem like they had time to lace the whole cavernous network with powder. Besides, I don't know if the Lord Commander would risk destroying so much of the Crags of Telsair. Isn't it supposed to be some kind of holy place to the Falcons?"

"That's another thing that doesn't make sense," Rem said. "Why would Dellan conspire to kill us? The Maker's Blades and hence the Maker's Hands are supposed to be important to the Mist Falcons, revered or something."

Willem smiled. "Do you feel revered, Aiden?"

Aiden offered a half-laugh. "Of course. Explosives are always a sign of extreme respect."

"Exactly my point," Rem said. "Why would Dellan want you dead? Why would he want any of us dead?"

"Maybe he's afraid Aiden is going to overshadow his authority," Lem chuckled. "You know—step in, smack him around a little, and take charge."

"I overheard a conversation on the sparring fields that our dear Lord Commander is a Twin Warrior of some kind," Aiden said. "I very much doubt he is overly concerned with me smacking him around."

"Don't be a git. You're a Maker's Hand, Den," Lem said wincing again as he leaned forward to look Aiden in the eyes. "I'm not sure if you noticed, but there doesn't seem to be a whole lot of those lying around Holmsguard."

Everyone fell silent for a moment. Then, Willem added, "I think there is another one, a Maker's Hand, I mean, or at least there was. I don't know, really, but when I was in the flames, listening in on Dellan and Tanbuary's conversation, before they figured out I was there and before Nathaniel had taken me to them, Dellan said something about one Hand being bad enough, but now having a second. It sounded an awful lot like they were talking about Aiden being the second Hand. Tanbuary said the other Hand had been dealt with though, something about a spirit, I think he said, so he might be dead. I don't know. Either way, though, Lem has a point, I think. They are trying to kill us, or at least kill you, Aiden. And, if the Lord Commander is in on it, who knows how deep the conspiracy goes."

"Not to sound pessimistic on such a bright shiny day such as it is," Rem announced, "but it seems to me that if Dellan wants us dead, our prospects aren't that great even if we make it back to the surface."

Everyone fell quiet again, obviously pondering the same thought. After a moment, Aiden stood, making up his mind. There was nothing for it. "We don't know enough about Mist Falcon politics to make a wise choice. I say we focus on getting to the surface. Once there, maybe we can find Thun and tell him what we've learned. He'll know what to do. For now, Will says there's nothing down that tunnel. That makes our choice easy. Let's see what's in the next room."

The next room held little to nothing, nor did the three chambers to follow. The going was slow. Amazingly, Lem had been able to limp along sluggishly. He wasn't grudging with his movements, but it was obvious that he was in pain. Most of the time he hobbled along, one arm around his brother, each step slow and short, over the uneven stone floor. Aiden did his best not to become annoyed with the slow pace. From what Willem explained, Lem had had hundreds of pounds of rubble trapping his foot and ankle after the explosion. It was nothing short of miraculous that the twin could walk at all.

They probably wouldn't have gone that much faster even with four fully healthy bodies. They were constantly searching the ground for more traps, while at the same time watching every shadowy corner for wild Elementals.

Aiden and Willem had both relit torches from the dying embers of their campfire before they had left it. Torchlight only cast itself so far, however, and they were all tense against attack, weapons drawn. Lem had surrendered one of his long knives into Willem's handling, and Rem had given up his sword. Most of his effort was being channeled into keeping Lem on his feet anyway, and the hatchet was easier to carry while supporting his brother. Besides, Willem had always been the best with a sword. Aiden had decided to leave his bow strapped across his back and draw his Maker's Blade in its place. He couldn't very well draw and loose an arrow while still holding his torch, and he didn't much care for the idea of dropping the torch to fight. If they had to flee, he would most likely end up abandoning it. He didn't like losing the range attack the bow offered, but they were blind without their torches. Aiden would take sight over reach in a fight any day.

Some of the chambers they entered had as many as three exits, not including the doorway they entered through. Their path in the near dark was anything but straight. More than once, they found themselves at a dead end and were forced to retrace their steps.

Hour relieved hour, trading shifts without the slightest change, save perhaps for a consistently heavier weariness spreading across the four of them. Lem and Rem were growing particularly tired—Lem due to his injury, Rem for his support.

Aiden was beginning to worry about their stock of torches. They had each been given two in their packs, and they were good, long-lasting torches—Falcon designed and made. They had even come upon a skeleton of bones in one of the passages, the remains of some other unlucky initiate. They had been able to scavenge an unused torch from the long-dead body. Still, they had used up a couple of their torches already and were burning through three and four readily enough. If they couldn't find their way out by the time they used up the last of the torchlight, they were as good as dead. They had discussed going down to only one torch burning at a time, and it may yet come to that, but one torch would mean less light to illuminate a chamber or tunnel, and less light meant an even slower pace.

Just as Aiden was going to suggest that Willem put out his torch for a while, they entered a chamber that pulled him up short. He hadn't been able to see it before they actually got to the doorway because they had been rounding a sharp bend. Now, though, he could see just fine, and what he saw was dazzlingly bright to cave-darkened eyes.

Huge crystals sprouted from every surface—wall, floor, and ceiling. They seemed to glow from some inner light, and reflected back each other's glow in an endless back-and-forth of shimmering beauty. The chamber stood in contrast to the rest of the cavernous Crags they had seen so far. The glow and beauty of the room drew Aiden forward, drew all of them forward, until they stood in the room's center, turning slowly in awestruck wonder.

A slender stream sliced a path through the room from end to end, dividing the room in half. Two silver trees stood as guardians on either bank, growing remarkably out of the stone. As they watched, a glorious figure emerged from the stream's depth. A beautiful woman's form seemed to grow straight up out of the water and hold there, delicate feet suspended on tiptoes above the stream, yet still touching the water's gentle flow. The figure smiled at them and motioned forward graciously with one hand. A sudden thirst came upon Aiden and he took an indecisive step forward.

Willem and Lem were faster, moving forward to drink from the stream's promise of cool, clear refreshment. Lem tripped partway to the stream, but continued forward, crawling, apparently heedless of the pain in his ankle.

Rem hesitated, his face showing a kind of inner struggle, a battle of wills. Aiden watched him intently, watched as Rem's willpower slipped away and he, too, moved forward to drink. Rem's hesitancy had been enough to break the spell for Aiden, however. He looked back at the watery woman, and it no longer seemed so beautiful or inviting to him. There was something disturbing about the form, unnatural as it turned its gaze upon Aiden's unmoving stance.

He felt the thirst tug at him again, this time a bit stronger—a bit more desperately. Oddly, the harder pull only made him want to pull back. This wasn't right. They shouldn't be here, shouldn't be drinking this.

He met the water woman's eyes. *Your feeling, your sight, your will.* He tapped Water and felt as much as he saw the figure change into something far more grotesque. It still had a female form—or mostly, at least, but it had dozens of rotating tentacles in place of arms and legs. Those cool, watery eyes no longer held the promise of peace and serenity. Now they offered only thirst. *Your feeling, your sight, your will.*

Slowly, he fought a battle with that thirst, forcing it back down into the stream, until with a final scream of agony and frustration from the beastly Water Elemental, Aiden pushed forward and the figure disappeared altogether with a light splash.

The room dimmed immediately, the crystals losing their brilliance, and Aiden's friends sat back, spitting out their most recent mouthfuls of water from the now-muddy stream.

"Water Elemental," Aiden said, breathing hard after the exchange, but he had no time for further explanation. At that moment, a ripping, cracking sound tore through the air as the two guardian trees wrenched themselves free of the rocky ground. They lumbered toward the companions, their forms shifting, growing arms from limbs and legs from roots.

Your feeling, your sight, your will, Aiden thought, trying to impose his will on the onrushing forms. His mind felt thick and sluggish after his encounter with the Water Elemental, however, and he could do little more than think the words.

Wooden limbs and clubs crashed down around the doorway as the companions retreated, stumbling and tripping. Rem more or less dragged Lem out into the tunneled hall just as the first blows fell. Running, falling, and scrambling, they fled back through the tunnel they had walked down only moments before. As they left the room with its crystallized light, they were left only with Aiden's torch to light their way. Willem had set down his torch to drink better from the Elemental's stream. At least it hadn't been his sword. At any rate, there was no going back for the torch now. The others were packed with no time to get them out. They'd just have to make due. The shorter doorway had bottle-necked the wild

Wood Elementals at first, but the crashing sound of rock behind them announced that it no longer held the terrifying tree forms.

They raced down the tunnel, Lem crying out from the pain of putting so much pressure on his injured ankle. There was nothing for it, though. The lumbering Wood Elementals gained on their prey as the seconds slipped past. Aiden led them through a doorway on their left and then took a right only a few feet into that tunnel. He paid no heed to which direction they fled—only to staying ahead of their pursuers.

Taking another right, Aiden found a chamber he was fairly certain they hadn't been through yet. Halfway across the room, Lem fell with a cry. Rem yanked his brother back up, but Lem fell another few steps further into the chamber.

"Just go," Lem said breathing heavily.

"Like Antice we will," Willem growled going back. He pushed his weapons and guitar out to Rem, who grabbed them in a jumble. Then, Willem bent down and, with Lem helping to bear some of his own weight, hoisted the fallen man up onto his shoulder. The twins were bigger than Aiden, but they still weren't large men. Willem had to strain in the lifting. Still, he could manage where Aiden and Rem would have been at a loss. The musician nodded to Aiden, and again they were off.

The Wood Elementals were obviously having trouble negotiating their large forms through the doorways. Aiden's quick turns had bought them a bit of time, but they had spent most of it here. Even as they reached the far end of the chamber and ducked through yet another archway, Aiden heard the crashing entrance of the tree forms into the room he and the others were abandoning.

Aiden didn't know where this would end. If the Elementals could smash through stone, then what escape were the four of them going to find by fleeing. He couldn't think of anything else to do, though, and so they ran.

He led the charge in taking two more quick rights and then another left. The mental map he had been forming since offering his farewell to the night stars upon entering the Crags was all but gone now. He was taking turns at random, hoping they might lead them out, or at least bring them to some kind of safe harbor. Rounding a corner, that hope died a little further.

Aiden only just had time to drop and roll, feeling the uneven rock floor rip scratches into his skin, as a handful of steel swords sliced the air. The metal blades hammered into the stone wall exactly where Aiden had been running a moment before. The others hesitated, taking a step back as they looked up at the Steel Elemental shimmering in Aiden's torchlight. Wasting the few seconds offered by the Elemental's missed attack, they all just watched.

"Golden Strings!" Willem whispered.

Your feeling, your sight, your will, Aiden thought, tapping Steel and pushing his way into the Elemental with his mind. The oversized, man-like form of the Steel Elemental turned back to him, its body swiveling and flowing rather than actually taking steps. The resistance in forcing his own will on this wild force was greater than any he had encountered. It felt like trying to swim through a thick molasses. "Your will, your will," he whispered to himself, trying to envelop and contain the Elemental before him. The defense of the Steel creature was just too strong, though. Aiden's mind gave out before he could accomplish more than a brief pause in the Elemental's action. He stumbled back, nearly fell, then steadied himself.

Breath coming in gasps, he did the only other thing he could think of beyond abandoning his friends: he drew his sword, his Maker's Blade, and prepared to stand his ground. Eight blades sprouted from the Steel Elementals torso. They grew to an impressive length, and then the Elemental attacked.

Aiden forced all thought into the moving metal. He could feel how it would flow, where it would flow. There was no ducking this time, no rolling to the side. The Elemental's blades came from different angles and different heights. If he dodged one blow, another would claim him. Instead, he stood his ground and watched. At the last moment, Aiden acted, forcing his blade this way and then that to block the onslaught of Elemental swords. Two of the attacks had only been feints and secondary plans in case Aiden tried to duck or charge. The other four came flying in, true and swift. The Maker's Blade snapped right, left, up, down, blocking each swing or thrust with perfect accuracy. As Aiden deflected the swords around himself, the Elemental let out a terrible howl as if it had been burned.

A moment later, Rem struck out with hatchet and short sword, driving both into the Elemental's back. A clanging sound reverberated through the narrow tunnel, but the Elemental seemed unaffected. Still, it turned to face this new opponent, swiveling its full torso again rather than moving its legs.

Aiden saw his opportunity and leapt forward, driving his sword into the Elemental's now exposed back before the wild creature could slash out at Rem with its blade limbs. His sword pierced the metallic skin of the Elemental driving several inches into the back. The steel Elemental reared up, howling more viciously than before.

"Come on!" Aiden yelled, and the others took hold of the opportunity to slip past the Elemental. With that, their little company was off running again.

Two more doorways lay ahead and only one direction to run. Plunging through the last archway, Aiden pulled up short. They had just entered an open chamber. Two doorways—besides the one they had just come through—stood along the walls. One of these lay completely blocked by rubble. The remains of a campfire still charred one spot of the floor black just where Aiden's group had left it. He knew exactly where they were now. They had fled back full circle. He didn't know if his mind had made choices for known paths or if the random rights and lefts had simply led here. Either way, they were stuck.

More crashing resonated behind them. Out of time.

"Quick, down the tunnel," Aiden shouted.

Willem hesitated, though. "Uh, Aiden, there's nothing down there."

"I know. Come on." Aiden didn't wait for further discussion, he just turned and started running toward the tunnel mouth. It spoke a great deal of Willem's and the twins' trust that they didn't try to argue further. After the briefest of hesitations, they simply plunged forward again after Aiden. He hoped he might prove worthy of that trust. What else could they do?

Aiden stopped a dozen paces into the tunnel and turned back toward the entrance. After gesturing for the others to continue on and get behind him, Aiden closed his eyes. Thinking back to just after the canyon battle against the Swaar, he tapped Stone and began working his mind into the stones around the entrance. The resistance he felt when trying to battle one of the wild Elementals or even the Elemental binding that had been in the canyon that day was not present here. Surprisingly, the stone of the surrounding walls, ceiling, and floor gave way to his will easily. It began to flow like liquid, over, down, and around, re-forming the doorway into a solid door. Only a tiny window of space remained peering into the far room. A crash resounded from that chamber and Aiden's eyes snapped open. He saw the Steel Elemental move into the room, followed by the two Wood Elementals.

The Elemental forms rushed the small portal that still lay open, and Aiden gasped, pushing on the stone around the doorway. He pushed too hard, and rather than the stone flowing the rest of the way together, rocks from ceiling and wall fell in to close off the remaining space. Control evaporated from Aiden's mind as the rocks continued to fall rapidly, filling the remaining space between Aiden and the rock pile.

Aiden stood, transfixed, even as the rocks threatened to engulf him. At the last moment, hands grabbed him from behind and tore him backward. Rock continued to fall and crash as the entry became more and more blocked. Finally, the quaking stopped and only dust fell around the rock pile.

Wheezing in the dust cloud, Aiden pushed himself back to his feet. Somehow the torch had stayed lit through all of the excitement. Aiden looked at his companions and saw in their faces the same realization that had just blossomed in his own mind. They were safe from the wild Elementals for the moment, but if Willem was right, this tunnel led nowhere. They were trapped.

Chapter 34

...and he will need you...

T he pain came in waves, sometimes fast and sometimes slow, but as surely as the ocean tides, the pain always came again after it receded. This time, it was more than Tako could bear in silence, and a cry escaped the prison of his lungs.

Mass was by his side in an instant, her concern a balm and an embarrassment all at the same time. "Bad?" she asked, as his breathing returned to normal, indicating the pain's lessening. Tako nodded, unable at the moment to offer more to the conversation. They had reasoned together that the pain came from the Shield of Ammereth's power trying to come to Tako's defense and finding itself quelled somehow by the shackles encircling his wrists and ankles. Tako was melded to the Shield's power in some way that he didn't yet understand, and being cut off from it like this felt like having a limb amputated time after time.

Tako's pain wasn't even necessary for Dal Tek's plan at this point. They were on a river barge heading for South Harbor and a ship. Tako was little more than cargo in transit and could easily have made his way as any other passenger. There was no reason for Tako to be chained into this cursed machine. Dante had tried to reason this point to the Dal, but Tek was having none of it. "We could be attacked at any point," he had said. "The Wolf Rider is good defense." This was only an excuse, Tako knew. The possibility of their barges being attacked by Mist Falcons, who were really the ones Tako's defense would have the most effect against, was very small. No, Tek kept Tako in the machine's shackles because he couldn't be controlled any other way, and Dal Tek feared what he couldn't control. Tako's pain would be seen to hold little consequence, except maybe to be approved of as punishment for Tako's defiance of Tek.

They couldn't even take the ring off. As soon as Tako's ring hand had been fastened into the shimmering chains, a domed cylinder had grown out from the hand's manacle and encircled the hand, ring, and stone altogether.

No, the ring was staying on Tako's finger, and Tako was staying chained into Tenlin's machine. There was little to be done but bear the pain and try not to let Whisper and Mass see the true extent of it. Tako could do that. He could carry this burden, at least for a while.

Along with the periods of pain, Tako had had little to do but think. After reasoning through the rush of his short time in Taalmor, he couldn't help but berate himself. It had all been a trap: Tako being brought into the Dal's confidence in Bellcross, the ensuing journey north, all of it. It had all been a trap, and Tako had sprinted straight into it, completely heedless of the peril. They had known—Tek, Olivat, and Gray Riller. Even Tuvry Quick Fist, had been in on the plot, Crones curse the man with all of his covert glances and his insinuated comments. Tako should have killed him in that alleyway. Yes, they had all known, or at least expected who Tako was and what he carried. Maybe they knew a bit of the Keeper's prophecy. If they had heard the line about the Wolf Rider, it may have been a strong giveaway.

Tako sighed. It didn't matter now anyway. He had been used. He was still being used, and the pain was payment for his idiocy.

"We could get you out," Mass whispered, bringing Tako back to the moment. She leaned her head forward as she offered him a drink from a bottle so that Tako would hear her nearly-silent words, but the guards posted near the hold's trapdoor wouldn't even realize she was speaking. "We could break these shackles and be gone before Tek could stop us."

Tako shook his head slowly. The chains that bound him were, he was sure, made from the same material that allowed the lights to dance in the cave he and the Keeper had walked through not so long ago. Dal Tek wore the only key to his shackles about his own thick neck, and Tako doubted very much if these chains could be broken by sword, axe, or hammer—at least, not easily. Tek's soldiers would flood this chamber the moment any fighting began. Whisper and Mass would not survive the ensuing battle, regardless of the Dal's sworn promise.

"No," was all Tako said in reply to Mass. "No more." She took the bottle away as if the water was all Tako was dismissing.

I will protect my companions—my friends, Tako thought, as he gritted his teeth against another wave of pain. Protecting, after all, is what shields do.

Chapter 35

...and all we have learned thus far.

———⁘———

"Alright," Rem said. "So Aiden just opens the stone around the door again, and starts hurling the big ones, the bigger the better, at the Elementals."

"While they're busy getting pelted with rocks," Lem jumped in, "we all make a break for it to the far doorway. If they get hit enough, maybe we can finish them off; if not, well, we'll be able to run for it again."

"And how will you run for it, Lem?" Aiden asked. "Even if I could do what you're saying I can, and I doubt very much it would be as dramatic as you say. I might be able to push some rocks at the waiting Elementals, but as for *hurling,* I'm just a man, not a catapult. But even if I could, well, let's face it, Lem: your ankle's swollen to double and you can barely limp around in here. How are you going to run?"

Lem just stared at Aiden for a minute. "Fine," he snapped, "the rest of you can make a break for it. I'll stay here."

"Now, don't be a git," Rem said.

"That's what he's thinking anyway," Lem said, "and he's right. I'm just dead weight at the moment. You boys can go on. Find the exit, get out of here."

Aiden shook his head. "That's not what I'm saying at all. Nobody's leaving anybody else behind. We came in together, and we're leaving together."

"How, then?" Lem asked.

That was the question exactly, Willem thought. They had been debating it, or around it, for hours. He wasn't really sure how long they had been trapped back in this tunnel. He wasn't sure how long it had been since he had transported into these Crags for that matter. They had slept here in this tunnel after the Elemental chase, and time was impossible to judge in the darkness. What he did know was that they were nearly out of both food and water, and they were down to burning their final torch. They didn't have long, Willem knew. They could go for a while even after their supplies gave out, but when that last torch died—well, they'd be pretty much done right then. A pitch-black world filled with wild Elementals? They might as well just lie down here.

They had searched the rest of the tunnel, of course. In truth, it was far shorter than Willem's memory acknowledged. His memory had not been faulty on the rest, however. No tunnels or doorways branched off from here, and this tunnel ended in a perfectly flat wall of solid stone. That struck him as odd for some reason—the flat wall. But stone was stone, and it offered them no escape.

So here they sat as their final torch burned away, arguing about what to do next. The twins' first idea had been for Aiden to just move the stone around them, creating a tunnel up out of the Crags. "What better proof of your Elemental mastery, mate, than to make your own path out of here?" Rem had laughed as if it were the simplest of answers to a complex problem. Willem had seen the immediate flaw: a massive amount of stone and earth lay between them and the surface. Aiden had been exhausted after moving the stone for their tunnel entry, how was he going to move the tons that blocked their way now? No, Willem doubted that even Thun could have done that. Aiden had dismissed the idea immediately, and they moved on.

Hours of arguing passed leaving them still just sitting here. Willem had his guitar in his lap as always. The world may have forced him to learn swordplay, but music would always be his first love.

He started to play, his fingers finding random notes and chords. Starting to hum, Willem realized that his random tune had again turned back to the same low tune.

"Down, down, down," he sang softly. He didn't know why his mind returned so continually to this same song. It drew him somehow, pulled his mind and his voice. "In caverns dark and dungeons deep—down, down, down. You'll find the treasure that you seek, but down, down, down."

Aiden shot him a look that said, *"Really? Again? The same song again?"* This wasn't Willem's first time through the tune since their imprisonment in this tunnel.

Willem smirked in response but didn't stop his quiet song. "Through open doors of solid stone, go down, down, down. And there you'll find your rest alone—down, down, down." The words simply resonated with him, perhaps because they reflected the mood of their current darkness.

"Reflect the mood?" he thought aloud as his fingers continued to find their places on the strings.

"What?" Aiden asked.

Willem wasn't listening, though. His mind raced, weaving connections of half-understood thoughts and lyrics. A completely flat wall at the back of a tunnel—a tunnel in which he had appeared magically after disappearing from a locked cell. He had been playing this song then, too. *Through open doors of solid stone, down, down, down.* But if you can go down, surely you can go up as well.

Willem leapt suddenly to his feet.

"What?" Aiden asked again, this time more emphatically, but Willem still wasn't listening. He moved off down the tunnel, guitar in one hand and his other sliding along the wall as he moved further from the burning torch and into darkness.

Willem couldn't explain yet; his thoughts were only half-formed and less than half- understood. He moved as fast as he dared as blackness began to surround him. As his pace slowed, the light grew, however. The interest of the others had been piqued and they were following with the torch. By the time Willem reached the far end of the tunnel and the flat wall that marked its boundary, the others had caught up, Lem leaning on Rem as he limped along.

"Willem?" Aiden started, but Willem held up his hand to forestall him. There was something here, something to be understood. He could feel it—understanding just beyond reach.

On an impulse, he strummed a chord and felt as it resonated with the flat wall. It was as if the stone absorbed the note somehow, swallowed it into itself like a sponge would a drop of water. If the stone could absorb the drop of a note, then what about the full stream of a song?

Willem started to play. "Down, down, down. Down, down, down." He felt the stone pulling the song toward itself in some real way. The song flowed easily as if wanting to be absorbed. A key and a lock, Willem thought, meant for each other.

His friends remained silent, apparently content to observe quietly for the moment. He was sure this looked strange—coming down to sing his same song to an empty wall. He couldn't worry about that right now. Something was happening to the stone in front of him. He couldn't see it, but he could feel it. Willem was close—not there yet, but close. He tweaked his song ever so gently, probing the stone with each note. He tried going higher but felt the stone's resistance grow. So he dropped lower, all the time holding his same song of "Down, down, down." He felt the resistance slacken to almost nothing—a sponge filled to overflowing.

Reaching the line, "Through open doors of solid stone," Willem moved forward on instinct, still playing. He reached the place where the stone should have been, but it offered no resistance as he slipped into—and then past—the obstacle. It felt like passing through a cool mist breeze. There was something there, but nothing he couldn't pass through easily.

His fingers continued to find their hold as he left the space of the stone, standing instead in darkness. The torchlight apparently couldn't penetrate the stone as Willem had. Without pause or giving himself too much time to ponder, Willem turned back around and once again passed through the cool, yielding stone.

"Angels' face!" Rem exclaimed as Willem reappeared.

"Willem," Aiden spluttered, "how...dregs and draught, man! What did you..."

Making sure he was clear of the wall, Willem stopped playing. "I don't know. It's kind of like what I did with the flame before, but totally different at the same time. Either way, come on; I think I've found our way out."

A few minutes later they stood before the flat stone wall once again, this time holding bags and weapons, ready for whatever might come next.

"Alright," Willem said. "I'll start playing. Give me a minute and then try the wall. We should be able to move through easily, like walking into a gentle breeze."

"Walking into a gentle breeze," Lem echoed.

"You've sung too many songs, Silver Tongue. Now you're singing them even when you're not." Rem grinned at Willem, Lem mirroring his expression almost exactly.

Willem smiled, but his mind only half registered their quip, so focused was he on the music and the stone. He took a breath.

Then, placing calloused fingers against worn strings, he began to play once more.

After the first few notes struck the air, Aiden moved forward and placed a tentative hand against the flat, solid stone. His hand rested there for a moment, his muscles tensed, trying to push in without success.

Willem could feel the growing tension in his companions. He could all but hear the anxious questioning: *"It's not working. What's wrong? Why isn't it working?"* Willem wasn't anxious, though. He could feel something the others couldn't—the stone's response to his song. The key turned in the lock, slowly, and then all at once, he could feel it click.

Aiden's arm shot into the now-open doors of solid stone. He stumbled forward a half step, disappearing halfway into the wall. Then he took another step and vanished from view completely.

The twins followed a moment later, their steps hesitant at the wall itself, but disappearing each in turn. The torch had gone with Rem last of all. So, in total darkness and still playing his song of "Down, down, down," Willem took his few steps forward and finally passed through the solid stone himself.

Chapter 36

I write this now, chiseled in stone and wrapped in wind... Do not be fooled...

―❧―

Ten more minutes, Aiden thought, glancing over at Willem and Lem in the near darkness. *We'll wait ten more minutes.*

They sat in an old storeroom they had found a few flights of stairs up from the smooth, stone wall—the doors of solid stone—as Willem's song composed. They were in Holmsguard. They had surmised that much. However, the castle was so large and sprawled off into so many basement floors and tunnel networks, that huge sections of the subterranean level went unused and nearly forgotten. With no one watching the doors below, it seemed a safe assumption that the magical entrance and exit had been forgotten by the order, but then, maybe Willem was the only one who had ever made the wall into a magical door. Aiden didn't know.

Either way, it seemed apparent that no Mist Falcons used this area—none other than the four of them now, Aiden supposed. They were out of the Crags of Telsair and they hadn't come out through the upper entrance. By the terms of their Trial, the four of them were in fact Mist Falcons. He smiled despite himself. He was a Mist Falcon, hero of legends. The problem was the Lord Commander of the Mist Falcons had been plotting all of their deaths in the Crags, and Aiden wasn't sure they would receive the warmest of welcomes if they simply came strutting into the Council Chambers. To further the trouble, Willem had been branded a deserter after being imprisoned by Lord Commander Dellan and his leashed dog, Tanbuary. Since the two of them were the only ones who could vouch for Willem's whereabouts, it seemed unlikely his story of appearing in the Crags with the rest of them would be very believable by the other Falcons.

They had decided to set up some kind of home base here in this storage room. Someone had apparently discovered this room in the last few years and decided it would be a good option for storing some supplies in. Either they had forgotten about the pursuit or abandoned it because a healthy layer of dust coated everything in the room. Fortunately for the four companions, the room's former owner had acted as a rather thoughtful patron. Wrapped and preserved salted pork, along with jarred peaches, sat on shelves along one side wall, while several bottles of wine were stacked neatly on a rack against the back wall. Two lanterns with four jars of oil lay in one corner just inside the door. Unfortunately, no cots or blankets graced their new hideaway. Even without them, however, and with the rather repetitive meals of old salted pork, peaches, and wine, the room offered far more than they had any reason to hope for. It would be enough to get them by for a short time, at any rate.

They had lain low for a few days, resting from their ordeal and trying to come up with a plan of what to do next. They had all explored the corridors directly surrounding their new home base. Even Lem joined in with the short expeditions after the first day, his ankle seeming to be better all the time. They discovered nothing and no one of any interest, though.

Finally, they had decided they had to look further. Rem had gone off some eight hours ago in hopes of locating Thun or, failing that, some news of goings-on. They needed a plan, and Aiden just didn't have enough information to make one. Rem was supposed to be back a couple of hours ago. It worried Aiden. He knew that the twin should be fine. They had sent him for several reasons. First, as Rem reminded them, he was a thief by profession and was accustomed to a sneaking life. Second, he should be fine even if he was discovered. He went into the Crags of Telsair and came back out alive. He was Mist Falcon now. He should be praised as a returning hero. It was a risk, but only a small one. In truth, Aiden and Willem were at the most risk if they returned. Even if Rem was found out, as long as he could convince Dellan that he was the last to survive, he should be fine and their hideaway here in the bowels of Holmsguard should remain secret. It would be too suspicious for the one survivor from the Maker's Hand's part to die mysteriously. Plus, if Rem were alive it offered the contrast that Aiden must be dead—a false Hand after all. Aiden didn't know if he should take comfort in the thought, but at least Rem should be safe.

Still, they sat in near darkness, burning one lantern at its lowest setting. They didn't want any light to escape beneath the closed door and betray them to any unknowing passersby.

"How much longer do we wait?" Lem asked, strain showing in his voice.

"Ten more minutes," Aiden said, repeating his silent mantra aloud. He'd been telling himself that same timeframe for hours now.

"Ten minutes, and then what?" Willem asked. "When we decide to stop waiting, then what are we going to do?"

"We should just all go, now," Lem said. "If we're found out hiding in the cellar, we're just going to look like we are guilty of something. Take it from me, mate: looking like you're guilty can be as bad as having done whatever crime in actuality."

"We don't know enough to do anything yet," Aiden said. "We'll just have to wait until..."

The door latch clicked and the old wooden construct swung open on silent metal hinges. Two men stood silhouetted in the doorway, their forms lit by the burning lantern held before them.

"Tell me," Rem's voice growled from the doorway, "what's the point of me being so careful as I sneak around if the three of you are going to be so bloody determined to bring the whole Angel-forsaken castle down here with your racket?" His voice was harsh, but his usual grin clung to his face as he moved into the room, stealing the reprimand from his words.

"About time, mate," Lem said. "I was beginning to think you had lost your touch altogether."

Rem just continued to smile. "Patience is a virtue, brother of mine. Besides, our dear friend here was a long time pilfering wine in the kitchen cellars before he finally saw fit to grace his apartments again."

At this, the second man moved out of the shadowed doorway and into the room at large. Aiden had been able to tell immediately that the man couldn't be Thunder—this man was too small. It wasn't until he stepped more fully into the light that Aiden saw the features beneath an upturned hood.

"Jumper!" he exclaimed, getting to his feet and letting his hand fall away from his sword hilt.

"Did you miss me, lads? I see you're all in one piece."

"No thanks to Dellan and Tanbuary," Aiden said.

"So Rem here has been telling me—daring battles in the deep, explosives, explosions, and a Heat Rider in the flesh." Jumper said this last, eyes sliding to Willem. "Is it true? You can spy, I'm sure, listen in to conversations being held miles away, but can you really ride it, body and all?"

"I guess." Willem shrugged. "I mean, that's how I got out of my cell and all. I don't know about riding the heat. Angels' mercy, all I know is that I have been doing some crazy things while playing my guitar lately." Silence held the small room for a moment as Jumper stared at Willem as if trying to read something intricate written on the man's face.

"Where's Thun?" Aiden asked after a minute, breaking the silent trance and pulling Jumper's eyes back to him.

"Gone," Jumper said. "Hiding. On the run. I really don't have the slightest clue. Officially, he is on mission, but Thunder hasn't gone on mission without me for years." There was the barest hint of angst underlying his usual flippant tone. Abandonment, maybe?

"I talked to him one day not long before you went into the Crags, and the next, he was gone without a word of farewell. Not that it matters much. At the time I assumed Thun had gone to take care of some personal matters, but then the word got around that he had gone on mission. I wasn't sure what to think. With Rem's story, however, I would guess Thun got word of some plot against him and made a run for it."

Aiden sighed. He had been basing a lot of their next actions on getting a plan from Thunder. It left a bad taste in his mouth, and Aiden thought he could understand the angst that Jumper felt. Thun was like the rudder of a ship. Without him, they were all just being carried in whatever direction the wind blew the hardest.

Trying to force his feelings aside, Aiden said, "Alright, what do we do now?"

Jumper smiled his sarcastic grin. "Well now, that brings up an interesting point. You see, you're all dead—the Hand Pretender and his friends."

"Except for Willem," Rem interjected.

"True; Willem is only on the run, a deserter with a death mark. Still, according to the Lord Commander, the rest of you didn't survive the Trial. So, it's a good question."

"Maybe Dellan thinks we really are dead after that explosion. But why does he want us dead? And why imprison Willem? What did we do?"

Jumper offered a nonchalant shrug. "It may be that he just fears your power will negate his own status. There have always been whispers that Dellan claimed his chain of office mainly due to his Twin Warrior status and not for his ability to inspire others. If he has based his leadership on his strength with Elementalogy, what is he to think when a Maker's Hand and possible Warrior Poet strolls through his door? It also may have little to do with you at all. This situation with Thun...I don't know. There was talk of Thun's name being put forward for the election that Dellan won. Thun squelched the rally behind him before it could gain too much traction. Then he ran off to Taalmor to save the Nine Cities again. I think he couldn't stand the thought of giving up ranging. Still, there are many who look to him for leadership. I'm sure you've seen how most of the Falcons look at him—awe is the word. He has been at the heart of every major move the Mist Falcons have made for twenty-five years. No, you may not be the only ones the Lord Commander has plotted against. In fact, you may just be pawns in something much larger."

Jumper blew out a breath and then smiled again. "Either way, we still have a question before us. Three dead men and one that will be killed on sight—what are you to do?"

The room was silent for a long moment as Jumper stared at them, eyes moving from face to face. Then he offered another of his casual grins. "Well, if none of you have a plan, it just so happens that I do."

Chapter 37

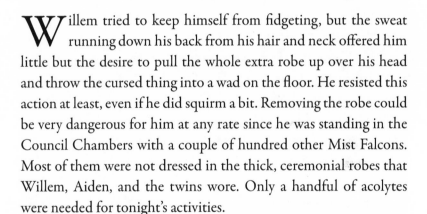

These may be my final words to you... Avoid my errors and do not follow...

Willem tried to keep himself from fidgeting, but the sweat running down his back from his hair and neck offered him little but the desire to pull the whole extra robe up over his head and throw the cursed thing into a wad on the floor. He resisted this action at least, even if he did squirm a bit. Removing the robe could be very dangerous for him at any rate since he was standing in the Council Chambers with a couple of hundred other Mist Falcons. Most of them were not dressed in the thick, ceremonial robes that Willem, Aiden, and the twins wore. Only a handful of acolytes were needed for tonight's activities.

Jumper's plan had been fairly simple. Every moons' turn, a meeting was called for all available Mist Falcons. Those whose duties wouldn't allow their presence—those on watch or out on assignment—were excused and would be filled in on events later. As best Willem understood, these meetings were a hybrid of a status and information session, disciplinary sentencing (when needed), and a ceremony of tradition to remind the Falcons who and what they were. Each meeting had nine robed Falcons that stood on the Lords' platform behind the table, facing the audience of other Falcons. These robed figures represented something that Willem didn't really understand. The important part was that beyond standing and sweating, these figures had little actual role to play in the meeting's activities. Moreover, Jumper had managed to attain four of the robed spots for the four companions.

This gave them a couple of important opportunities. First, they had the chance to stand before the great majority of the Mist Falcons and possibly speak their case in a situation not totally under Lord Commander Dellan's control. Second, it offered them the anonymity to wait for the proper timing before raising their voices in protest. Willem's grandfather had always told him to "wait for kairuq" in his music. "Don't rush it," he would say, and Willem had learned the truth of that. Either the word was from some old language Willem didn't know, or his Grandfather had made up the term altogether. Either way, he was right. A well-timed note could be the difference between a masterful performance and a subpar one. In their situation, kairuq quite literally could mean the difference between life and death.

Willem saw Jumper sitting near the back of the hall at the far left of the podium. A small smirk tugged at his features, and he leaned back against the footrest for the seat behind him as if nothing of any import was going on. Threll sat on the other end of the room, her face grim in all the ways Jumper's was flippant. She wasn't in on their plan, but Willem hoped she would back them when the time came. He didn't see Tanbuary anywhere, but he had always seemed to be the type to hide in shadows.

With the main body of Mist Falcons seated in the half-circle of benches, the torch fires in the wall sconces dimmed. Willem had no doubt this was done by some kind of Elemental manipulation. These were torches, after all, not lanterns or lamps. There was no dimmer switch—no physical one, at any rate. With the light dimmed thus, the Council of Lords flowed in, swift and powerful in dark robes. At their head strode Lord Commander Dellan, a beautifully-carved staff of ceremony in one hand and an honor guard in mail marching to either side of him.

Willem looked from face to face in the slithering line of Falcon Lords, searching for Thunder. He wasn't to be found, however—not that Willem had truly expected him to be there among the others.

They moved down the steps before finally claiming their seats, all in a row facing out toward the waiting Falcons now, rather than in a circle to debate issues of importance. Willem supposed theirs was to be a uniformed front in these meetings. Thunder's seat and the other seat that had been empty when they first arrived and Holmsguard remained notably bare—the chairs present as a marker, but empty.

"When battle comes—" Dellan boomed in his orator's voice.

"The mist rises," the body of Mist Falcons intoned in unison as a response.

"When darkness threatens—"

"The Falcon hunts."

The litany finished, Dellan struck the floor once with the butt of his carved staff. "This meeting of the tenth moons in the month of Hendu will now come to order. First in line for business is Lord Jabren with a word on the Hellantor situation."

Jabren stood, addressing the hall at large. "As you may have heard, the uprising at Hellantor has escalated with the Regent of the Western Quarter being publicly executed by the group calling themselves the White Bearers. From reports in the area..."

The sallow man droned on in his nasally voice, but Willem had a hard time concentrating on Jabren's words. He knew that Hellantor was someplace in the southwest, but he had never traveled that far. It didn't really matter—this was not their part. Their part was waiting for kairuq.

After what seemed like forever, Jabren sat and Lord Commander Dellan reclaimed the floor. "Thank you Lord Jabren. We must, all of us, be on the ready for further developments in Hellantor in the coming days. I will see to an exploratory ranging there.

"Now, my dear brothers and sisters," Dellan started again, "I feel we must discuss a situation that has been floating about in whispers of ones and twos. We must bring the hushed voices out of the dark corners and into the light before us all. Most here have met, seen, or at least heard tell of the young Hand Pretender and his small group of followers."

Wait for it, Willem thought. *Let him dig himself in deep.* The move wasn't his to make, but he willed patience toward his friend with all his might.

"They came here," Dellan continued, "making certain claims, offering sleight of hand and forgery as proof of the Pretender's claim to being a Maker's Hand."

Willem saw several of the Lords in front of him stiffen or squirm at this. They had tested the Blade, he knew. Willem had been there for it. They weren't so sure the Maker's Blade had been a forgery. It seemed that at least some of the Lords weren't buying Dellan's lies as completely as the Lord Commander might like.

"In wisdom, this Council declared that these newcomers should be tested by Elementals in the form of a Trial. They agreed to this, perhaps not understanding that their trickery would not work in the Crags of Telsair. One of their group realized his danger, but too late, and fled. The other three went into the Crags, where they were consumed by the powers that hold residence there. None survived the Trial, and we should rejoice that we have been rid of the Pretender and the desolating influence he might have wielded if not checked here. Let us be on guard for such theatrics, my fellow Mist Falcons. Let us not grow corrupt."

Okay, Willem thought. *Okay, he's in deep. Go.* But, Aiden didn't move as Dellan continued on. *Has he lost his nerve? Kairuq, remember. This is it.*

"And how did these Pretenders, these charlatans, come to us?" Dellan said, finger raised vehemently in pronouncement. "By one of our own. Was he tricked, taken in by the superb performance given? Perhaps, but then—where is he to answer for such a mistake? Would not this Council offer leniency and understanding in such an event? But it pains me to say, he too has fled from us—absent without leave, gone from Holmsguard without assignment. This is not the way of the code. As hard as it is, my brothers and sisters, I must regrettably announce the removal of Lord Jak Thunder Klapp from this Council of Lords and a declaration of Deserter be placed on him until such a time as he can be brought to this Council to answer for his crime of bringing this near-calamity down on us. All you who can hear my words, let it be known that Jak Thunder Klapp is to be captured at any cost and brought back to Holmsguard for trial and questioning. The use of force, even lethal in the event that Thunder becomes violent, is acceptable, if unfortunate."

Murmuring broke out and grew in volume amongst all the Falcons seated in the Council Chambers.

Dellan didn't halt his message but simply raised his voice to shouting so as to be heard over the tumult of voices. "The herald of the Hand Pretender must not be allowed to escape at risk of more Pretenders rising to his cause."

The room bubbled as people stood and murmurs became shouts, Falcons coming down on both sides of the argument. The storm grew for a moment and then ceased all at once, like a candle being blown out.

Willem looked to his right and there Aiden stood on the table, which the Falcon Lords sat behind. His discarded robe lay pooled at the base of Thun's empty chair, which Aiden had used to climb onto the table. The entirety of the room had fallen silent. No whispers or murmurs declared the situation. Not even any gasps broke the sudden stillness.

After a moment, Aiden reached to his hip and drew free his sword holding it aloft like some hero from childhood stories.

The drawn blade was apparently enough to shake Dellan from his stupor. "What is this?" he demanded, throwing as much outraged indignation as he could muster into the question. "Who dares draw a blade at a moons' meeting?"

Aiden regarded the still-silent body of Mist Falcons for a second longer, ignoring Dellan's right to challenge him. Then Aiden turned to the Lord Commander and said, "The Maker's Hand dares to draw his Maker's Blade to show the assembly of *my* brother and sister Mist Falcons the proof of my life, which apparently has been in slanderous question."

He lowered the tip toward Dellan. The two of them were a dozen paces apart, but still, the move looked menacing. Aiden stood proud and powerful, his small frame doing nothing to quell the strength emanating from him. Willem couldn't help but wonder at the change his friend had undergone in the few months since their first meeting at the slavers' fire. Aiden was no longer the sullen boy tied into the wagon every day. Willem knew that a good portion of Aiden's show here was just bravado. Jumper had instructed him to be confident, but still, Aiden had grown. The old Aiden couldn't have done this.

"I declare you a liar, Dellan—a liar and an attempted murderer," Aiden started again. "I am so pleased to tell you, your trap failed. Your explosives in the depths failed to consume us, and we are very much alive." At this, the two figures to Willem's left stepped forward, tearing off their hooded robes to reveal Rem and Lem.

"It also happens that when you falsely imprisoned my friend Willem, you underestimated his skill with Elementalogy, because he escaped your cell and joined us in the Crags so as to come out the other side a Mist Falcon." Willem, sensing his moment, finally tore the Angels' cursed robe over his head and dropped it to the floor as he stepped forward.

More murmuring broke out at Willem's appearance. Then, apparently deciding on the easier target, Dellan pointed his ceremonial staff at Willem and shouted, "The deserter! Seize him! Kill him!"

The Council Chambers became a torrent of activity as each Mist Falcon tried to choose a side. Two of the actual acolytes in the ceremonial robes dropped their hoods and made to grab Willem. Another robed acolyte, a big one with broad shoulders, intercepted them, crashing a fist into one's face before sweeping the legs from beneath the second. This last maneuver forced the big acolyte's hood back revealing a face Willem knew well.

"Thun," he croaked.

The big man winked at him and then boomed out to the assembly, "Stop! Enough madness; stop!"

Aiden found himself in the middle of a building storm as Mist Falcon argued with Mist Falcon, many coming near to blows. The Lords behind the table he stood upon toppled their chairs and rose to take action. He was reminded that these were not your average bureaucrats who might be expected to flee or hide when fighting broke out. Rather, these men and women were the most accomplished wielders of the Elemental arts. He was rather sure that any one of them could strike him down in a fight. What was worse, he had no idea who might have been swayed to his side, if any. Instead of risking a battle with any of them, he turned his eyes on an even more dangerous adversary.

Lord Commander Dellan turned away from Willem and back to Aiden again. The man's eyes narrowed in a fierce, smoldering anger. The Lord Commander pulled free a honed long knife from his belt and brandished it beside his wooden staff. Aiden pointed his blade at the man once more, considering a charge and first strike when he heard a familiar voice cry out to stop in a rich, traveling baritone. Aiden hesitated, and a moment later the huge form of Thun had joined him on the tabletop. Thun's appearance had a quieting effect on the room. The man was respected, Aiden knew. He had heard the whispers and the stories, but he hadn't known people would listen to him enough to stop the beginnings of a brawl. Still, there they were, looking up at Thunder, waiting on his words.

"I am here to answer your allegation, Dellan, and it just so happens I have a few of my own," Thun said in a deep, steadying voice. "You would murder a *true* Maker's Hand and despoil the sanctity of an Elemental's Trial simply to hold the reins of power a little tighter. Explosives and kidnapping, Dellan? You know the prophecy, of the words spoken by the First Poet himself, and you would endanger us all."

Thun shook his head, his chest heaving now as anger built in his face. "You disgust me. The Falcons have no place for snakes like you. We soar above such things. May the Maker himself brand you with a traitor's brand for all of eternity, and may he give you to Antice, that you might burn. I say you are no Lord Commander, no Lord. I say you are no Mist Falcon. And, before these brothers and sisters, I will prove it through a Challenge of Right given to every Mist Falcon by the code laid down by our forbearers."

Dellan sneered, "Who are you to say? Who are you to challenge? You know nothing. I won't fight you. I don't have to. I am above your ranging ways, Jak Klapp, you and your pet Hand. He was supposed to die in the Crags, but you would bring destruction down on us all. I am above the Mist Falcon code, though, Thunder. And I will lead us out from this peril for I am Lord Commander of the Mist Falcons." He spat at Thun's feet, and then barked, "Seize the traitor!" But no one moved to obey. Dellan looked from face to face around him, in surprise, searching for an ally. Even Jabren refused him, though, and the Lord Commander met nothing but hostility encircling him.

"If you would deny my Right to Challenge, a vote of confidence, then," Thun intoned in an almost remorseful growl. Then he stretched out his hand with a thumbs-down gesture. In turn, each of the other Lords still near the table did the same.

"Fools," Dellan spat. "None of you understand what's going on. None of you understand what I do for us, for you. You want to betray your oaths. You want mutiny. Then you can have the consequences." With that, Dellan hurled himself up and backward, propelled by Wind of his own calling. Aiden thought he would smash wholly into the stone wall, but when the man reached the wall, it simply accepted him, melting around him like water before returning to its former solid appearance.

A few cries of pursuit went up, but before anyone could act, the horns began to blow.

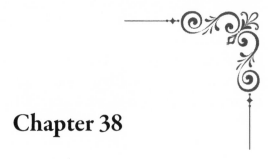

Chapter 38

...you may yet be saved...Do not be fooled...so rarely as they seem...

⟨⟩

Aiden watched as the room exploded into activity, Falcons sprinting toward the four main exits.

"Come on," Thun shouted and started up the stairs without waiting to see if Aiden and the others were following. "Those are neyrlon horns," Thun explained as Aiden caught up to him. "It is said their cry is so resounding that men can hear a single horn blow from five leagues away. They blow in Holmsguard for only one reason. We are under attack."

Aiden found the thought laughable. The thought of someone attacking this fortress guarded by hundreds of Mist Falcons was simply preposterous. It was suicide. Who would throw their lives away in such a manner? Still, the horns were blowing.

Thun led their small party up onto the wall to look out over the expanse toward where the sentries were pointing. It was evening and twilight was nearly upon them, but still, the light was enough to make out a fleet of dark-hulled ships racing toward the coast, their white sails billowing in the wind.

"Angel-cursed fools," Thun muttered. "Dregs and draught, what are they thinking, coming here?" Then, turning back to the Falcons lining the wall, he yelled, "Wind Cannons to the front." That command was enough to snap the men from their gawking and into action once more. They knew how to do this. They had been trained for it.

A few dozen Falcons moved up to the front of the wall. Once in place, they raised their hands outward as if preparing to push the oncoming fleet away with nothing but their arms. They looked confident, ready, capable, and Aiden found his own courage bolstered.

"Fire!" Thun bellowed, and a rushing crash exploded from in front of the line of Wind Cannons. The air tore itself as wind raced out from empty, outstretched palms of Falcons along the wall, obeying the command of so many masters. Trees toppled and branches broke as the wind's onslaught raced for the coast. Aiden watched with anxious eyes as the dust and debris marking the wind's progression reached the waterline. He watched expectantly, waiting for torn masts and crashing sails. He waited, and nothing. The wind dissipated as if it had grown lazy at the last moment. Aiden doubted if the marauding force of sailors had felt so much as a gentle breeze play across their skin.

He looked up at the Wind Cannons. Their arms were still raised, but their look of confidence had melted away, leaving puzzlement and fear in its wake.

"Torches, to the front," Thun boomed. "Woods, get me some empty barrels for kindling. Wind Cannons, relax and reload." The men scrambled to obey, the Wind Cannons dropping their arms and relaxing. A moment later Thun was yelling again. "Barrels up! Light 'em! Cannons, blow 'em away!" Working in an amazingly dancelike harmony, the Woods, Torches, and Wind Cannons worked the barrels into the air, lit them on fire, and shot them toward the oncoming ships faster than an arrow can fly. The attackers were nearly at the coast now and still showed no sign of slowing. Apparently, they were going to run their ships ashore, rather than take the time to send off the longboats.

The flaming barrels hurtled toward the ships, but with half the distance to the water still to go, they died out. The flames were snuffed as if by a huge, invisible hand. The wind lost its strength, and the half-burned barrel husks dropped to the ground, cracking and crumbling.

"Waters, sink those ships!" Thun called, voice still strong but face looking worried. The Water Mist Falcons along the wall reached out, but nothing happened—no bubbling of the water, no waves, nothing.

Silence fell for a brief moment as the realization of what they were facing fell over the Mist Falcons. Everyone just stood, watching as the ships drew closer. Then, just as the first ship was going to make land, its sails caught as if in a massive wind from below and the ship soared up into the air, racing over the ground of Castle Isle and thundering toward the gate of Holmsguard. The sheer strength it would take to lift and propel the ships was astounding.

"Storm Eater," Thun said distantly. It came out as barely a whisper. If it hadn't been for the silence ruling the wall, Aiden never would have heard the utterance.

Everyone still just watched for a moment, staring as their own power—all that had made them special for hundreds of years—turned against them.

"Thun," Aiden said, and then louder, "Thunder."

The man snapped back to himself as if from a dream. "Muskets!" he yelled. "Muskets, cannons, and blades! Falcons to arms! To arms!"

Men and women raced to collect their gear. The few cannons on the parapets boomed out huge iron balls, which broke into the lead ship. The cannons were just too few to be any kind of main defense. They did some damage, but the time to reload seemed to stretch for eternity.

Moreover, few Falcons other than those on watch duty had thought to bring any weapon but their Elementals, and why would they? No attacker could ever get close enough to the castle for a musket shot. They had all been dead the moment they decided to attack the Mist Falcons—every attacker until now, at least.

Thun grabbed Aiden to steady him as the lead ship struck the gate like a giant's battering ram. The wood of both splintered and broke, shaking the ground itself. The gate still held, its steel support lending the wood strength. Then the second ship struck the wide gate, breaking the hinges on one side.

Aiden caught a glimpse of men sliding down ropes from the other ships which had skidded to a halt before the walls of Holmsguard. Then Thun forced him back and away along with Willem and the twins. He led them at a run to an interior stair, down and away from the outer wall. After several minutes and several turns, he came to a stop before a small door. He fished a key from around his neck, unlocked it, and led them inside a small room. Opening a large trunk, he gave each of them a musket, a small bag of gun powder, a smaller bag of metal balls, a black leather jerkin with the falcon emblazoned on the chest, a gray cloak that all Falcons wore, and a Mist Falcon brooch. He also grabbed Willem's guitar from the corner and thrust it into his hands.

"Jumper gave it to me for safekeeping today," he explained.

"I'm sorry this ceremony can't be more formal, lads. There is usually more celebration to accompany new brothers joining our ranks. You have had to go through more than most and yet I can offer you no pomp—no roasted meats, no cake, no wine. All I can give you is a name and a title—an identity. You are Mist Falcon now. That is your name. That is your title. That is your life's identity. Regardless of what happens today, know that you are Falcons—fully and truly."

His short speech given, Thun looked to Willem. "Jumper said you're a Heat Rider. He said you do it with song. It's time to sing, my friend. Use the torch. Get the four of you to safety."

"What? I don't know how to..." Willem began, but Thun cut him off.

"Just have them touch you when you go; they'll come along for the ride the same as your clothes and weapons."

Then turning to Aiden, the big man held out what looked like a tightly-wrapped scroll. "Take this and keep it safe. Once you're out..."

"But—" Aiden tried to cut in even as he accepted the scroll and tucked it into the inner pocket of his new cloak.

Thun stopped him off with a quick gesture. "You haven't been trained for this, not yet. And we can't afford your loss due simply to inexperience. Once you're out, you must find Janaral Bear Hammer. Seek him out in Nyrn."

Just then, a huge explosion shook the castle as if a monstrous thunderclap had swallowed all of Holmsguard.

"Now, go!" Thun shouted, pushing Aiden toward Willem. Then, on stone-strengthened legs, he turned and sprinted toward the wall and the waiting battle.

"Wait!" Aiden shouted, but the big warrior was already gone. Aiden waited for a heartbeat and then, making his decision, said, "Angels take this." He took off his cloak, pulled on his new Falcon jerkin, fastened the cloak back on with the brooch, and ran after Thun.

Willem watched Aiden run for the door and only hesitated a moment before following, pulling on his jerkin as he ran.

"Aren't we leaving?" Lem shouted as the twins matched Willem's pace.

"Great idea," Willem snapped. "The only problem is, I don't have any idea how to ride the heat. I can't transport us out of here. I did it once, by accident, in desperation, and after hours of playing. It's not a switch. I don't know how it works."

"Sure you do, mate," Rem said, jogging behind him. "Start playing that Antice-begotten fiddle of yours, and let's go."

"It's a guitar."

"Whatever; just play."

By then they had come back out into the main courtyard and found a world on fire. Willem had no idea where Thun had gotten to, but holes peppered the walls and dead Falcons lay strewn across the training yard. Cruel-looking men with axes and swords were battling the remaining defenders. Swaar, Willem realized. This is what they had been planning.

The Mist Falcons were holding their own. They were, after all, trained in all sorts of combat, not just in Elementalogy. Still, it had always been the Elementals that offered the Falcons their edge. Now, without it, they were too few against far too many.

Aiden could hear his friends following behind him as he crashed through the door and back into the courtyard. The world was a torrent of violence and death. He saw Thun on top of the battlements, facing down a handful of Swaar, amongst them the largest man Aiden had ever seen. The man made Thun look small, and that was saying something. As Aiden watched, Thun took down two attackers with a complex swirl of his axe before being forced backward by the huge man. At the edge of the outer battlement, the giant brought down his war hammer in a mighty arc. Thun had to leap back to avoid being shortened by a couple of feet. He dodged the blow, but it cost him his footing. He slipped, seeming to hang at the edge for a moment, lingering. Then, an arrow leapt from a

Swaar bow and struck Thun's chest, burrowing in past his leather jerkin. The big Mist Falcon's mouth opened in a gasp, and then he toppled over the far side of the wall, plummeting to the waiting ground below. Just like that, Thun was gone.

"Thun! No!" Aiden cried, but his words could not bring the man back.

Without thought, he drew his Maker's Blade and felt as it shifted from the form of a short sword, elongating into a six-foot spear made entirely of shimmering metal, thick and strong but lighter than any spear Aiden had held before. Anger pumped, burning in his veins like liquid musket powder. He launched himself into battle with reckless abandon, whirling this way and that, dancing out the katar Sevion had taught on the Champion Sands. Tapping Wind to gain speed in his attack, Aiden barely noted that his Elementalogy had done the work commanded of it when all the other Mist Falcons' art had abandoned them. His only thought was for battle and getting to Thun.

Swaar died around him as if he were Antice himself come to claim these poor souls. Death, death, death—that was the mantra of each swing and thrust, and the Swaar around him danced to the tune his spear played. He tried to force his way toward the stair that would lead to where Thun fell, and to the big Swaar still standing there, watching, waiting. He waited for Aiden, and Aiden would not disappoint his patience. He fought wildly, feeling as he used the Elementals around him for battle on occasion, but not really knowing how he did it. It was more instinct than skill. He just wasn't accomplished enough to simply command anything. Everything seemed to take time, and that was the one commodity that battle stripped from all its combatants.

Aiden tried time and time again to get to the stair that would lead him up to the man waiting there, to find where Thun had fallen, and time and time again he was repelled. Every Swaar he killed was replaced with two more through the broken gates. He could feel the tears of frustration slide down his cheeks as he snapped his spear out, releasing a blast of wind and fire that consumed a dozen Swaar, knocking them back twenty strides, burning and screaming.

Seeing his opportunity, he plunged forward toward the stairs again even as more Swaar descended to meet him. He felled two quickly with a swing and a thrust, but as he pulled his spear free again, he felt a fiery pain burst to life inside his left shoulder. Glancing over, he saw a blade protruding from his arm. Instinctively pulling back from the pain, he dropped to his knee.

Glancing up, he was close enough to see the big man upon the wall looking down on him. Anger and something else that looked like fear—but couldn't have been—smoldered in the giant's eyes.

As Willem and the twins reached the doorway to the courtyard, Aiden already had his Maker's Blade drawn into an amazing, long spear, and was fighting several Swaar with reckless speed. The small man was astounding, leaping here and there, demolishing the Swaar line of attack. He fought with abandon, opening himself to almost constant peril. Somehow he always slipped past the strikes and stabs of the Swaar, though. Willem slung his guitar over his shoulder and drew his long sword. There was nothing to do but help. He fought forward, trying to reach his friend, but there were so many Swaar.

Finally, an explosion of fire erupted from Aiden, and the space between him and Willem cleared. Again, Aiden tried for the stairs. Just as Willem reached him, Aiden took down two attackers before a third drove the tip of a sword into Aiden's left shoulder. Aiden cried out, spinning away from the pain, his motion pulling the blade free. The Swaar raised his sword for another strike, but then

Willem was there, plunging his blade through the man's leather armor and into his chest. The man screamed and fell.

Willem pulled Aiden up from the knee he had fallen to. More Swaar were approaching from the stairs and gate, hunger in their eyes. Willem and Aiden tried to retreat but the Swaar were coming in fast. Willem parried the first Swaar's axe swing, but the blow knocked him to the side slightly, opening his right torso to attack.

Two small blasts sounded from behind. The axe-wielding Swaar and the invader coming up behind him both fell. Willem turned and saw Rem and Lem both lowering their new muskets to reload. The two of them *would* figure out how to use the crow-begotten things first. By Dentar's golden strings.

The Swaar's deaths gave Willem and Aiden enough time to get back to the door they had come out of moments before. A few other Falcons were coming to this same escape route. The Mist Falcons wouldn't hold much longer; they couldn't. For every Swaar dead in the yard, six more were scrambling in to take their place.

From the left side, Threll staggered up with two men Willem didn't know. All three of them looked absolutely exhausted. They were covered in blood and gore, like characters in some kind of sick mummer's show.

"Where did they come from?" Threll muttered. "All this killing—from where?"

Willem had an idea of that. He had seen the Swaar at Bellcross. They were conquering from the east. He couldn't believe they had come this far, but wasn't this what they had been doing in the Nine Cities for months?

"Come on," was all he said. "Inside." He ushered her and Aiden both in through the doorway, and Threll's two companions followed. Aiden held the doorframe for a moment, looking back at a large figure descending the stairs that Willem recognized at once. "Dal Tek The Rock Giant," he said and then finished pulling Aiden through the door. The twins let loose one more volley with their muskets and then came in behind.

They didn't get far before the sound of fast pursuit came from the courtyard. The two men who had been with Threll turned to face the onslaught. One died with an arrow through the eye. The other struck down a Swaar attacker before being felled with a mace blow to the head. The two men's sacrifice had given the other five time enough to reach the room the four had abandoned only a few minutes before, slip in, and slam the door.

They immediately set to work piling everything in the room in front of the closed door, which had no deadbolt and whose key still lay around Thun's neck. Luckily, the room had a large cabinet and a couple of chairs to offer some kind of barricade.

That done, everyone threw their weight against the furniture, trying to keep the door closed. Willem was struck by the full circle this event offered to his first encounter with Swaar. There had been escape out the window in Bellcross, though, and countryside to race across. Not this time—this time they were in a room built of stone in the center of an island. There was no escape, unless.... He looked over at Rem, who nodded and made a shooing motion with one hand.

Willem released his hold on the barricade and pulled his guitar around. Beginning to play, he did as Thun had suggested and fixed his eyes upon the torch flame in the sconce on the wall. He played the first thing that came to him, no words this time, just the slow, resounding tune of "Down, down, down."

At first, there was nothing, just the flame and the song—separate, independent. He glanced to the doorway as the Swaar started to batter against the outside of it, shaking the very doorframe, longing to open it.

"Will?" Rem shouted.

Willem looked back at the flame and then at the slowly breaking door again, all the while playing his tune. Something clicked then, something about the door wanting to open, the flaming door, though, not this wooden one. He changed his tune slightly—the key in the lock again. This was going to work. He could do it. He could feel it. He didn't understand it, didn't understand how this could work when everyone else's Elemental art had abandoned them, but it *was* going to work.

"Grab on to me," Willem heard himself say from some remote place. He wasn't there anymore, with his voice, not really, not entirely. He was in the in-between, and the flame was calling him on. "Grab on to me," he repeated, turning his head back to that distant place where his body still stood. This time he saw as Threll released her hold on the barricade and grabbed hold of his shoulder, followed shortly by the twins. Still, Willem waited, looking back.

Rem followed Willem's gaze, released his hold, grabbed Aiden, and pulled him back to where the music met the heat.

As soon as Willem felt the other holds on him, he let go of his anchor. As the door to the room finally gave up its noble defense and crashed open, the five of them vanished into heat and flame.

Chapter 39

But if not, remember, for one may yet come after, and he will need you and all we have learned thus far.

Tako screamed out his anguish. He could feel his power's misuse. Olivat had been down into Tako's personal abyss in the hold of another ship off and on for a week. Poking and prodding Tako and fiddling with the machine's controls, Storm Eater had finally figured out what he had been attempting.

"And there we have it, Wolf Rider," the man had said with a laugh and left back up the ladder.

Tako hadn't understood at the time, but he did now. Tenlin had designed this machine of his to do more than simply hold the Shield of Ammereth and release its power in small waves. It was not just an emitter, dampening attack and strengthening defense. Tenlin and now Olivat had found a way to weaponize Tako and the power which he held.

He could feel as his strength, a strength given him to protect, was instead used to strip away protection and offer desolation in its place. Tako was being used to kill hundreds of people—not kill to protect, but murder for the sheer malice of it.

Tako felt as each life was squelched due to him. It resounded jarringly in his chest as a physical force, and he cried out in anguish and despair, fighting an unwinnable battle against the obliterating chains that shackled him.

Chapter 40

Blessings, my friend.

———————

The sun had set fully now and the others sat around a campfire that Threll had sparked to life. Her Elemental ability had returned with their arrival here in this wooded clearing. All of theirs had.

Willem had first brought them to a grassy area a mile or so out from North Port. They had some thought of going after the horses they had left stabled there, but the town was in flames, cries of battle and death filling the air. The Swaar had anticipated and blocked this possibility of help or retreat. That explained the weapons cache they had found in the canyon after battling the Swaar during their journey to Holmsguard with Thun and Jumper. One of several weapons caches, Aiden had no doubt. They would find no succor here.

Willem had watched the dancing flames of the burning town, strumming what was now becoming something of a theme song. Once he was ready, everyone had grabbed hold a second time, and off they had gone, appearing a moment later in a forested area. Willem had crumpled to the ground almost immediately, a cold sweat dotting his brow and his breathing a shallow rasp. The Heat Riding just seemed to steal so much energy from him. There had been several moments of panic, but slowly, Willem returned to himself.

He rested now with the others around the fire.

Now, Aiden cradled his wounded shoulder. Threll had used her ability with Water Elementalogy to see to the cleaning of it. Unfortunately, they had no Vellen to expedite the healing. Still, Threll had bound the shoulder and told him to try not to move it. It would heal.

He sighed, wincing at the pain as he prodded his shoulder too hard. Taking an involuntary step back as if to retreat from himself, Aiden felt a lightweight click against his side. Only then did he remember Thun's scroll. He pulled it out slowly with the hand of his uninjured arm and unrolled it.

He was surprised at what he found. Though the scroll seemed to be parchment on the outside, unrolled, it revealed an inner layer of thin, hard stone. Once fully unrolled, the scroll snapped into a rigid tablet and hovered slightly of its own accord, just over Aiden's hand. The text inside appeared to have been chiseled. He read:

These may be my final words to you, and to those who come after. Offer my apologies to the rest of the Council, and know to you personally, if I do not return, I am sorry for my failure. Still, I will not stop now, not after coming so far and gaining such a close purchase. The Traitor stands before me and I will not let him slip back into his shadows again.

I write this now, chiseled in Stone and wrapped in Wind, with the hope that you may yet be saved from my folly. Avoid my errors and do not follow in my footsteps, save in greater preparation and wisdom than I have shown. Do not be fooled by the appearance of things. They are so rarely as they seem in this. Remember the teaching of the past, that two waterfalls may yet form one river, and even wide, swift rivers cease when swallowed by the ocean. Trace the heat and ride the waves, my friend. Know that I have left the item we discussed. It is hidden safely six days shy of a month and a month past a day's worth of counter spin. You'll remember the spot, I have no doubt. Perhaps I will follow this message shortly myself, and we will laugh at all our extra caution. But if not, remember, for one may yet come after, and he will need you and all we have learned thus far. Blessings, my friend.

~Spirit

Aiden read the letter through twice, pondering over its meaning and why Thun would give it to him. What had Thun said? *"You haven't been trained for this. Not yet, and we can't afford your loss due simply to inexperience. Once you're out, you must find Janaral Bear Hammer. Seek him out in Nyrn."* Had it really only been a few hours? He couldn't think of how Thun would have gotten away. Their escape had only come through Willem's gift, and Aiden had watched the big man fall from the battlements, an arrow driven into his chest. A tear slid down Aiden's cheek unbidden.

"You haven't been trained for this," he had said. "Find Janaral Bear Hammer." Fine. Aiden knew that he needed more training. He knew that he needed more information. If this Janaral Bear Hammer, could tell him something, he would listen. Aiden would find Janaral, and once he had learned what he could, Aiden would add a few more names to his list for vengeance alongside Semlie's murders. He would start with Dal Tek The Rock Giant—him and Storm Eater, whoever and whatever that was.

Wiping away his tears and cradling his wounded arm, Aiden turned back to the fire. There would be work to do and answers to find, but that was for tomorrow. Taking a deep breath, he walked back to join his friends.

The Warrior Poet Archives continues in Book Two:
Rising Shadow.

Books by Ryan J Doughan

The Warrior Poet Archives:
Mist Falcon
Rising Shadow
The Touch Heist: A Warrior Poet Archives Story

About the Author

Ryan J Doughan is the author of the epic fantasy series, THE WARIOR POET ARCHIVES, which begins the journey in MIST FALCON. Doughan grew up on a steady diet of Narnia and Middle Earth, quickly falling in love with the magic of fiction. This love of stories led him to Northwestern College where he received an English degree in Writing and Rhetoric with a Religion minor.

Ryan lives in Iowa with his beautiful wife and children where he pursues both his writing and his love of family.

Read more at www.ryanjdoughan.com.

Made in the USA
Middletown, DE
10 January 2023

21776230R00248